L.S. WALKER

# The Witch and the Woodcutter

*First edition*

*ISBN (paperback): 978-1-7640854-0-3*
*ISBN (hardcover): 978-1-7640854-2-7*

*This book was professionally typeset on Reedsy.*
*Find out more at reedsy.com*

# Preface

Dearest reader,

Thank you for taking the time to open my book. Hopefully you will stick around a while longer and get a taste of the tale I have spun within these pages. Before you do, be forewarned – some readers may find the content within disturbing. This includes references to sexual violence, violence against women and children, as well as religious and cultural violence. For that reason, perhaps a little background is needed.

I am an avid fantasy reader – it is without a doubt my favourite literary genre. And while I enjoy even the darker sides of the genre, those labelled *grimdark* and such, there are some traits and tropes that frustrate me. Too often when I read fantasy, I am confronted with the gratuitous and unnecessary use of violence (often sexual violence) against women, used as what I consider mere 'set dressing'. It is as though an author will sit down before their proverbial typewriter and think to themselves, "I need to make my reader feel immersed in this fantasy world. It will need dragons, yes… swords, of course… oh, and rape!" Of these things, one is imaginary, one is an antique and the other continues to exist in our present day (in numbers far higher than most would think imaginable). Why, therefore, is this treatment of women so needed to weave the tapestry of a medieval-coded fictitious world? That is not to say just because something is unsavoury it cannot be written about. On the contrary, there are things so detestable that happen every day, yet much of the population goes about their lives in blissful ignorance (until they too are robbed of that bliss).

That brings me to the second point from which this story was born. When I'm not writing or reading, I work in a field (my 'real job' if you will) dedicated to intimate-partner homicides. In this job I write slightly different stories; the stories of *real* women who were treated detestably by men who they thought they were safest with. Stories that I will never be able to repeat to my partner or my family; stories that I will carry until the day I die. And the *quantity*. Quantity unimaginable to the average person. While undertaking several particularly gruesome reviews involving arson femicides, I was confronted by the statistic that more women in my home state had been burnt alive in recent years than during the entirety of the Salem Witch Trials (the number of the latter being, despite popular belief, zero). And thus, the inspiration for this story was born. Even as I was writing this novel, another woman was set alight, but thankfully escaped with her life.

To tell this story, I had to break my own rule. This is a story, first and foremost, about the violence women endure. Not in medieval times. Not in a fantasy world. But now, today. As Margaret Atwood said about the inspiration for her novel, *The Handmaid's Tale:* "Nothing went into it that had not happened in real life somewhere at some time. The reason I made that rule is that I didn't want anybody saying, 'You certainly have an evil imagination, you made up all these bad things.' I didn't make them up."

So that is what I would like to leave you with as you embark on the journey I have crafted for you. Many of you, especially the women, will not need such a stark reminder that such atrocities exist. But hopefully, for some, this story may act as a conversation starter, an eye opener. Because none of the atrocities that occur in this story are fictitious. All of them have happened at some point in history. Many of them continue to happen today.

I didn't make them up.

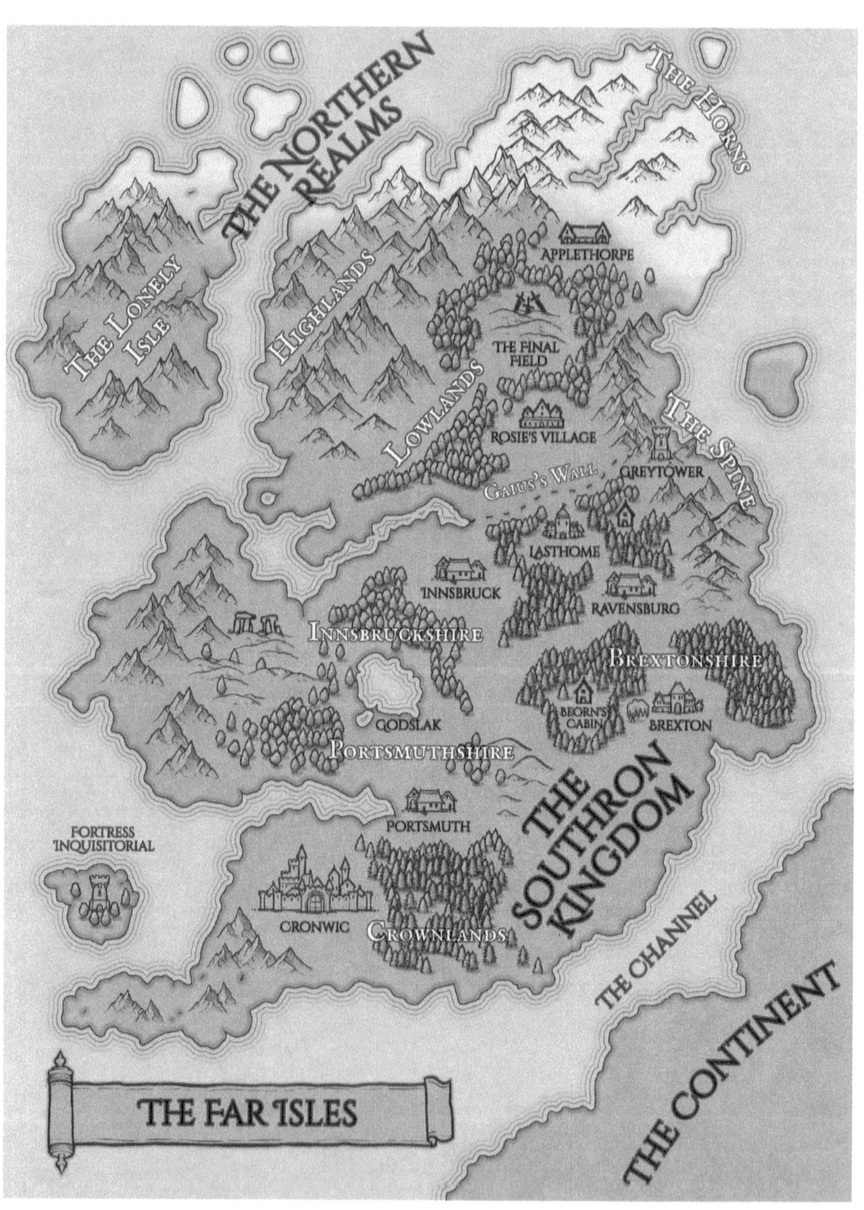

THE NORTHERN REALMS
THE HORNS
THE LONELY ISLE
HIGHLANDS
APPLETHORPE
THE FINAL FIELD
LOWLANDS
ROSIE'S VILLAGE
THE SPINE
GAIUS'S WALL
GREYTOWER
LASTHOME
INNSBRUCK
RAVENSBURG
INNSBRUCKSHIRE
BREXTONSHIRE
GODSLAK
BEORN'S CABIN
BREXTON
PORTSMUTHSHIRE
FORTRESS INQUISITORIAL
PORTSMUTH
THE SOUTHRON KINGDOM
CRONWIC
CROWNLANDS
THE CHANNEL
THE CONTINENT
THE FAR ISLES

# I

# The Bystander

*"He who sees evil and does naught is just as complicit as those who stain their hands with the act."*

# Chapter 1

P*ick it up.*

Beorn opened his eyes to the rising sun creeping in through the cracks in his shutters. A thin sheen of sweat clung to his brow. His chest heaved up and down, lungs sucking in breath like a drowning man. Steadily, his heart slowed from its frantic hammering. When he'd resumed his composure, Beorn levered himself onto an elbow, swinging his legs over the side of the pallet bed.

As the sun rose, light continued to break through gaps in the cabin's wooden walls, washing away the lingering remnants of his accursed dreams. Some men woke from their slumber unable to recall the details of their dreams, good or fearful. Not Beorn. For him, the dreams came every night, curling up on his chest while he slept, restricting his breath, torturing his mind, and depriving him of rest. And in the morning, when the sun rose to wake him from his torment, the memories remained. There was no escape.

The pallet creaked as he lifted his bulk from its makeshift mattress, straw spilling from a split in the side. The hardwood floor was cool under his bare feet as he strode over to the window and threw open the shutters. Light spilled into the one-room cabin, illuminating its stark interior. Besides the pallet bed, the room sported a stone hearth with the low-burning embers of the night's fire, a thin table for preparing food scored with knife marks, a single three-legged stool, and a heavy chest at the foot of the bed.

A shallow wooden bowl sat upon the windowsill, filled with clean water. He stooped, cupped the water cooled by the morning air, and splashed it onto his face. Droplets ran through a coarse black beard, fighting a losing war against an invasion of greys as he rubbed the sleep from his eyes. Outside the window, sunlight made its way through the verdant forest canopy to fall upon a floor littered with pine needles. To his left stood a dilapidated shack made of three walls. Inside, a large draught horse stood chewing at a bale of hay. Next to the shelter sat a wooden cart. The wood was dark brown with repeated varnish, save for several newly repaired spokes showing its heavy use. Piled high in the cart's bed was a mountain of firewood, bundled roughly five logs apiece with hemp rope. To the right, another enormous pile of split logs loomed. A thick stump sat at the base of the mound and embedded in its ancient rings was a sharp iron axe.

Beorn picked up the wooden bowl and brought it to his lips, draining the remaining water and soothing a throat strained by his nocturnal cries. He turned and walked towards the cold hearth where a string of clothes hung; washed and dried from the previous day's labours. He stepped into a pair of worn trousers before slipping a roughspun tunic over his head and tucking it into his waist. Sitting on the three-legged stool, Beorn leaned forward to slip on two worn leather boots. As he did, long black ropes of hair fell around his face.

*I should shear it off while I'm in town,* he thought. *Lest I get lice.*

Beorn took no pride in his appearance. No mirrors existed in the small wooden cabin. Beorn did not care for the eyes that stared out of them.

Rising, his eyes fell upon the chest by the bed. Like all aspects of the cabin, the chest was bare of any adornment, built solely for utilitarian purposes. Beorn considered the weather. It was mid-autumn, and while the days were still pleasant, winter storms were regularly arriving without herald. He strode towards the chest and knelt to open the lid. Within were the few other earthly possessions Beorn owned. His eyes glazed across them, pushing objects and spare clothing aside until he glimpsed his travelling cloak near the bottom of the chest where he had stored it at the onset of last spring. Drawing out the grey-dyed woollen cloak, he shook it free of dust, briefly inspected it for any moth-eaten holes, and flung it across his shoulders. As he reached out to close the chest, he spied another bundle of neglected fabric within its depths. The cloth concealed a long object hidden from the eyes of men and God, and showed only faint signs of its former heraldry…

*Enough.* Beorn let the lid close with a heavy slam.

Birdsong and insect chirps greeted him as he pushed open the cabin door, its hinges creaking. It would take Beorn an hour's ride on his cart to reach the nearest human dwelling, and another hour yet to reach any semblance of civilisation.

*Best get a move on then.*

As he started across the yard, he swung past the stump and extended his hand for his axe. It was possibly his most cared-for possession; the haft was smooth from frequent use but protected from the elements with a strong coat of linseed oil; the head kept free of rust with a beeswax blend, and the edge kept sharp and clean of sap. Beorn pulled the blade from the stump without missing a step and strode towards the laden cart. Depositing the axe onto the bench seat, he turned to the powerful cart horse gnashing at the loose straw.

"Morning, Godfrey." The horse did not deem an answer necessary and continued to chew. Just as Beorn preferred. Godfrey was a mighty horse of deep bay colouring, with four white socks and a white stripe down his nose. His mane and tail were as dark and long as Beorn's own hair. At two meters tall and weighing roughly a tonne, Godfrey made simple work of clearing felled trees and pulling the heavy cart to town. His feathered hooves clomped through the mud of the yard as Beorn led him to the cart. Godfrey gave a single shake of his head and a snort through his large nostrils once the bit was in place, and the pair were ready for the pilgrimage to town.

The path from Beorn's cabin was dirt, two trenches carved into the earth by the cart's repeated procession from cabin to town, town to cabin, and back again. The birds continued their chorales, calling to one another amongst the branches. On one or two occasions, Beorn caught sight of a doe grazing on the long grass of the forest floor, rarely raising her head in search of foes. There wasn't many a predator in these parts of the woods. Those lurked further out.

Steadily, the forest thinned, and Godfrey led them out of the last of the tree cover. As they proceeded down a hill, Beorn raised his head to the grey clouds forming on the horizon. The warm sun that had greeted him that morning still shone against his back, but up ahead, a tempest was preparing itself to inflict the people of this land with wet socks and muddy streets. The brewing storm sent an icy breeze as its forerunner, and Beorn was thankful he had brought his travel cloak.

An hour into the journey, Beorn and Godfrey came upon their closest neighbour. The squat messenger station wasn't more than a shack, but still put Beorn's cabin to shame. The stable behind housed two horses, fresh and ready to be swapped at the need of any royal messenger. Food and shelter were also available should a royal runner require; or to a lowly traveller for a small weight of coin. Beorn spotted the station master sitting on his step as he regularly did.

"Good morrow, Beorn!" shouted Alan Reed. The station master was a stout little man well past his prime, if in fact he had ever been in it. Missing every second tooth and with more hair on his shoulders than pate, Alan was not a seemly visage. His personality fit the mould. It was not for honour that Alan took his post far from friend or neighbour, offering support for the King's messengers. It was for the gossip they carried, and for the opportunity to swindle desperate travellers out of their coppers for watery gruel, stale bread, and a patch of floor in his stable. Regardless, the information gained from royal and impoverished traveller alike was useful to a man as far removed from civilisation as Beorn.

"What tidings?" Beorn offered in reply once Godfrey had crossed the distance to the messenger's station. A dull copper coin leaped from Beorn's thumb into Alan's weathered hand. *Friend* would be a gross overvaluation, *acquaintance* would suggest some level of knowledge of each other, and *associate* implied some shared business. Beorn got his news from Alan; Alan in return got a copper from Beorn.

"There's a storm on the horizon." Alan was sceptically inspecting the copper.

"I have eyes," Beorn retorted.

"Steady on. Was only making small talk."

"Didn't pay for small talk, Alan. On my way into town to sell my wares; eager to know if I'm expected to be waylaid by bandits, set upon by roaming hounds, or if God Almighty in his infinite wisdom has seen fit to raze Brexton from the face of the earth, saving me the trouble of a wasted journey."

Alan Reed gave a chortle. "A'right, a'right. I can't speak to any bandits spotted in the area; the King's men keep the road safe enough. And the only hound that's given me any trouble is Matilda here, spreading her damnable fleas all over the place." He nudged a sleeping bloodhound, snoozing by his feet. Its coat was dull, skin pulled tightly across its ribs, and a sprinkling of white hoarfrost speckled its hanging jowls. The beast opened its eyes sheepishly at the mention of its name - for all the good it did; both were milky with blindness. "As for Brexton, we'd only be too lucky if the Good Lord erased that den of sin from this plane." Alan leaned forward and spat brown phlegm into the mud. "But, short of such a feat, He has seen fit to send his emissaries to Brexton to root out the cause of all our ills in these lands." Beorn stared down at Alan without comment. Sensing he wouldn't get a response, Alan saw fit to explain: *"Witches."*

Beorn's skin prickled and his hands squeezed tighter around the reins. "The Inquisitorum?"

A wide, gap-toothed grin spread across Alan Reed's ruddy face. "Aye. Word has it Brexton's been infested with the devils, to the point their cells are practically burstin'! The King has sent his Inquisitors to tend to the heretics. I must confess I'm a touch jealous of you headed into town. I 'eard there's to be a grand execution today." Alan gave another chortle. "That bein' said, I got my fair share of entertainment last eve' as the Inquisitorum rode through."

"Meaning what?"

"Meaning they left a message at the message tree." A sly wink, and Alan Reed turned and limped back inside his messenger's shack.

Beorn sat for a moment, staring at the road ahead. Finally, he gave a shake of the reins and Godfrey resumed his slow meander along the path towards Brexton. Not far from Alan Reed's run-down messenger shack stood an ancient oak with branches as thick as Beorn's waist. At its base was a notice board littered with missives for passers-bye. Recruitment flyers calling men to arms to spread the king's law and the word of God to those distant kingdoms not yet within the Gilded Father's embrace, advertisements from local physicians hawking miracle tonics and balms, and letters from desperate mothers beseeching any information of their lost children. And above the notice board swayed four naked corpses, hanged by their necks from the boughs of the ancient tree. Each bore the signatures of the Inquisitorum: nails torn from their nail beds, stripes of burnt flesh from hot iron rods, and elbow and knee joints twisted at sickening angles. Several had breasts cut from their bodies. One was missing her eyes. Prior to her hanging, or the work of the congregating crows, Beorn could not be sure. The sky above the tree was dark with them.

From rope around each poor soul's neck was attached a board that read: *"Here be sinners, heretics, and witches."*

Someone should have taken them down. Someone should have buried them... Beorn did not slow his wagon and passed on towards Brexton.

Time passed, the sky grew darker, the road slowly transformed from mud to gravel to stone, and an hour after parting from Alan Reed's shack, Beorn arrived at Brexton's gates. It was mid-morning by this point. He had made good time. Beorn joined the queue of peasants waiting for entry, come from across the countryside to sell or to buy. He settled into the cart's bench-seat, his mind turning once more to the Inquisitorum currently behind those gates. The line moved slowly, each peasant showing their wares or stating their business for entry. The guards weren't usually this stringent, more concerned with their bawdy tales of the previous night's conquests than with the security of produce entering Brexton's market. Perhaps the presence of Church officials had produced special orders: that being, the doing of their jobs.

It had not been five minutes before the guards spotted Beorn in the queue.

"Ho, Beorn!" An energetic wave and a wide smile accompanied the greeting. Despite himself, a return smile crept into the corner of Beorn's mouth. "Move aside, you lot! Let the cart through! This is your lord's woodsman and about your lord's business!"

Beorn shook the reins and trotted past the still lengthy queue, much to the displeasure and silent curses of those who were before him. "Greetings, Hollock. How fares guard duty?"

The man, who in truth was barely more than a boy, blew out his hairless cheeks. "The captain has us all out on duty today. An envoy of Inquisitors rode in, dead of night," his voice lowering. "They come escorted by a squad of Holy Guards. There's to be some execution in the town square at noon. They've already started hearing trials for the prisoners confined to the town gaol."

"Aye," Beorn growled. "I saw those the Inquisitors have passed judgement on already, on the journey here." The limp bodies swayed on their ropes behind Beorn's eyes.

The boy-guard nodded. His expression was part-fear, part-elation. Brexton did not experience this level of entertainment often. A travelling bard or roving caravan now and then. Never trials. Never the Inquisitorum. "And those were just the standard proceedings. Trial and judgements held behind closed doors, executions in private. Likely just blasphemers, adulterers and the like. But whatever they've got planned for today is *different*."

"Well," Beorn interjected, keen to be on his way. "I dare say I'll be too preoccupied to attend. What will it be today?"

"Three bundles, Beorn. We were running on coals last night, freezing our cocks off! Ha!"

Beorn reached back and began pulling out bundles of split logs. Hollock stacked the bundles at the side of the gate, near the guard tower's door.

"My thanks, Beorn."

"My thanks to *you*," Beorn reciprocated, nodding at the queuers who were growing more and more disgruntled by his interjection. Beorn regularly exchanged firewood for skipping the queue at the gate. Hollock had even taken to keeping apples in the guards' quarters for Godfrey.

*Perhaps here is an associate?*

The queuers were becoming restless, not only from Beorn's line-cutting but now from the added holdup of his and Hollock's pleasantries. "Best be off before you have a riot on your hands."

"Aye. Fare thee well, Beorn! And you too Godfrey." The boy-guard gave the draught horse a pat on his solid hindquarters before trotting off through the city gates. *City* was generous, but it was the largest town in the fief and where the local lord made his home (albeit high upon the hill away from the filth and muck of the city proper). The cart's uneven wheels *click-clacked* across the street's cobbles, taking him on his usual route. Waste flowed in the gutters as people emptied their chamber pots from the prior evening. Stray dogs roamed the alleys, looking for anything from which they could salvage a meal. The occasional rat scampered across the road, darting between cover. It was hardly metropolitan. The city's economy revolved around trade; in virtually all sectors, a market atmosphere prevailed. Grains, meats, and dairy products flowed in from the surrounding countryside. Craft production focused on ironware and timber work. There was wealth among the local aristocracy, high upon the lord's hill; but there was poverty and vagrancy too, down here among the common people. A local saying in Brexton went, *"The gold flows uphill while the shit flows down,"* though never within earshot of the town guards.

The culture in Brexton was less varied. Lord or peasant, baron or farmer; all worshipped the Gilded Father. In times past, religious worship in Brexton stretched from the pantheon of Old Gods brought over by the Carthians, to the Sun Gods of the Distant South, to the forest gods of the northern druids, and even a dozen richly developed cults clamouring for attention. There may even have been some Leyanites permitted within the city walls, albeit in small numbers and constrained to ghettos. Then the Church of the Gilded Father burst forth onto the scene. The old deities were pushed out little by little, and those believers who remained eventually found the sharp end of a spear. Ghettos burned down, idols were toppled, temples sacked, and in their place rose towering chapels and churches adorned with the square cross.

Ironically, the Church had risen from the embers of the Carthian Empire, only to tear down the statues and shrines dedicated to the Old Gods of

Carth. The Church decreed these were false idols, guises of the Adversary, used to lure mankind away from the Path of Light. The fall of the Empire and its preceding Republic proved this. *Democracy* was an insult to the Lord Above, for only He could anoint the leaders of man: nobles, lords, *kings.* Democracy was mankind playing God, seeking to exert their will unto the world. It was the *illusion* of choice. The Church decreed men were sheep, and the King was their shepherd (though every man, cur, and rat knew it was the Church who stood behind the throne). Beorn cared little for that rhetoric. He'd much preferred to swing the axe than to be the livestock.

Attached to a pole next to his seat was a bell; rope hanging out, knotted at the end. Beorn's first stop was the bakery. *Clang, clang,* the bell went. Beorn swung out of the cart's bench and landed with a *thump* on the street. Upon hearing the bell, the baker made his way out of the shop and greeted Beorn with a nod.

"Greetings, Beorn." The hot air from his multiple ovens came wafting out after the baker, nicely holding at bay the continued drop in temperature brought by the coming storm. With it came the rich scent of rising bread.

"Greetings, Sampson," Beorn replied. "The usual?"

"We'll take an extra bundle today. There are big events occurring in Brexton! Members of the Holy Order have blessed us with their presence! Executions tend to get people's blood pumping, and that makes them eager for drink and vittles. And the latter I plan to have at the ready. Freshly baked trenchers in every tavern from here to the town square. Same price per bundle as last time?"

"You can pay for the extra bundle with one of these freshly baked loaves you're boasting of."

"Ha! I like the way you barter. Martha! Bring our friendly giant one of the fresh loaves. And grab some of that cheese we were gnawing this morn!" He turned back to Beorn. "Splendid stuff, nice and sharp."

Martha, the baker's wife, followed her husband out of the shopfront holding a small cloth bundle, emanating with the scent of freshly baked bread. The older woman wore a homely smile. As she reached her husband's side and stepped forward to hand Beorn his meal, the toes of her sandals caught on an uneven cobblestone, sending her sprawling into the street. The bundle bounced and rolled, landing between Beorn's boots.

In an instant, the baker had his wife by the elbow, hauling her to her feet. "What the devil is your problem, woman?!" And fast as lightning, he drew back his hand and cracked her across the face. She spun in a half circle, bending over with her cheek cupped in her hands. "Get back to the ovens! God help you if any of those loaves burn."

Martha stood. Her cheek was already swelling. With eyes cast down, she turned back to the store, the homely smile left in the street where she'd fallen.

Sampson, the baker, sighed. "My apologies, Beorn… I can retrieve another loaf if you'd like…?"

Beorn bent to retrieve the bundle between his boots. He dusted a layer of dirt off the roughspun fabric's exterior. "That won't be necessary. My thanks for the cheese."

The cart's wheels resumed their *click clack* down the cobbled street, the incident with the baker's wife lingering for only a moment. *I don't get involved;* Beorn told himself.

Next stop was the smithy. Beorn heard the rhythmic strike of a hammer on an anvil before he saw the blacksmith's sign hanging from the gables of the workshop. The smithy had an open storefront. Beorn saw apprentices running back and forth, retrieving tools and pumping bellows. The heat of the forge erupted into the street in a league above anything the bakery could have produced. Journeyman smiths were quenching white-hot blades in vats of oil, before pulling them out to inspect for warping.

Beorn rang his bell and reined Godfrey to a stop. A thick-armed blacksmith strolled out of the heart of the smithy, sweat streaming from his forehead. Constant squinting against the furnace's heat had left his face lined with deep furrows. Soot clung to the coarse layer of hair coating his forearms. In one hand he held a hammer, in the other a near finished shortsword. The tip still glowed a dull orange where the smith had been hammering it into shape. He slid the hammer into a loop of his leather apron and strolled out of his shop, sword in hand.

"Just in time, Beorn. I've an order of horseshoes for the lord's stables and my furnaces are about to run cold."

"Never fear, Elias. The Lord provideth."

Elias whistled to two apprentices to come unload the required number of bundles. While they were unloading, the smith counted out the required coppers and handed them to Beorn, who began his own count. Seeking to fill the silence, Elias spoke. "Have you heard about Brexton's latest visitors?"

Beorn *humphed*, continuing to count.

"Any plans to attend the demonstration in the square? They're executing a witch."

"I saw the outcome of several Inquisitorial executions on my way into town, hanging from the boughs of the message tree. I've no taste to see any more corpses today."

Elias shook his head. "From what I've heard, this is different. They're pulling out all the stops. It's to be a burning."

That made Beorn raise his head. He pocketed the coins. Elias had skimmed him several coppers, but he couldn't bother to haggle. "It's rare the Inquisitorum bother to burn their heretics, at least this far from the royal court."

"They want to send a message, I hear. They want the crowd to see what happens to heretics and heathens who turn away from the Gilded Father."

"And will you be attending this o' holy of exhibitions?"

Elias surveyed the street. The foot traffic was slow in this quarter of town. The oncoming storm front had now obscured the sun, making it difficult to determine the time of day, but noon was likely nearly upon them. "Day in and day out, I work with fire. I've felt its kiss more times than that of my wife. I've smelt the stench of burnt hair and seen the skin slough off my inept apprentices more times than I can count."

Elias paused a moment as a bald-pated friar waddled past the woodman's cart. He smiled at them both and crossed himself: left shoulder to right hip, right shoulder to left hip. Both brawny men repeated the gesture.

"But the thing I've learnt most working with the flame all these years," Elias resumed when the friar had passed, "is the fear it puts in men. All beasts fear the flame, and man is no different. That's why the Inquisitorum burn their witches. To strike fear. Not just in those they seek to burn, but in those who gather to watch." He shook his head. "I've no interest in seeing that fear in someone's eyes."

By now, the sweating apprentices had piled the purchased firewood against the side of the smithy. Apparently, they had made a game of it, with the taller of the two revelling in his victory.

"Well," Beorn finally said, "good thing we both have work to keep us busy this day."

Elias grunted. Looking down, he seemed to remember the sword he had been hammering. The tip had cooled now, leaving the steel a mottled blue. He hefted the blade up and presented it for Beorn's appraisal, hilt first. Beorn did not take the handle, but inspected the blade with his eyes. He nodded his approval. "A good blade. I can see the distinction between the core and outer steels. Softer steel in the centre to absorb the shock when struck, yet stronger at the sides to keep a keen edge. You leave a deeper fuller than other smiths. To lighten the blade?"

"You know your swords."

"I recognise good craftsmanship, is all." *How many men will that weapon fell?* Beorn lamented. "I must be off, Elias. Other customers to attend."

Elias nodded. "Lord protect you, Beorn."

"And you, Elias."

Continuing his route, Godfrey brought them out of the working quarter and into the residential areas. Beorn unwrapped his prize from the baker and broke his fast on warm bread and strong cheese. Coming to their first stop, Beorn rang his bell and waited for the owner of a small clay-walled house to come out. As the wooden door creaked open, a small, hunched-back old woman appeared. At the sight of her, Beorn openly grinned. Her, he would call a friend.

"Good morrow, Adeline," Beorn greeted.

"Good morrow to you, Beorn," the old woman responded. Beorn slid from the cart's bench as she shuffled down her stoop to stand before him. "Keeping well fed, I see?" She reached up a bony hand to brush crumbs from the greying tip of his beard.

Beorn chuckled. "Demand for firewood is high, especially with autumn ending." Again, the chilling breeze of the imminent storm blew through him. He saw it bite into the older woman and whip her tattered shawl into a flurry around her narrow frame. "Let me get you your bundles." Beorn turned and reached into his cart. Adeline was a widow. Her husband had fought honourably in the northern campaigns. He did so for the promise of coin and a more comfortable life for his wife and children. Never mind that he was already well past his prime. Nonetheless, he swung his sword with an unexpected strength and felled many a foe. That didn't prevent the pagans from slitting his throat while he slept, along with the rest of his company. Adeline never got to bury his bones. *'Too far out in heathen territory for retrieval,'* the regiment liaison had told her. *'Untenable.'* But the King gave her his *'heavy thanks for her contribution to his holy crusade.'* Not that it mattered to Adeline. She had been too old to remarry and without a husband to bring in coin, the family had suffered. Their children followed him into death two winters later. The fool should have stayed home.

Beorn finished stacking four bundles of firewood at her feet. "I can't afford that many, Beorn. I'm struggling enough with the two I usually buy."

"A gift for a frequent customer," Beorn replied.

Tears crept into the corners of the widow's eyes. "Bless you, Beorn. You do the Lord's work." She made the sign of the cross, shoulders to hips. Beorn bit back any quarrel with the statement and nodded his acceptance of her blessing. He turned and reached up to the cart's bench when a voice cut through the air.

"You! Woodcutter! Halt!"

Beorn peered through the ropy black hair at the corner of his vision. Stomping down the dirty street was a stout man with a sword strapped to his waist. This was no city guard. The armed man wore heavy chain mail under a black surcoat, and a pointed half helm with a noseguard. Blazoned across his chest was a heraldry depicting two silver keys, crossed.

*The Holy Seal.*

This man was part of the Holy Guard escorting the Inquisitors, come to rid Brexton of its heretics. Guilty or innocent, catching the attention of the Inquisitorum never bode well. Beorn's hand, still on the bench of his cart, made a slow creep towards the butt of his axe.

"Woodcutter," the Holy Guard puffed when he finally stood before Beorn. The man's neck was red and sweaty, as though he had been running. "I received word that you would be in these quarters."

The tips of Beorn's fingers now rested on the grain of his axe handle. "And for what purpose," Beorn retorted in a monotone drawl, "do you seek me out?" He tried to keep any malice from his voice, anything that may provoke the man to anger. A difficult task when, at near seven feet tall, Beorn stood two heads taller than the armed guard. Small men often like to fight large battles.

"By order of his holiness, Inquisitor Constantine Julius Herodotus, I have come to seize your wares to undertake the holy mission of the Inquisitorum."

Until that moment, Beorn had maintained a blank expression; but at the Guard's words, it darkened. His brow furrowed and eyes narrowed. "Seize?"

The Holy Guard swallowed but stayed his ground. "Perhaps… *acquisition* would be more appropriate."

Again, Beorn remained silent.

The Holy Guard, unfamiliar with anything short of total obedience and abasement, was growing frustrated. A vein was bulging in his stout neck. "I'm here to purchase your firewood, you imbecilic behemoth! On behalf of the Inquisitorum! Consider this a great honour."

Beorn took a long time considering, although in truth there was very little to consider. The Inquisitorum were second only, in authority, to the King, and depending on who you asked that was being generous… to the King. Their word was law, interpretations of divine will, and defiance was tantamount to heresy. Despite this, abiding the little man's request soured Beorn's soul.

"Unfortunately, I've already promised much of this wood to others. I have regular customers who depend on my deliveries to guarantee their livelihood and heat their homes. Without, they will go cold and hungry." In truth, Beorn cared little for this detail. A man didn't choose to make his home miles from the comforts of civilisation and humankind's hospitality because he cared for his fellow man. "Johan, the lord's woodcutter for the western forests, should be among the fishing quart–"

"Johan is dead." The small guard snorted deep and spat a phlegmy wad into the dirt. "Hanged by order of the Inquisitorum. He spoke ill of his liege lord and the quality of the woods granted to him to make his livelihood. To speak ill of the local lord is to speak ill of the King who granted him this fief. And to speak ill of the King is to speak ill of the God who ordained his ascension. And to speak ill of our Lord God is *heresy*." The Holy Guard stared icy daggers up at Beorn through long and unruly eyebrows.

Beorn had known Johan, if only as a colleague. A fellow woodsman for the local lord, granted the woods opposite the River Brex to maintain, permitted to sell the timber of any tree that needed felling. They had crossed paths occasionally in town but usually sold their wares in opposing quarters to not interfere with each other's business. He had liked to whittle. From what Beorn could remember, he'd had a family; a wife and two sons. And in the eyes of the Inquisitorum, the sins of the father...

*More's the pity.*

Beorn let out a defeated sigh, and let his fingers slide from the haft of his axe. There was no fighting the whims of the Inquisitorum. "How much?" he grunted.

"The lot."

"My other customers..."

"Can go cold and hungry for all I care. The needs of the Inquisitorum go before all else!"

Beorn stared coldly down at the small man before reaching up to grab Godfrey's reins to comply.

"And those as well!" The Holy Guardsman pointed a stumpy finger at the four bundles of wood piled next to Adeline's feet.

"Those are paid and bought..."

"Enough of this!" The guard had apparently reached the end of his generosity. "Bring your wares, including those bundles, with me now or I will impound your horse and cart for my purposes and have you thrown in the city gaol." His right hand gripped the hilt of his sword, knuckles white with rage. "I speak with the voice of the Inquisitorum. The Inquisitorum speaks with the voice of God! And to defy the voice of God–!"

"Is heresy," Beorn finished through gritted teeth. Beorn picked up the pile of firewood from Adeline's feet without making eye contact with the old woman and threw them into the back of his cart. She did not argue, despite the cold that would creep into her bones tonight. She did not protest, despite the hunger that would twist her stomach, her gums unable to make do with dried hardtack. She did not beg, despite the rats that would come crawling in without the protective light of the hearth. For Adeline had lived longer than most, in no minor fact because of her knowledge that when the Church *'asked',* you obliged. A moment later, Beorn was leading Godfrey down the cobbled street at the heels of the satisfied guard.

They made their way along the wynds and alleys. As they passed, the masses of people became thicker and more fevered. It took Beorn a moment to realise they had joined a current of bodies, all moving in the same direction. He realised a moment later, to his dread; it was towards the town square.

*'There's to be some execution in the town square at noon.'* Hollock's words rose from the waters of Beorn's mind.

*'It's to be a burning,'* Elias's words followed.

In his blatant disdain for the Holy Guard, Beorn hadn't even bothered to wonder what the Inquisitorum required with a cartload of firewood at a moment's notice. They needed wood for their pyre. The town square fell in Johan's agreed-upon area of sale.

*Suppose they didn't think of that when they strung him up,* Beorn thought with dark humour. No wonder the Holy Guardsman had looked so dishevelled upon finding Beorn. The Inquisitors had promised a show to the peasant folk, and a guaranteed way to stoke mass insurrection was to deny the people their entertainment. Beorn knew these spectacles served other purposes though.

*Even so, why a burning?* he pondered as the crowd encased them.

"Make way! Make way! I'll crack your skulls if I have to!" the stout guard shouted. The throng of peasants reeking of soiled garments, unwashed bodies, and cabbages parted for the two men and the giant draught horse. In the gap of bodies, Beorn sighted the stake. A thick trunk fixed atop a wooden platform. All were fresh pine; the wood light and aromatic. Felled, planed, and constructed for the sole purpose of being reduced to ash. Around the platform stood a troop of Holy Guards, all dressed identically to Beorn's guide. The silver keys on their surcoats looked dull grey in the shadows of the massing clouds. Each man wore mail, with a sword sheathed at his waist. "Here will do," the short guard grunted when they were near to the stage.

*Stage,* thought Beorn. *For that's what this is. It is theatre.*

The guard gestured for two of his comrades to unload the cart. They unbundled the firewood and stacked it in orderly columns under the stage, allowing spaces for airflow. Some of these gaps they stuffed with dry hay. They were proficient at their task, obviously having done it before.

*How many times?* wondered Beorn.

When they were done, the short guard reached into his surcoat and withdrew a leather pouch heavy with coins. He threw this at Beorn's chest, his hand rising quickly to catch it. Beorn pulled the drawstring and caught sight of the dull glint of gold.

"That should more than cover the cost of your wares. Now begone with you," the short man chided and turned his attention away, as though Beorn no longer existed. Beorn made no complaint and began leading Godfrey away, the cart in tow. He didn't get far, for the crowd had reached an impassible density. People stood shoulder to shoulder, packed tight like lumber for transport. Without the authoritative bark of the Holy Guard, the people had no interest in parting for some lowly woodcutter and risk losing a prime view of the execution. Beorn sighed and ceased his efforts. Instead, he patted Godfrey on the nose before leaning against one of the cart's wheels, folding his arms and turning his gaze towards the stage.

The Holy Guards had resumed their perimeter, now turned to face the crowd, eyes scanning for any potential issue. It wasn't long before murmurs rippled through the crowd, signifying something was occurring. A moment later, three figures appeared upon the stage. On the left, another Holy Guard, indistinguishable from his brothers. Next stood a hooded figure wearing a dress of stained roughspun material. Their hands were bound before them with thick hemp ropes, the skin around them red and raw. The legs that were visible below the shift were black with grime. Beorn could not see from this distance, but he wondered if the gaol's rats had riddled those legs with bite marks. And last, on the far right, stood the Inquisitor.

He towered above the other two and was thin as a reed. His priestly robes were dyed black, the blackest cloth Beorn had ever seen, save for the white square of his clerical collar at his neck. Atop his head sat a broad-brimmed hat, as black as his cassock and wider than his shoulders. He raised his head towards the crowd and from underneath his hat was a countenance of skeletal complexion. His skin was pulled taut around his features. He turned his neck and Beorn swore he could see the imprint of the Inquisitor's grinning skull under his gaunt cheeks. Even at this distance, Beorn could see his eyes were black pits, deep enough to drown the man who was unfortunate enough to catch his gaze.

*The reaper has come to Brexton,* thought Beorn, *and he brings death in his wake.*

The Inquisitor raised two long bony arms, hidden beneath the sleeves of his black cassock. Instantly, the furtive crowd fell silent. The Inquisitor opened his mouth and spoke; "I am the Inquisitor, Constantine Julius Herodotus. His High Holiness, Innocent the Tenth, and King Aethelstan the Third have ordered me to attend this wretched hole of sin and depravity and deliver you all from the vile wickedness that has infested your ranks."

His voice carried power and authority, stemming from the surety from which he spoke. He knew his voice's power, and he imbued his words with it. The articulation, the roll of his *R's*, the superiority in his tone. It cut through the peasant folk like a scythe, telling them this man was of a different world. He sat at the table of kings, sampled wine from the casks of his High Holinesses' personal cellar, and could deliver death with the point of a finger.

"The cells of your gaol," he continued, "teem with filth of the lowest form:

whoremongers, blasphemers, cheats, and *heretics*." He spat the word. "We of the Inquisitorum have commenced our judgements. Many repent and walk the path of penitence and flagellation. Their backs run red with their sins, but their souls are now pure. Those deemed beyond the saving Grace of our Lord have had their souls delivered unto the River of Penance and begin their long pilgrimage upriver, into the Light of God." Beorn pictured the women hanging from the message tree.

The Inquisitor paused, either to let his words sink in or to catch his breath. Regardless, he did not hurry. The world spun around this man, and he knew it.

"But there are some for whom redemption is impossible. There are those who have turned their backs to our Lord and accepted the cold, dark embrace of the Adversary!" A choir of gasps from the crowd and the quick movements of the four pointed cross being enacted. Inquisitor Constantine took a deep breath through his thin nostril before bellowing, "*Witches!*"

The crowd erupted in anger; curses and obscenities shouted out. The frail figure between Inquisitor Constantine and the Holy Guard flinched at the cacophony, blind behind the rough hessian hood. "*This* treacherous whore is accused of cavorting with the Adversary, giving herself to him body and soul, and spreading her dark magics amongst us!" The crowd was in a frenzy now; the Inquisitor had stoked their fears and anxieties and they were ready for blood. "But above all else, her greatest sin… the murder of the innocent; of the unborn!" Women in the crowd broke into a sob, men began flinging rotten vegetables at the hooded prisoner.

Inquisitor Constantine raised his hands again, and slowly the crowd fell under his spell and quietened, their boiling blood barely contained. "Her guilt in these matters is certain. Our investigations have proven it." A feigned look of remorse fell across his face, but the phantom grin of his skull remained. "Undoubtedly, she must be punished. But punishment does not take primary place in today's proceedings, for punishment ought to be for the correction and good of he who hath sinned. Today is for the good of you, the public, in order that others may become terrified and weaned away from the *evils* they would commit. And with this in mind, I have sentenced this heretic to death… by fire!"

At this, the Holy Guard at her side ripped away the hessian hood, revealing the young witch to the crowd. At the same instant, she heard the Inquisitor's words and saw the platform, the stake, and the cheering crowd awaiting her death. A veil of bright red curls fell around her head as the sack was torn away. Deep purple bruises ringed her eyes, but within them were green pools full of terror. The eyes of a cornered rabbit, with a wolf at the mouth of its warren. She was young, maybe fifteen summers, and frail.

Beorn stared at her, shocked.

*She looks just like…*

The girl had obviously not been aware of her fate. Death, she obviously would have known, awaited her at the end of her walk from the gaol, but not upon the pyre. Her frail chest heaved, and she sucked in air, frantically looking around her as if searching for escape. The Holy Guard at her left went to guide her towards the stake. Her wrists had been tied before her rather than behind. An oversight by her gaolers, or perhaps her frail figure and short stature, had prompted no cause for concern. A mistake. The girl swung her clasped hands into the stomach of the guard; an inconsequential blow considering her size and the mail he wore, but enough to drive some air out of his lungs and give her time to wrap her twig-like fingers around the hilt of his sword. With a long step, she had drawn the blade from its scabbard and stood with its tip pointed at her captors' faces.

The crowd froze. Beorn had not removed his eyes from the girl's face since the Guardsman had torn away the sack. The Inquisitor and guard stood as statues before the shining blade before them. Even in the hands of the inexperienced, two-and-a-half feet of razor-sharp steel would put a fear into a man.

But the girl had never held a sword, and it showed. Her arms quivered with the weight of the blade, and try as she did with all her strength, knowing her very life depended on it, she could not keep the tip of the blade level with her enemies. The Inquisitor let out a chilling laugh which was soon joined by the crowd and the Holy Guards. The stout guard who had chaperoned Beorn drew his sword and handed it to his comrade atop the stage.

"Cut her to ribbons, Devon!" he shouted.

The Inquisitor's face became suddenly stony and joyless. "She is a witch, a child-killer. She dies by the fire."

The guard beside him nodded and advanced upon the little witch with his borrowed sword. The girl frantically swung at the advancing man. He barely had to move to avoid the blow. She had no clue how long the blade was and missed by a mile, the weight of the weapon carrying her in a semi-circle. The crowd erupted in laughter. What had once been an execution was turning into a mummer's farce. Well, entertainment was entertainment. Only the Inquisitor's eyes maintained their desire to see the girl burn. The advancing guard made a tentative jab with his blade, the girl swinging hers in response. He braced, and the girl's sword bounced off his with a *clang*, her arms vibrating from the clash. She swung once, twice, cutting nothing but air. She was exhausted. Tears and sweat ran down her face, leaving lines in the grime. Her skin underneath was so pale.

The guard seemed to take pity on her. "Listen girlie, just drop the blade. I don't *want* to hurt you. Don't make this harder than it need–" The guard had been reaching out a gloved hand towards the girl, as though approaching a wounded dog. With speed and strength Beorn had thought beyond her, the girl yanked her blade from where it rested with its tip on the platform's planks and brought it in a silver arc up over her head. As the guard leaned in, arm extended, the tip of the blade caught his cheek, leaving a bright red gash. The wound wasn't deep, but he'd never be pretty again, if ever he was.

"You little *cunt*!" Spittle accompanied the curse. Pure, unbridled anger replaced his previous attempts at comfort. With a single powerful backhand, he swung his sword at the girl. She raised her blade to intercept, but her strength had failed. The guard's sword collided with hers and sent it spiralling into the air. It spun in a silver arc, over and over and over, before falling to earth and embedding in the ground before Beorn's boots.

The crowd had followed the arc of the sword and now stared at Beorn.

Beorn stared at the sword.

His reflection in the blade stared back.

Beorn heard the stomp of the stout guard's boots upon the cobbles as he made his way across the square to where the sword stood fixed into the ground. The crowd was silent as they watched the events play out, an intermission to their scheduled entertainment. Beorn saw the guard's black boots appear on the other side of the blade, but his eyes remained locked on the glistening steel. His own dark eyes stared back at him.

*Pick it up.*

A voice that wasn't his echoed the words from the back of his skull. The fingers of his right hand curled and uncurled, as though imagining the feel of the leather grip. The fuller was not so thick as the blade Elias had shown him, but the blade looked sharp. It would rend through flesh with ease.

The guard noticed his fingers and followed his gaze to the blade. A thin smile creased his face. Amusement danced behind his beetle eyes. He leaned over the sword's hilt and came into Beorn's line of sight. "Go on, big man. Take it. Make a grab for the sword. Play the hero I know you want to, like you tried to for that old bitch back there."

*Pick it up.*

The voice was louder. Stern. An order.

"Reach for it," the guard hissed through his yellow teeth. The smile was almost a snarl. "You'll never touch it. Make a grab and I'll have it at your throat before you can blink. I'm a killer. I've killed more dumb bastards than I can remember, but never one as big or as dumb as you. Go on. Do it. Then I can take my gold back from your giant, lifeless corpse."

*Pick. It. Up.*

The voice was unrelenting. It clawed at the back of his skull. His fingers were numb from flexing open, closed, open, closed.

*Save her, Beorn.* A different voice. His eyes darted from the sword to the girl on the stage. She stared back at him, her eyes wide, pleading, begging for him to do something. Her lips mouthed the word repeatedly: *please.*

The guard saw where his gaze landed. "Go on, big man, save the girl. I'll cut you down before you can move an inch."

*Pick it up!*

*Save her, Beorn.*

"C'mon! Do it!"

The girl's eyes pleaded. Fresh tears welled from her already bloodshot eyes. The wind snatched hungrily at her hair. *Please.*

Beorn closed his eyes. The world went black. The voices stopped.

"No? More's the pity." The guard pulled the sword from the ground and sheathed it at his waist, turning back to the stage. "Stupid fucking peasant. Too dumb to even rise to the bait–"

The blade of Beorn's axe stoppered the word in his throat. He pulled it free of the Guardsman's neck and crimson blood sprayed into the air, across the cobbles and the closest of the shocked onlookers. Chaos erupted. The spell that had held the crowd silent broke and screams echoed across the square. People began darting into the streets and alleys, fleeing the scene. Holy Guards ran forth from the stage, steel leaping into their hands. With a deafening crack, the heavens opened, and rain pummelled the earth. The closest guard reached Beorn with his sword raised high above his head. *Stupid.* Beorn's heavy axe head darted forward like a striking serpent, breaking the guard's nose before his sword could fall. He staggered back, stunned. A second later, the axe bit into his cheek, cleaving his head apart. His body was still falling when the next guard was upon them. He favoured a leftward swing across the body, which Beorn intercepted with a swing of his own. The axe was heavier and sent the guard's sword bouncing back. Beorn charged into the gap with a burly shoulder and knocked him to the ground. He lay there, stunned, as the axe came down hard between his eyes. Blood spattered Beorn's face.

The fourth guard had been hot on the heels of his comrades, but their quick dismissals from the mortal plane had installed a healthy level of trepidation. He pulled up just outside Beorn's reach and began circling to his right. Beorn countered by circling left. The haft of the axe was slick and sticky between his fingers. He saw the guard from atop the stage jump down and begin skulking towards him. His present foe continued to circle. A few more steps and Beorn would have one in front and behind. *Not good.* Fortunately for him, the guard in front wasn't planning that far ahead. Beorn feigned a look over his shoulder at the foe from behind, and the one in front lunged forward with a thrust. A mistake. Beorn spun in the direction he had turned, twisting away from the sword thrust. The guard stood off balance, leaning forward, his belly outstretched. Beorn's momentum carried him in a full circle, and he used this motion to drive his axe into the guard's exposed gut. The blade bit through surcoat and chain mail and embedded in his flesh. He dropped his sword as Beorn ripped his axe free. Blood and meat from the guard's insides immediately filled the space the axe had occupied a second before. He fell to his knees, trying to hold himself together, but his viscera continued to bleed through his fingers. He rolled onto the ground, moaning in pain as his blood spread to mingle with that of his companions.

Beorn turned to the last guard; a giant bear of a man staring down at its prey, covered in the lifeblood of four men-at-arms. The guard stared up into Beorn's dark eyes. The slash inflicted by the waif was still bleeding down the guard's cheek, but he could no longer feel it throb. Warm piss spread across his breeches. His fingers could no longer keep a grip on his sword, and it clattered to the muddied ground. He spun and fled, sprinting towards the nearest alley.

Beorn let out a breath he hadn't realised he'd been holding. The Church would kill the guard for fleeing. But Beorn was grateful that it wouldn't be his hand that dealt the blow. He cast his gaze across the square. *Four lives, snuffed out in a matter of minutes.* He did not grieve their deaths, but he couldn't bring himself to look at his stained hands. Instead, he looked up at the girl. The Inquisitor was nowhere to be seen. The square was now empty but for the girl and Beorn. The rabbit and the bear. The witch and the woodcutter.

The rain had plastered the girl's hair against her face. The guards' blood had done the same to Beorn. Both were crimson red.

# Chapter 2

The streets were bare as Beorn steered his cart through the downpour. The townsfolk had sought refuge in their hovels to escape the bite of the rain. Beorn sat atop his cart's bench, rain plastering his travel cloak to his hulking form. The rainfall had washed the carnage from his face, and his clothes were so darkly soaked that the bloodstains were near invisible. The axe leaned against the bench beside him; next to it sat the girl.

Her hair hung limply around her face, her roughspun shift soaked and heavy. Her eyes stared blankly ahead.

*Why did I do that?* Beorn thought to himself. *I don't get involved. I don't get involved. I don't get–*

Across the city, the echoing clamour of church bells rang. The deep, hollow *clang* resonated through the air, making the raindrops vibrate with each heavy toll. They had discovered the massacre in the town square. Beorn gave Godfrey's reins a shake. *"Hyah!"*

The draught horse's great feathered hooves gouged through the mud covering the cobblestones, hot breath steaming out his nostrils.

*Just make it to the gates, make it to the gates.*

The cart turned one corner, then another. Past Adeline's dark cottage, past Elias's now-quiet forge, past Sampson's silent bakery.

*Almost there, almost there.*

Beorn blinked furiously through the rain as it assaulted his eyes, teeth gritted against the cold.

*One more corner ...*

His heart turned to lead and sank in his chest. A great throng of people gathered before the western gate. Guards shouted back at them from the gate's arch, spears in hand.

"No one in or out, by order of the Inquisitorum!" one burly guard shouted at the crowd.

"But what 'bout my wares? No one will come to market in this weather. Do you expect us to sit in the rain and give our goods over to the damp?" shouted back one merchant from the mass.

"You can leave after the Inquisitors arrive and your wagons are searched. Until then, stay put or you'll find a spear in your bellies!"

Beorn's hands tightened around the reins. What would they do? They could turn around and try another gate, but the bells were audible throughout the city. The Holy Guard would bar all exits until they completed their sweep. They could try to hide? But where? Brexton wasn't an overly large settlement and at near seven feet tall, Beorn didn't exactly blend in with a crowd. They could make for the river, try to swim for it. But that would mean leaving Godfrey, something he was loath to do. What if…

"You! On the cart!" The words cut through Beorn's planning like a dagger. His left hand fell from the reins and came to rest on the butt of his axe. Through the downpour, a guard to his right was pushing his way through the crowd. Beorn heard the rain ringing off his kettle helm over the mob's disgruntled complaints. Beorn cast his eyes around.

*Three guards at the gate, plus the one in the crowd.* Another three were atop the wall with bows. On any other day, the numbers would be half what they were. But with the presence of the Inquisitorum, the sergeant had fully garrisoned the gate. The odds were not good. Rain made visibility poor. The crowd left no room to manoeuvre, and he had exhausted himself in the town square. The blood of the Holy Guards still clung to his fingernails.

The guard had reached his cart. Beorn's hand closed around the haft of his axe. Lightning split the sky above. The guard tilted his kettle helm up to meet his gaze.

"Beorn! God, I thought that was you! I can't see shit through this rain!"

Hollock squinted up at him through the downpour. Beorn could almost have laughed.

"Hollock. What's all this about?"

"Some drama in town. We got orders to close the gate and not let a soul through. They're sending down a troop of the Holy Guard and an Inquisitor to check anyone wanting to leave the city. No clue why. Jerrod reckons they lost one of their witches. Ha!"

Beorn was thankful the storm obscured his reaction. "And how long until that occurs?"

Hollock shrugged. "Nary a clue. I expect it'll take the rest of the day to search this lot, one by one. You seem to have had a profitable day! Not a piece o' kindling left in this cart o' yours."

Beorn felt the weight of the pouch of gold hanging at his waist. The coins would be red with blood. "Aye. Lucrative."

Hollock was giving Godfrey a thorough scratch on his right haunch, a grin plastered across his face. The boy had no clue what had transpired in the square. He had no clue what their orders meant, or what would happen when the Inquisitorum arrived. What would he do when they dragged Beorn from his cart and put him to the sword? Beorn had seen Hollock at this gate since he was a boy of eight, annoying his father while on duty (annoying him while playing dice would be more apt). The giant woodcutter had enamoured Hollock ever since he'd laid eyes on him and his monstrous cart horse. *Look at his size!* he'd call to his father. *'If I was his size, I'd be the greatest knight the land had ever seen!'* As a boy, Hollock had dreams of joining the army and going to war, fighting back the pagans to the north, and earning himself a knighthood. But by the time he could swing a sword, the northern campaigns were already won, the pagans suppressed, and the glory taken by others. For a small-town son of a guardsman, the closest he could hope for was following in his father's footsteps. Still, Beorn knew the sight of Godfrey brought up those dreams in the boy-guard whenever he came to town. *'What a warhorse he'd make, eh Beorn? Look at his size, his strength! What I wouldn't give to ride a beast such as him into battle...'*

"Hollock," Beorn called down at the boy as he patted Godfrey's flank. "I need to be on my way. Godfrey isn't as young as he once was. Too long in this weather and he'll catch rain rot. I couldn't bear to see him succumb to such discomfort."

"Discomfort?"

"Pain, in fact. Scabs and scores across the body. Lesions that matte the hair."

"God, I had no idea…"

*You wouldn't, would you? You simple town boy.*

"I couldn't bear if anything happened to him… and I fear I couldn't afford a new steed…"

"A new steed? Can this rain rot really be that fatal?"

"Aye." *No.* "I need to get him undercover, and dried before the rot takes in."

Hollock stared up at him for the longest moment. Boy and guard warring behind his eyes. Finally, the boy, with fantasies of riding a mighty warhorse into battle, won out, and he turned to the massed crowd. "Oi! Move it, you sods! Make way!"

Curses and cries of anger erupted from the mass of bodies as Hollock led Godfrey through the throng.

"Why's he get to go through?!" shouted one especially enraged peasant.

Hollock spun on him. "This here is the lord's woodcutter. Would you deprive our lord of a fire in his hearth? In weather such as this? Is it your whim that our lord catches a chill? That he perish and leave our land to the bandits and villains of the road? That, to me, sounds like treachery!"

The peasant backed away; hands raised. "A'right, a'right good sirs, I meant no treachery. We is cold, that's all."

"And you can be cold a while longer," Hollock barked. He guided Beorn past his fellow guards, under the gates, and through the other side. "On your way, Beorn. But keep this between us."

"You have my thanks, Hollock." Godfrey gave a shake of his mane, water droplets flying in all directions. "Mine *and* Godfreys." Beorn shook the reins and Godfrey trotted away. Beorn's heart thumped heavily in his chest. His knuckles were white upon the reins. All he wanted was to give Godfrey leave to race away from the gates at full speed, putting as much distance as he could between himself and the town square. Were the bodies still there? Had anyone moved them? Had enough rain fallen to wash away the blood?

*No rain will ever be enough to wash away that blood,* Beorn mulled.

Godfrey had taken twenty paces when, from behind, a shout: "Wait!" Footsteps thumping into the mud. The jingle of mail, the slap of a sword in its scabbard against a thigh. The ping of rain off the top of a kettle helm. Hollock appeared again at Beorn's side.

*Please don't make me kill this boy,* he prayed.

Hollock's arm shot out. Something green and round grasped between his fingers. *An apple.* A smile cut across the boy's face. "For Godfrey. I save him the green ones from my rations. I know they're his favourite."

Beorn tenderly took the apple and nodded back at the boy. "My thanks." And with that, he was off again. Hollock watched the cart make its way down the winding track. Only as it disappeared over the hill did the guard notice the small frail figure sitting at Beorn's side, vibrant red hair made dull by the rain.

*  *  *

The corpses hanging from the message tree stared down at them as they passed. The crows that had darkened the sky on Beorn's procession into town now lined the branches of the old oak, sheltering from the storm. A hundred small black eyes followed the woodcutter, the witch, and the cart horse as they plodded past.

*Murder,* Beorn thought. *A murder of crows.* An apt name.

Alan Reed's hut was dark as they passed. The porch was empty except for Matilda, the bloodhound who continued her lazy doze under the awnings. As they passed, the sickly hound raised her head, opening her blind eyes. The milky pupils stared at the girl on the cart until they were out of sight, and even then, Beorn swore he could feel their empty gaze follow them into the tree line of his forest.

*What did they train her to hunt?* Beorn wondered. *Will I wake tonight to the sound of the bloodhound's nose sniffing the crack under my door, hunting a witch?*

Beorn shook the notion from his head. He hadn't given two thoughts to the waif of a girl sitting beside him since they'd left Brexton's gates behind. She hadn't said a word. He'd tried to offer her his cloak to shield her from the rain, but she'd flinched from his hands as though they were vipers.

The cart continued down the dirt path into the woods. The rain was lighter under the canopy of trees. Birds were no longer singing, and any trace of the sunshine that had awoken Beorn this morning was long gone. The hut rose from the undergrowth like an oasis in a desert. Beorn allowed himself a breath of relief as he pulled up beside Godfrey's shed and began working at untethering the horse from the cart. Once done, Godfrey meandered into his makeshift home and resumed gnawing at his bale of hay, unfazed by the events of the day.

*Oh, to be a horse.*

Beorn sloshed through the mud towards his door, stepping through a curtain of rivulets trickling from the wooden shingle roof. The rain continued its relentless assault; the wind whipping Beorn's cloak around his ankles. Putting a large palm against the door, he pushed and was greeted with the sight of normalcy. His pallet bed was as he'd left it, his chest sat closed, the hearth remained cold. It was a comforting sight. He was about to step inside when he stopped and looked behind him for the girl. She wasn't there. For a second, he thought she had run off into the woods, but there she was, still sitting in the rain on the wagon's bench.

"Are you coming?" he shouted at her over the downpour.

She had been sitting there, eyes unfocused, her mind likely trying to make sense of the events that had taken her from gaol to executioner's stage to a woodcutter's cabin. At his shout, she turned to Beorn's bearded face before letting her eyes drop. Beorn followed her gaze to the blood-stained axe in his hand. What did she see when she looked at him? Saviour or murderer?

Beorn placed the axe against the frame of the door and backed into his home. With his now empty hand, he gestured in what he hoped was a reassuring way. The girl looked past him into the warmth the cabin promised and appeared to decide it was worth the risk. Once inside, Beorn worked at getting a fire going; scraping the remains of last night's ashes into a wooden bucket, laying the fresh kindling, and sparking the flint against the steel of his kitchen knife. Once the fire was burning steadily, he fed a few decent sized logs into it. During this, the girl had not dared enter further than the threshold of the cabin. She pressed her back firmly against the door, as though ready to run at any moment. However, Beorn could see the promise of warmth was battling her instincts for self-preservation. Her tentativeness was irritating him. Years of solitude had not helped his people skills.

He kicked his single stool in front of the hearth. "Sit," he ordered. The girl considered, and then obeyed. Beorn saw the colour returning to her face as the heat of the flames licked at her cheeks. Her shift dripped puddles around the stool, but Beorn guessed better than to make her hang it over his drying rope. From under his sodden cloak, Beorn pulled a small cloth sack and tossed it at her feet. The remains of his breakfast spilled out before her. "Eat."

This the girl did not protest. She snatched up the remains of the bread, now cold and hard, and began tearing bites out with her teeth like a savage beast. Bite, swallow; bite, swallow; bite–

The girl heaved once and then vomited all over the floorboards. Her first three bites of the bread swam in a puddle of acrid green bile. She coughed twice and winced in pain.

"Easy, girl," Beorn offered. "Take it slow." The girl resumed her feasting at a less frantic pace. When the bread was gone, she snatched up the cheese and began gnawing. She sat with hands clasped around it, eyes closed as if in prayer. City gaols didn't have a reputation for good cooking.

Beorn threw some ashes on top of the vomit before taking a seat atop his wooden chest. As he settled down, the weight of the day's events finally sank in. Tension slowly released from the muscles of his shoulders and his fingers uncurled from fists he hadn't realised he'd been making.

*Why the devil did I do that?* But he knew why. *Because she looks like...* Except she didn't. Her hair, while of a similar colour, was far more unruly. Her eyes, which he'd first thought green, were grey, and her skin was too pale. Not to mention this girl was older. *Older than she'd ever been allowed to grow.*

"Are ye a knight?"

The question froze him. Not only because it was the first thing that he had heard the girl say, nor because of the content of the question; it was her accent that gave him pause.

*She's a northerner. I murdered four Holy Guardsmen for the life of a northern witch.* "I… I am not. What makes you ask that?"

"Ye killed four men. Men with swords. And ye without."

"I was a soldier. But no longer."

The girl considered him with those grey eyes. "Ye must have been quite the soldier."

Beorn nodded slowly. "Suppose I was." A long silence fell inside the cabin. What did you say to a girl the Church had condemned as evil? What did you say to a man who could kill four warriors without a proper weapon? The fire crackled in the hearth. Finally, Beorn braved a question. "What do I call you?"

The girl considered him for a long minute. Thoughts danced behind those eyes, as if contemplating what power her name might give this man over her. "Morrigan," she finally answered. "And ye?"

"Beorn."

"Well, Beorn the Woodcutter," the girl said. "What happens now?" He saw her eyes glance at the straw mattress behind him. *What is the price for my life? she means.* Everywhere the girl looked, she saw dangers. Part of Beorn found it annoying; another part considered the events that had led her to that pyre. He looked past her eyes to the dark bruises surrounding them.

"Well," he sighed, "I suppose my time as the lord's woodcutter is over. Might be I'll need to be finding a new cabin to rest my head, and a new wood to swing my axe and earn my bread. I've no clue where that might be just yet. What of you? Have you any family?"

Morrigan nodded. "Aye. Though… I'm nae sure how I'm t' get back to them."

"And why is that?"

"They're in a village far t' the north. In my homeland."

*You could have guessed that one, you great fool.* Beorn sighed to himself. "Aye. That poses a problem… for *you*. I must be on my way come sunup. Perhaps I can take you some ways, but I have no business headed north." *Only ghosts lie that way.* "And truth be told… I'm not sure what chance a creature such as you has of making it the length of the kingdom unscathed. Might be a better plan is to look to the future, rather than running whence you came. You could make a life down here. Albeit far from Brexton and the Inquisitorum. If I were you, I'd find myself a nice quiet village with a nice quiet convent and give myself over to the Order of the Faceless Sisters. Take a vow of modesty and shave off that hair and a vow of silence to hide that accent, and the Inquisitors will never be the wiser. A nice comfy life, muttering prayer and being well-fed."

Beorn wasn't sure if it was the hearth reflected in her eyes, but a fire burned there. "I'll nae spend the rest o' my life on my knees for yer southern *God*." She spat the word like a curse. "I will return t' my homeland even if I have t' walk the length o' the kingdom barefoot."

Beorn chuckled. "A barefoot pilgrimage? You're halfway to being a Faceless Sister already."

"I'm nothing like ye southern savages."

Beorn regarded her quietly. *The army drafters had said the same thing about you northerners all those years ago.* "Truth be told, I don't care what you do. Take your chances on the road for all I care, even if you are most like to end up as a head in a ditch somewhere. Or stay here, take my cabin. But don't curse my name when the Inquisitors find you and string you up by the boughs of the message tree. At daybreak, we part ways. In the meantime, we both need rest." Again, her eyes darted to the bed. "You take the pallet, girl. I'll take the floor."

His cloak was nearly dry by the time he laid it out on the floorboards. The floor was hard and unyielding, but years of sleeping upon the hard earth while campaigning made him grateful that it was at least modestly dry. As he closed his eyes, he heard the girl crawl into the straw bed. He could hear her breathing, fast and steady. She was obviously waiting for him to go to sleep. Beorn was happy to oblige. He had nothing worth stealing other than Godfrey, and the girl wouldn't even be tall enough to mount the horse on her own. And if it gave her some manner of peace to see him sleep before she did, then so be it. Beorn let himself slip under and into his nightly torments.

He knew when he woke without opening his eyes that it had been hours but was not yet sunup. He kept them pressed closed and maintained his even, rhythmic breaths. It was the sound of steel scraping wood that had woken him, so very much like the sound of a sword being drawn from a scabbard. The girl's footsteps were light as she padded towards him, but not quiet enough to be masked from his sensitive hearing. He could hear her ragged breaths as she got closer, shaking from nerves.

"If you're going to stick me with that thing, make it quick and make it count. I won't give you another chance." He opened his eyes. She stood over him with both hands gripping the hilt of the kitchen knife, the tip pointed at his chest. Her arms didn't shake as they had with the sword in the square. There was a determination in her eyes. "What's the plan? Kill me, take my horse, and ride like the wind until you're back amongst your mountains and moorlands? And what of the dangers of the road? Brigands and rapers will be the least of your worries. The Inquisitorum will not stop their search until they find you. They won't let a witch escape them."

"Then perhaps I'll take ye with me. Safer t' travel with a man."

"Ha! Do you plan to keep me at knifepoint the entire journey?"

"If I must."

Slowly, Beorn sat until the tip of the knife pressed into his chest. A small bloom of red appeared on his tunic where it stuck him. "I've faced down armies of swords, girl. I'll not meet my end upon the blade of a kitchen knife." He waited for her to retreat, but she did not, nor did she run him through with the blade. She stood defiantly, unwilling to withdraw.

"Take me north." Not a plead, but just short of an order.

"No."

Fire returned to her eyes. "Why did ye save me if ye plan t' just let me die on the road like some sick dog?"

"Forgive me for sacrificing what menial life I'd built for myself here, so you might have a chance at freedom. The truth is, I regretted saving your life the moment the first body hit the floor. Everything after that was self-preservation." *A lie.* "I was a fool to get involved, and I'd be a fool to help you any further. You asked if I'm a knight, and I told you; I'm not. There are no heroes here to escort the fair maiden across the land and defend her honour. There is me. And there is you. And naught betwixt us. Die on the road like a dog for all I care, but don't give me the plague before you do."

"Ye're a monster."

"I'm just a man."

Something creaked just outside the cabin door.

They both turned towards the sound. A shadow appeared across the threshold, then vanished. Beorn thought of that blind bloodhound and his skin prickled despite the warmth of the fire. The wind continued its banshee cry through the rows of pines outside, shaking the shutters in their frames.

"Stay here," he ordered as he sat up, brushing her and the knife aside as if they'd never concerned him in the slightest. Beorn padded over to the shutters and delicately cracked one open. Four figures stood in the mud outside the cabin, shadows hiding their faces. But the moonlight shone clearly off their bared steel and the silver keys crossed upon their chests. "Shit," Beorn cursed. He turned towards the girl. Her hands still gripped the knife like a drowning man to a lifeline. "Keep that thing handy. We have company."

Beorn stepped out into the cold and wet night. The four swordsmen raised their blades as the cabin door opened. It was only out in the full light of the moon that Beorn realised the last of the four men did not wear the raiment of the Holy Guard, but that of the Brexton city guards.

"Evening, Hollock," Beorn called. The boy-guard stared back at him with a pained expression. Fear, dread, anger, and betrayal all fought for dominance on his face.

"We're 'ere for the witch," shouted one of the Holy Guardsmen.

"Hand her to us," called another.

Beorn did not respond or move to comply. He slowly cast his eyes across all four warriors before him. He observed how they held their blades, how they planted their feet in the mud, and what armour showed beneath their surcoats.

"Please, Beorn," Hollock begged. "They just want the girl. I vouched of your character, how you are an honourable man and a loyal servant of these lands. We understand the witch has ensorcelled you. Beg forgiveness before the Church and take your penance, and all will be as it was. Just, *please*, drag out that foul creature so we might vanquish it."

Beorn looked over his shoulder. Morrigan was staring at him through the cracked door. Her grey eyes did not plead as they had upon the pyre stage. She would not beg him to save her again. She held her knife defiantly; whether to use in defence, or to give herself a quicker end than she knew these men would allow her. Beorn pulled the door shut behind him. "No."

"Please… Beorn, I beg you… the Church will show you amnesty if you comply…"

"No, they won't. They deceived you, Hollock. The only thing I see in these men's eyes is murder. They will take the girl, and subject her to all the earthly horrors they can imagine while keeping her alive just enough for the Inquisitors to use in their demonstration. As for me, if they don't cut me down here in the mud, they'll burn me, brand me, and flay me until finally gibbeting me as a warning to the townsfolk."

Hollock glanced down the line of his accomplices. None of them made to dispute Beorn's words. The young guard set his jaw. "Then so be it. If it is the Church's will that you die, it must be done. Bring us the girl and I will give you the honour of a clean and quick death."

Beorn sighed. "I don't think that's how this will play out…" He reached with his right hand for the axe he'd left by the door. His fingers groped the empty air.

"Looking for something?" called the third guardsman. Beorn's axe fell from his hand and plopped into the mud. The men advanced.

*Shit.* Beorn's mind raced for a solution. *Inside the cabin, hidden at the bottom of the chest…* No. Beorn strode into the mud to meet his adversaries.

The rain continued to fall as his eyes combed the yard for anything he could use… *There!* Next to Godfrey's shed, a shovel stood, used for mucking out the stall. Keeping his eyes on the guardsmen, Beorn sidestepped towards the shed. The three Holy Guards advanced with swords raised. Hollock remained where he stood.

The guardsmen kept a wary distance. They had obviously seen the bodies in the square. This gave Beorn the room he needed to back into the shed, unopposed. Without taking his eyes from the advancing men, Beorn's fingers wrapped around the shovel's shaft and brought it up.

"Ha! What are you going to do with that, woodcutter?"

"First, I'll kill you with it." Beorn said it as fact. "Then I'll dig your graves with it."

The guardsman smiled back with rotten teeth. "I'd like to see you try." He lunged, sword first. Beorn swung the shovel. The spade sailed past the Holy Guard's head, missing by an inch… "Ha!" … and struck Godfrey firmly on his left flank. The draught horse bucked and kicked out with his two powerful rear legs. An iron-shod hoof caught the guard firmly in the face, pulverising his skull. Body and blade dropped into the mud. Beorn surged forward in the ensuing shock; shovel held like a spear. The second guardsman half raised his sword in time, but Beorn struck it aside and thrust the tip of the spade into the guard's throat, crushing it instantly. He dropped his blade and brought both hands to his neck. Each attempt to draw a breath resulted in a raspy whistle. He was dead on his feet. Beorn turned toward the third, just in time to block a sword strike.

The third man hammered him with blows, which Beorn deftly blocked with the haft of the shovel, but the man did not give Beorn a second to counter. Again and again his sword came down on the wooden haft until finally it gave. The sharp steel blade bit through the old wooden handle, which splintered into two halves. The blow caused the guardsman to overstep and lose his footing in the mud. Beorn took his opportunity and barrelled into the man, taking them both down. His advantage only lasted a moment. Beorn's exhaustion from the previous day's events had only deepened after two more murders. The third guardsman wrestled Beorn to his back, two callused hands wrapping around his throat. The woodcutter sent two left jabs into the man's kidneys, but the black oiled mail under his surcoat only served to bruise Beorn's knuckles. Beorn's vision darkened at the edges, and the pressure behind his temples was close to bursting. His lungs burned, desperate for air. Spittle sprayed from between the guard's bared yellow teeth.

"Die you fucken' dog!" the man swore.

Beorn tried desperately to get leverage and buck the man off, but his feet kicked uselessly in the mud, unable to find any purchase. He began groping with his hands in the surrounding muck, looking for anything he could use. A stone, a stick, a…

His fingers closed around the shattered haft of the shovel. Once, twice, thrice Beorn stabbed the splintered end into the guard's armpit where the mail was weak. The fingers instantly slackened, and Beorn rolled the Holy Guard onto his back. Black blood mixed with the black mud. Beorn brought the stake down again and again into the man's neck until he had long stopped jerking with each thrust.

Beorn's panting breaths frosted in front of him. The rain plastered his muddied hair across his face. The bloodied shovel fell from his fingers. Two boots stepped in front of him. Hollock stared down, holding Beorn's axe.

Slowly, Beorn stood, towering over the younger man. He felt the burn in his muscles and the bruises rising on his neck. Hollock thrust the axe out in front of him. "Take it."

He stared down at the boy-guard. "What?"

"Take it. And my sword too, if you must, as a sign that I will do you no harm. Take your axe and the girl and let me leave. I hold no ill will against you." He stared up at the woodcutter with the eyes of a boy. Before today, he had never seen a man die, and in five minutes, he'd seen three men murdered before his eyes. He had no desire to join them. "Please Beorn… I've known you so long. I don't know what any of this is about… but please, let me live and be on your way. Far from anywhere the Inquisitorum will find you."

Beorn considered. "Did you lead them here?" He gestured to the corpses with a nod.

Hollock's face was white in the moonlight. "They knew... they knew I let you through the gates. They threatened my family... God, Beorn! Why did you get me involved in any of this? I'm just a guard!"

*A guard who'd dreamed of becoming a knight,* Beorn thought. *An acquaintance, an associate... a friend?* Reaching out slowly, Beorn took the axe from Hollock's outstretched fingers. "Go. Because of our history, and the service you did me today at the gates; go." A spark of hope lit up the boy-guard's eyes. He nodded and turned to flee. "And Hollock?" The guard stopped to stare back at the woodcutter. "I am sorry." Hollock waited a moment, then nodded his acceptance, and turned to leave.

The head of Beorn's axe arced through the air and crushed the back of Hollock's skull. He fell limp, face down into the mud. He did not move again.

"Why did ye do that?" The voice drifted over from the cabin's door frame. How long the girl had been standing there, Beorn could not say.

"I couldn't let him leave. He'd brought them to me once; he'd do it again. He would have killed me if I'd let him."

"I dinnae mean why'd ye kill him," the girl said with little sympathy. Four more dead southerners did not seem to trouble her much. "Why'd ye make him think ye were letting him go?"

Beorn did not answer right away. He stared down at the body of his friend, the boy he'd seen grow from running under his father's feet in the guardhouse to wielding a spear of his own. He would never go to war, never experience glory, never know a woman's love, never hold a child...

Finally, Beorn answered. "I didn't want him to see it coming."

Morrigan gave a slow nod. "A kindness."

Beorn's boots waded through the mud and up the steps to the cabin porch. "Go inside and pack any food you can find. It's a long road north, so we'd better prepare."

Her grey eyes filled with hope. "We...?"

"Aye. Don't pester me about it, or I'll change my mind."

"O' course... erm... okay." And she darted off to do as she was bid.

Beorn set to reining Godfrey to the cart (the giant horse was none too pleased with Beorn after the strike he'd given him with the spade) and then stepped inside to pack up his life. It took roughly two minutes. After sorting his food and possessions, Beorn went to his wooden chest and retrieved an older travelling cloak than the one he'd worn the previous day. He handed this to Morrigan. "Braid your hair and keep the hood up whenever we come by other travellers. The colour is too noticeable." The girl nodded and took the cloak, striding out of the cabin to wait on the cart. Beorn was about to close the chest when his eyes fell on the faded heraldry that he'd noticed the past morning. Without thinking, Beorn grabbed the bundle out of the chest, dust falling from the musty fabric, and walked out of his cabin for the last time. He did not glance back. It had always been temporary.

Seating himself beside the girl, hood drawn and reins in hand, he took a last moment to take in the sight and sounds of his forest. It had been peaceful while it had lasted. But eventually, all things must end.

"All right then. Let's go."

He gave Godfrey's reins a shake, and the cart started into motion. The storm broke, and the rain stopped. A few birds began to sing.

# Chapter 3

Alan Reed's hut was dark as Beorn's cart pulled up beside it. It was unlike Alan to not be sitting on his porch, watching for travellers and the gossip they carried, upon which his livelihood depended. The storm had passed, but the sky was still dark. Every window in Allan's hut was dim, not a flicker of a candle to be seen. The door stood slightly ajar.

"Alan?" Beorn called. Nothing but the wind answered.

The Holy Guards would have needed to pass Alan's hut to reach Beorn's home. They would have stopped to question the station master. After all, no one could have travelled along Brexton's western road without passing Alan's message station.

"Stay here," Beorn told the girl, slipping from the cart bench, axe in hand.

The door's rusted hinges screamed in protest as they swung open. The dull arc of light from the door illuminated the gruesome scene within. Alan Reed lay sprawled across his dusty floor, a wide red smile grinning from his opened neck. Blood had spread across the floorboards, streaked and smeared with the marks of Alan's violent death throes. Had Alan seen Beorn pass by the day before from his darkened windows, with a malnourished, redheaded girl seated beside him? Had he told the Holy Guardsmen where to find Beorn's cabin? And if so, had this been his reward - silenced to suppress the Church's failure of losing a witch? Or had Alan seen nothing and therefore been able to disclose naught? Would the outcome have been any different, regardless?

The left half of Alan's face was gone. Matilda the bloodhound stood hunched, worrying away at the remaining skin of Alan's face. She raised her head at the sound of Beorn's entry, staring up at him with milky blind eyes. The grey fur around her jowls was dripping red from her recent meal. A houndsman in the army had once told Beorn that dogs were the most loyal of beasts. He'd detested cats - saying that if you died with a cat in your house, they'd start eating you before your skin had even gone cold. But dogs wouldn't touch you for days - not until they were *starving*.

Beorn got back on his cart, gave Godfrey his reins, and trotted past the hut without a backward glance.

The clawing, arthritic branches of the message tree waved at the unlikely duo as they neared. The storm had done no services for the four hanging corpses. Rain and carrion birds had removed patches of skin from several of the bodies, some of which were sloughed in piles below them. Without slowing the cart, Beorn turned the reins to the left and began their journey due north.

Half an hour passed before Morrigan spoke up: "I knew some o' those women." Beorn didn't reply. In his experience, silence usually begot silence. The girl, however, seemed unaware of this rule. "I met them in the gaol. One o' them told me she was there because her neighbour's cow had fallen ill. He'd claimed the pair had quarrelled the day before about a shared fence. When the beast turned lame, he claimed witchery, and they dragged her t' the city gaol in chains. Another woman told me she'd been bathing in the river with some o' the other townswomen. Some old harridan noticed a mole on her back; claimed it was a *'mark o' the witch'* – some superstition from the Continent. Witches supposedly suckle imps from their flesh, and these marks are testimony t' their sins. That mark was enough to send her t' the rope. The third woman I met had been raped. Nothing superstitious or devilish about it. A man raped her. When she came home and told her husband, he beat her, called her an adulteress. They executed her for her 'infidelity'."

Morrigan fell silent for a moment.

"None o' those women deserved t' die… so why am I alive, and they aint?"

Beorn didn't want to answer, but she was looking up at him with those storm grey eyes, waiting. "Providence?" he ventured.

Morrigan threw her head back and laughed. There were tears in her eyes by the time she stopped. "Providence? 'Twas God trying t' burn me at the stake; he had no hand in sending ye. The only thing that brought ye t' that square was a purse o' coin."

Beorn gave a nondescript grunt that could mean anything. The pair lapsed back into silence. The road was dirt initially, but several hours into their journey, their small path fed into the northward highroad; a stone marvel of the Carthian age. One and a half thousand years earlier, the Carthian expansion had reached the shores of the Far Isles. For the next four hundred years, the Carthians built roads, cities, catacombs, and other marvels that the world could not replicate since. Their technologies were so great that people still travelled their roads today; the lifeblood of their once great empire. Now, the uneven wheels of Beorn's cart *click clacked* over the stones, smoothed by over a millennium of use.

Beorn could tell the silence disquieted the girl. She kept sneaking furtive glances in his direction and opening her mouth as though to speak, only to close it just as fast. Eventually, she built up the courage to ask him a question. "In the square... why didnae ye pick up the sword?" The cart's wheels *click clacked* atop the stones. Minutes passed. Eventually the girl ventured again: "I said, why didnae ye–"

"I heard what you said." *Click clack, click clack.*

"Well... are ye gon' answer?"

It took another full minute for Beorn to respond. "I took a vow."

"Against what, exactly?"

*God, will she never stop speaking,* Beorn thought, irritated. "I vowed never to pick up another weapon. Never to wield one intending to kill."

Morrigan considered these words. "Right. But... and I dinnae mean t' sound ungrateful... but in the square with ye axe..."

"My axe isn't a weapon. It's a felling axe, not a battle axe. A tool with a specific purpose. It was forged to fell trees and split logs, not rend flesh. I refuse to use a blade made for murder, but I won't stand by and let myself be killed, either. I'll defend myself, and I'll use what I have at hand to do it."

"What's the cause o' this vow?"

"How about I ask you a question?" Beorn retorted, uninterested in diving into his past. "How long were you the Inquisitorum's prisoner?"

Morrigan snorted. "*Prisoner* implies I committed some crime."

"The Inquisitorum would imply that you had."

The name of the institution, so nearly the cause of the girl's death, made Morrigan snarl. "I cannae be sure. They moved me around, kept me in dark cells, tortured me..." She drifted off, receding into memories that Beorn knew would stay with her until her final breath. "Dinnae matter. I did nothing worth what they did t' me."

"*Hmph.*" Beorn grunted his acceptance of the statement. He let the conversation return to blissful silence. It did not last long.

"Where did ye soldier?" the girl queried. She stared at him from the corner of her eyes. She'd asked the question flippantly, as though she couldn't have cared less what his answer was. Beorn knew better and had hoped to steer clear of the topic.

"The same place we all soldiered." The hatred between the Northern Realms and Southron Kingdom was as old as the world itself. With every passing war, bloodshed watered the roots of animosity. New grievances grew from the wounds dealt, festering during peacetime, until the cycle began anew. The Church of the Gilded Father's rise to power threw fuel on the flames. Pushed by the Church, King Edward V launched a full-scale invasion into the north. These campaigns lasted twenty years and when Edward died, he passed them to his heir, King Aethelstan III. By their end, hundreds of thousands had died on both sides, but the south emerged victorious. The southerners occupied the land, building churches and destroying northern idols and temples. Soldiers put druids to the sword and punished any worship of false gods as heresy. The Far Isles were at last united under a single king, and, more importantly, a single God.

"And how many," asked Morrigan, "o' my brothers and sisters, did ye butcher t' raise yer southern God's chapels?" It was a baited question. But Beorn saw no reason to lie.

"More than I can remember."

"The way ye swung that axe, I can imagine. Tell me, what did my people do t' cause ye such personal offence, that ye felt the need t' march thousands o' miles t' subject us t' the sword and torch?"

"Nothing. But I was a good soldier. And good soldiers follow orders."

Beorn's answers were only enraging the girl. "Aye, a good soldier. And tell me, what is it about war that turns these 'good soldiers' into rapers, eh?"

"That I couldn't tell you. I'm no raper."

"And what o' ye brothers-in-arms? Can ye say the same for all o' them? When ye finished butchering the *heathens* that threw themselves in front o' yer swords, what happened t' their women?"

Beorn considered his response. "I saw no rape."

"Then ye have selective blindness."

Beorn resorted to silence.

"He who sees evil and does naught is just as complicit as those who stain their hands with the act."

The girl had irritated him. "You'd like to talk of evil? You were being led to that pyre for murder as much as witchcraft, from what I recall. And that of a babe, not yet free of the womb. Would you like to speak to those crimes?"

Morrigan glared back at him. "I already told ye, I committed no crime. But if ye want t' keep yer past a secret, then suppose I'll keep mine as well." And with that, she sunk into sullen silence, much to Beorn's relief.

The highroad passed through hills and meadows, before eventually cutting through thick and shady woodland. Beorn felt at ease surrounded by the trees. The road had been quiet, with nary a fellow traveller to be seen, and since the terse conversation, the girl had kept silent. Perhaps she was wondering what her family would think when she arrived home with a southern soldier, who may or may not have slaughtered her kin. Despite enjoying the silence, a question was pestering his thoughts. To appease this inner disquiet and as a peace offering to the girl, Beorn sparked up the conversation again.

"If you're a northerner, and your family is in the north, why were you being tried in Brexton?"

"I'm a seventh daughter. Too many mouths for Ma and Pa to feed, so one year when a travelling cunning woman came a'calling, they gave me up. It is said that seventh daughters possess special healing abilities. I dinnae know none about that, but I made a decent enough healer. The cunning woman took me in, trained me in her arts. We travelled the Isles, north and south, bringing our craft t' those in need o' it. The Inquisitorum arrested us in a nearby hamlet. My mistress didn't survive the gaol…"

Beorn could see the toll the loss took on the girl. "Seven daughters," he said, shaking his head. "Not enough for your folks to do during the day, eh?" he joked.

Morrigan gave a faint smile. "Pa wanted sons. That's the truth of it. The first few bein' girls he could forgive. But as each one came with not a pecker in sight, the more and more angry he got. Became paranoid his neighbours were laughing at him 'hind his back. Millicent said t'was after the fifth he started t' beat Ma." She stopped.

"A harsh man. I… can sympathise." Beorn whispered the words.

Morrigan looked up at him, and then *through* him, as though peering into his mind. "Ye can, can't ye? Anyway," she continued, looking down, "what's a man t' do with seven daughters? All they are, are mouths to feed. He tried his best to marry off as many o' my sisters as he could, but many a suitor turned up their nose, complaining of *'poor stock'*. What husband wants a wife that'll only bear daughters?"

"Many a man would trade his left arm for a daughter," Beorn replied, meaning it.

"Aye. T'were only my Pa such a man. But anyway, that's how I came to be in that grey town square and not nestled amongst the forests and moors o' my homeland."

"You mentioned a 'Millicent'?"

"Aye, my eldest sister. Millicent, Marigold, Melina, Margery, Marian, Mathilde, and me; Morrigan." The girl's face glowed while speaking of her sisters. "Margery's been married off t' some brute, Marian's in love with an archer, Marigold's a ripe tart, and Millicent–"

"Quiet."

"It was ye that asked *me,* remember–"

"Quiet, girl!" Beorn cocked his head. In the distance, he could faintly hear a low rumble.

Morrigan looked up. Although the sky was still grey and cloudy, rain did not appear likely. "Thunder? Should we try t' seek some cover? I dinnae know about ye, but after yesterday I still feel…"

Beorn ignored the girl and swung down from the cart bench to the paved road. He knelt and placed a palm on the stones. The tips of his fingers vibrated ever so slightly. Leaning down, he placed his ear against the stone and listened. Shooting upright, he looked at whence they'd come. A small cloud of dust was visible beyond the rise they just passed. Beorn grabbed Godfrey's reins and began leading him off the road and into the thicket of trees.

"What are ye doing?"

Beorn didn't bother answering. He was too busy trying to prompt Godfrey off the road. The cart horse reluctantly followed him between the bushes that lined the highroad and deep into the tree line. The canopy cover made the day seem closer to twilight. When the horse and cart were far from the road, Beorn tied Godfrey's reins to a tree. The road behind them was a blurry line between the foliage.

"Stay with the cart," Beorn spoke up to Morrigan. "Don't make a sound until I return." And with that, he was off at a slow trot towards the road. As Beorn got closer, he approached in a crouch, and the last hundred yards he crawled until he was peering at the highroad through a thicket. The sound was unmistakable now, the distinct *clang* of steel horseshoes striking the road face. Beorn estimated, from the size of the dust cloud, that multiple riders approached, and he was soon proven correct.

Over the hill, silhouetted against the bleak sky, came three black riders. Their mounts were massive war horses, with iron hooves ringing like church bells, sword and mace hanging from their saddles. Each rider wore a knight's armour, but every plate and chink of mail was obsidian black, all adorned with visorless great-helms. Wearing these helms while on horseback led Beorn to assume they had taken a vow of modesty and could not remove their helms before witnesses; a common fairy tale trope, but rarer in reality. The two knights at the rear of the procession wore slate-coloured surcoats with a pair of silver keys embroidered upon their chests. The giant knight in the lead wore no surcoat, but upon his breastplate was a crimson hand enamelled into the armour. Upon his helm, the knight wore a crown of iron thorns. Each thorn appeared to be a black carpenter's nail, heated, and twisted upon each other to form a rough ring which was welded tightly upon the black great-helm. Though the helm hid his eyes, Beorn sensed a dark stare from behind the steel. The horses were panting as they passed, their coats foaming from exertion. The knights were riding their beasts hard with little regard to the outcome. In an instant they were gone, shooting down the highroad.

"Who were they?"

Beorn turned his head to meet Morrigan's grey eyes. "Thought I told you to stay with the cart."

The girl shrugged. She nodded after the knights. "Well?"

"Knights Inquisitorial," Beorn replied. "Although the peasantry prefers to call them the *Inquisitors' Dogs*." The Dogs were a class of knights all to their own. Taken as boys, the Church trained them in the most gruelling circumstances imaginable. Day and night, body and soul; everything they did was for the benefit of the Church. They were a monastic order, and unlike landed knights, gave up all claims to land, title, or lineage for the honour of serving the Church. Each man, as well as being a tested warrior, held the powers of a priest and a magistrate. As such, they were vital to the witchcraft inquisition. A single knight could empty a gaol with the stamp of a seal, without trial or due process, sending man, woman, or child to the gallows. And from what Beorn had heard, they relished this power.

"Are they looking for us?"

"Likely." The thought made Beorn uneasy. "These are probably foreriders. They'll be riding ahead of a more thorough search party to spread word of us. They'll split up to cover as much ground as possible, but we don't want to meet even one of them on the road."

"Should we turn back? Find another route?"

"No. Loathe as I am to follow in their footsteps, so close on their heels, at least we know we're behind them. If we take a different route, a detachment of their brothers could easily take us unawares from behind and ride us down. No, we stay the course and watch the horizon, lest they double back."

"And if they do? What will we do then?"

"Die, most like."

* * *

It was another two days before the pair chanced upon another traveller.

Back upon the highroad, Godfrey was making good time. Despite their conflict about Beorn's previous occupation, the girl continued to make attempts at conversation. Beorn, likewise, was trying his best to shut them down. Not that this seemed to dissuade the little witch. She would continue to pester him with questions about the Church, the Inquisitorum, himself (a topic he was reluctant to discuss in any depth), and anything else that caught her eye.

"What type o' tree is that?"

"Spruce."

"Did ye ever campaign on the Continent?"

"Yes."

"Is it true all roads lead back to Carth?"

"I don't know."

"What's ye horse's name?"

"Godfrey."

"Why'd ye call him that?"

"It means 'God's peace.' And before you ask your next question, I chose it because, unlike *other people,* he has the good graces to *stay. Fucking. Silent.*"

The girl chose not to take the hint. "I like him. He's a good horse. Strong, with kind eyes. He'd like it up north. We let our horses run wild, grazing the moors and forest floors. A barn is no place for such a beast. They need t' *fly.*" And with that, she finally drifted into a serene quiet, possibly thinking of the horses of her homeland, manes flowing through the Highland breeze.

The ensuing peace, however, was to be short-lived.

As the cart made its way along the highroad, Beorn sighted a scene up ahead. A caravan of wagons and travellers were blocking the road. As they got closer, Beorn realised the issue was a baggage cart whose rear axle had snapped. Several of the men were crowded around, looking busy, expertly diagnosing the problem (a broken axle). A few more drifted over to look, crouching down under the cart-bed, nodding knowledgeably before standing to state the cause for concern (still a broken axle). Nevertheless, as Godfrey came to a stop behind the stranded vehicle, Beorn assumed his role in the age-old act and called down to the congregation: "What seems to be the problem?"

"Broken axle," eight gentlemen called back in unison. Beorn grunted. It was then he noticed the travellers' garb. Broad-brimmed hats shaded the men's tanned faces; loose trousers covered their legs; and ornate vests adorned their linen shirts. Each was as different as the next, but they all carried the same motif, as though signalling a fraternal bond. Looking around the caravan, Beorn saw women as well. The younger girls wore their dark hair in thick braids, while the older wives wrapped their hair in scarves of various colours. They all wore their linen blouses tucked into beautiful, brightly coloured pleated skirts that hung down to their ankles. The women embroidered their long skirts with woven family stories, just as their brothers and husbands had embroidered their vests. Intricate carvings, bright paints, and scenes from poems wrought in beaten gold and silver decorated the wagons lining the highroad, as richly as the people who rode and slept inside.

*Rovers*, Beorn thought to himself, and not kindly. Rovers were nomadic peoples, having emerged far to the Continent's east, and spreading across the Channel to the Far Isles. They were not well liked; often preceded by stories of Rover men defiling local girls, Rover wives hexing townswomen, and all-round fears they would eat up crops, befoul streams, and leave the towns they passed looted, desolate, and barren. People often spoke of Rovers with the same derision reserved for locust or lepers. Not that Beorn believed the rumours, *per se*, but nor had he seen any evidence to pronounce their innocence…

"Ho, traveller!" called one of the cart inspectors. A short man with a clean-shaven face and a gold ring in one ear.

"Well met," Beorn called down to him, giving him a nod that was not hostile, but neither was it inviting. "You appear to be having cart troubles."

"Got two good eyes on you! Aye, we've broken an axle." His posse nodded their agreement with the diagnosis. The ear-ringed man nodded to Beorn's axe, sitting against his thigh. "You a woodworker? Don't suppose you could fashion us a new axle?"

"Wood*cutter*. I fell the timber, not shape it."

"Ah, blasted shame! What ever will we do?" He let the statement hang in the air with a pregnant pause. His eyes were blue and cunning, like a fox in man's flesh.

"You could start by pushing your cart off the road. We've a distance to cover, and don't need any delays."

The short man was eyeing Beorn up and down. Then he looked over at Morrigan. He lent down and peered up under her hood to meet her eyes. "Well met, young lady. If you don't mind my saying… you seem to be in quite a state." It was true. She still wore her roughspun shift, her feet still caked with the gaol's grime. Thankfully, the bruises around her eyes were healing, and she could pass them off as tiredness. The meagre rations of the food Beorn had provided were slowly filling out her gaunt features.

Morrigan stared back at him, as though trying to read his mind.

"Times are tough," Beorn interjected. He didn't elaborate. A good story was a simple one.

"Aye," the blue-eyed man nodded, "that much be true. Say… I see that cart bed o' yours is mighty bare. What say you help an old Rover out and aid us on our way? There's naught chance of getting this axle fixed out here, and it's unlikely another passer-by is like to come this way anytime soon. It's still three days' ride to the next township, and we've no room to offload our goods into the other wagons. What say you, *big man*?" Something about those last words made Beorn wary.

"No." "Yes," the woodcutter and the girl said in unison.

"Splendid! I'll have the lads move our things over and then push the cart off the road. We'll purchase a new axle in the next town and come back for the cart." The man was off to relay the good news to his fellows.

"What was that?" Beorn hissed at the girl.

Morrigan shrugged. "I have a good feeling."

*Female intuition or something more supernatural?* Beorn wondered. Regardless, Beorn felt the opposite. His own prejudices aside, Rovers drew unwanted attention. *Keep your eyes on the Rover,* the saying went, *lest he steal the sleeves off your shirt.* The last thing Beorn wanted was anyone giving them more than a passing glance. Not to mention the risks from the Rovers themselves.

*Could they know?* Beorn wondered. *About me and the girl?* But what other choice did they have? The Rovers blocked their only way forward, and he doubted they would move their cart to let them pass without the promise of aid. The axe leant against his knee. They certainly weren't warriors, but sometimes a skilled man with a thin knife was just as dangerous. He looked down at the eight tallies he had carved into the axe's haft. Eight bodies since Brexton. *No. No more where it can be helped.* That wasn't him anymore.

In no time at all, the Rovers had unloaded their cart, rolled it to the side of the highroad, and transferred their luggage to Beorn's. It was true he'd had little enough in his own cart. Their rations and Godfrey's saddle, mainly, and the few possessions Beorn owned. Now the bed was laden with the Rover's goods. Tents, blankets, trunks, and miscellaneous knickknacks. Lastly came the blue-eyed man. He climbed up into the cart, crawling over the Rovers' belongings and made himself comfortable behind Morrigan, his eyes towards Beorn.

"Hope you don't mind, big man? Not that I truly believe you'd ride off with our worldly goods, but as you rightly said, times *are* tough."

Beorn grunted, and with that, the caravan was on the move. Beorn's cart was to the rear of the procession, so there wasn't much chance of them being able to make off with the Rovers' goods. Not that Beorn cared much for their odd belongings, but the march of the caravanners was slow. Perhaps the only benefit was the added camouflage. It was easy to blend in with a crowd, especially one as gaudy as this. As they travelled, the caravanners played their Rover songs on their Rover instruments between their Rover wagons (*vardos* they called them), and carts. At times the whole caravan joined in, shouting their location for all to hear, even the deaf and dumb. Beorn detested the breaks between their songs just as much. The blue-eyed Rover was as much a talker as Morrigan. He'd informed them his name was Danior, and he was some kind of unofficial leader to this troupe of travellers. He spent much of the remaining day explaining their customs to an inquisitive Morrigan. When he wasn't talking, Danior would sit there staring at the back of Beorn's head with those cool fox-eyes.

"So, big man, where is it you and the girl are headed after you drop us at the next town?" Beorn couldn't put his finger on what it was about the way Danior said, *big man*, that put him so on edge.

"North."

"Ahh, there's quite a bit o' the world to the north. Care to be more specific?"

"More north than where we started."

"Ha ha! I respect your trepidation. These are dangerous times and you've got to be careful who you trust." He nodded his head at Morrigan. "You're Da's a smart man."

"He's not my Da." The words left the girl's mouth faster than Beorn could blink.

"Oh, my mistake. Didn't mean no offence. Just naturally assumed, is all. After all, what other business could a man of such advanced years have, travelling the kingdom's roads with such a young thing as yourself…?"

The man was clearly fishing. He left the accusation hanging in the air, hoping Beorn's pride would prickle and he'd defend the insult with the truth. Morrigan had already given him more than Beorn was comfortable with by admitting they weren't blood. Beorn instead turned the questions on Danior.

"And where is it your troupe are off to in such numbers, congesting the highroads?"

"Death is the ultimate destination, but we must make stops along the way."

Was he a wise-arse or philosopher? Beorn couldn't decide.

"Those being?"

"Well, first and foremost we make for Innsbruck for the nuptials of my dear sweet Esmerelda." Danior's face conveyed he'd had a thought. "You'd both be welcome to come! As a token of our gratitude. Rover weddings are something to behold, and as father of the bride I could get you both places of honour at the high table. Why, without your timely arrival, we mayhap have missed the ceremony all together! Can't have a wedding without a bride!"

"A generous offer," Beorn replied in a voice lacking gratitude, "but we can't afford any deviations."

"Of course, of course. Wouldn't want to waylay you on your trip… *north.*"

As the sun went down, the caravan veered off the highroad and into a clearing amongst the trees. The wagons formed a half circle, and Rovers jumped down to set up camp. Beorn reined Godfrey to a halt behind the wagon he had been following. Danior jumped out of the cart and stretched his arms high over his head.

"I must thank you again, stranger," the Rover said to Beorn as he climbed down from the cart's bench and began untethering Godfrey. "Allow me to repay your kindness with the hospitality of my fire, food, and drink." He spread his arms like a performer, gesturing to the camp coming to life around them. Fires were being started, barrels tapped, and meat skewered for roasting.

"Your hospitality is noted," Beorn replied, "but we carry our own provisions, and I'm well-versed in starting a fire." Beorn felt Morrigan's glare on the side of his head. They'd brought some salt beef from his cabin, and they'd scavenged some nuts along the road, but neither had eaten anything fresh since the baker's bread and cheese three days past. Regarding the fire, it was no lie that Beorn could start one easy enough; though in truth, they hadn't since they'd started their journey. Beorn was too paranoid the fire would attract attention, either that of their pursuers or just fellow travellers wishing to share the flames' warmth. Both were equally unwanted.

"Ye can eat yer nuts and leather, but I'll take anything that's offered," replied Morrigan.

"Splendid!" Danior clapped his hands together. "My wife will be getting things in order as we speak. In the meantime, might I suggest... a costume change for the young lady?" The Rover eyed her prison garb up and down.

"I haven't anything else."

"Naught to worry. You're about the size of my dear Esme. We'll be sure to find something suitable. It is, after all, the least I can offer for your help. Come, come!"

"No." Beorn's interjection was sharp.

"I think ye forget," Morrigan retorted, "yer not my Da."

The woodcutter glowered down at her but didn't say anything further.

Danior waved Morrigan over to the camp three wagons down. "My wife, Sibella, will see to your needs." And with that, the dirty young woman was off. Beorn and Danior watched her walk away. The Rover shook his head and chuckled. "So fiery at that age." He turned and caught Beorn's eye. "What a sprightly little witch." And with that, he was off, walking across the clearing. "You're welcome to come join our fire once you're finished with your steed!" Danior shouted over his shoulder.

Beorn's teeth clenched as he watched the fox walk away.

*He knows.*

Turning back to Godfrey, Beorn finished freeing him from the cart, feeding, watering, and brushing the horse. When he was done, Beorn left Godfrey tethered to a stake and walked off into the woods to collect kindling. The clearing seemed to be seldom used, and the forest floor was littered with fallen branches. Taking his axe, he set about cleaving through the larger ones and compiling a healthy pile of firewood. As he chopped, he thought.

*We should leave in the night.* Chop.

*What if they tried to stop us?* Chop.

*Then I'll cut them down.* Chop.

*There are children in the troupe...* Chop. Images of Brexton appeared behind his eyes. Townsfolk running and screaming as he desecrated the town square with gore. His thumb slid over the eight tallies on the axe's haft. *The axe isn't a weapon. It's a tool with a specific purpose.'* Yet here were eight scores that spoke otherwise. In the dark of the woods, the tree sap that beaded on the axe's blade was dark, almost red. *'Yer a monster.' 'I'm just a man.'*

Beorn lowered the axe and looked around. The forest floor was littered with split branches, more than they would ever burn in a night. Sighing, he collected as many as he could under one arm and walked back to camp.

"I've come to take up your offer," Beorn said as he strode into Danior's campsite. The Rover was sitting on a stump next to a roaring fire while a comely woman of middle years was mixing a large cauldron over the flames. Beorn dropped the armful of logs into a pile next to the campfire. "I brought kindling."

"Looks more like half the forest, ha ha!" the Rover jested. "Come sit. There's a stool here for you. Sibella, my love, go and check on our dear friend's ward. See how she's finding those clothes." The woman dipped her scarved head as she passed and kissed her husband gently atop his head. Beorn watched her as she vanished into the back of the ornate wagon.

"Ah," mused Danior, who'd been watching his wife walk away for altogether different reasons. "Aren't I a lucky man? She's been with me since we were children. And look at what a woman she grew into… Anyway! Good to see you changed your tune, big man, and came to your senses! A man who spurns meat and mead is good only for the madhouse."

"What do you know?" Beorn's tone was flat, but not yet aggressive.

Danior seemed to consider the question. "A great many things, really. Some astrology from me Ma, some whittling from me Pa, the entire collection of Cesare's limericks, the secrets of a woman's touch–"

"About me and the girl."

"Ah. Not in the mood for jests, I see." Danior's fox eyes waited for a response, but Beorn only glowered back. "Very well. Here it is. Two days before you chanced upon us, a trio of black-garbed knights pulled us to a halt. A large man with a thorned helm advised us to be on the lookout for a young witch and a *big man*." He gave Beorn a wink. "Naturally when you came upon us, I knew you were the pair our armoured friend had been speaking of."

"I will warn you now. If you try anything, I will cut you down."

"Oh, I don't doubt it."

"But... I would rather not. So, what are your intentions?"

Danior smiled back, his grin just as fox-like as his eyes. "I have no intentions. What? So surprised? Expecting me to blackmail you, lest I hand you over to the Church and Inquisitorum? You may find this difficult to believe, but my people have little love for the Church, and less still for their witch hunters.

"Think of everything you've ever been told of my people. Think what went through your head the second you saw us on the road. Half of whatever you've heard originated from the musings of the clergy. *'The Rovers! They'll steal your children and swap them with changelings! Dirty tax-avoiders and criminals, and worst of all: impious.'* And to what result? Pogroms, lynchings, public executions... You must admit, witch-hunting bears an obvious similarity. The difference is witch-hunting finds the despised 'other' within its own ranks. All communities have a pool of possible 'witches'. A 'supporting cast' if you like. When it's not witches, it's Leyanites. When it's not Leyanites, it's us. Someone to cast the blame for any and all the town's ill fortunes. It galvanises the community and solidifies their devoutness.

"There is, of course, an issue with that, which no Holy Man has yet been able to answer for me: If God is all powerful, why does he permit witchcraft to exist in the first place? The answer - He doesn't; the *Church* does. Witch trials are functional. The witch epitomises the personification of evil. They are the Adversary incarnate; they show us what the Church deems the most dangerous of behaviours. Healing practices that don't follow the holy teachings, folk who question the divine doctrine, women who don't conform to their 'God-given' roles... At least that's how it started. But then it extended beyond the simple boundary markings of right and wrong, but to boundary *preservation*. You following?"

"Not an ounce."

"The *fear* of being labelled a witch keeps the populace on the Holy Path. Doctrine about morality mutated into a potent instrument of social control. Witch hunting at its core is an instrument of Church-ordered *control*; after all, the easiest prisoner to keep is the one who can't see his own chains. But it goes further still! An accused witch serves to deflect hostility from other targets and to concentrate blame, like a boil on the body that pulls in toxic fluids. To execute the witch is to lance the boil and release the toxicity.

"As I said, there have been other scapegoats, of course: pagans, Leyanites, and the like… but persecute a group long enough and you're bound to either drive them away or deplete their numbers. Therein lies the beauty of the witch. They can be *anyone*. Anyone who's ever spurned you, anyone who's ever done you wrong, anyone you've ever secretly wished ill. Anger and fear; fear and anger. The two great drivers of witch-hunting."

Beorn sat silently, mulling over the Rover's rhetoric. He'd never thought much about the Church's claims of an infestation of witches. He'd seen the bodies, though, and to him it looked the same as every other kind of bloodlust. Since the conclusion of the northern campaigns, King Aethelstan had declared this as peacetime. Beorn just saw a war of a different kind.

"Well?" Danior prodded. "Any thoughts?"

"You should use smaller words."

"You should learn how to read."

"A soldier need only know how to read a map." He was a lettered man, in truth, but didn't feel like letting that be known. It was unusual for a simple soldier to be educated.

The Rover smirked. "I clocked you for a soldier the second I saw you. It was how your eyes looked us over, taking in all the possible dangers."

"So, you have no ill will towards me and the girl? You swear it?"

Danior nodded. "If I were to drag the witch before the Inquisitors' Dogs, they'd be just as like to string me up as well. But enough of this talk. We needn't trouble our ladies with the worries of the world." He nodded towards the wagon.

Sibella exited the wagon and resumed her stirring. Another girl with features identical to Sibella's and no more than fourteen winters trotted down the wooden steps, followed by another girl, slightly taller and far fairer of skin. It was a moment before Beorn realised he was looking at Morrigan. Since the second he first saw her, Morrigan had looked right at home in a town gaol. But now Beorn glimpsed the girl she may have been before, among the redwoods and black mountains of her homeland. Beorn hadn't a comb or brush, so she had made do with her fingers when she'd braided her hair back at his cabin. While still tied back, it had obviously been thoroughly brushed and re-braided. She had washed her face, and nearly all traces of her bruises were gone. The Rovers had dressed her in a green linen tunic tucked into one of their long, pleated skirts of a deep red ochre. Her feet, once caked in grime, were now enclosed in a sturdy pair of laced boots. As she walked up to them, she tossed the remains of her filthy prison shift into the fire and burned away all traces of that place. She looked at Beorn expectantly, although for what, he couldn't tell. All he could think that dressed as she was, combed and cleaned, the resemblance that he'd first seen in her was near non-existent. Perhaps it had been a trick of the light. Danior interjected in Beorn's absence.

"Well, don't you look the fine maid, straight out of a folktale! *Let down your hair, let down your hair*, ha ha! Come, sit by the fire dear and have yourself a bowl." Sibella was ladling the stew into five wooden bowls and passing them round. As Beorn took it, the warmth of the stew spread into his hands. Delicious vapours crept into his nose and his stomach growled like a bear. He hadn't realised how famished he was. A thick, rich gravy filled the bowl. Chunks of carrot, potato, and rabbit floated within. The fragrant scent of rosemary, thyme, and peppercorn made his mouth water.

"Sibella, pass the big man some of that bread, dearest."

The comely woman reached around the fire to hand Beorn a piece of warm, aerated bread. "Here you go..."

"Beorn."

"Here you go, Beorn." Her eyes were dark chocolate. Danior was right, he was a lucky man.

The stew was gone in minutes. Beorn used the last of his bread to scrape the bowl clean before setting it aside. That was the soldier in him. Eat fast, and fully, lest you not get the chance to eat again. As the night grew late, the camp became quiet. Fires burnt low, Rovers retired to their wagons, while stars glistened brightly overhead. Sibella told a folktale while Danior lit up a long, thin pipe. It was a habit Beorn had never picked up, but the smell of the smoke was settling. Before long, his eyes were heavier than they had been in an age.

"Well, we should be retiring," announced Danior with a yawn and a stretch. "We'll want to rise early to get the most out of the daylight."

"Agreed," announced Beorn. Morrigan stood to follow.

"My thanks again, big man," said Danior. "Without your cart, we'd be up a creek without a paddle. I promise you'll be rid of us by the next town."

Beorn gave the Rover a nod. "And my thanks to you, for the… conversation. It was…" He thought for a word. "*Enlightening.*" He had read the word on the spine of one of his father's books. As Beorn and Morrigan walked across the darkened camp to their own cart, Beorn worked up to what he had failed to say earlier. "You do look… uh… *clean.*" Clean? Apparently, his exchange with Danior had spent whatever sparse lexicon dwelt within his mind.

Morrigan, however, did not seem to find anything ill with the comment. "Thank ye. I feel *clean.*" She said it with what sounded like relief.

# Chapter 4

Beorn woke before the sun had risen, sweating and panting. Slowly, the night terrors released their talons, and his heart steadied its frantic pace. Above him, the stars still glowed, incandescent. The Church would have you believe they were the eyes of a thousand watchful angels. *To watch over you while you slumber,* some Churchmen said. *To witness the sins of the night; lust and malice and greed,* others proclaimed. All Beorn saw were stars.

"Please... please don't... no... no..." the soft voice whimpered beside him. Morrigan lay curled under her blanket, asleep on the grass. Creases and furrows marked her face. "... Please... don't hurt me..."

The corpses hanging from the message tree appeared behind Beorn's eyes. Torn nails, burnt flesh, severed breasts... all hallmarks of the Inquisitorum. Beorn stared down at the girl and wondered what she had endured. The bruises on her arms and face were near healed, but what else had laid beneath that filthy prison shift? The saying went, 'time heals all wounds,' but Beorn knew that wasn't the truth. Time only dulled them. And being stabbed with a dull knife was not the same as having not been stabbed at all. The scars on the outside may heal, but the scars on her mind never would.

The camp was dark and quiet as Beorn got to his feet. Once awake, there was no returning to slumber for him, and truth be told, he preferred to spend as little time as possible in the cruel embrace of his dreams. As he cast his eyes about, a small red light glowed into life across the clearing. It faded slowly before flaring again as Danior took another drag of his long pipe. Beorn made his way quietly across the grass to the smoking Rover.

"Trouble sleeping?" Danior queried as Beorn took the stool across the remains of the fire.

"Call it the legacy of a soldier." A lie, but only half of one. Truth be told, there was very little about the events of war that disturbed his sleep. He had never taken pleasure in killing, but it was something he had done with proficient skill. *Good soldiers follow orders.* "What of you? Does the leaf have such a hold of you that even sleep will not part you from its kiss?"

Danior smiled his fox smile, thick smoke seeping from the corners of his mouth. "Nay. It merely helps to pass the time." He nodded to the bundle at his feet. A warm woollen blanket lay between him and the smouldering fire. A small face, haloed by black hair, poked from beneath it, eyes gently closed against the night. Shallow, even breaths made the blanket rise and fall in the way that put every parent's heart at ease. "She likes to sleep 'neath the stars," Danior explained. The younger version of Sibella from dinner did not stir at their words, so deeply was she asleep. "I have no doubt the clearing is safe, but it never hurts to be cautious." The Rover took another long drag of his pipe, smoke drifting slowly from his nostrils. "And truth be told, I'm trying to savour every second I have left with her before her wedding." He reached out and stroked the girl's silken hair. "My little Esme."

"Esme? As in Esmerelda, the daughter to whose wedding you're headed?"

"One and the same. This here's the blushing bride-to-be."

"She's a child." Beorn said the words without thinking of any offence it may cause. But it was the truth. The girl he'd eyed as fourteen winters could easily have been younger as he looked at her in the moonlight. Her cheeks were full and soft as a child's often are, her face unlined with the stresses of the world, her eyelids spider-webbed with thin blue veins.

Danior stared down at his daughter, drinking in the sight of her like a man dying of thirst. "She is, I suppose. But by Rover traditions she is old enough to wed. And it's for the better if she does so, sooner rather than later."

Beorn saw nothing but a child before him. The thought of her being wedded and bedded... "And how is it you figure that?"

Danior didn't take his eyes off the girl as he answered. "We are not a wealthy people. We have no lands from which to grow our fortune, no estates through which to channel our wealth. The only assets we have are the ones we carry with us. This nomadic lifestyle was not ours by choice. Persecution and discrimination have dogged us since our eviction from our homeland centuries ago. We travel out of necessity, picking up at a moment's notice as the populace grows weary of our presence. Annoyance so quickly turns to animosity, turns to hatred. Then come the mobs. So, we caravan across the lands, making our homes wherever we can, living just short of poverty and destitution. We trade the… '*purity*' of our girls as an asset. The bridegroom's family will pay a hefty sum for a lovely young bride. That coin will support our troupe for a time, and the groom's family ensures that their line will live on. We face extinction otherwise."

The Rover hadn't taken his eyes off his daughter. Was he remembering her as a babe not so long ago? "You said it was best if she marries young. You meant best for you."

"And her. '*All the good men marry young*': a saying amongst my people. Wait too long in seeking a match for your daughter and you're left with the old and infirm, the husbands no one else will court. As her parents, if we wait too long, we risk a terrible match; a man who will beat her, force her into servitude, or worse… That, or she ends up a spinster. Another mouth to feed, with not enough food to go 'round."

Beorn was understanding the rationale. But he struggled to align this with the sight of the child before him. "So, she will be wed as a sort of… political alliance? As the kings of the Continent do? Strengthening alliances by marrying princesses to neighbouring states."

Danior chuckled. "I'd never thought of it as such, but I suppose you're right." He reached out and stroked Esmerelda's cheek. "My little princess."

"A marriage in name. But… as for the functions of that marriage…?" The implication hung in the cool morning air. Wedded and bedded. Marriages required consummations.

Danior didn't reply at first. His fingers traced the curve of his daughter's cheek. "There is a ceremony," he announced at last, a sombre tone to his voice. "A ritual, really. We call it 'shirting' the bride. The day before the wedding, the bride-to-be dons a white shirt and is taken to bed by the groom. When they return, the boy will display the *'evidence'* of her purity to the wedding guests; a red stain on the white linen shirt. The guests will dance with joy around the shirt and the marriage will proceed. If the shirt is not stained, the wedding is off; the bridal family shunned… Without the promised bridal price, they might starve." Danior's tanned face had gone pale. Or was it only the moonlight? Was he thinking of what awaited his daughter, or the risk to his troupe if things didn't go as planned?

"You're selling her."

Danior looked Beorn in the eyes for the first time since he'd sat down. Beorn saw something close to anger behind those fox-eyes. "I'm giving her a life better than she could hope for with us. The family she's joining is wealthy, and well known amongst the Rovers. I arranged the match myself. He's a good lad. He'll treat her right. And beyond that, I have a responsibility to my troupe. I cannot spare her from her responsibilities just because she's mine own daughter. What would you know? Have you a daughter?" Beorn did not reply. The pair stared at each other for a minute. Danior saw something in Beorn's eyes that made him look away. "I apologise. For all my talk of responsibilities and tradition… it is still no simple thing to bid farewell to a piece of yourself."

"What of your wife? What does she think?"

"Sibella understands. She and I met the same way when we were no older than Esmerelda. I still remember the first time I saw Sibella, the day before our wedding. A beautiful girl, dressed in blue. She looked up at me from under that sapphire veil and I nearly drowned in those chocolate eyes. She was everything I'd ever wanted; my father had chosen well. You can imagine my excitement at the shirting ceremony, a green boy of fifteen who'd never had a woman before. She looked an angel as she walked into that room with naught but a white shirt, so thin I could see the lines of her underneath. My body was hot from wanting her, my mouth was dry from nerves. She pulled me in with those chocolate pools beneath her lashes. Her lips were the softest of silk as I kissed her, but as I ran my hands up her arms… I realised she was shaking. She didn't open her eyes as I pulled away. She just stood there, waiting. I think if she'd opened her eyes, she would have cried… not the experience I had been expecting.

"There was a knife in the room, on a platter of fruit. I took it and drew it across my palm. Sibella only opened her eyes when I smeared my bloodied hand across her white shirt. I spent the next two years courting her until she finally felt comfortable enough to welcome me into her bed willingly. They say it's impossible for one person to be everything you need, but that's what Sibella is to me. We fell in love, proper, and haven't looked back since. I pray Esme's husband is as kind a man… or *boy*, I should say."

Between them, the girl continued to sleep.

* * *

The Rovers struck camp at daybreak. The caravan had packed and was ready to move faster than they'd made their camp the day prior. Golden fingers of sunlight reached through the treeline to caress a sleeping Morrigan. Beorn stared down at the girl, resting so soundly while the camp bustled to life around her. The worry lines of her nightmares had dispersed, and she looked for all the world like nothing more than a resting child. Placing a large hand upon her slender shoulder, Beorn made to shake her awake. Her arm shot out like a viper, thin fingers grabbing his wrist. In her other hand, Beorn's kitchen knife sprang forward, the tip stopping an inch from his throat. It would have continued on its path were it not for Beorn's quick reflexes, grabbing the knife-wrist with his own remaining hand. Morrigan's eyes stared blankly at the situation for a full second before she finally realised what she was looking at. Her fingers released the knife, and it fell to the grass.

"I'm… I'm sorry," she stammered as Beorn released her wrist, and she his.

"Don't be," he replied, meaning it. "You have good reflexes. It took me sleeping with one eye open, surrounded by enemies to hone my reflexes so."

"A woman in this world is always surrounded by enemies."

He made no argument there.

As dawn cleared the tops of the pines, the caravan was on the move, once again with Beorn, Morrigan and Danior at the back of the procession. They passed through little groves of blackthorn and comfrey. When Beorn's cart came within reach, Morrigan would lean out and snatch up various parts of the plants. A stalk here, a branch there; here, a berry or two.

"Careful, girl," Beorn warned. "We don't need you attracting any more attention than necessary with your witchery."

She gave him a glare. "Ye'll be thanking me for these herbs when ye fall off this cart and break a leg. Comfrey also goes by 'boneset' and has amazing medicinal properties. It can be applied to the skin t' treat pain and swelling."

"Uh huh. And the blackthorn? I heard witches make their wands out of blackthorn."

She rolled her eyes. "Aye, and we use its thorns t' stab poppets and bring pain t' those whose likeness they share," Morrigan lamented sarcastically. "Its sap is an ingredient in ink. A useful thing t' trade, should we need. And I've half a mind t' record some o' what's happened to me since I left home. Otherwise I'm like t' forget. Not that my sisters will believe me anyways."

"Well, aren't we the little dendrophile? I thought comfrey was poisonous?" Danior interjected from his lounged position in the cart. He seemed to be more trusting of Beorn since their conversation in the early hours of the morning, and no longer appeared to be riding with them out of any duty to his worldly possessions, but more-so for the free ride devoid of any responsibilities he might find in the caravan-proper.

"Only if brewed incorrectly," Morrigan replied, "and in too high a dose. This, on the other hand-" she reached out to a passing bush and pulled off an umbrella of small white flowers "-is hemlock, and will kill ye dead if ingested."

"Make sure I never drink tea brewed by you," Beorn scoffed, only half joking.

Danior was regarding the small flowers and the girl that held them. "The ability to heal and the ability to harm are so intimately linked. It's no wonder the Church hangs or burns so many cunning folk these days."

"The Church fears what it disnae understand," she replied.

"All men do."

"So, how proficient are you in the healing arts? Really?" Beorn queried. She was so young and still seemed so frail. Surely she couldn't do half of what she boasted of. Beorn had known many a barber-surgeon in his days of soldiering, and mostly, they seemed to recommend amputation for any and all ailments a soldier might have.

Morrigan eyed him warily. "I'm proficient enough t' set a leg. Stitch skin, salve wounds, and stave off rot. Those'd be the things yer askin' about, eh? Soldier things. Really, though, the most impressive things my mistress taught me concerned the ways o' the birthing bed."

Beorn grunted. "Lie on your back, push hard. Doesn't seem all that impressive a craft to me."

"I can turn a baby in breach. Without those skills, the mother and babe both die. I can clear a mother's swollen teat. If not, the babe goes hungry, and the mother succumbs to infection. I can staunch the bleeding of a birthing tear better than any soldiering barber-surgeon. More mothers die in the birthing bed than knights upon the field, but the singers only write ballads for the latter."

Beorn was silent.

Danior spoke first. "A noble calling. Truly. Without your ilk, the world could not continue."

"Aye," Beorn added. "I meant no disrespect." His mind went back to a room, the early hours of the morning. Candles burnt low, dogs howling in the yard, having caught the scent of blood. Screams coming from the other side of a door that Beorn had been too terrified to go through until finally the screams stopped, and a quieter infantile wail replaced them.

"Well, ye exceed rather well at something yer not intent on doin'."

"I remember the day Sibella brought our Esme into the world," Danior cooed, trying to dispel the tension. "She laboured for three whole days. Slept nary a bit. By the third night, exhaustion prevented her from pushing. The physician we'd sent for said she was likely not to make it, nor the babe. Unless he cut her out."

"Cut?" Beorn frowned.

Danior nodded. "Some old Carthian thing that birthed one of their great emperors. Only downside is…"

"The mother's not like t' survive the procedure." Morrigan didn't turn when she spoke, just looked out at the road as though reliving another moment. "What did ye say t' the surgeon when he asked?" She had the same look as when she'd asked Beorn where he'd soldiered; feigned disinterest, when really she wanted badly to know.

Danior shook his head. "I didn't get the chance. Just at that moment, Sibella pushed the healer aside and got down on her hands and knees. The physician tried to haul her back onto the bed, but Sibella broke the man's nose! She was there but a minute when finally something gave. I jumped behind her to help, but she pushed me away! She pulled little Esme out with her own hands." Danior was beaming with pride. Beorn could think only of the door, the screams, the barking dogs from his own past.

"What would ye have chosen?"

"Hm?" Danior, lost in his memories, missed Morrigan's question.

"What would ye have chosen? If the winds hadn't changed at the eleventh hour? If ye'd had t' make the choice, between her and the babe, like the physician said?"

Danior's skin had gone a shade more pale than his usual sun-beaten brown. "I don't know. I was saved from making that choice."

"Ye do know. Ye'd made a choice, even if ye hadn't spoken it." Morrigan did not seem impressed by the choice she had concluded Danior would have made.

"P'haps. But either way, I was saved from ever having to speak it aloud. Then or now."

"Well, we can agree on one thing. The physician was a quack."

Danior laughed deeply. The tensions dissipated like morning mist. "Aye!"

"Should have let her get on all fours t' begin with. Men can't help stickin' their noses in a woman's business and telling her how she aught to be or not be doin' this or that. Womankind've been birthing since the gods first sculpted us from clay and ash. Long before *man* decided it was something that needed his attention."

"Well, you'll get no quarrel from me, girlie. Should the day ever come when I'm graced with a grandson, I'll be sure to call for you especially."

"Won't be very long, from what I hear," Morrigan whispered with no small pang of resentment.

Danior either didn't hear or chose not to.

The caravan rolled along at a steady pace until slightly before noon, when the wagon train came to a steady halt.

"Well," sighed Danior, jumping down from his makeshift bed in the back of Beorn's cart, "better see what the holdup is 'fore my boys start running around like headless chooks. If it's another broken axle, I swear to…" He trailed off as he walked towards the front of the caravan.

"What's all this 'won't be very long' nonsense?" Beorn hissed when Danior was out of earshot. "You been talking to Esmerelda?"

"Oh, ye mean the child bride? I have, as a matter o' fact."

"He's doing it for the good of his people," Beorn said, only half believing himself. "Not to mention he's doing us a mighty favour by not turning us in to the nearest authority. Anyway, how old were your sisters when your father started marrying them off?"

"I'll nae hold my father as the standard for the men o' this world. We all deserve better than that."

"Quiet, he's coming back."

Danior strode towards the cart from the front of the caravan. "As charitable as you've already been," he called up to Beorn, "I must ask another favour. Bring the axe."

Beorn and Danior walked towards the front of the wagon train until Beorn saw the problem. A giant pine had fallen across the road, its mighty trunk blocking the path. Likely, the storm that had swept through Brexton had felled the ancient tree. Beorn observed the thickness of the trunk, bark as hard as armour. How many kings and emperors had this single tree outlived? Had the Carthians camped beneath its branches as they marched north? Only to be felled by a strong breeze and torrential rain.

"I'll get some of the other lads to come help," Danior said. Beorn didn't waste any time waiting for reinforcements. He unlaced his travelling cloak and flung it to the side, then methodically rolled up his sleeves. Beorn squared his feet, gripping the axe haft below the head and above the pommel. One practice swing, the blade lightly kissing the timber. Another practice swing, and then *thwack*! The blade bit deep into the wood. Beorn rolled his shoulders and pried the axe out and swung again. *Thwack!* By the time Danior's men came along with their own axes, Beorn was well and truly into his rhythm. The axe flowed in an arc over his shoulder, through the air, and into the growing wedge of the pine trunk. Danior's men took up their positions at intervals along the felled tree and began to chop. Soon, shards and splinters of fresh pine wood littered the road. The air was fragrant with the aroma of pine sap.

As Beorn neared the end of his wedge, a mighty crack filled the air. "Clear!" Beorn called, signalling the others to step back. With one final blow, Beorn brought his axe down and the tree trunk split in two. The Rovers in the caravan gave a cheer and applause filled the air. Beorn, now drenched in sweat, raised his axe slightly in acknowledgement and stepped away to let the others finish the task of chopping the tree into pieces small enough to be hauled off the road. Picking up his cloak, Beorn strode away to a copse of trees beside the road where the waiting Rovers had decamped for an impromptu lunch. Beorn did not join them but strolled past towards the sound of running water. Just past a low hill, Beorn found the source: a small stream meandering through the countryside with a shallow bed lined with smooth stones. The water looked clear and cool.

Beorn stopped beside the stream and ladled ice cold water into his mouth greedily. He splashed his face and rubbed it into his neck before sitting down beneath a leaning ash tree. He closed his eyes. The combination of his early rise and the exertion of cutting through the fallen tree had taken their toll and before he knew it, Beorn was sinking into a shallow sleep, lulled by the rhythmic sound of axes biting into timber.

"… ye cannae go through with this!"

"What choice do I have? No, I didn't pick this for myself, but… it could always be worse…"

"Oh, how? He could be forty years yer senior and sell yer body t' his family?"

The two voices cut through Beorn's waking sleep. His eyes slowly opened to see the sun was lower in the sky than he'd expected. The voices were coming from behind the tree he slept under, unaware of his presence.

"Better to have a match arranged for me than to be bride-snatched by a neighbouring troupe! You don't understand the risks! At least this way my family, my people, get something out of it. My virginity buys them food and clothing and safety."

"Yer virginity shouldnae be a commodity t' be sold and bartered with!" Beorn recognised the voice now as Morrigan's. The other, young and female with the twang of the Rovers, must have been Esmerelda.

"What other choice do I have?" the Rover girl snapped.

"Come with me," Morrigan pleaded. "Come north. We can keep you safe."

"And what of my parents?"

"Why d'ye care? They're treating ye like a show pig!"

"If I don't show at the wedding, the groom's family will want retribution. Either in coin or blood. I can't… Besides, these are traditions as old as my people. Traditions dating back to the Old Country before the Carthians came with sword and flame and forced us onto the roads of the Continent."

"Tradition is just a word oppression hides behind to make it easier t' swallow."

There was a long pause. The silence hung thickly in the air. "You know nothing of my people, or our ways. I like you. But you overstep. I too long for the day that mine own daughter won't have to be sold like a brood mare, but until you can change the natural order of this world, can raise my people from poverty and persecution, then I must live in the *real* world. I saw your ribs when you changed in our *vardo*. I *know* you know something of which I speak. I don't know what the Inquisitors did to you in those black cells, but my people have suffered the same treatment since we arrived on these shores. We must keep our traditions alive in order to keep intact our identity and to survive. Survival. That's what this is truly about. And if I can do this one thing to ensure the survival of my people, shouldn't I?" A pause. "Shouldn't I…?"

"Esme…"

But the hurried stomp of the Rover child's boots through the grass drowned out Morrigan's words as Esme ran back to the caravan. Morrigan sighed and stepped into sight as she crouched before the stream, head in her hands.

"That not go as you expected?"

Morrigan flinched at Beorn's words, but recovered her composure quickly. "How much o' that did ye hear?"

"Enough to know you never would have convinced her. For her to listen to you, she would need to forsake her very view of the world. It would break her. People will rationalise, ignore, and deny anything that threatens to shatter that safety."

"I wanted t' help her."

"You can't help those who won't first help themselves."

A bell rang from back at the caravan. "The tree must be cleared," Morrigan stated, standing. "We should get back."

* * *

The caravan proceeded without further incident for the rest of the day. As the sun fell, they again made camp beside the highroad. Beorn and Morrigan ate with Danior and his family. Beorn watched silently the loving looks between Danior and his wife, his fatherly teasing of his daughter, and her childish giggles in response. A family of three, soon to be devoid of a daughter. Morrigan and Esmerelda seemed to have repaired their friendship and spent the night whispering and laughing like a pair of school children at the back of the class.

The next day went much the same. The Rovers played their fiddles as the wagon wheels *click clacked* across the stone road. When the caravan stopped that afternoon, Morrigan and Esme ran off to explore the woods. Beorn heard from one of the Rover women that Danior had spotted some game in the trees and was gathering his lads to go hunting before the light died. Beorn didn't bother to protest that these were the King's woods and any game within was, by law, his alone to hunt. Being labelled as poachers was likely low on the Rovers' list of pressing worries. But as he arrived at Danior's wagon, he realised, to his disappointment, they were already gone.

"Looking for my husband?" a rich voice called down from the back of Danior's wagon. Sibella leaned out of the *vardo*, the light of a lantern in hand cutting through the dusk.

"Aye. Though looks like I've missed him."

Sibella shrugged. "Fate goes ever as it must. If you were meant to have caught him, you would have."

"I'm not one to put much stock in *fate*."

"And what *do* you put your stock in?"

"What I can put my hands on. What I make happen for myself."

Sibella contemplated Beorn's words a moment before answering. "And if," she offered, "I could give you a glimpse of what fate had in store for you? Would that incline you more to believe in it?"

Beorn was sceptical. "You flirt dangerously close to heresy."

She smiled a performer's smile. "The orthodoxy of one age becomes the heresy of the next. I speak only of things my foremothers have practiced for time immemorial. Come." Blowing out her lantern, she shrank into the darkness of the *vardo*.

Beorn stood a moment in the darkening gloom of the camp. The blackness from inside the wagon had enveloped Sibella. Something about stepping into the *vardo* alone with a married woman gave him pause, but after a moment, he mustered himself and stepped up into the gloom.

For a moment, everything was black. Then a small flame flared as Sibella lit a single candle on the table before her. The dim light danced across a world few outside a Rover's own troupe had ever laid eyes upon. Inside the *vardo* was a world of whimsy. Colour-rich tapestries hung from the walls, segregating the small space into sleeping and living quarters. Velveteen drapes, dark like the midnight sky and adorned with tassels, fringe, and mystic symbols, lined the windows. Tales of ancient lore were woven in their threads. The scent of sandalwood and patchouli emanated from the burning candle.

A cramped, yet cosy world of wonder and mystery. In every nook, a treasure trove of trinkets lay, souvenirs of their travels. This movable sanctuary, a home wherever they might roam. A symbol of freedom - or oppression? Never to own land; a place for parents to grow old and hand down to their children when their time came.

Beorn sighted a gilded mirror hanging on the wall. The man that stared back at him was old and haggard. His beard going to grey, his hair unkempt, his eyes dark and puffy from lamented sleep. His father's eyes gazed back at him. Beorn turned quickly away.

Sibella eyed him over the lone candle. She sat behind the small round table, draped with an amaranth cloth. A deck of cards sat before her. "Please," she offered, gesturing at the chair across from her, "sit."

Beorn did so gingerly.

"Cut the deck, if you would be so kind."

Beorn indulged her and split the stack of cards in two roughly equal amounts. Taking the stacks, Sibella deftly shuffled them together, the cards dancing between her fingers. When she was done, Sibella returned the stack to the tablecloth. With a fluid movement of her hand, the Rover woman spread the cards across the table in a line.

"I will now read your past. Choose a card."

Beorn was hesitant. The ritual reeked of heresy. The Church could execute the entire troupe for the possession of a single card, and here Sibella was, *reading* them. "I thought you were to satiate my scepticism of *fate*. I already know my past."

"Yes, but I do not. I will first read your past, then your present. The accuracy of these readings should satisfy your qualms with my abilities. I will then pull your future. Choose a card."

Beorn observed the line of overlapping cards. They were each painted black, with inlaid borders of gold leaf. Constellations of glinting stars pierced the black paint, as though each were a pin-pricked hole in the fabric of space. A card on Beorn's right caught his attention. Indistinguishable from the rest, it lay nearly entirely overlapped by its neighbours, as though hiding from sight, doing everything in its power to avoid being chosen. Beorn reached out and tapped it. The card was cold underneath his finger.

Sibella took the card and placed it face up between them. A pale horse stood atop a field of broken bodies. On its back sat a rider, robed in black, a long scythe held in skeletal hands, with a skull peaking from beneath an inky hood. Beorn thought of the Inquisitor from Brexton, and his skin prickled.

"Death. A major arcana," Sibella's voice was a whisper. "You have experienced great loss. I am sorry." Beorn could tell from her tone that she meant it. He did not speak, he just stared at the skeletal smile grinning up at him and the bodies beneath the pale horse's hooves. "The Death card signifies that one major phase in your life has ended, and a new one is going to begin. You must close one door, so that a new one may open. The past need be placed behind you, so you can focus your energy on what lies before you."

*Save her Beorn,* a voice called from the recesses of his mind.

Sibella waited for Beorn to speak, to query, to argue. It was a comfortable silence of one who was, themselves, comfortable in silences. Finally, Beorn spoke: "Easy enough to infer death in a man's past. There's not a soul on these retched Isles who hasn't suffered loss in some way. I wouldn't call that satisfying my qualms."

Sibella didn't show offence, but simply gestured to the cards. "Choose your next."

Beorn turned his eyes back to the cards, trying with all his will not to look at the Death arcana. The stars on the cards winked at him. He was sure of it now. They couldn't be merely paint. One to the left glinted brighter than the rest, guiding him towards it like a sailor lost at sea. Sibella flipped the card and placed it next to his previous choice. A figure in a black cloak hid their face in despair. Before them lay three cups, violently cast asunder, while at their back stood two remaining chalices, filled to the brim with vibrant wine. A river flowed through the background, painted in a rich cerulean.

"The Five of Cups. A powerful card, representing feelings of disappointment and sorrow over the past." Her eyes slid back to the Death arcana. "The card displays five cups before a figure, three of which have fallen, while two remain. The figure, however, takes no notice of his good fortune at having two remaining cups, but laments the loss of the three before him. This card represents the emptiness that comes with significant loss, but it also warns of the risks of missing out on the opportunities of the future. You are at a crossroads Beorn, staring ever back at the road you have travelled without taking the time to glance at the path ahead… and who is at your side as you travel it."

Beorn was no fool and could see plainly what she was hinting at. "The girl made it plain when we first met your husband. I am not her Da. And nor do I have any desire to be so. As for what I have lost…" His own eyes returned to the pale horse and its rider. "I have not lost three cups, nor four, nor five. What I have lost cannot fit on one of your cards. Nor would I think to disrespect my grief by imagining I could simply look to the path ahead. It is a beast that stalks me, waiting for me to turn my back so it may drive me to my knees. Staring it in the eye is the only thing that keeps it at bay. Now read the last card." He reached out and flipped a card at random, letting it fall haphazardly across the two others.

They both stared down at its illustration. A solitary stone tower rose menacingly at the centre of the card. Flame and smoke poured from its uppermost windows while violent waves crashed against its foundation. Storm clouds gathered behind, with forks of lightning streaking the sky.

"The Tower." Sibella's voice was firm, unwavering. "Danger. Crisis. Destruction. Your future…"

"Don't bother, Sibella," Beorn growled, rising to his feet. "There's only one tower I care about, and it has no place in my future. I will never return there." Beorn turned to leave.

"This is not an omen to make light of. You should heed what awaits you on your journey."

It was not the Rover woman's fault. She had not chosen the cards; Beorn had. There was no way she could have known the effect they would have on him, but they had regardless, and Beorn had sunk into a sour mood. Because of this, he lashed out. "If you wish to speak of what awaits us on our journey, would you care to speak of what awaits you? Or, more importantly, your daughter? The *bride?*"

Sibella looked down at her cards. "My daughter. The bride." Deft hands began collecting the cards into a stack. Cutting it in two herself, she shuffled them together with her eyes closed. She shuffled and shuffled, fingers expertly moving the deck until a single card fell and landed face up before her. The card depicted a man, hanged by his ankles from a stake in the ground. "The Hanged Man. Self-sacrifice. Surrender."

"Is that what she is to you? A sacrifice?"

"To ensure the continuation and prosperity of her people, yes." Sibella's voice was small. She spoke with surety, but as though she loathed what had to occur.

"Danior told me of your own engagement."

Sibella raised her eyes to meet Beorn's. They truly were the richest of browns. "What did he tell you?"

"He told me how fetched he was with you from first sight. He told me how excited he'd been for the shirting ceremony… but also how you'd shaken as he touched you, and what he did for you instead."

"What he did *for* me." Sibella nodded, then shook her head. "It wasn't fear, you know."

"Sorry?"

"I wasn't shaking from fear. When Danior entered that room, when he put his hands on my body, it was *anger* that made me shake. Anger at what my father had done. Anger that my mother, my sisters, and every other woman in my troupe had allowed it to happen, knowing full well I was a girl of thirteen and what would be expected of me. Anger at the world that sold little girls between caravans like sheep at market. Anger at the boy before me, two years my senior, ready to take me despite my youth, despite never having laid eyes upon me 'til that morn."

Beorn wasn't sure what to say, so he just continued to listen.

"*What he did for me.* Yes, you're right. Danior didn't rape thirteen-year-old me. I suppose that makes him a noble hero?"

"He said you both waited two years…"

"Well, I could hardly put it off any longer. He was insistent enough with his 'courting'. The pawing, the fondling. And at the end of the day, I could have done a lot worse. He's a good man. As good as 'good men' go. And a great father."

"Did your mother say the same of yours?"

Sibella shot him a dark look. "I suppose we're just hypocrites to an outsider. But I was a girl then. I'm a woman now. I have responsibilities to my people."

"An outsider might say you have responsibilities to your daughter."

Sibella nodded. "Aye. A daughter determined to fulfil her own duties to her people." She paused, searching for the words. "I cannot interject in this match. Danior and the groom's father brokered a substantial dowry. Any attempt to alter the agreement will be met with bloodshed. Even if I could interfere, Esme is determined to fulfil her duties. However... if an outsider were to take umbrage with our traditions... and make off with the bride..." Sibella eyed him through her eyelashes as her unspoken question sank in.

Beorn could not speak for a moment. When he finally found his answer, it was concise. "No."

Sibella looked down. "I shan't beg. And if you won't interfere, I ask you to keep your opinions of our customs to yourself."

Beorn turned to leave, but a question lingered. "In the two days I've been with your troupe, all I have observed between you and Danior would appear to the world to be nothing but unadulterated love and adoration. If what you've told me tonight is true, is that all... just a lie?"

Sibella smiled a sad smile. "It would be easier if it were. Somewhere along the way, I truly did fall in love with Danior. He *is* a good man. At the very least, he could be far, *far* worse. And he truly is a great father. If it started as a lie, it was a lie I told myself, until eventually the line between deception and reality blurred to the point of indifference. Life is what we make of it. And this is the life I chose to make for myself. One of the few choices I had control over."

* * *

As the sun was setting on the third day, the caravan rolled into the village. It was a small settlement, only a hundred households, and lacked any name. Small farms formed the outer village, while a single street with houses on either side comprised the village proper. As the caravan marched past barns and stables, the village peasantry ambled out of their homes to watch. The dirty villagers leaned on hoes and pitchforks, their rusted tools gleaming wickedly in the dying light.

Danior sat on the cart bench beside Beorn, while Morrigan rode in his *vardo* with Esmerelda and Sibella. "You're being especially laconic this afternoon, Beorn." Beorn did not answer, but eyed the Rover. "It means quiet," he added.

"Then say 'quiet.'"

"Not afraid of a few villagers, are you?" Danior was jesting, but his eyes watched the growing reception as they neared the village centre, just as much as Beorn's did.

"How quickly a few villagers can transform into a violent mob."

"The Rovers are no strangers to a mob. The trick is to know how to disperse the tension. A joke, a smile, and more importantly, a coin usually helps dispel any unpleasantness." His smile, though, didn't quite touch his fox-like eyes.

By the time the caravan pulled into the village centre, a large crowd of residents had come out to see what was about. The Rovers watched their audience with furtive glances. Beorn reined Godfrey to a halt outside a small building with a cart displayed on its signpost. A small man with a bent back and a lengthy grey beard came hobbling out of the front door as Danior jumped down from the cart.

"Excuse me, good sir!" Danior said, smiling. "Would you happen to be the wainwright?" The Rover gestured at the signpost.

The old man eyed Danior from beneath a pair of bushy brows. "I may be. What's it to ye?"

"Well, my troupe has found itself in a bit of a bind, and need the expertise of a master craftsman such as yourself." The Rover laid on the compliments thickly, his fox-like grin on display for all to see. His eyes, though. His eyes remained cool and calculated, assessing and reassessing their situation.

The old wainwright leaned forward and hawked a wad of phlegm that landed beside Danior's boot. "I don't sell my services to wagon-ridin' drifters. Begone before I have my boys run you outta town." A murmur of agreement drifted through the crowd. Beorn's eyes scanned the various farming implements held in tense hands.

Danior's smile did not waver. "Well, my good man. The issue at hand is naught more than a broken axle. Something I assume is a simple task for one with your skills. And I could reward you handsomely, far more than such a job would usually warrant..."

While Danior had been attempting to appeal to the man's vanity, he had instead struck at his pride. The wainwright's face reddened under his beard. "You fecking Rover dog. Do I look like some beggar in need of your stolen coin? Get out of our village! I'll not waste quality timber on the like of ye! So you can carry off our daughters as you roll away? Child snatchers!"

The crowd was becoming unruly. The door behind the old man swung open and two young journeymen came out of the shop, each with a hammer in hand. Someone from the mob threw a stone that shattered one of the *vardos'* windows. Someone shouted an obscenity. Beorn saw another shove a Rover woman.

"Now, now," Danior said, hands raised in the air passively. The crowd was becoming a single beast, the hive mind spreading. "There's no need for such unruliness, all we need-"

"*Danior*," Sibella hissed, having jumped down from their wagon. "We need to *go*."

"What we need is our cart repaired," Danior whispered through the teeth of his smile.

"At what expense? The children are growing scared. Someone just threw a rotten potato at Lebushe."

"I have the coin," Danior reiterated, raising his voice over the growing din, "and you have the services. Surely there is an accord to be made?"

"I'll not make deals with heathen vandals," leered the wainwright. His journeymen, sons from the look of them, were flexing the arms wielding their hammers. The graybeard's comment nearly broke the levy.

"Heathens!" someone called out.

"Blasphemers!" yelled another.

"Child snatchers!"

"Thieves!"

"Danior," Beorn called down. "Put your coin to better use. Buy my cart instead. Let's begone from this hovel." Beorn kept his eyes locked on the two journeymen, hand resting on the pommel of his axe, daring each of them to try him.

Danior looked from Beorn to the wainwright, to his wife. "Very well. My apologies, good man, for taking up your time. My family and I will be on our way." He climbed back onto the cart bench and the caravan began rolling. Danior kept his eyes forward and face unreadable, as though a hundred peasants weren't calling him the most heinous names from the Far Isles to Old Carth.

"It was kind of you to offer your cart," Danior finally said when they had left the village in their tracks. "But I won't part you from it. We'll find another way to move our possessions."

"I wasn't saying it just for your sake. I'd been thinking about it for a while. The girl and I will move faster without it, and it's not as though I have much in the way of possessions myself. They'll fit in Godfrey's saddlebags."

"You do me too many kindnesses for one who knows me not."

"I know you well enough; more and more, as each day passes. You and your family."

Danior gave a slow nod. "Aye, Sibella mentioned she'd read your cards. The Tower - an ominous reading. "

Beorn did not deign to answer.

"The cards predict your journey is fraught with peril. A dangerous path for one so young to walk." Beorn saw Morrigan laughing with Esmerelda in the wagon ahead. "There is safety in numbers. And it's been an age since I led my troupe north." Danior left the offer hanging in the air between them.

"You're offering to take the girl home?"

"Possibly."

"So eager to replace the daughter you're about to relinquish?"

Danior did not respond in anger. "You have helped us greatly. First on the road, and now in that village. I simply wish to return the favour. You would both be welcome, of course."

"I offered to take the girl home only because she had no other options. It was that, or she'd surely die on the road. If another chaperone were made available, I would have no further business with her."

"You would be rid of her so easily?"

Beorn eyed the Rover. "She said it herself. I'm not her Da."

"Well," Danior replied after a pause. "Something to sleep on."

$$* * *$$

The Rover caravan made camp among the crumbling stone walls of an abandoned farmhouse on the outskirts of the village. Beorn lay down and stared up at the glimmering stars and tried to fall asleep, but his head was abuzz with thoughts. He considered Danior's offer.

*She'd be better off with them. Danior said himself, the Inquisitors' Dogs were looking for a young woman travelling with a big man. I'm only hindering her chances. She would be camouflaged among the Rovers. She's already dressed like one. Add a headscarf over that flaming hair and no passing traveller would be any the wiser.*

Beorn turned his head and looked at the sleeping mass to his left. Morrigan looked all her fifteen years as she slept. Not more than a child.

*But Danior's giving his own daughter away to a stranger. How safe would she really be with them?*

Morrigan's chest rose and fell with each gentle breath. The wind blew a crimson curl across her face. Tentatively, Beorn reached out and brushed it away. She screwed up her face and shuffled under her blanket before falling back into an undisturbed slumber.

*How safe is she with me?*

Beorn could not answer his own question. Instead, he drifted away into his nightly afflictions...

A hand wrapped around his mouth, stifling any noise he might make.

"Beorn," a voice croaked. It was strained and breathless. *"BEORN."*

Beorn opened his eyes to the sight of Danior leaning over him, grasping his own throat. No. Grasping at Beorn's hand *around* his throat. The Rover's face was going purple. Beorn opened his fingers and Danior sucked in a ragged breath, taking his own hand off Beorn's mouth.

"If you're this dangerous asleep," the Rover wheezed, "I'd hate to cross you awake."

"What are you doing, Danior?"

His face was serious. "You need to leave. Both of you. Now. Esmerelda is saddling your horse. You'll need to leave the cart. There's no time."

"Why? What's happened?"

"The villagers. They're marching down the road with torches and farm tools. It's a pogrom. They're out for blood. I may be able to cool their tempers or pay them to leave us be, but the others have decided it's too dangerous for you to be found with us." Danior's eyes passed between Beorn and Morrigan. "If you understand me."

"But what of your offer? To take the girl the rest of the way north?" There was frustration in Beorn's voice. Had he come to a decision without realising it? Could he have walked away from the girl so easily?

Danior was shaking his head. "A fool-hearted notion from a fool-hearted father, grown sentimental with the thought of losing his own daughter. But the others are right - it's too dangerous for us to take her. She must go. You both must."

"And what of 'returning the favour'?" Beorn growled.

Danior was growing obviously impatient. "For God's sake, man, I know you not! Not really. I have me and mine to consider. I can't risk our very lives for a girl being hunted by the Inquisitorum. Not when we're as much a target for the Church as you are. Now *go*." And with that, he was off through the ruins towards a growing light in the distance. Beorn could hear them now, the shuffling footsteps of the mob, and angry curses under their breaths. Beorn shook Morrigan awake.

"We're leaving. Get up."

She blinked the sleep out of her eyes and Beorn explained. The pair were on their feet a moment later, skirting the tumbling stones of the farmhouse walls, ducking between the wheels of the *vardos* until they came upon Godfrey, saddled and prepped by a frightened-looking Esmerelda. Beorn gave a quick check of the saddlebags, tallying the possessions he'd had in the cart before swinging up into the seat. He reached out a hand to a waiting Morrigan. The girl hesitated before turning to Esmerelda.

"Come with us," she pleaded.

Esme took a step back. "What?"

"Please. Ye have to. Ye'll be safer with us, free from this sham marriage, free t' do what *ye* want."

"This *is* what I want. I *want* to take care of my people, my *family*. I'm not a victim here. This might have been my father's decision, but I *agreed*."

"Against what other choice? That or be bride-napped against yer will? Please, Esme, I'm begging ye."

Esmerelda stared at Morrigan blankly. Morrigan stared back with pleading eyes. This would go no differently than the argument by the stream. From atop Godfrey, Beorn saw the villagers entering the Rover camp. Danior was walking out to placate them, smile wide and hands parted.

"Morrigan," Beorn barked. "We must go."

Beorn heard breaking glass from somewhere else in the camp. The smell of smoke drifted into his nose. Somewhere, a woman screamed. Esmerelda turned towards the cry, eyes filled with panic. "Ma!" she shouted, running towards the sound.

"Esme!" Morrigan shouted and made to follow, but Beorn had grown impatient and snatched the girl from where she stood, flinging her up behind him. He dug his heels into Godfrey's side and the giant horse made for the road. "Wait! Go back! You have to help them!"

Beorn didn't answer, aiming Godfrey through the thick underbrush. Suddenly two gap toothed yokels stepped out of a thicket. "Stop, yew!" one of them shouted. He raised a shovel towards them.

Beorn dug his heels in deeper, and Godfrey whinnied angrily and charged at the two men. One screamed and lunged away, but the other raised his shovel and swung. The result was as if a rabbit had charged a bear. Godfrey flattened the man, bones crunching under two thousand pounds of muscle and sinew. Beorn took a furtive glance over his shoulder. Several of the Rover's wagons were ablaze. Villagers were running throughout the camp swinging their weapons at any man, woman or child that crossed their path. Beorn caught no sight of Danior, Sibella, or Esmerelda.

"Go back!" howled Morrigan. "Go back! Ye can help them, ye can fight!"

The Rovers' screams drowned out hers, and both drifted into the night sky with the smoke from the burning caravan.

# Chapter 5

They rode through the night, never stopping until the sun crept over the horizon. The stars slowly dwindled away and the black blanket they'd rested upon shifted through shades of cherry and umber. As the shadows fled back into the recesses of the forest and the sky lightened, Beorn reined Godfrey to a halt, vaulting down from the saddle and leading the horse to a shallow stream to drink. Morrigan slid tenderly from the saddle, rubbing the inside of her legs, pain visible upon her face. Beorn himself sank down against the trunk of a tree, legs cramping from the hard ride.

The pair sat in silence for a long time. The only sounds were the babble of the brook and the slapping of Godfrey's lips as he gulped from it.

"I'm sorry," Beorn said finally. "About Esme."

Morrigan didn't answer. She just sat in a deflated silence.

"They'll be all right," Beorn tried to reassure. "The Rovers are survivors." *Pests*, he might have said before their three days on the road with the troupe. *Cockroaches are hard to kill,* he had often heard it said of the Rovers. Beorn was loath to admit it, but getting to know them had changed his perspective on many things.

"I know," Morrigan answered faintly. "But even if Esme is alright, it still means she has t' go marry that boy, that stranger. I just wish she'd come with us." Beorn opened his mouth to answer her, but Morrigan cut him off. "Please, let's nae talk about it any more. I'm sick and tired o' the whole topic. And I suppose it disnae concern us any longer." They spoke no more of Esme's betrothal.

The pair resumed their silent brooding for a time. Godfrey had taken his fill of the stream and had turned his attention to the grass beside it, meandering about, tearing tufts from the soil. Beorn could see Morrigan rummaging through her skirts, but paid her no mind until he heard her curse, "Fuck."

Beorn looked over and saw her open palm, scarlet with blood. Beorn's skin turned to ice, his tongue became too big for his mouth as he struggled to find the words. "What… how… are you hurt?" Beorn remembered those villagers, the one with the shovel. Had it struck her? How much damage could a shovel cause? His memories supplied the answer with images of the Holy Guards who'd come for him and Morrigan at Beorn's cabin. Beorn's shovel had damaged them plenty.

Morrigan winced and rubbed her stomach. "Find me the small red pouch in the saddlebags. Hopefully Esme remembered t' pack it."

Beorn rifled through Godfrey's saddlebags until he came upon the pouch in question. He knelt down beside Morrigan and watched her open its contents. Morrigan had sorted herbs she'd collected along the road into smaller wax-cloth pouches, along with a needle and cat-gut thread. Morrigan rifled through them all and pulled out wads of red-dyed cloth. She rose, discomfort on her face, and made for a line of trees.

"Wait, where are you going?" Beorn pondered. "Let me help."

Morrigan frowned at him. "Help?"

"With your injury."

"Oh. No injury."

"But, the blood…"

"Aye. Blood."

She stared back at the large man like he was a simpleton. Realisation slowly (too slowly) dawned on Beorn. "Oh."

"Yes."

"It's your… moon… uh… your monthly… flux…"

"It's my period."

Beorn nodded, eyes suddenly looking everywhere except Morrigan and, least of all, her blood-stained hand. Morrigan rolled her eyes and strode off towards the tree line. Beorn waited silently until she returned, repacking her supply pouch.

"That pouch?" he broached, eventually. "From Esmerelda?"

Morrigan shook her head. "Sibella. Esme hasn't bled yet."

"Were you expecting…?"

"Well, obviously. Eventually, hence the supplies. But I wasn't sure when. I haven't bled since Brexton. The stress o' the ordeal, I suppose."

Beorn nodded, eyes on the dirt. Morrigan noticed his strangeness and scoffed.

"Oh, come off it. S'not as though yer any stranger t' northern blood, now are ye?"

Beorn cleared his throat. "Should we… rest? Until your time passes?"

"Do I look like a porcelain doll? I'll be fine, just a wee more uncomfortable than usual."

"So they aren't too difficult? Your… *periods?*"

Morrigan eyed him suspiciously. "Nay. Not in the scheme of it all."

Beorn nodded. "I… knew a woman, once. Her times were quite difficult. Pain and heavy bleeding. She was often bedridden 'til they passed."

"Oh my," grinned Morrigan, wryly. "The reclusive soldier Beorn fraternising with *'a woman'*. Let me guess; yer favourite camp follower while ye were campaigning? What? Did she enjoy a wee chat between tumbles?" Morrigan chuckled.

"My wife, actually."

Shock replaced the levity on Morrigan's face. "Oh. Yer wife. Is she…"

"Dead. Yes. Many a year now. Come; if your blood won't hinder your travels, we should get a move on." And so they did.

* * *

Their journey continued, much the same as it had before joining the Rovers. They did not speak again of Danior, Sibella, or Esmerelda. Beorn feared to bring them up, lest Morrigan continue to blame herself for failing to convince Esme to join them. They rejoined the northward highroad and made steady pace. A week after their departure from the Rovers, Beorn and Morrigan came across the first major town since Brexton.

Forest gave way to farmland, gave way to whitewashed plastered wattle-and-daub homes. Outside the town stood a wooden sign with *RAVENS-BURG* painted in large black letters. A roost of the town's namesakes sat perched atop the crooked signpost, staring at them as they passed with beady black eyes. Black wings fluttered with glimmers of cobalt blue. *"Caw!"*

*An 'unkindness', Beorn mused to himself. An unkindness of ravens; a murder of crows. What had the black feathered birds done to warrant such unfortunate plurals?*

There were no town gates, as there were no walls encircling the town, allowing them to drift in unnoticed and unchallenged. Roofs of thatch and tile shadowed over the horsed duo as they meandered through narrow and unpaved winding streets. The town was not wealthy, lacking any buildings made of brick and mortar. Many houses showed cracked and peeling plaster, with thatch and soil spilling out. As they ventured deeper into town, the streets widened, filling with bustling foot traffic. Eventually they came upon a wide lane, filled with market stalls. The crowd was too dense to continue riding, and Beorn tethered Godfrey to a post so they could continue exploring on foot, hoods drawn against inquisitive eyes. In the week since parting from the Rovers, the pair had resumed their meagre diet of foraged berries, nuts, and the hard jerky Beorn had dried himself back at his cabin. The market promised proper food again, and plenty of it. The coins in Beorn's purse weighed heavily on his hip.

Merchants, artisans, and traders were hawking their wares over the sound of clanging hammers on steel. Livestock *squawked, mooed* and *baaed* from pens made of sticks as customers looked them over. The aroma of wood smoke and baking bread wafted through the crowd before the stink of human waste and garbage, that couldn't help but arise wherever people congregated in large numbers, cut through it.

Beorn strode straight up to the first stall he saw. "Two," he ordered, slapping down a coin. Beorn didn't even know what he was ordering, but his nose knew he wanted one. The merchant returned with a smile and two steaming hot pies. Beorn took one and Morrigan the other. The pastry was flaky and crisp, with liquid mince spilling from the centre with each bite. The pies were gone in an instant, and the pair were off to the next stall. A pair of skewered smoked sausages found their way into their hands, then their stomachs. Next came a duo of cob loaves, hollowed out and stuffed with mutton, cabbages, and leek. They washed it all down with a pewter mug of hoppy ale. Beorn took Morrigan's off her when she'd drunk half and finished it to the sound of her lacklustre complaints. The pair sat on some empty casks outside the ale merchant's stall, allowing the food stupor to pass over them.

"What good fortune," Morrigan sighed, "that we arrived on a market day."

"Aye. I'd lost track of the days."

"Unless it's to mark some special occasion?"

"Aye. We should make the most of it while we're here and gather supplies for the journey ahead."

Having satiated their hunger, they continued with their shopping, making wiser purchases than they would have on empty stomachs. Despite this, they couldn't help but indulge in some more perishable provisions than would be advised. Morrigan demanded they buy a dozen fresh, hen-laid eggs, white and speckled. Beorn packed the eggs, which they had delicately wrapped in cloth, in a sack with the bacon he'd purchased at the previous stall. It was as they were haggling over the price of some onions that church bells rang nearby. An unexpected excitement swept over the market and bodies moved towards an adjacent street. The merchant settled on a price and handed Beorn his onions before quickly closing his stall and running off with the crowd. The crowd swept Beorn and Morrigan through the market lane and a series of adjacent streets, depositing them in a cobbled square before a large church.

Any mortar or stone the town had access to had been dedicated to erecting the church. Its walls were stone grey, supported along both lengths with buttresses. Slate tiles covered its steeply pitched roof. Tall narrow windows lined the walls, adorned with stained glass depictions of the Father Above, often in the act of smiting the Adversary. The lone spire loomed above the square, its iron church-bell still ringing. Expertly carved gargoyles adorned all corners of the building, their sunken eyes staring down at the gathered crowd in judgement.

The gallows rose menacingly in the middle of the village square.

In contrast to the stage built for Morrigan's execution, this structure's wood was old, weathered, and grey from many days of sun and rain. Two mighty posts held the crossbeam from which many a criminal had met their premature end. Beorn saw dark stains running down the posts that held the platform aloft, and he did not think they were tar or varnish. The market food that had moments ago sat deliciously in his stomach turned sour.

Three witches stood upon the gallows' platform. Around their necks hung thick hemp nooses. Their dirt covered feet teetered gingerly atop three rickety stools. The leftmost accused was barely more than a maid, younger perhaps even than Morrigan. She was staring around wide-eyed at the gathered crowd, as though too shocked to truly grasp what was about to transpire. To her left was a woman grown, the maid's mother, perhaps. They shared the same heart-shaped face, the same flaxen hair. The woman was sobbing though, chest heaving with rattling breaths. A court of crows stood in judgement over them, talons perched atop the gallows' crossbeam.

"P-p-please," Beorn could hear her begging between sobs. "'Twas only the wind. 'Twas only the w-w-wind…"

The final of the three was an old crone. Deep lines scored her brow, and her skin was dark and leathery from a lifetime in the field. Of the three, she alone stood defiant. With her shoulders back and spine straight, she set her thin lips in a harsh line. She stared down at the gawking crowd with open derision in her gaze. Dishevelment, starvation, and battering marked all three women. The wind showed the outlines of their frail bodies under their filthy shifts.

A man was walking up the steps of the gallows, followed by a hulking black figure. Beorn's mouth went dry.

*The knight from the road.*

The man under the armour must have stood at seven feet tall, and that wasn't counting the height added by the iron thorns upon his helm. The hilt of a giant greatsword stood sentry over his left shoulder. His black plate armour shone in the muted light of the cloudy afternoon, and the enamelled red hand print upon his chest plate stood out like an open wound.

The crowd quietened as the first man reached the gallows platform. He raised his hands and gestured for anyone lagging to cease their chattering. He wore the clothes of someone with authority; not decadent, but at least clean; which, in a place like this, was the closest thing to luxury. Around his neck hung a gold chain of office.

*Gold in colour, if not in material.* Beorn couldn't see this stinking hamlet having more than two silver groats to rub together, let alone enough gold to make the official's chain of office. *Likely it's copper, tinted with some fool's gold to add the shine.* Even then, it was unlikely the man wore it out on any but formal occasions.

"Good people, good people, may I have your attention! As you know, I am Alaric Benedict, the constable of this God-fearing hamlet, and it is my solemn duty to uphold the King's peace and His divine law. We are honoured today, to be joined by a holy member of the Inquisitorum and captain of the Knights Inquisitorial." The knight nodded his crowned head. His armour seemed to drink in joy and sunlight. "Before you," continued the constable, "stand three women accused of a most heinous charge. That of witchcraft."

The crowd gave the expected response of gasps, disgruntled mutters, and angry shouts. Having seen more than one of these spectacles, Beorn was wondering if townspeople across the country met regularly to practice for these events. Or, more likely, the genuine thing happened regularly enough for everyone to learn their lines by heart. Groups of women whispered to each other: *"I never did trust her... always been a malicious woman... to think such an innocent child..."* The men were more open with their malice, shouting insults and vulgarities at the prisoners.

"Dorothy, Beatrice, and Marika Tiller stand accused, that on the first day of this lunar cycle, they raised a tempest so as to flatten and destroy the harvest of their neighbours, John and Martha Kent." Two disgruntled peasants at the front of the crowd – the aggrieved party, no doubt – began nodding in earnest. "It is alleged that through dark and seditious arts passed down via the distaff line of the family, the Tillers were able to call upon the malignant forces of the Adversary and unleash his malicious and envious wrath upon the pious Kents! These three acted out of resentment, no, *hatred* for their victims, and coveted their bountiful harvest!" The crowd jeered angrily.

*How easily one's own embarrassing failures or unexpected misfortunes can be laid at the feet of another*, Beorn thought.

Constable Benedict waited for the mob to quiet before continuing. "Through vigorous questioning-" Beorn could see the edges of bruises creeping from the hem of the crone's shift, along the mother's legs, and blatantly across the right cheek of the young maid. "-my men and I were able to obtain a confession from Dorothy Tiller, admitting to the family's dark entanglement with the Adversary. It is with this evidence we bring the entire coven to justice."

"I just wanted to go home," the little girl muttered, turning to her sobbing mother. "He said if I told him we'd done what he says we'd done, he'd let us go. Mumma…" But her mother wasn't listening. She just continued with her deflated begging.

"P-p-please… 'twas naught but the w-w-wind… p-p-please don't h-hurt my daughter…"

"Beorn." Morrigan's voice was a whisper at his side.

"Quiet," he snarled back at her. Throughout this all, Beorn had not taken his eyes off the giant knight atop the platform. The slits in his great helm were dark, but inside Beorn could feel his eyes scanning the crowd.

"Beorn, ye have t' do something," Morrigan hissed.

"What?"

"Those women. They didnae do anythin'. Ye have t' help them. Help them like ye helped me. For God's sake, the youngest is naught but a girl-"

"What the *fuck* do you expect me to do? Have your eyes gone blind, or do you not see the hulking armoured knight atop that stage? Have you any idea what a knight in full plate can do to an unarmoured peasant? No. We stand. We watch. Then we go."

"I winnae stand here and watch three innocent women be put t' death…"

Beorn grabbed her elbow firmly as she made to leave. "We're not going anywhere. These executions aren't mandatory, but do you know why? They don't *need* to be. Everyone from the entire hamlet is in this square, and two figures walking in the opposite direction are going to draw attention. We stay." His tone let her know that there would be no arguing.

"But… I cannae just watch this."

"Then look at the ground." He could feel the rage radiating off the hooded girl, but she did as she was bid.

"Coward." She was looking at the stones when she said it, but Beorn knew it was for him.

"Are there any amongst you–," Constable Benedict continued, "–who would proclaim the innocence of these women? Any amongst you who would champion their cause?" The crowd responded with a deathly silence. Beorn could see Morrigan's clenched knuckles turn white. "No? Then it is my sworn duty to deliver justice, punish wickedness, and maintain the safety of this community. For the crimes of blasphemy, heresy, vandalism, and above all else *maleficium*, I sentence all three of you to hang by your necks until dead."

Morrigan could not hold herself back. She went to step forward. Beorn grabbed the back of her cloak. The giant knight kicked the first stool from beneath the young maid's feet. Her mouth went to form a word she would never get to speak. The rope went taut, her neck snapped, the life left her eyes.

The mother screamed. *"PLEASE-!"* Kick went the stool; snap went her neck. Another pair of lifeless eyes stared out at the mob. The giant knight came to stand beside the eldest of the three witches.

The old crone stared down at the crowd like they were ants. Those eyes revealed neither shock, nor fear, nor sorrow. Not even anger, only the blatant loathing of a woman staring at something beneath her. She did not turn to look at the black knight as he came to stand beside her. Nor did she close her eyes in anticipation or attempt to speak any last words. The knight did not hesitate in his mission; his boot sent the stool flying, the old woman dropped, and the noose tightened around her throat. Her neck did not snap as her daughter's and granddaughter's had. She hung there choking to death slowly, feet kicking at the air.

The thorn-crowned knight stepped forward. "My name is Sir Brutus Thorne. Captain of the Holy Order of the Knights Inquisitorial. I have been known as Brutus the Red, and often the Red Hand of God by my enemies... of which few remain." His voice echoed from beneath his wicked helm. The hand print upon his chest shone dully in the grey sunlight. "It is my sacred vow to uphold the King's peace and enforce the holy doctrine that governs our lands." Behind his head, the crone's feet continued to jerk. Her face had gone purple, the noose cutting into the skin of her neck. "Some weeks past, a similar demonstration of holy justice took place in Brexton, to the south. However, before the witch in question could be brought to justice, she summoned forth a demon in the form of a bear-man to free her. The pair enthralled the city guardsmen and made off into the woods. We believe they are headed northward."

Beorn's innards were tying themselves into knots. If the Inquisitorum had sent outriders forward to the towns to the north, this journey would be far more cumbersome. Where would they buy provisions, who would offer them succour?

"It is the responsibility of every God-fearing man, woman, and child to hunt down these heretics, lest they spread blasphemy and sedition in our land. Anyone found harbouring them–" Captain Brutus reached back to the still struggling crone. With a powerful jerk downward, the knight snapped her neck and her kicking ceased. "–will meet the same fate. The girl is young and red of hair. Her familiar - bear-like and demonic - may take the appearance of a man. Tall, dark of hair. Anyone with information is to come to me." And with that, the captain turned and strode down the wooden stairs and out of sight.

The crowd began to murmur and break apart. Blacksmiths went back to their forges, tanners back to their hides, and grocers back to their wares. The three corpses hanging from the gallows watched them go with bleeding eyes. Men and women who had once been their neighbours, their customers, and their friends left the three women to be picked at by carrion birds. A gap-toothed peasant to Beorn's right, perhaps spurred by Brutus's words, seemed to have noticed for the first time his unusual size and was attempting to peer under his hood. Grabbing Morrigan by the arm, Beorn started shouldering his way through the crowd.

From the edge of the market, a bald friar was shouting at the dispersing mob: "Turn not to charms and totems to protect you, lest the Adversary corrupt you also! Such counter-magics are but a devil's shield against a devil's sword! Prayer and prayer alone are the only true protection from witchery! Witches are everywhere, multiplying upon the earth as worms in a garden…"

As they marched through the alleys, hoods drawn against watchful eyes, Beorn noted many of the townsfolk were ignoring the friar's pleas for piety, and instead had clung to the old folktales. Townsfolk hung bundles of barley leaves from windows and nailed horseshoes atop doorways. As the crowd dispersed, the market stalls closed shop, the main event now being over and their customers meandering back to their insipid lives or into squalid taverns to drink away the boredom. Beorn couldn't help but feel the eyes of those lingering in the streets fall upon him as he passed. Were they sizing him up while recounting Brutus the Red's words? *Tall, dark of hair.* Were they trying to peer under Morrigan's hood to catch a glimpse of her red locks? Small towns were always nosy, he tried to tell himself, but he couldn't shake the sensation of eyes on him. That knight, Captain Brutus, was still in town. If someone ran to fetch him, and if they were stopped and questioned… Beorn remembered the giant greatsword's hilt over the hulking man's shoulder. Unarmoured and lacking any actual weapons, it would shear them in two. As they arrived at the hitching post Beorn had tied Godfrey to, an inquisitive local stepped out of a shadowed doorway and in front of Beorn.

"'Scuse me, big fella, you wouldn't happen to 'ave–"

Beorn's fist struck like a viper, knuckles pulverising the cartilage of the man's nose as the words were leaving his mouth. Too stunned to make a sound, even to cry out in pain, the man fell against the door frame he'd emerged from clutching at the remains of his nose. Bright red blood pumped through his grimy fingers as Beorn hefted Morrigan into the saddle and then hoisted himself up behind her. They were down the street and headed for the hills by the time a good Samaritan approached the injured bum to enquire what had occurred.

Godfrey's hooves carried them away from the town, the gallows, and the three corpses that were undoubtedly still hanging there. The sun was at its zenith, its heat cutting through the chill of the autumn day. The town became a speck behind them, and it was only when there was naught around but yellow-leaved trees that Beorn let Godfrey slow to a canter.

"What the fuck was that about?" Beorn hissed at the back of Morrigan's head. They hadn't spoken since the square, and he could see the tension in her shoulders through the heavy wool of her cloak.

"Ye could have helped them." It was hard to place the emotion in her voice. Anger? Sadness? Disappointment?

"You know that's a lie."

"It's not!" she snarled back at him, half turning her head. "The lie is the one ye tell yerself, that ye are powerless t' help these people. That all ye can do is sit back and let the atrocities unfold. Just like ye did today. Just like ye did when those villagers came for the Rovers; for Danior, Sibella, *Esmerelda*." She hissed her friend's name at him. "Ye pretend that ye're just a bystander t' the events o' this world, but ye are as much a part of it as they or I. The only difference is ye hold the power to *do something!*"

"To what end?" He was shouting now. A flock of birds alighted from a tree. "To get myself killed? I am not an army; I cannot take on a mob of pitchfork wielding villagers, let alone one steel-plated knight. And even if I could. What would I achieve?"

"One less monster in this world."

"The world will always birth more men, girl, and more women for them to torment. It would take power beyond that which I or any other man might possess to rearrange the natural order of this world. Besides, it's not my hand that tied the noose or led them to the gallows. There were a hundred others in that crowd. Go lay those deaths at their feet, not mine."

"He who sees evil and does naught is just as complicit as those who stain their hands with the act." Morrigan said it as a whisper, like a silent prayer.

"You've said that to me before."

"It bears repeating."

Beorn clenched his teeth, his jaw aching. "I told you once before, I am no knight. I will not scour the countryside for maidens to save. But nor am I a monster who will run them down or string them from a tree. I am just a man."

"Monster and man. How often the two look alike." And with that, the conversation ended.

The silence that followed dragged on for several hours. Sparrows chirped, grasshoppers clicked, and Godfrey's steel hooves steadily beat a rhythm on the road. Despite the physical closeness of their bodies, the distance between Beorn and Morrigan was like an abyss. Any steps taken at bridging this distance in the time since fleeing Brexton had been undone. Beorn felt as if he shared the saddle with a stranger. As much as he craved the silence, the air between them was heavy with words left unspoken, and those that had.

*Coward...*

He didn't care what she thought of him. But it had been a long time since he'd contemplated what he thought of himself.

Several hours after fleeing the town, as Godfrey made his way up a steady slope, Beorn heard the brutish laughter of men coming from ahead. "Keep your head down and say nothing," Beorn ordered. Morrigan didn't answer, but her hood lowered towards Godfrey's mane. As they crested the hill, Beorn's stomach sank. Lining the road were a series of gibbets, the arms of the upside-down-L structures reaching over the road. Corpses in various states of decay hung from most. Beorn reined Godfrey around the feet of the lower hanging cadavers. Clouds of carrion crows scattered screeching as they passed.

As they weaved their way through them, Beorn sighted, for the first time, the cause of the noise. A pair of boorish-looking men were passing a wineskin between themselves as they stood beneath a gibbet. On a rickety stool between them stood a frail young woman, wearing a dress and apron. Her frailty, despite being unhealthy, did not have the look of a prisoner. She was likely some common peasant, probably from a nearby farm. As they got closer, Beorn could make out flour clinging to the hem of her dark woollen dress. Beorn had no interest in stopping to investigate, but by the sheer fact that the gibbet hung over the road, the three of them were in his way. *Say nothing*, he willed at the back of the girl's bowed head, but she didn't even look up at the commotion. *How many of these damned scenes must we witness?*

Godfrey's hoof falls came to a stop before the two men and their captive. They stared up at Beorn as though they'd not even registered his approach until now. "Ho!" shouted one man. They wore studded leather armour and wore a band around their right arms. Soldiers? The constable's men, more like. Certainly not Holy Guards. Both men were cherry-faced from the wine; one swayed slightly on his feet. The woman between them cried silently, not bothering to look at Beorn. If she had any hope that his arrival offered any chance at salvation, she did not show it.

"Well met," Beorn nodded to the men.

"For you, it is indeed!" shouted the other, as those too far in their cups often do.

"And why, for me?"

"Haven't you heard? On this road, there be monsters." His partner laughed drunkenly, an ugly *huh huh huh* sound.

"Monsters?" The corpses behind Beorn swung in the breeze.

The first man nodded. "Aye. And being that we're deputies, but more importantly, God-fearing men and honourable citizens of the King, it is our sworn duty to route out wickedness wherever it may be. Evil must be vanquished."

*Evil must be vanquished.* "And what… *evil* has this poor wretch enacted to deserve her fate?"

The two drunks looked at each other for a moment, a quiet mulling going on behind their eyes. "Ah… this one's… what was it again? A temptress! She sought to bewitch us with a glimpse of her comely ankles. She stirred a fire within our loins that was most ungodly."

"And then did naught to soothe it," laughed the second. *Huh huh huh.* The first man gave him a jab with his elbow, sloshing wine from the skin, but did not hide his smile.

"Whatever her crime," the first continued, "it need not concern any God-fearing man such as yourself. Be on your way and let us do our duty and save your lass such a ghastly sight." Morrigan didn't answer, even to correct the man that she'd seen more ghastly sights than this. What was one more corpse on a mountain of femicides?

For the first time, the noosed woman raised her head and looked Beorn in the eyes. She had pale eyes, sorrowful eyes. There were no silent pleas behind them. She did not scream out and beg for his mercy. There were not desperate appeals, or last second desperate attempts at freedom as Morrigan had made on the Brexton stage. Her pale eyes took him in, then lowered back to the road. The rickety stool wobbled unevenly beneath her. The two deputies waved Beorn along, and Godfrey resumed his trot, nipping aggressively at one drunk as he passed. Drunken laughter resumed behind them as the road curved away. *Huh huh huh.*

Pale eyes stared back at Beorn. "Why didn't she ask us to help her?" Beorn hardly registered the words had left his lips. He certainly hadn't meant them to.

Morrigan's shoulders shrugged in the saddle before him. "Why would she?" the girl replied, her first words since their argument hours earlier. "Who are we t' have helped her? She probably just saw some other *man* in ye. Better t' just die with some dignity than abase yerself by begging a man for help. They have enough power over us in life. Let us meet death on what terms we can claw for ourselves."

The face of the crone stared at Beorn from the backs of his eyelids. Her look of blatant disdain glaring down from the gallows. The blank, pale eyes of the girl on the gibbet taking him in like some oddity she was trying to name.

*I don't get involved,* he reminded himself.

*'Yer a monster.'*

*I don't get involved.*

*'I'm just a man.'*

*I don't get involved.*

*'Coward.'*

*I don't get involved.*

*'He who sees evil and does naught is just as complicit as those who stain their hands with the act.'*

*I don't get involved.*

*'Evil must be vanquished.'*

Beorn pulled Godfrey's reins and the draught horse came to a halt. Morrigan turned slightly and looked up at him over her shoulder. But Beorn stared ahead, at something no one else could see. Stones crunched under his boots as he vaulted from Godfrey's saddle. Morrigan said nothing as she watched him turn and walk back towards the gibbet. The two deputies were just as unperceptive during his approach as they were the first time. Midway between horse and noose, Beorn knelt as though to lace his boot. His fingers slid across the stones of the road until they wrapped around a heavy piece of granite the size of his palm. Standing, he walked the rest of the way to the drunks. The first drunk took no notice of him until Beorn's shadow fell across his face. It was then the deputy realised the sheer scale of the man before him, first making eye contact with Beorn's barrelled chest before seeking his dark eyes on high.

"Let her go."

Drunk number one stared vacantly back at him. "*Wut?*"

"The woman. Cut her down. Let her go. Then leave."

Slowly, through the haze of drink, the second deputy clued on that something was amiss. "Hey, what's your issue, big fella?"

"I told you. Let her go."

Perhaps without an audience, and several wineskins earlier, the deputy would have realised the danger he was in. As it stood, he figured this was just some other peasant he could bully into getting his way. That or just cut him down. Beorn carried no sword and no other visible weapon. "Listen here, blockhead. I don't know if you didn't hear us earlier, but we *are* the law. And unless you want to end up on one of these gibbets yourself, you'll turn 'round, get back on your oversized mule and fuck off into next year."

"Last chance. Take her down, or I take you down."

"The fuck you say, cunt?" The deputy's hand went for his sword. Unfortunately for him, Beorn's hand was faster. With the power of a man who spent his days felling trees, Beorn's arm arced out in a wide circle, bringing the heavy road-stone he grasped crunching into the deputy's temple. The man's head snapped to the side and his body fell heavily into the dirt. Beorn turned to the second deputy. The man, seemingly forgetting his sword, threats, and status as *the law*, turned tail and legged it back down the road. Beorn let him get another ten yards before pulling back his arm, then launching the stone through the air and into the back of the man's head. It struck deftly, decimating the back of his skull, and lodging itself there. The man fell face first into the earth, twitched once, then died.

Beorn turned to leave when the first deputy groaned from where he lay in the dirt. Apparently, Beorn's strike had not been as precise as he first thought. Now devoid of his stone, Beorn cast his eyes about for another tool. It was then his eyes met those of the woman still on the gibbet. She had observed the entire scene silently, not daring to pray this was salvation. As she stared into Beorn's black eyes, she still couldn't tell.

Beorn had found his tool.

"You'll pay for this," the deputy slurred down at him (more-so now from the head wound than the wine) after Beorn had tied the noose and strung him up. He wobbled unsteadily atop the stool. Beorn had left little slack in the rope, and the deputy was standing on the tips of his toes to keep from choking. "Who the fuck do you think you are? Huh!? What gives you the right? Who are you?"

The man's shouts fell against Beorn's back as he walked back to Godfrey. "Haven't you heard?" he shouted over his shoulder in response. "On this road, there be monsters."

Mounting Godfrey, Beorn turned to the pale-eyed woman standing next to the rickety stool which moments earlier had swayed beneath her feet. He gave her a nod and Godfrey resumed his trot. A minute later they heard the telltale sound of a noose-rope going taut, the strained grunts of a man flailing against empty air, then the slow rhythmic creak of a still body swinging from the rope. Beorn could not see Morrigan's face, but he knew she was smiling.

# II

# 'Good men'

*"Good and evil isn't black and white. It's a spectrum. There are men who'll sell their own daughters but feel bad about it, men who'll string up innocent women by the roadside, men who'll torture little girls in dark cells, and men who'll stand by and watch it happen."*

# Chapter 6

"I want ye to teach me how t' fight."

Morrigan was staring at Beorn over the eggs and bacon frying on their breakfast campfire. Beorn stoked the coals without looking up. An egg popped and sent grease flying.

"What?"

"I want t' learn t' fight. Like ye. I'm sick and tired o' relying on others t' save me."

"No."

The girl scowled. "And why not? Some nonsense about me being a girl? *Fighting's not for girls,*" she mocked, "*they should care only for dresses and poppets.*"

Beorn looked up at her. "A blade cares not what's between your legs, only that when you plunge the steel into another man, he dies." He returned to stoking the fire.

"So what's the issue, then?"

"I have no desire to. Simple as that."

"Oh bollocks. Yer a grumpy old man who won't abide a sword in the hands of a girl, and that's that."

"Are you a killer, girl?" Beorn snapped, harsher than he had intended. His axe lay beside the fire, two fresh notches carved into the handle. Maybe he hadn't kicked the stool from beneath the last one, but he'd tied the noose.

"I can be. If ye'll teach me."

Beorn shook his head. "That's not how it works. You either are a killer, or you aren't. It's something you're born with. Those who aren't and commit the act anyway, break inside. And there are no decoctions or physicks in this blasted world that can put them back together."

Morrigan was angry. "I'm not weak."

"It isn't weakness, it's humanity. Too much of it and the killing will break you."

"And what if I *am* a killer, eh? What if I can take it?"

Beorn was silent for a moment. "Even more reason for me not to teach you. I have no desire to make you into a monster."

"Like ye?"

The pair eyed each other off, venomously. Beorn stood silently, then kicked dirt over the fire. Sand sprayed over the pan with the sizzling eggs and bacon. "Eat your breakfast."

* * *

Morrigan rode atop Godfrey while Beorn walked at his side, reins in hand. Despite the draught horse's power, Beorn wouldn't burden him with carrying two unless necessary. They made slower time than they had with the cart, but so too were they no longer hindered by its bulk and lack of versatility. Beorn could easily lead Godfrey around a broken-down wagon or fallen tree, and would hopefully dissuade any future appeals at charity. Beorn had made a bet that this would hasten their journey in the long run.

They skirted villages and towns where they could, recent experiences having left a sour taste in both their mouths. Their need to take smaller back roads meant they had left the highroad shortly after their escape from Ravensburg. The paths were dirt mostly; or mud when it rained, which it did often in the Far Isles. Autumn had closed its icy fingers, and the trees bared the shades of yellow and umber as evidence. It was on an especially bitter day, travel cloaks wrapped tightly around themselves, that Beorn, Morrigan and Godfrey encountered their next ordeal.

As the trio were nearing a small bridge that crossed a stream, two thugs stepped out from behind a nearby tree to stand in the middle of the road. Beorn stopped ten yards from the men. He could tell they were road men by the look of them. Unwashed clothes, rotten teeth, and wicked steel hanging from their hips. Both wore simple leather armour, mismatched and clearly stolen from various victims. One man was using a long, thin dagger to pick under his nails.

"Greetings travellers," called the knife-wielder. Sunlight danced across the long silver blade.

"Greetings," Beorn responded.

Neither party said anything for a moment, each sizing the other up, taking stock of visible weapons, making calculated guesses at concealed ones. Finally, the knife-man spoke again. "I am Brown Tom. This here," he gestured with the knife, "is my associate, Silent Bob." Silent Bob opened his rotten mouth and wagged the stump of his tongue at them. He seemed amused by the scowl this elicited from Morrigan.

Beorn did not make to respond with their own names. Sensing he wouldn't get a reply, Brown Tom went on: "We are tax men, and collect the lord's toll for this bridge from any who wish to cross."

"I see no heraldry on your person."

This seemed to trouble Brown Tom, who didn't appear used to people questioning his credentials. He recovered quickly enough, though. "This here is the only heraldry I need bear," he replied, waving his dagger through the air.

Beorn shrugged. "A pity we have no coin to pay the toll," he lied, purse still heavy with the Holy Guard's gold. "We'll have to ford the stream."

"*Up bup bup*," tittered Brown Tom. "The stream is the lord's private property and no lowborn cur may pass through it without paying the lord homage. Homage in the form of a toll." The robber's eyes gleamed wickedly.

"As I said, we have no coin."

Silent Bob made a guttural noise in the back of his throat while staring at Morrigan. "That's a'right," reassured Brown Tom. "We take all forms of payment. Your horse, for example. And the girl."

Beorn saw Morrigan's knuckles whiten around the saddle's pommel. "That would be a no on both counts," Beorn replied coolly.

Brown Tom *tsked*. "More's the pity. We would have given her back. When we were done."

Silent Bob laughed. An ugly sound, like a frog croaking. Both men drew their swords.

Beorn sighed and pulled his axe from where it hung on the side of Godfrey's saddle. "This is your only chance, lads. Walk away from this now, or don't walk away at all."

"No," Morrigan called down from the saddle. "You heard them. They're rapers. They die here."

"Is it really rape, if deep, *deep* down she actually wants it?" Brown Tom pondered. Silent Bob croaked his frog laugh.

Beorn looked back at Morrigan. "Fair enough," he conceded and stepped forward.

When it was over, Silent Bob had added a hand, an ear, and the bottom of his jaw, alongside his tongue, to the list of body parts he'd never be growing back. Brown Tom had taken an axe blow to the gut and was making a noisy display of dying as he used one hand to hold in his innards, while the other clawed at the earth, trying to crawl away. Beorn stalked slowly behind, the axe resting on his shoulder.

"Please... please don't kill me..." Brown Tom's blood made mud of the dirt as he crawled.

"Oh, I'm not going to kill you," Beorn growled. "Girl! Get down here." The girl slid from the saddle and moved tentatively to Beorn's side. "Still got that kitchen knife?" She nodded. "Good. Then finish him."

"What?" she gasped.

"You told me you had what it took to be a killer. And just now you told me these men had to die. Well, as I see it, if you're so quick to pass judgement, you should have a hand in seeing their sentence carried out. So, finish him."

Morrigan looked down at the snivelling man, his innards spilling from his fingers. Slowly she drew forth Beorn's kitchen knife, its thin blade chipped, the tip snapped off. The robber stared up at the redheaded girl. "Please, girl... don't do this... I beg mercy..."

"Would ye have shown me mercy?" she asked. Morrigan held the knife in both hands now, breathing deeply. "After ye'd dragged me from my horse and into those bushes?" There was a fire growing in the girl's eyes. Her hands were trembling. She was steeling herself for what she was about to do.

"Please… I didn't know any better… I'm just…" Brown Tom raked his mind for any iota of sympathy he could draw forth. "…I'm just somebody's son. I'm just somebody's little boy."

Morrigan's hands stopped shaking. Her knuckles whitened around the hilt. "And how many daughters," she hissed through bared teeth, "have ye left bleeding by the roadside?"

Brown Tom realised his mistake, but all he could do was continue to beg. "Please… I can do better…"

"On that, we agree. Ye can die." Morrigan roared and lunged forward with the knife held in both hands. Beorn's hand caught her wrists a moment before she skewered the robber. Beorn saw the puddle of piss spreading beneath his crotch. "What're ye doing?!" she wailed.

"Stopping you."

"But this was *yer* idea! He deserves t' die. He's a monster."

"Aye. Don't mean you need to be the one to do it." Beorn's axe swung through the air and lodged its blade in the dying man's neck. He didn't make a sound as he died, only stopped clinging to his ruined stomach. Morrigan stared on, bewildered. The man's lifeblood spattered across her cheeks, hiding among her freckles. "So you've got what it takes to be a killer. Fine. You want to learn how to fight, I'll teach you. But I'll not hear any complaints, and no moral grandstanding about rights and wrongs. You fight to kill your opponent before he kills you; end of. And I'm not training you to carve chickens, so throw that piece of scrap away. We won't bother with a sword - I saw your arms tremble when you snatched the blade off that guard in Brexton. Here, this'll do." Beorn kicked Brown Tom's long, thin dagger over to Morrigan's feet. "Pick it up."

* * *

Training became as integral to Morrigan's days as eating and sleeping. She began wearing Brown Tom's dagger immediately, sheathed in leather at her waist, despite not having a clue how to wield it properly. Their first training session went about as well as expected.

"Take out your dagger," Beorn told the thin-armed girl as they paused in a glade the following afternoon.

Morrigan obliged, drawing out the foot of cold steel and gripping it in both her hands.

"What are you doing?"

Morrigan blinked at him. "Holding the dagger."

"Yes, I can see that. But why are you holding it like a longsword?"

"How else am I supposed t' hold the damn thing?" Her cheeks flushed the colour of her hair.

"Here," said Beorn, picking up a stick roughly the size of her dagger and imitating a fighting pose. "Copy me." Morrigan did, taking one hand off the dagger and spreading her feet apart. "You don't have a shield, and even if you did, it'd do shit all unless you had a weapon with any sort of reach. You've only got a foot of steel in your hand, which means in order to use it, you'll need to get close. The easiest way to do that is to let *them* get close to *you.*"

"And what do I do when they try t' stab me once I've let them get close enough?"

"You grab their weapon."

"You mean the sharp, deadly thing they're tryin' t' stick me with? Shouldn't I, I dunno, try to dodge it?"

Beorn rolled his eyes. "You're not some sword-dancer from the far east. And despite what you might have heard in fairy-tales and stories of chivalry, blade fights don't go on and on, full of parries and ripostes; steel clanging off each other for hours and hours. A short fight is a good fight. You stick the other man before he gets a chance to stick you. You wait for him to lunge and you grab his wrist and before he can blink, you drive that blade between his ribs. Now, lunge at me and I'll show you."

Morrigan eyed the sharp steel in her hand and then the short stick in Beorn's. "With... this?"

Beorn nodded. "And don't pull your strikes either, or I'll know."

Morrigan took a tentative step forward. Then another, hands raised like Beorn had shown her, like a grappler. Beorn kept his hands at his side. Morrigan took a quick step forward and jabbed the knife towards Beorn's side, only half-seriously. Beorn's hands moved lightning fast, one wrapping around her knife wrist like a vice and the other bringing the stick down hard against her outer thigh.

"Ow! You fucker!" she cursed.

"I told you not to hold back, but you did anyway. In a proper fight, you'd be dead."

"But it's not a proper fight, ye fucking brute!" She limped away, rubbing her thigh. It would welt before the day was out.

"You asked me to teach you to fight. This *is* fighting. This is not a game. This is not farm boys playing at being knights with wooden swords. This is me teaching you to take lives. If you can't handle the brutality that it takes to mould you into a fighter, then it's not for you."

The glare she gave him made her dagger look blunt. "And what happens when I make you kiss this blade?"

Beorn scoffed. "You won't. That's why I told you not to hold back."

Morrigan was determined to prove him wrong. Again and again she lunged, feinted, counter-feinted, trying to get past his defences. Each time he'd catch her wrist, or knock it away, and in the opening, bring his stick whistling down against a different part of her body. The stick wasn't thick enough to do any lasting damage, but where it kissed her, it left stinging red marks. After one particularly inventive thrust, Beorn struck Morrigan's dagger with his stick and sent it flying over her head to land in the dirt ten yards behind. As she'd turned to retrieve it, Beorn brought the stick down across the backs of her knees. She screamed and fell to her knees.

"Ye fucking cunt of a man! I'm unarmed, ye bastard!"

Something hot flared in Beorn's chest. "And you might very well be the next time two brigands stop you at a bridge seeking to exact their 'toll' from you. Disarmed does not mean defenceless. You're lucky I'm going so easy on you-"

*"Easy?"*

"Yes! If I'd made half the mistakes you've made today when I was a soldier, my quartermasters wouldn't have stopped with a single lash. They'd have kept beating me until I'd picked my weapon back up!"

"Well, I'm not a soldier!"

"That much is plain! Now get your weapon and *pick it-*" Beorn bit back the last word. An eerie silence overcame him as he found himself transported back in time to a courtyard beneath a tall grey tower, his wooden sword at his feet. The knight before him, blotting out the sun, his face in shadows. "I'm sorry," Beorn spat. "This was a mistake." And strode away.

Morrigan found him some time later, shaded beneath a tree sharpening his axe. The grindstone slid slowly down the blade in steady, even strokes. Beorn eyed the four fresh tallies that had joined the existing eight since they'd fled Ravensburg. She said nothing to start with. She simply sat beside him and watched him work. Somewhere in the long grass, a cricket sang.

"What happened?" she finally broached.

"I reminded myself of someone I'd rather not have."

"Yer father?"

Beorn stopped sharpening the axe and stared at her. How could she know? Witchcraft?

"Something ye said on the road from Brexton as we spoke of my own Pa. I could see it in yer eyes. It's easy to see those who grew up in the cold."

Beorn nodded. "A great man, my father."

"Great by whose standards?"

"The realm's. The King's."

"Yers?"

Beorn did not answer. "A great warrior then," Beorn offered at last. That, even he could not deny. "He taught me everything I know in the red arts. He forged me the way a smith forges a sword. The perfect killing weapon."

"Not the perfect son?"

"...No. I don't think that's how he's likely to remember me."

"When did ye see him last?"

"Maybe... twenty years ago? Or near enough to make no matter. I've been on my own so long the years have blurred together."

"Why did you walk away?"

Beorn closed his eyes and let the currents of time take him back to a different life. A life of war, of bloodshed, and unbridled anger. And then…

"I fell in love."

A small smile appeared on the corners of Morrigan's lips. "Yer wife?"

"Aye. We met during the northern campaigns. She… changed me."

Realisation dawned on Morrigan's face. "She's the reason for yer vow?"

Beorn nodded solemnly. "She loved me… but said she'd never marry a killer; that she'd never take a violent man as a husband. So I swore to leave it all behind. To never raise another weapon as long as I drew breath. Even if it meant losing her."

The warmth of phantom flames licked his face.

*Save her Beorn!*

"How…?"

"No." The cricket continued to sing. "I won't talk of it. And I'm sorry for today. It was a mistake to train you. I won't become… him."

"Then don't." Morrigan stood, wincing slightly from her bruises, and dusted off her skirts. Her dagger still hung at her hip. She extended a hand down to Beorn. "Don't be what he made ye. And don't be what ye were. Be better."

Slowly, he reached out and gently clasped her wrist. He stood, their hands still clasped.

"So. Ye gonnae keep training me?"

Beorn took a breath and exhaled slowly. "Aye."

"And yee gonnae be less an arse about it?"

Another, deeper breath. "Aye."

"Good. Then what are we waitin' for?"

* * *

The falling leaves told the story of autumn's slow march towards winter. The days grew shorter and nights grew colder. Any moment they weren't on the road, Morrigan was practising her drills. Beorn had taught her to sketch the outline of an opponent on trees, highlighting the critical strike points.

"This here is where the liver would be. Here, the kidneys. Lungs, here. And here, the heart." Beorn pointed to each with the charred tip of a stick he'd pulled from the fire to draw the figure. "Each of these will kill a man. Anything here or here will just wound him. He'll bleed out, aye, but it'll take days for him to die. He can hurt you in that time. Better to end it quick. Give it a try."

Morrigan stepped up to the tree, dagger in hand. She swung her arm, the tip of the dagger embedding in the bark.

"Good. Again."

Swing, stab.

"Good, now liver. Good; heart. Good…"

Over and over, she swung and stabbed until Beorn could leave her to run the drills on her own. When they paused near a river, Beorn waded out into its waters and returned with a hefty river stone.

"Here, take this and hold it over your head."

Morrigan looked at him, puzzled. "Why?"

"Your arms are the size of brittle twigs. It's all well and good to be able to find the kill-spots on a man, but if you lack the strength to drive the knife deep enough, it'll be for naught."

Morrigan took the stone and, with some effort, hoisted it above her head. She gritted her teeth and her face turned red. "How… long…"

"As long as your arms allow." A few seconds later, she dropped the stone to the ground with a crash. "Good. Rest a moment, then do it again." So she did, this time for slightly longer. She trained like this whenever time permitted, finding heavy stones and hoisting them overhead for as long as her shaking arms granted. Gradually, Beorn gave her larger stones and her arms shook less while holding them. Her strikes became more precise. Beorn taught her where a man's arteries lay hidden beneath his skin, how you could easily nick one and dance away while waiting for your opponent to bleed out and weaken. Her knowledge of the healing arts was an asset;

she already knew which wounds a man could come back from and which ones were fatal. All Beorn was teaching her was how to inflict them.

Beorn also taught her patience; how to wait, how to stalk. Morrigan practiced lying in wait along game trails, hidden in the foliage. He couldn't expect her to bring down larger prey with naught but her dagger, but now and then a hare would stumble along and stop to nibble the berries she'd strategically left in front of her hideout.

After one such successful ambush, Morrigan sat on a log, skinning her kill while Beorn worked at a fire. The afternoon sun was kissing the horizon, the sky cloudless and clear.

"For one so invested in the healing arts, why the sudden interest in killing?" Beorn asked as the kindling caught and flame flickered to life. "Not that I'm a religious man, but doesn't the Church preach turning the other cheek? That violence begets violence?"

Morrigan's bloodied fingers deftly parted the hare from its skin. "Violence is the inheritance o' the privileged. King, Church, *men* - take your pick. They'll never shirk from using violence if it means maintaining their control. And they'll never relinquish that control willingly. Not when they benefit from it so.

"Violence *is* a privilege. They determine who can and who cannae use it. Who's rewarded and who burns for it. But I winnae be controlled any longer. Violence *does* beget violence - but their violence begot mine. I am *owed* this violence; I have a right to it. Only through such violence can we truly achieve freedom from oppression."

"Is it your experience as a northerner or as a woman that draws you to such a conclusion?"

"Why cannae it be both?"

✳ ✳ ✳

Beorn and Morrigan lay on opposite sides of the fire. Embers rose into the sky in a desperate attempt to join the stars, before dying out in the cool night air. Their lives were so short, burning for but an instant; but giving warmth and light to those around them.

Beorn lay on his back, eyes lidded but still awake, trying to stave off sleep and the nightmares that accompanied it, for as long as possible.

"Beorn?" Morrigan whispered from the other side of the fire.

"Mm?"

She paused, as though rethinking what she'd been about to say, before finally deciding to go through with it. "Why did ye change yer mind? About taking me north?"

Beorn mulled over his answer. *I don't know*, he went to say. But that was a lie. He knew why.

"Something my father told me once." Beorn paused, but Morrigan didn't prod. She knew better by now that sometimes Beorn just needed a moment. "We were hunting in the woods near our home. I was young, younger than you are now. I don't think I'd yet killed a creature. As we strode through the underbrush, I heard a sound in the bushes. My father bade me move forward, bow raised. It was a deer, but a young one and gravely injured. I'd lowered my bow, thinking this was not the game we were tracking. The poor thing was near dead.

"'*What are you doing?*' my father snapped at me.

"'*It's a fawn,*' I protested. '*And it's injured.*'

"'*We came here to hunt deer,*' he'd said. '*I see a deer.*' He'd raised his own bow to nock an arrow, but I couldn't stand to see him kill something so defenceless. So I pleaded for him to spare it. I remember the way he looked down at me; disappointed.

"'*You get involved,*' he told me, '*and it's your responsibility.*' And he left me there with it. I wasn't sure what he'd meant at first. I tried to get close enough to carry it home with us, but it wouldn't let me; stumbling away on a broken leg, more likely to bleed itself to death before I could catch it. So I left it there. The next day, I returned to see how the fawn fared, bringing water and food for it. I thought if I could keep it fed while it healed, it could survive. All that remained was a torn apart carcass." The fire crackled between them.

"Had ye seen death before?" Morrigan queried.

"No."

"Must have been quite a sheltered life."

"In its own way. Though I was no stranger to cruelty. I understand now what my father had been trying to teach me. By interfering, I hadn't saved the beast, only prolonged its suffering and delayed its death. Better to have died quickly on my father's arrow than ravaged by wolves. What he'd meant for me to learn was that if I truly wished to interfere, I'd need to see the task through - either that or not get involved at all." Beorn turned his head. Morrigan's grey eyes were staring back at him. "What would be the point of saving you from the pyre merely to leave you to the perils of the road? I won't lie and say the fire would be a cleaner death than if you'd met the same fate as the fawn, but at least it wouldn't have been on my conscience. No, I'd already broken my rule - I was involved. So now you're my responsibility."

They stared at each other a while before Beorn turned back to the sea of stars.

"Beorn?"

"Mm?"

"Why *did* ye save me to begin with? I understand why ye couldn't help those women in Ravensburg, and even Esme... but why me? What make's me any different?"

"You... reminded me of... someone. Someone I couldn't save."

They were silent for a time. The fire burned low and Beorn was sure Morrigan had drifted off to sleep when her quiet voice crept through the night air again.

"Do I look like her?"

"Her?"

"Her." She fixed him with that look that unnerved him so, the one that saw past his eyes and into his soul. "Yer daughter."

Memories of a scream came from behind a closed wooden door as Beorn paced back and forth restlessly. Then, a smaller, shriller cry. A wail. The door opened, an older woman in a blood-stained apron came striding out, smile upon her face. *'It's a girl.'*

"Yes - or rather, what she might have become... a chance she was robbed of."

# Chapter 7

The road was littered with bodies a mere mile from the next town. They wore the black surcoats emblazoned with the crossed silver keys of the Holy Guard. The stench of decay intruded upon Beorn's nostrils, watering his eyes. Flies formed dark clouds above the bodies and covered the corpses like writhing black death shrouds. Beorn covered his nose and mouth with the crook of his elbow, to little avail. Godfrey pulled at his reins restlessly, great plumes of steam billowing from his flaring nostrils.

"They've been dead a while," Morrigan noted. She was right, of course. Trust a cunning woman to be well-versed in the stages of decay. "What d'ye think happened?"

"Highwaymen most like." Wounds from blunt and violent weapons assaulted the eyes all around. Cudgels, hatchets, and farm tools. "Violent men with nothing better to do now that there are no more wars to fight." Beorn spat out a bloated corpse fly that had tried to worm its way between his lips.

"What were they doing here? Looking for us?"

"A possibility, I suppose. But I wouldn't be so sure." Beorn took a count. "Ten bodies. Seems about right for an escort number. Can't be sure what they were escorting, though. Church gold likely, now long gone in the pockets of brigands. Even so, we should see what they left behind."

"Ye mean loot the corpses?" Apprehension tinged Morrigan's voice.

"Aye. They've no further use for any of it. And if we don't, the next passer-by will." Beorn set to work patting down the dead men. Sure enough, there was little of value left on their persons. That being said, Beorn was lucky enough to score himself a fresh pair of travelling boots, some flint, hardtack, and a signet ring which fit on his pinkie finger. Morrigan scored a new whetstone and leather belt which fit her better than Brown Tom's old one. Once they were done, they remounted Godfrey and left the site of the slaughter for the flies and carrion birds.

Shortly enough, they were riding through the gates of Lasthome. As the name suggested, Lasthome was the last settlement before crossing into the Northern Realms. Once upon a time it had served as the last stop for soldiers to provision before marching north to war. Beorn himself had stopped here a lifetime ago, though the settlement seemed to have expanded a great deal since then. What had once been a quaint wooden fortress was now a bustling town, filled with merchants and hawkers, inns, and whorehouses. Everywhere they looked, business was teeming and life passed by at breakneck speeds. They steered Godfrey towards the town centre, where Beorn recalled there was a fine inn well known for its hospitality and beef stew. His stomach growled at the thought of a hot cooked meal and a warm hearth. Disappointment sank in as Godfrey strode into the town square and Beorn's eyes drank in the sight where the inn had once stood, now with the sign for a haberdashery hanging over the door.

Beorn slid from the saddle, helped Morrigan down, and lashed Godfrey to a hitching post beside a stone statue in the centre of the square. A black-robed priest sitting atop a stone bench beneath the sculpture was scratching away at a piece of parchment. His cassock extended to his ankles, held together by a line of gold clasps in the shape of praying hands. Charcoal blackened his fingers and the white cuffs of his undershirt. Depicted upon the parchment was the visage of the woman sculpted above them.

She lay reclined atop the plinth, robed only in stone cloth cascading from her waist. Her chest was bare, firm and pert breasts bared to the world. The detail was exquisite; each lock of hair, each fold of cloth, the tears spilling down her cheeks. In her right hand, the blade of a dagger pointed at her heart, the tip poised to take her life.

"Beautiful, isn't she?" smiled the priest. Beorn was taken aback by his age. No older than twenty winters, his face was devoid of lines, cheeks still plump and lacking whiskers. He tilted his parchment to show Beorn his depiction of the stone woman, sketched in charcoal. It was a remarkable likeness, though Beorn noted some liberties taken to the priest's depiction of her chest. "Lucetta of Carth. One of the greatest beauties in history; sometimes referred to as the idealised depiction of the female form. Since the fall of the Carthian Empire, artists have used Lucetta's figure to explore the nude female form and symbolise womanly virtue."

Beorn lacked an artist's eye, but he recognised the craftsmanship of the piece. The elements had taken their toll on the stone, once a near alabaster white, now weathered and covered in lichen and moss. Everywhere but her two heaved breasts.

"Why does she hold a dagger to her heart?" Beorn queried.

"She was raped," answered Morrigan, coming up beside him. "According t' the oral histories, Lucetta was a noble woman and indeed a great beauty, but so much more. A sharp mind, an amazing poet, and much loved by the masses for her kindness and charity. Alas, t'was her beauty that caught the eye of the Carthian Prince, Tarkin. This was before Carth became an empire, when a king still sat the throne. Enamoured by her ethereal beauty, Prince Tarkin tried t' steal her away from her husband but she stood loyal. Not t' be denied by the likes o' a mere woman, Tarkin took what he wanted, regardless.

"Lucetta pleaded with her husband and father t' exact vengeance on her behalf, t' defend her honour. But they were loyal subjects o' Tarkin's father and would not rise against their liege. Devastated and betrayed, Lucetta saw only one path left for her t' take back control o' her life. She drove a dagger through her stomach, killing herself and the bastard babe Tarkin had planted within her.

"The peasantry, outraged that their fair lady had been denied justice, rose in anger and overthrew the king and his son. Some legends say they escaped, spirited away on horseback; others say the vengeful mob tore them limb from limb. From that day on, the Carthian Kingdom made way t' the Carthian Republic."

The young priest chuckled. "Your daughter knows her annals well. Aye, there are records that Lucetta's story had some impact on the Carthian transition from kingdom to republic. Though in truth it was likely a much more complicated net of politics and internal feuds that a young girl such as yourself wouldn't quite grasp. It makes for a decent story, though." The priest went back to sketching the statue's pointed nipples.

"Somewhat of a salacious subject for a priest to be taking an interest in?" Beorn said.

The priest chuckled. "There are some within my fold who would agree with that statement. But I would argue that a proper understanding of history is needed if we are to avoid repeating the missteps of the past. Take Lucetta for example. Her salaciousness *allegedly* brought down a kingdom and replaced it with a mummer's farce government. Democracy, of course, is an illusion; an attempt by man to impose his own will upon the world. For all those who follow the Golden Path, know that kings and rulers are chosen by God On High. It is only for He to choose who would lead us. Any attempt by man to 'elect' a leader is just a blasphemous attempt at playing God.

"Nevertheless, as dictated in the philosophies of Machiavel's *How Women are a Cause of the Ruin of States,* he expresses clearly how women have been the occasion of many divisions and calamities in past nations, and have wrought great harm to rulers. It is for this reason the Church preaches modesty, servility, and humility to the women of our kingdom, lest they once again tempt a great man into abasement and bring ruin to our lives."

Beorn *humphed.* He could feel Morrigan seething at his side. "Why is her chest bare?"

The priest blinked up at him, then the statue, as though searching for a reasonable answer. "I would suppose… artistic liberty? Sources *did* describe her as a great beauty. And her likeness has been used by artists for many generations to demonstrate their proficiency with human anatomy." He smiled at his own answer. "Some artists, such as this one, use the point of her suicide, while others may choose to use the rape itself to show their mastery of the female figure."

Morrigan ground her teeth.

"What I meant," interjected Beorn before the girl could lash out, "was why are her breasts *clean*."

"Oh!" laughed the priest. "That's simple. Many a traveller passing through Lasthome on their way north will rub one of Lucetta's breasts as a symbol of good luck. A silly superstition, really, and one I wouldn't repeat around the more pious of my Brothers, but it's obviously well practiced." The priest nodded at the pair of stone breasts, rubbed clean of any water stains, lichen, or moss. They stood out alabaster white where the rest of the sculpture was a dull grey. One nipple had been rubbed so much it was now significantly flatter than its counterpart. A detail the priest was meticulously replicating on his own parchment. Her face, however, appeared to have been left somewhat more rudimentary.

"There used to be an inn here," Beorn said, changing the topic. "What happened to it?"

"An inn?" frowned the priest. "Goodness, it's been a haberdashery for as long as I can recall. When was the last time you rode through this way?"

"An age."

"Ah yes. Well, the march of time stops for no man. If it's an inn you seek, I shall escort you back to my own lodgings. They are warm and dry, and the lady of the house informed me she'd been suckling a pig all day to prepare for tonight's vittles."

Beorn's stomach growled in response. "That would be appreciated. Lead on."

Through winding streets and back alleys, they followed the young priest until they emerged before a respectable-looking establishment. A small stable boy came out at once to relieve Beorn of Godfrey's reins. He gave the draught horse a pat upon his massive nose before heading inside. The warm embrace from a blazing fireplace greeted them as they pushed through the thick oaken door. They left the icy chill of the ride at the threshold, and the sweet aroma of braised pork immediately filled their noses. A large fat cat lounged atop the bar, deep *purrs* vibrating the air. A portly woman wearing an apron was sweeping the floors with a straw broom.

"Sara, dear!" called the priest. "I've brought you more customers."

The woman smiled. "Well thank ye, Father. The charity of the Church knows no bounds, I see."

"A room, if it please you," Beorn said, "for me and my ward. And some of whatever I can smell coming from your kitchens."

"I'll have me boy prepare a room for ye and the girl. Take a seat and I'll bring out some supper. Anything for yerself, Father?"

"The usual please, Sara dear."

Beorn and Morrigan took a seat at a table in the far corner of the common room. The priest joined them immediately, seating himself on the remaining stool. "Hope you don't mind if I join you, travellers?"

Beorn and Morrigan eyed each other across the table. "Well, I can't-" *unfortunately* "-see any reason to refuse you… Father." It felt odd using the title on one so young. Was he really an ordained priest? He looked more like a choirboy.

"Splendid! Then allow me to introduce myself: Father Emanuel, Ministerium of Virtue and the Prevention of Vice."

Morrigan scoffed.

"Bless you, child," replied the priest entirely sincerely.

"Forgive my potential ignorance, but you seem quite… *young* to hold the title of Father?"

The young man chuckled merrily. "Indeed, your assumptions are correct. I am the youngest to hold the title in a hundred years, the last being Saint Nikolai the Young. He was ordained after he performed the miracle of turning water into vodka."

"Both clear liquids," observed Morrigan. "Somewhat less impressive than wine. Sure it wasn't vodka t' begin with?"

Father Emanuel chuckled. "You have a critical mind, young one."

"And what spirits did ye transmute t' earn yer title?"

"Nothing so extraordinary, in my case. I simply had an idea. Have you perchance heard of a Madelena Laundry?"

The pair stared blankly back at him.

"No? Well, let me explain. I was not born into comfort, and I spent my early years running the streets, as many wayward boys do. My sister shared my misfortune and, well… young girls in such circumstances are prone to experience particular *hardships*. The Cloth provided an avenue of escape for myself. However, for my sister, tainted as she was, the Sisterhood was not an option. It was several years later I heard of her passing, dead in the street of some pox or other venereally contracted disease." He shook his head solemnly. "Her death weighed heavily on me. If only there was a place within the arms of the Church for fallen women such as her. Then I realised there could be. Therein lies the birth of the Madelena Laundries - named for my late sister. A place for fallen women -prostitutes, victims of seduction, unmarried mothers- to find meaning in their lives and seek forgiveness for their transgressions. The Church applauded the idea; a way to address the growing vice and immorality amongst the kingdom's young women. They appointed me a position within the Ministerium of Virtue and the Prevention of Vice and granted me a parish in the Northern Realms, to spread the gospel and erect further Laundries to our heathen neighbours." He smiled back at them like a schoolboy proud of his work, awaiting the praise of a teacher.

"And what," grilled Morrigan, "do these 'fallen women' do in these laundries o' yers?"

"Oh, a range of things. *Laundry*, for starters." The priest laughed. "Washing, ironing, and sewing of garments for the Clergy. Some domestic work such as cleaning, cooking and the maintenance of the institutions. And of course daily prayer and recital of scripture at the direction of the Sisters who oversee them."

"And are these women free t' leave yer institutions?"

The priest looked perplexed, as though he had never considered this notion. "Why would they want to?"

Just then, Sara brought out their food and a pewter jug filled with ale alongside three mugs. Conversation ceased as Beorn and Morrigan took to their bowls ravenously. Thick brown stew, with pulled pork, soft boiled potatoes, and carrots, filled each bowl. Father Emanuel's plate, in contrast, contained nothing more than warm bread and simple cheese. He filled his own mug with clean water.

"For all your boasting of this establishment's vittles, I'd have thought you'd at least partake?" Beorn said between mouthfuls.

"As aromatic as it smells, those of the Cloth may not partake in the consumption of swine. But a meal of bread and cheese is enough to satiate the needs of my earthly vessel."

Morrigan, in response, having finished shovelling the potatoes and pork into her mouth, brought the bowl to her lips and downed the remaining liquid in a long, loud slurp. Beorn reached for his pewter mug, bringing it to his own lips. The looted signet ring from the roadside massacre winked at the priest across the table.

"Oh!" exclaimed Father Emanuel, looking for all the world as though he'd uncovered some grand discovery. "I mean," he said, lowering his voice, "I hadn't realised… how could I have been so blind, the square had been the predetermined meeting place, hence why I was loitering there… Captain Lawrence?"

Beorn peered at the young man from over the lip of his mug. *Captain Lawrence?* Was that the name of the Holy Guard who'd owned this ring? How to proceed…?

Seeing Beorn's hesitation, the priest appeared to have another realisation. "Oh wait! Of course-" and went ruffling through the folds of his cassock before drawing out an identical signet ring. "Forgive my ignorance of such measures, but here is my own proof of office." A gold signet adorned with the crossed keys of the Holy Seal.

"Yes. Captain Lawrence. That's me."

The priest beamed. "Excellent!  I have been anxiously awaiting your arrival, sir! The Sisters and I are eager to be on our way to the border. I must ask, though… where is the rest of the escort?"

"Dead," Beorn answered. The best lies were nestled within the truth. "Killed by bandits. Only I remain."

"Oh, dear… and this girl?"

"An orphan. Taken under my protection. She tends to my steed."

Morrigan glared from the corner of her eye, but said nothing to contradict his story. She'd clued on immediately to what was happening. To admit anything different was to admit to looting the sacred corpse of a Holy Guard.

"Yes, yes, I see. Well, what are we to do? The Church promised us an escort of ten men-at-arms. The roads from here to the border are treacherous, to say the least. Should we send word for reinforcements?"

"No," Beorn responded immediately. The last thing they needed were more churchmen anywhere near them, let alone headed in the same direction. "The Lord has provided you with me. With me, you will make do."

"Of course," nodded Father Emanual. "The Lord provideth."

"What sisters do ye speak of?" queried Morrigan.

"Faceless Sisters, my dear. A congregation of acolytes accompanying me north to establish a convent and, with any luck, many more Laundries for the sinners of the Northern Realms."

Beorn was contemplating his options when the matron of the inn returned to clear their plates. "Good news, Sara! My escort has arrived! Captain Lawrence here will be delivering me to the border."

"Oh, bless ye deary. I knew the Lord would come through for the young Father here so he might continue his good work for our neighbours. Lord knows they have need of him. The things I hear from travellers coming south, of the way they treat their women and the way their women abase themselves for their men. Like animals rutting in heat."

Morrigan kept her mouth shut, but Beorn noted the way she slowly caressed the pommel of her dagger.

*This complicates things*, thought Beorn. *Now there's a witness to our involvement with the priest, and my defrauding of a Holy Guardsman.*

"When will we leave?" Beorn queried as the matron bounced away.

"On the morrow would be best. The Sisters are eager to be away from Lasthome. The sins of man are legion here, and they disturb their delicate dispositions."

"Very well. We will meet you in the yard on the morrow. Good day."

The priest seemed unaccustomed to being dismissed and lingered a moment, mouth hanging agape as though he had more to say. But after a second he stood, wished them a pleasant evening and headed up to his room.

Morrigan shifted her stool closer to Beorn's. "What now?" she whispered.

"I'm not sure. At first I thought we could just make off at night, but now the innkeeper thinks me a Holy Guard. It wouldn't be long until some other travellers brought word of the massacre on the road, and then we'd look guilty of their deaths. Then I thought we could just... *do away* with the priest after we left town. But the presence of the Sisters complicates things."

"We can't leave the Sisters." Morrigan's statement was flat and certain.

"You want to go through with this farce? Escort a priest of the Church of the Gilded Father to the border with his brood of nuns? We're wanted by the Church for *witchcraft*. We should steer as far away from every man of the Cloth we meet."

"And what will happen t' those girls if we don't escort them t' the border? Their escort is dead, and the priest is right; the sins o' man are legion in this place. Won't be long before some traveller or passer-by wonders what they're hiding under their habits. The priest knows this too. If we don't help, he's like t' brave the road north without protection. And what was it ye said when we first met? 'Brigands and rapers would be the least o' my worries'?"

Beorn considered her thoughtfully. "I know you couldn't convince Esme to come with us. But if you think you'll fare any better with these maids..."

"This has naught t' do with that," snapped the girl. "It's about doing what's right."

Beorn considered. The priest appeared to have no qualms in accepting his identity as this Captain Lawrence. And if he had heard any tell of the witch and her familiar wanted by the Inquisitorum, he gave no sign of it. Travelling with a clergyman may hide them in plain sight. No one would suspect heretics so close to a man of the Cloth.

"Fine. It's decided. We'll travel with them to the border, but only because we're going the same way. Any sign of trouble though and we leave them in our dust, regardless of the dangers."

Morrigan nodded, hiding her smile of satisfaction at having convinced him.

* * *

"What in the hells is that?" Morrigan asked.

Beorn, Morrigan, and Godfrey were waiting in the yard outside the inn. The amenities, as promised by the priest, had been comfortable. Clean sheets atop a dry straw mattress and a warm room. The stable boy had fed and watered Godfrey and had even given him a brush down (with the expectation of an extra copper, of course). Now they were awaiting their new wards for the journey north.

First out of the inn's door was the priest, smiling his genial smile, golden hands glinting modestly down his cassock in the morning light. Behind him came a train of five young nuns. Their robes were white as snow, freshly fallen upon a forest floor. Atop their bowed heads were five gossamer veils of scarlet. From what Beorn could see through the scarlet sheen, each was of an age with Morrigan, maybe slightly older. Upon their backs, they carried all their earthly possessions: blankets, tents, provisions. And at the rear of the procession came the cause of Morrigan's exclamation.

The nun wore a habit, black as sin, inlaid with religious scenes and stories stitched with golden thread. She clasped her hands before her in prayer; they emerged from her cavernous sleeves, clad in satin gloves as colourless as the acolytes' robes. Her own veil was the same black as her habit, but beneath it she wore a featureless porcelain mask. Genderless and devoid of emotion, the mask concealed her identity entirely. It was flawlessly smooth, but for the two bottomless eye holes.

"A Faceless Mother," Beorn whispered in response to Morrigan's question. "Highest rank within the Order of the Faceless Sisters."

"Why is it... why does she *look* like that?"

"Modesty is the highest virtue around which the Order is based. Novices must ensure they dress modestly from the time they take up the Cloth, lest they tempt the hearts of men. The higher the girls move through the ranks, the more they must cover themselves to set an example for others. Acolytes, like those girls, must wear the scarlet veil and speak only when necessary. For one to achieve the rank of Faceless Mother, she must denounce her physical form to the world, covering every inch of skin so the sins of men may never blight her piety."

"That's ridiculous. If the Church is so concerned with the sins o' men, they'd be better t' burn out the eyes o' those who might be tempted."

Beorn grunted. "I heard tell once of a man who laid eyes upon a Faceless Mother as she removed her mask to drink."

"What happened?"

"She was executed for allowing herself to be shamed in such a way."

Morrigan ground her teeth. "Once a society deems a woman's body provokes sin in men, no amount o' covering will ever be enough."

"Salutations!" pronounced Father Emanuel as he crossed the yard.

"Good morrow," replied Beorn. Morrigan stood silent, casting her eyes over the line of girls before her. She dared not look directly at the Faceless Mother. The black holes in the nun's mask stared down at the girl, taking in the sight of her. Beorn wondered what the Mother saw: Rover skirt, heathen complexion, dagger at her hip, hair uncovered for the world to see. Though the Mother's gloves may have been the softest silk, Beorn knew the hands inside likely bore the calluses of someone who easily wielded the flail and paddle.

"Captain Lawrence, may I introduce you to the Faceless Sisters who will accompany me north to establish the Church of the Gilded Father's newest convent." The girls did not look up or speak at the introduction, nor did Father Emanuel introduce them by name, as though they were not individuals, merely the collective.

"Well met," answered Beorn. "We should be on our way. Have you horses?"

"Nay. We travel as the Gilded Son did, with naught but our feet to carry us."

"Wonderful," Beorn muttered.

* * *

Lasthome slowly disappeared behind the column as they made their way north. The bustle of the town gave way to fields of crops before eventually surrendering to the untamed wilderness of the frontier. They left the stink of civilisation behind to be replaced by the rich earthy redolence of primordial forests. While winter was still some time away, and snow had not yet graced the pine needles with its tender kiss, the air had developed a bite.

Morrigan rode atop Godfrey with Beorn walking by her side, travel cloaks pulled tight and hoods low over their faces. Father Emanuel led the five acolytes in single file, while the Faceless Mother brought up the rear; her hands remained held in prayer at all times. Her habit slid across the gravel with barely a whisper. If she had appeared through a veil of mist on a moonless night, you would have been forgiven for mistaking her for a spectre.

The Sisters were in stark contrast to the Rovers as far as travel companions went. Where Beorn had wanted nothing more than for Danior to cease his incessant chattering, the Sisters' eerie silence chilled him. Father Emanuel attempted to broach conversation, though Morrigan had nothing to say to the man. Beorn caught her eyeing the young acolytes whenever she thought he wasn't looking. Did she hate them - defenders of a faith that had put her homeland to the torch? Or did she pity them - unwilling victims of the Church's beliefs, as much as her?

It was noon when the topic of witchcraft arose. Father Emanuel had been chattering away about the Ministerium of Virtue and the Prevention of Vice - and his prominent role within - when the conversation (if you could call one man talking *at* another, such) steered towards the Inquisitorum.

"… but unfortunately, that's just how these things play out. So often the poor wretches who make their way to our Laundries are already beyond hope, sullied by the sinful tendrils of the Adversary. It's only so long before what they are eventually reveals itself, and the Inquisitors come knocking. Witchcraft is, if nothing else, a parasite to its host; the community." A beat. "That isn't to say," the priest added hastily, "that witchcraft is prevalent within our institutions." He laughed nervously. "*Anyone* could be a witch."

"Yes," said Morrigan. It was the first she'd spoken to the priest since their departure from Lasthome. "But in practice, those executed for witchcraft *are* mostly women, nay?"

Father Emanuel cocked his head, as though thinking of this for the first time. "Well… yes… I suppose in practice…"

"And practice counts most o' all here. For it's only fallen *women* that get corralled into your Laundries, is it not? A ready band o' scapegoats for whenever the Inquisitors need someone t' string up or burn? Keep it in the public eye, lest they think the issue is dissipating. And if there're no witches left, there's no need for the Inquisitorum."

Father Emanuel looked at her incredulously for a moment, then burst into a jovial laugh. "Oh, my dear! You have the inner workings of a philosopher, if I'm not mistaken. While I can see how you might come to such a conclusion, your evidence is circumstantial. The truth of the matter is women are simply more impressionable, and feebler in mind and body than men. These qualities separately - let alone together - naturally invite the attentions of the Adversary. On top of this, women are liars by nature and so naturally more inclined to deceit. And lastly… and I am reluctant to discuss such matters in front of the Sisters and yourself… but I suppose the truths of the world are not comely. Very well: women are simply more carnal. Their appetites are insatiable, hence the need for chastity and protection of virtues. It is for this reason alone that men find themselves so drawn to temptation. For what is a woman but a foe to friendship, an inescapable punishment, a natural temptation, a desirable calamity, a vice painted with fair colours like a poisonous frog?" The good priest sighed. "It is no wonder there are many more women than men found infected with the heresy of witchcraft."

The Sisters did not raise their heads at his comments, merely continued walking single file, heads bowed as though listening to a sermon. One they had likely heard many times before.

"Ah, yes," Morrigan responded sarcastically. "How unfortunate men are t' endure such *temptations*. Speaking nothing, o' course, t' whether the temptresses in question are willingly seeking these advances. No, priest: men do what they like, and women pay for their avarice."

Beorn saw something flicker behind the priest's eyes. "On that, my child, you are part right. There is evil in men; no doubting that. And their appetites can be legion. But make no mistake: young boys may suffer from such appetites as easily as any woman... but let us change the topic from such grim things. Captain Lawrence - indulge me with your past exploits." The priest grinned at Beorn.

"What do you wish to know?"

"Well, as a captain of the Holy Guard, surely you must have some tales to tell."

As always, Beorn decided a lie closest to the truth would be most believable. "I was a soldier most of my life. When you're good enough at killing, you get the attention of your superiors. Promotion is the only logical response. Not much more to say than that."

Father Emanuel nodded. "Modesty is a godly trait, Captain. I take it you wet your blade in the northern campaigns?"

Beorn glanced aside at Morrigan. "Aye, as did most men of fighting during those long decades."

"I'm curious to know more of these northerners from your experience, Captain. What do you think they will make of our mission? Our ways?" *Our God* was the undertone.

"The northerners are a strong-willed people. They do not bend easily. If you come at them with force, they will never hear your message. But you should ask the girl. It's her homeland, after all."

"Of course. What do you say, child? Is the Captain's assessment correct?"

"Aye. The Carthians broke their armies against our borders without ever driving us t' kneel. Gaius's Wall stands in testament t' that. I'd like t' see yer flowery words and veiled Sisters have any better luck o' driving the northmen to their knees - either in servitude or prayer." Beorn could hear the pride layered upon her voice.

"Ah, but you forget - the Northern Realms *have* been driven to kneel. Where the Carthian Empire failed, our good King Aethelstan has succeeded, for he is anointed by the Gilded Father and no man can stand before the Light of God. But I would not expect a member of the gentler sex to understand the nuances of warcraft. The female sex is just naturally the more submissive of the two. They crave structure and direction, and lack much free-thinking of their own."

"Yet men make the better soldiers..?" Morrigan mused under her breath. Beorn couldn't help but chuckle.

The train of pilgrims continued their slow march north.

It was nearing sundown when Morrigan first caught sight of the Carthian ruins towering above the treetops. "By the gods… what *is* that?"

"While I take issue with your casual blasphemy, my child," the priest said, "I think the Lord will forgive you in this case. Those are Carthian aqueducts."

As they continued through the forest path, more and more of the colossal ruins revealed themselves. Made of countless arches, the structure towered above them. Stone after stone had been carved and placed in position until a structure, not unlike a giant bridge, split the countryside in two. While some columns had crumbled and given way, for the most part, the feat of engineering stood against the ravages of time. Moss and lichen spotted the aqueduct, and thin trickles of water streamed down from its top. The party pulled up beneath one of the arches.

Carved into the stone of this arch was a giant man, naked as the day he was born. The artist had chiselled away each muscle with intricate detail, as well as his flowing beard. He held his arms aloft, supporting the weight of the structure above, his back bearing the load of the column behind him.

"One of the Carthian Pantheon, I suspect," Father Emanuel guessed. "Heathens to the last, but you can't dispute their artistry." The Carthian artists had captured every detail of his naked form with chisel and hammer. Beorn could have sworn several of the Faceless Sisters were blushing beneath their veils; or perhaps it was the way the setting sun filtered through the crimson fabric.

"Look," Morrigan said. "There are others."

The line strode down the length of the aqueduct. A different figure was imposed on each subsequent archway, supporting the ancient wonder with what remained of their divine strength.

"These are women," Morrigan pointed out.

She was right. Six arches they passed. Six colossal women stared down at them, all as naked as the first. What did the veiled Sisters make of their nakedness? Sisters who represented all things modest and chaste, faced with detailed stone carvings of the female form twenty feet high, each as different from each other as the Sisters were uniform. Thin, wide, supple, lithe.

One held a sickle; the next a bow; another a basket. So on, and so on; all representing a different aspect of Carthian life. Farmers, hunters, bakers, warriors. Providers and protectors. Each of the five girls and Morrigan stopped before one of the giant goddesses. Stone eyes, a thousand years old, gazed down at girls of soft pink skin.

"Each of them had their role," Beorn observed. "More than just mother and wife." The goddess before Morrigan held a pair of scales in one hand, and a long stone sword in the other. "She represents justice."

"How can ye tell?" Morrigan asked, transfixed.

"The scales display the balance needed when determining a man's fate. Punishment versus forgiveness."

"And the sword?"

Beorn eyed the dagger hanging from her waist. "You should know more than most that sometimes the only true justice comes at the edge of a blade."

They made their camp under the ancient gods. The fellowship encircled the fire, eating their provisions; dried meat for Beorn and Morrigan, stale bread and still water for the acolytes and Father Emanuel. The Faceless Mother sat as impassive as ever, kneeling on the grass, hands joined in prayer. She made no move to eat. Morrigan sat slightly away from the rest, sharpening her dagger the way Beorn had taught her. The Faceless Sisters sat with heads bowed, but one was subtly sneaking glances at Morrigan as she honed the blade.

"Sisters," Father Emanuel announced as he stood. "I must give confession. Revise verses eleven through seventy-five of the Book of Atonement before sleep. Captain Lawrence, I entrust their safety to you." And with that, the priest disappeared into the trees, the Faceless Mother close behind, prepared to mutely hear whatever sins he may have accumulated on the day's journey.

As soon as they were gone, low whispers filled the campsite; the Sisters huddling together and chattering like schoolgirls whose teacher had left the classroom. Giggles and teasing, hands covering mouths as though releasing any pent-up thoughts they'd suppressed through the day. Morrigan's hand continued to glide down the length of the dagger.

"Can you truly use that?" The angelic voice had come from the Sister who'd been secretly eyeing the northern girl. It was the first Beorn had heard any of them speak.

"Aye," Morrigan said, without taking her eyes off her work.

Gasps and more giggles from the girls.

"Have you killed anyone?" the girl enquired.

"Not yet."

"I heard a story once," chimed another, "about a fierce she-warrior from the far side of the Continent. She was the admiral for a great God-King. She conquered his foes for him and even brought the Carthians to heel. Will you be such a warrior, do you think?"

"P'haps," Morrigan replied. "In time." Her eyes didn't leave her dagger, but Beorn could see her cheeks reddening in the firelight. Beorn smiled.

* * *

They broke camp at sunrise and the second day progressed as smoothly as the first. On the third, however, trouble struck.

As they crested a small rise, the sight of a man seated in the centre of the road greeted the group. A patchy brown cloak, stained enough to be a tablecloth, shrouded him. His beard was shaggy and his eyes sunken; those of a man who'd not eaten his fill in a long time. A knot formed in Beorn's stomach.

Father Emanuel appeared to have no such concerns. "Greetings, traveller!" shouted the priest.

A hand extended from the wayward man's cloak, holding a tin mug. "Spare a coin for a lowly sinner, Father?" the man said.

Father Emanuel strode towards the beggar, but Beorn snatched him back by his cassock. "It's a trap."

A twig snapped to their left. Two rough-looking men emerged from the

140

treeline. Three more emerged from Beorn's right. The beggar on the road had risen, his tattered cloak falling from his shoulders. Underneath, he wore boiled leather. In his hand, a steel longsword, the pommel stamped with the crossed keys of the Holy Seal.

Morrigan noticed it, too. "These are the men who killed the escort," she whispered. Beorn nodded. Several other swords appeared in the hands of the men who were encircling them. Others held the crude weaponry they'd used to brain the Holy Guardsmen.

"How can we be of service, traveller?" Father Emanuel said, with not nearly enough fear in his voice.

"Do you speak for God, Father?" enquired the beggar.

"I suppose… in a way. Yes."

"Can you ask him something?"

Father Emanuel brightened at the prospect of meeting a sinner seeking forgiveness. "I am his chosen vassal. Speak unto me, and he shall hear you."

"Why did he kill my daughter?"

The silence that filled the air was heavy. Beorn slid his axe from Godfrey's saddle. Morrigan's hand rested on the hilt of her dagger.

"I beg pardon?" stammered the priest.

"My daughter. Taken from me last winter. And my wife; taken in the spring. I would ask God for what purpose?"

Father Emanuel stood dumb, unable to formulate a response.

"And my acquaintances," he continued, gesturing with his sword at the band of cutthroats. "Children, families, crops, cattle… all lost. Lives destroyed. In church, they told us that all ills experienced on Earth were a necessary part of God's plan. That we should trust in Him, put our faith in Him… It's hard to put faith in a God who drowned your daughter in her own blood. So I will ask you again. Why?" The beggar stared into Father Emanuel's stunned eyes, waiting. He wanted an answer.

"Here," Beorn called, untying his coin purse with one hand. He hurled it to the beggar's feet, coins spilling across the gravel. "Take this and be on your way. We want no trouble."

The sunken-eyed beggar stared down at the coins, deep in thought. Then stepped over them. "Your coins won't bring back what was taken from me."

Men to the left and right began closing in. This wasn't simple highway robbery. This wasn't about money. This was about retribution. Justice. Why else would they have attacked the escort? No everyday bandit would try to take on a squad of Holy Guardsmen willingly. But this was personal. This was an attack on the Church, and anyone who represented it. This was a group of hurt men exerting their wills upon the world, trying to prove they and their lives were more than mere pawns to be moved about the board and sacrificed at a cosmic whim.

*Fate goes ever as it must*, Sibella whispered in the recesses of Beorn's mind.

"Take out your dagger," Beorn ordered. Morrigan complied.

The first man reached them and swung a sword at Beorn's head. A mistake considering Beorn stood above him by a good two feet. The swing left the bandit off balance. Beorn stepped out of reach at the last second and the sword carried the assailant stumbling forward. Beorn drove the blade of his axe into the back of the man's head. First blood had been spilt.

The next two came at once, one from either side. Sword and club rained down on Beorn. He parried, dodged, swung his axe in return. The Sisters were screaming. As Beorn deflected the swing of a club, he caught sight of one highwayman to his right dragging a Sister away to the treeline. Before he could say anything, Morrigan was running after them.

"No!" Beorn bellowed, but the fight quickly consumed him. Between blows, Beorn saw the redheaded girl slide beneath a sword swing and dart after the stolen Sister. Beorn felled the two men he'd been battling and turned to go after Morrigan. The haft of a hardwood staff struck him across the face.

Beorn's axe fell from his fingers and the hard gravel of the road rose to his back. Images swam across his eyes, sky and earth vying for the positions of up and down. Beorn couldn't breathe. Something was pressing into his neck, cutting off his airways. The yellow eyes and grey teeth of the man who'd struck him glared down as he pressed his staff into Beorn's throat. Vision fled like shadows before a rising sun. Twilight encroached upon the corners of his eyes. His face felt close to bursting. A waterfall raged in his ears, drowning out all sound… until a scream burst through.

*Morrigan!*

But struggle as he might, the man atop him wouldn't budge. With every passing second, his strength ebbed away. Beorn sank deeper and deeper below the surface, unable to draw breath.

Spittle dripped from the gritted teeth above him. "Die you fucking bast-"

The bandit lurched forward, cutting short his curses. With all his strength, Beorn heaved and threw the man off him to land face first in the dirt. Father Emanuel stood over him, shaking with fear, a heavy fallen branch held in his hands, snapped where it had struck Beorn's would-be murderer in the back of the head. Beorn rolled to his feet just as the staff-wielding bandit took another swing at his head. This time Beorn caught it and wrenched it from the man's grip, swinging it around to crack against its owner's face. Neck and staff broke in sync and the bandit fell to the ground like a sack of rocks.

That left only the beggar and his sword. The man stood stunned at seeing his men reduced to corpses. Beorn took advantage of his disbelief and charged at him. The beggar got over his shock and drew his hand back to swing the sword; a mistake.

*Not a soldier then*, figured Beorn. *Just an angry farmer with a stolen sword.*

Beorn dived into the beggar before he could bring his sword down. The pair crashed into the earth; the wind driven from the man's lungs. Beorn brought his fists down on the frightened man's face, sword forgotten as he frantically raised his hands in pitiful defence. Again and again, knuckles connected with skin, and then bone. Beorn stopped only when the blood in his eyes obscured his vision. He tried to wipe the gore away, but his hands were too covered in blood, splinters of skull, and chunks of brain matter.

*Morrigan!*

Beorn shot up, racing to where Morrigan had disappeared, and pulled up short. Morrigan was staggering back towards the group; face, chest, and arms drenched red. Her eyes were half-lidded; vacant. Her boot tripped on a stone and she fell, landing softly in Beorn's arms. He hadn't remembered moving towards her.

"Morrigan," he called, trying to corral the girl. "Morrigan! Are you alright? Are you injured?" His eyes darted over her, seeking a wound, the source of the blood. "Priest! In the saddle bags! The small red pouch! Get it-"

Morrigan was shaking her head. "Not mine," she whispered. "Not my blood."

"Good God," Father Emanuel gasped at the sight of Morrigan's blood-stained dagger, still clutched tightly in her bloodied hand. "What they say is true. When the Adversary cannot come, he sends a woman."

* * *

Father Emanuel knelt before the line of corpses, hands raised in prayer. The priest had demanded Beorn line them up, so he may give the brigands their last rites. "Father, forgive these men their trespasses. They knew not what they did. The whispers of the Adversary clouded their minds. May they embrace your Light and find peace at the end of their pilgrimage up the River of Penance. Amen."

Beorn bristled. "You would pray for the men who tried to kill you. Kill the Sisters? And God knows what else if they had half the chance?"

The Sister that Morrigan had saved stood silently beside the priest, staring down at the man who had tried to drag her away. A hole in his stomach stained his tunic red where Morrigan had slammed her knife into him too many times to count, the wounds blending together in one giant wet mess. Where the other Sisters avoided the sights of the bodies, she stared directly down at the man who had tried to hurt her. There was a thinly veiled satisfaction in her eyes.

"All sin is washed away as our souls swim upstream through the daggers of the River," the priest said. "They cut away our faults, and through this pain, we repent for our mortal transgressions. For at our heart, all men are created good. You cannot let their actions make you think otherwise."

Beorn scoffed. "There was no good in those men. Their souls were tainted black with their *actions*. There is no penance for that. Some men are just born monsters. Others are made. But at the end of the day there are two groups of men who walk this earth: those who harm, and those who protect."

"Ye're wrong," Morrigan whispered. "Both o' ye." She stared down at the blood still caked under her nails. Her fingers were red raw from trying to scrub them clean. "It's so tempting t' believe that most men are good, and those who are evil hide within the crowd like wolves among sheep. An island, kept apart from the rest o' us by the crush o' waves. But the truth is far more sinister.

"Good and evil isn't black and white. It's a spectrum. There are men who'll sell their own daughters but feel bad about it, men who'll string up innocent women by the roadside, men who'll torture little girls in dark cells, and men who'll stand by and watch it happen.

"Are all o' these men evil, or just some? What if those actions are pardoned by royal or holy decree? Is the man who murders the girl by order o' the Church any less evil than he who kills the travelling woman out o' his own carnal desires? And what o' the man who watches?

"Aye, there are outright evil men in the world. But it's the ones who ye trust, who ye let past yer defences that are the most dangerous."

# Chapter 8

The motley group continued their trek north, stepping over knotted roots and broken stones. The sea of green foliage gave way to shades of vibrant oranges, bold reds, buttery yellows and even the occasional plum-purple. Low-hanging branches slapped at their faces with autumnal-shaded leaves. Night drew her curtains earlier and earlier each evening, and seemed more and more reluctant to raise them with each passing dawn. It became harder to rise early each morning, the temperature slowly creeping lower each night.

Beorn allowed the Sister that Morrigan had saved to ride atop Godfrey following the fight, her weight hardly noticeable to the giant draught horse. Morrigan's actions had prevented any physical harm befalling her, but she remained shaken. Morrigan had not spoken willingly of the event, and nor had the Sister; however, Beorn knew it had bonded them. He caught them sneaking glances at each other when no one else was looking. Morrigan would help her mount and dismount Godfrey until she was strong enough to continue walking afoot, and even then the pair often walked the road abreast.

The party had stumbled across a shallow stream the day after the attack. Father Emanuel, Beorn and the Sisters took the opportunity to refill their canteens and water Godfrey. Morrigan went off with her newfound shadow to scrub the blood from her clothes. The pair's absence lasted quite some time, and upon Morrigan's return, Beorn noted she had freshly brushed and re-braided her hair, the scarlet rope hanging down her back, mirroring the hue of the Sister's veil. She looked for all the world like her usual self, all traces of the ambush scrubbed and scoured from her outward appearance. Beorn knew better than most, though, that some things never left you.

"Do you wish to speak of it?" he asked as they walked along the dirt road. "The attack? What you did?"

Morrigan wouldn't meet his eyes, finding any and everything else to look at. The leaves crunching underfoot; birds swooping over their heads; a doe, frightened by their appearance, bolting through the trees. "What good would it do t' speak o' it?"

"Sometimes it helps."

Morrigan chewed her lip before finally speaking. "I… I didnae expect the blood t' come so fast. After I stuck him that first time. And after I had, he just stared dumbly down at the wound… I wisnae sure if once would be enough, so I stuck him again and again…"

Beorn nodded. "At the end of the day, we're just giant sacks of blood. Poke a hole in us and we empty." Morrigan didn't answer. *She'll speak more of it when she is ready.* So instead, Beorn changed the topic. "You and the girl appear to have grown close."

"Aye. Her name's Joanna. But dinnae let on t' the priest that she told me. They're hardly meant t' speak, remember, let alone tell us their names. But I figure, ye save a girl's life, least ye can expect is her name in return."

"She tell you anything else?" Beorn cared little about the Sister, but he was glad Morrigan was talking again. Silence was the gateway through which guilt and regret crept into the world, and the girl needed no more of that.

Morrigan frowned and lowered her voice. The Sisters and Father Emanuel were a way ahead of them up the road, and the Faceless Mother brought up the rear several yards behind. Beorn had not heard her mutter a word since their journey began, nor even when her own acolyte was being dragged through the underbrush to God-knows-what fate.

"She told me more about these Madelena Laundries," Morrigan whispered.

"What did she say?"

"They're workhouses. Some o' them are more strict than prisons."

"I thought the priest said they reformed wayward women?"

Morrigan shook her head. "They strip them o' their names, they shave their hair, and impose a rule o' silence. Friendships and contact with the outside world are forbidden. The priests force the girls t' work from morn to eve; washing, ironing, packing laundry, sewing, embroidering, or doing other manual tasks. If the girls refuse t' work, they're deprived o' meals, beaten, locked in brick rooms, and forced t' kneel and be humiliated. She said many feel like they'll die. Some do…" Morrigan dropped her voice even further. "Joanna says the Faceless Mothers secretly bury those who perish, in mass graves behind the Laundries."

Beorn turned his head slightly. The black-clad figure stalked seven yards behind them, ivory hands clasped together, the lifeless eye-holes within her porcelain mask staring forward.

"So all these girls," Beorn whispered, "the acolytes… they'll be working in these Laundries?"

Morrigan shook her head. "They'll be *overseeing* the Laundries."

"Is that better or worse?"

Morrigan shrugged. "I dinnae know. Better t' receive the pain or inflict it? Joanna told me she's scared. Scared at how easily she could have ended up on the other side o' the deal - one of Father Emanuel's 'fallen women', rather than a Faceless Sister."

Beorn begrudgingly spoke before Morrigan could ask. "You know we can't…"

"I know we cannae take her with us. We cannae take any o' them. Already, we're wanted for witchcraft and murder. We cannae afford t' add kidnapping a churchwoman as well. I just… wish it didnae have t' be this way."

That evening, they all sat around the fire, pulling out provisions to satisfy their collective hunger from the day's long walk. Father Emanuel and the Sisters brought out their now-stale bread and cheeses and began chewing lustfully. As the priest brought his hardened loaf to his lips, Beorn cleared his throat.

"Father, would you care to share some dried meat I procured before we left Lasthome?" Beorn offered the strip of pink salted jerky to the holy man.

Father Emanuel considered. "Is there perchance enough to share with our dear Sisters?"

Beorn shook his head. "Unfortunately not. However, we still have a way to go, and you must keep up your strength. Your mission requires you to make it across the border healthy and strong."

Father Emanuel considered for a moment, stroking his non-existent whiskers. "Well… I suppose a little wouldn't hurt." The priest took the jerky and bit into it heartily. It was good too. Freshly dried and salted just right, still slightly pink within. "What manner of beast is this, might I ask?"

"Venison, Father."

"Delectable," he muttered between chews. When he was done, the priest sucked the remaining salt off his fingers. "Ah. With that, I must take my leave and provide confession. Mother Superior, if you would be too kind."

As the pair wandered off to a secluded glade to share the priest's sins, Morrigan leaned over to Beorn and whispered, "We didnae buy any venison in Lasthome?"

"No," said Beorn, taking another bite out of his cured pork. "We didn't."

Morrigan grinned knowingly. "Mighty hard to confess to a sin ye dinnae know ye've committed."

"Mayhap it will even out all the ones his God forgives."

It was several hours later that evening when Father Emanuel and the Faceless Mother returned from confession. The Sisters all slept soundly across the fire, and Morrigan leant close against the trunk of a tree close by, eyes closed, hand resting on the pommel of her dagger. Beorn had the watch.

Father Emanuel sat beside Beorn, warming his hands against the fire. His eyes appeared red, as though he had been recently crying. Once again, Beorn found himself wondering at the content of the priest's confessions.

"Father," Beorn said, "why must you make confession every night? Why so frequently? What sins could you possibly commit throughout the day that require your immediate repentance?"

Father Emanuel smiled as he sat on an overturned log. The sky above had turned grey near noon, and was now a roil of shifting shadows. The crack of distant thunder promised a storm. There would be no sleeping under the stars tonight. "Surely they teach the importance of confession within the ranks of the Holy Guard?"

Beorn, while not devout, was well aware of the beliefs of the Church. He'd shed northern blood in the name of those beliefs. Brought 'peace' through the sword for those beliefs.

"Aye, Father. But daily?"

"God saved me from the streets, Captain Lawrence. I owe Him everything. And in response to that devotion, I am granted a place at His side once I leave this mortal plane."

"So you do it for the promise of Paradise? A gilded afterlife?"

"I suppose, in a way. Isn't that why we do anything - the promise of divine reward? It is the foundation our laws are based upon. It is the Path of Light that keeps mankind honest. Without it, we would devolve into sedition, sadism, and sacrilege."

"So… let us say, there was no Holy Doctrine. There were no Church. There was no… *God*; people would hold no morality?" Beorn stepped tentatively, his words bordering on blasphemy.

Father Emanuel did not mind, though. He spent his days reassuring the worries of those losing faith, converting the unbelievers. What was a captain of the Holy Guard engaging in some philosophical debate compared to rank heresy?

"There is good in all. It needs merely to be uncovered. Unfortunately, the filth of this mortal life can sometimes bury that goodness deep. Through penance we can shovel that mountain of filth away, one confession, one good deed at a time." The priest looked solemn for a moment, but perhaps it was merely the shadows cast by the fire. "Perhaps I have more to atone for than you assume. Perhaps I merely need to be reassured that… it wasn't my fault."

Beorn wasn't sure for what the priest craved forgiveness. The treatment of the women in his Laundries? The ones dragged out by the Inquisitors and thrown on the fire? The mass graves? Beorn thought it unlikely.

"Besides," winked the priest, "who wouldn't want to jump the cue up the River of Penance where they can?"

*The River of Penance*, Beorn thought. A Stygian cascade, full of icy daggers.

The Holy Texts described how a person's soul, upon death, would enter the River and swim upstream to Paradise. Throughout their pilgrimage through the icy waters, they would be cut over and over again by daggers carried on the current. Your sins on Earth determined how far down the River you began your pilgrimage. The more pious emerged from the waters near the banks of Paradise. But regardless, all must suffer to achieve enlightenment. Even his High Holiness must wade through several feet, or so it was said.

*Not all*, thought Beorn. *Surely there are those so pure of heart they wouldn't need to bear such torments. Surely she...*

The priest stood, making to leave for his tent the Sisters had erected for him earlier, while they themselves slept under the night sky. "Fret not, Captain Lawrence. It is all part of His plan. It is not for us to question it. We are but the flock, and He is our Shepherd."

*And sheep are so easy to lead*, thought Beorn as the priest's black cassock disappeared into his tent.

Morrigan appeared at his shoulder, taking a seat beside him.

"Were you listening the whole time?"

She nodded.

"Any thoughts?"

"If the only thing keeping a person decent is the promise o' divine reward, then that is not morality. It's bribery."

"Or control," added Beorn, thinking back to his conversation with Danior. *...Witch hunting at its core is an instrument of Church-ordered control...* Was that all any of this boiled down to? Controlling the masses? Did the Church truly care so deeply about the souls of its subjects - or was it merely the need to be *in* control?

* * *

They came upon the crucifixes the following day.

Despite their lost technologies, the Carthians left behind three things still found in abundance across the Continent and Far Isles: roads, castles, and crosses.

They lined the road; four giant X's erected along the path. And four corpses hung from the crosses, arms and legs extended to their limits along the four even planks. Beorn could see the deep grooves gouged into the earth where each prisoner had been forced to drag their crucifix to the site. Where had they come from? Lasthome was days behind them, and there were no other settlements up to the border. And why place the crosses here? Was it a sign for those travelling north? But for what purpose?

*Sometimes violence needs no purpose*, Beorn reminded himself.

Each of the Sisters crossed themselves; shoulder to hip, shoulder to hip. Father Emanuel raised his sleeve to cover his nose. The air was putrid with the stench of decay. Old blood stained the wood of the structures brownish red. The first they came across hung limply by the nails through his wrists and ankles. The weight of his emaciated body had ripped each shoulder from its socket, tearing deep red fissures through his flesh. His rib cage jutted out from his chest, each rib visible through the near translucent skin. The crows had already taken his eyes and several of his toes. The second corpse resembled the first, except that repeated whipping had left red welts across his skin. Likely, he had struggled to carry his cross more so than his peers. Whoever had herded them out here had not taken kindly to his tardiness.

The third man took a breath.

All five Sisters shrieked, one fainted, and another turned to run for the hills but was met by the impassable stone wall that was the Faceless Mother. She said nothing to console the young women, but parted her praying hands to place them on the shoulder of the acolyte who had made to flee. With gentle but firm hands, she turned the girl to face the crucified men.

Morrigan too had broken into a run at the crucified man's intake of breath, albeit in the opposite direction of the fleeing Sister. Canteen in hand, Morrigan sprinted to the man and raised the waterskin to his lips. Despite her best efforts, however, she was a few feet too short.

"Beorn!" she bellowed.

Without thinking, he was at her side. He took the flask from her hands and raised it to the man's lips. For a moment, he did not respond. But slowly, his eyes cracked and a pair of pale blue orbs stared back at Beorn.

"Drink," he urged and tipped the canteen up. A slow trickle of water ran into the man's mouth. His cracked and bloody lips went unnoticed as the water slid over the wounds and down his throat.

*Cracked lips are likely nothing compared to his other injuries.*

"What happened to ye?" urged Morrigan.

"They came..." gasped the man. "They came for us..."

"Who did?"

The man shook his head. A small, pitiful movement. "Neighbours... friends... led by the knight in black... thorns upon his helm..."

Beorn's skin prickled at his words. *The knight from Ravensburg? Surely not.* Beorn had been right to use the paths less travelled. If the knight had come upon them on the highroad...

"Why?" Morrigan asked, befuddled. "Why would yer neighbours do this to ye?"

"Morrigan," whispered Joanna. Beorn saw the Mother's porcelain mask turn towards the young girl, bottomless eyes boring holes through her scarlet veil. The girl, defiant, spoke anyway. "They're Leyanites."

*Leyanites?* thought Beorn. *But they look... just like... us.* Everyone had heard tales of Leyanites. The Church painted them as a blasphemous offshoot of the Church of the Gilded Father. Some attributed the death of the Gilded Son to the Leyanites, naming them turncoats and traitors. Beorn knew it was likely much simpler than that; they were outsiders. Much like the Rovers, the Leyanite faith originated across the Channel and the people of the Far Isles had little tolerance for that which they didn't understand. Those that weren't run out of villages and towns were forced to live in small ghettos, bereft of the facilities the wider settlement likely had access to, such as a running water supply, fresh produce and, above all, space. Authorities forced many to wear identifying marks whenever they left the ghettos.

Some attributed this hatred to the historical persecution against the Church of the Gilded Father by the Leyanites themselves - though this was thousands of years ago, not long after the fall of the Carthian Empire. Regardless, this lingering feeling of persecution by the Church led to frequent pogroms and expulsions of Leyanite communities. Throughout the centuries, the Church had waged dozens of crusades across the continent to take back holy sites from the Leyanites, leading to fresh blood feuds and retaliations. Ultimately, the Church emerged victorious, leading to its proliferation across the Continent and Far Isles, and the subjugation of the Leyanite peoples. Beorn couldn't help but draw a parallel between what had occurred to the Northern Realms.

"They likely tried to hide their identities," Beorn wagered. "When their neighbours found out who they truly were... *what* they were... well..." The evidence was plain to see.

"Cut him down. Beorn, cut him down!" Tears beaded Morrigan's eyes. Joanna stood behind her, hands raised to her veiled mouth.

Beorn's legs carried him back to Godfrey to retrieve his axe. When he returned, he set about assessing how best to get the man down. The nails were thick iron. He would need to cut the entire structure apart to have any chance of removing the poor soul. But as he readied himself to swing his axe, Morrigan shouted, "Wait!"

The man's lips were moving, but the air was leaving his lungs. They were barely more than a whisper. Beorn leaned in close to hear the dying man's words. His head rested limply against his shoulder, matted hair splayed against the freshly cut timber.

"M...my f...father was a... carpenter," he struggled. "This... smells like... home..."

Beorn watched as the light faded from his eyes. A new slackness overcame his body that could only be achieved by one now free of pain. A single tear rolled down Morrigan's cheek.

A cough came from their right. "Help..." wheezed the last of the crucified men.

"Beorn! Hurry! I'll get my pouch, we still might-"

"No." The voice was stern and unfamiliar. It took Beorn a moment to realise it had come from Father Emanuel.

"*What?*" roared Morrigan.

"Look around his neck." The priest was bone white. Each hand was curled into a tightly balled fist. A thin trickle of blood dripped through the fingers of his right hand where his nails had bitten into his palm.

Morrigan and Beorn stepped tentatively closer to the final Leyanite. Around his neck hung a leather cord. Tied to the end were two fleshy...

"Are those...?" Morrigan trailed off.

Beneath the man was a large pool of blood, continuing to grow from a steady drip originating from his crotch.

"They are," Beorn said.

"That is a punishment reserved for those who befoul children," Father Emanuel spat. "The most lowly, the most sadistic of sinners." He trembled like a leaf in the wind.

"Father," Joanna said, "surely we must show mercy. Whatever his sins, this man shall suffer his punishment in the River of Penance. It is not for us-"

"No!" the priest bellowed. "Captain Lawrence, Sisters - let us be on our way." Beorn looked down at Morrigan. In her eyes swam confusion. Her desire to help, the desire of a healer, clashing with her knowledge of the things a man could do to warrant such retribution. "Captain Lawrence," the priest reaffirmed. "Might I remind you I am the overseer of this journey? Remind your ward as well."

Morrigan's internal conflict had settled into apathy. She turned away from the man dying on the cross. He could do little more than wheeze in protest as they walked away, Joanna by Morrigan's side. Beorn saw the Sister reach out subtly and brush her fingers against Morrigan's. When they were far enough away that the crosses disappeared over the rise of the earth, the priest gave a sigh.

"I apologise for that. I just can't stand such barbarity. To think anyone would perform an execution using such archaic means. Truly, it's a mercy the Inquisitorum took up burning as their preferred method for heresy."

"*Mercy?*" Beorn spat. "Have you any idea what happens to a human body when it's set alight?" Flames danced across his vision, climbing wooden beams, thatch bursting aflame. A woman's scream: *Save her Beorn!*

"Well," stammered the priest, "I assume... burn?"

"Eventually," spat Beorn, standing over the small man. "But first they *melt."* Father Emanuel's face took on a greenish hue. "Have you ever seen a burning? Perhaps you looked away until the screaming stopped and all that remained was a charred black husk? Well, let me illuminate, *Father*.

"First the skin blisters, then weeps, then sloughs off the body. The fat underneath liquefies and runs down your legs. Your blood begins to bubble and evaporate, turning to pink mist. All the while your lungs are afire, burning for air, but all you suck down is the stinging acrid smoke of the kindling and your own flesh. If you're lucky, you die of the smoke before your body can properly take light. If not, the flames themselves will find their way into your lungs." Father Emanuel blinked like a fish on a hook as Beorn towered over him, his wroth palpable. "I once saw the Inquisitors burn a woman alive, years ago. The flames caught hold of her clothes and melted them to her flesh. She'd tried to close her eyes to the pain, but the flames took her eyelids, forcing her to stare out at the crowd who cheered for her death. Then the flames took the ropes that bound her and she lurched off the pyre into the mob. She tried to run, tried with every ounce of her being. But every step she took left a disfigured print of flesh in its wake, the soles of her feet peeling off the bone and sticking to the cobblestones. Eventually, she fell to the floor and tried crawling. Her blackened skin glued itself to the ground, tearing itself from her body as she dragged herself onwards. Underneath her charred flesh, she was white like a fish."

The priest looked as though he was about to be sick. "Well, I only meant... compared to the alternatives... perhaps 'mercy' wasn't-"

"And do you know why the Inquisitors insist on fire for heretics and witches?" Beorn barrelled on, ignoring the priest's stutters. "Purification and cleansing, some will tell you. Eventually it became for the sheer spectacle of it; something for townsfolk to congregate for. But no, the original reason was *modesty*.

"The original sentence for traitors and heretics, including those caught practising witchcraft, was drawing and quartering. But as the Inquisitorum flushed out witches like a ship's cat hunting rats, a problem arose. As you yourself said, women are so *easily misled* by the Adversary, and naturally, more and more witches were being found within their ranks. What to do? They couldn't draw and quarter women; executions are well-attended affairs, and once the horses tear those legs and arms from their torsos… a woman's modesty isn't exactly kept *intact*. So some genius magistrate had the grand solution that women ought to be burnt for their crimes. More modest. More virtuous. More *humane*." Beorn stepped to Father Emanuel. The small man skittered backwards, nearly tripping on his cassock. "Tell me, Father. If you watched a girl, no older than your Sisters, cry her own eyeballs out… would you call that mercy?"

Beorn's body was tight as a bowstring. The tendons in his neck strained like the rigging of a ship battered in a hurricane. His fists ached, clenched tight enough to turn coal into diamonds… or to crush the thin neck of a young priest.

*Save her Beorn!*

"Y-y-you forget yourself, Captain," stammered the priest. "You speak against your Church. To speak against the Church is to speak against God. And to speak against God-"

"Is heresy." Beorn stared down at the small man. "Heard it before. Come Father, we've still a long way to go to the border."

As Beorn walked away, Morrigan fell into stride beside him. "As satisfying as that was t' watch, it seems ill advised." Beorn did not respond. He gazed past the horizon, past the towering trees and rolling hills, through time to memories he longed to bury. "Who was she?" Morrigan asked. "The one to stoke such anger in ye. Not some random woman atop a pyre, I'd wager. Which of ye loved ones did they burn?"

Beorn took a deep, rattling breath. "My daughter."

The pair walked in silence for the longest time. The hum of cicadas resonated through the darkening sky, interrupted only by the crunch of their boots upon the gravelled road. Morrigan reached out and took Beorn's hand, gently sliding her fingers into his. Neither of them spoke. Neither of them needed to.

* * *

Beorn felt as though he'd never been further from civilisation than on the frontier between Lasthome and the border. The forest slowly crept forward to surround the travellers like a rising tide to a marooned sailor, cutting off all options of escape. They were drowning in the foliage.

The hairs on the back of Beorn's neck stood perpetually on end. Invisible eyes stared out of the treeline, watching their journey. A constant cover of cloud had settled across the sky. Combined with the denseness of the forest, the difference between day and night became hard to identify. It was only the eerie calls and cries that filled the night air that told Beorn the sun had set and the moon had risen. Despite his best efforts, folktales and faerie stories filled his waking thoughts. Stories of white-gowned weeping women with ankle length black locks that obscured their faces. Beorn's ears pricked at each sound from the gloom that clung between the trees, waiting for the unearthly wail that was said to foretell your death. When the clouds cleared enough for the ethereal pale light of the full moon to break through the tree cover, Beorn could hear far off howls. Were they the call of wolves, simple earthly beasts? Or something more sinister? Beorn spent many a night at the campfire as the others slept, sharpening his axe as he scanned the darkness, waiting to meet the gaze of two golden reflective disks.

Father Emanuel had become far less talkative since their dispute. The Sisters too, while still as silent, were exuding a glumness that was new. Their once virginal white habits were slowly becoming more and more mired with the filth of the forest. As they journeyed farther from the Church's borders, the dirt and mud of the roads stained their hems, mirroring a gradual staining of their souls. Father Emanuel would continue to leave for his nightly confession, but the acolytes' chatter during these brief periods of freedom had steadily declined. The Faceless Mother remained unwavering; hands in prayer, empty eyes watching silently. Always watching.

Morrigan alone remained unchanged. She and Joanna continued to sneak furtive conversations when the others were not watching. Beorn even glimpsed the red-veiled young woman giggling once at something Morrigan had whispered. Morrigan herself continued her drills with her dagger every evening when they made camp. She would find a tree and mark out the rough locations of a man's vital organs, practising piercing them one by one with deft precision. Her arms, which had once been gaunt and frail, were now showing the beginnings of sinuous muscle. Dagger in hand, they would lash out like striking serpents. When she had worked herself into such a sweat that one might have washed their hands on her hair, she would return to the fire and sharpen her dagger, sheath it, then sleep. Joanna was always close at hand.

One evening, as the others made camp, Beorn strode off into the trees to collect firewood. Fallen branches littered the forest floor, and he set about collecting them into a bundle. Striding back to camp, branches under arm, Beorn rounded a tree, stopped, and quickly retreated until the trunk concealed him. Leaning slowly forward, he peered around the bark and through the greenery.

Morrigan and Joanna stood close to each other under the canopy of a low-hanging branch. Shadows played across the acolyte's scarlet veil, a mirror to Morrigan's own braid. The pair were talking in low voices. Sadness bled visibly from Morrigan's eyes. She was asking Joanna something. Begging. Was the poor girl imploring the Sister to come with them? To abandon the cloth and all it stood for, along with her future in an oppressive Laundry, standing over the acid-etched fingers and steam blistered brows of less fortunate women held there against their will? Joanna was slowly shaking her head, her hands reaching out and taking Morrigan's own. For whatever reason, Beorn knew the girl would never abandon her faith. As oppressive as it was, as hypocritical - it offered some measure of safety. The safest place from the scalding eyes of the Church was within it.

Morrigan nodded slowly, understanding. Beorn recognised the pain in her eyes. She didn't want to say goodbye. But they had to. The border drew nearer, and with it, their inevitable farewell. Joanna turned to leave, robes gliding through the fallen leaves of the forest floor. As she went to step, she paused, spun on her heel, and planted a kiss upon Morrigan's freckled cheek. Lips pressed against face, the gossamer veil hanging betwixt the two, as though the thin fabric were enough to nullify the sin they committed.

It lasted but a moment. Joanna pulled away, staring into Morrigan's eyes.

The grey-eyed girl stared back, cheeks ablaze with blush. Then the acolyte turned and ran through the trees, back to camp. Morrigan watched her go, tips of her fingers gently touching her cheek. After a time Morrigan slowly followed in Joanna's footsteps, headed back to camp, vanishing in the growing shadows that fell upon the forest.

Beorn hadn't noticed the smile that had spread across his bearded face. The sight transported him back to another time, in another place, to another young woman standing on her toes to plant a kiss upon his own cheek. His heart thudded with the memory, joy settling into his stomach. It was the first time in the longest time that such a memory had not filled him with sadness and grief. Still grinning, Beorn turned to make his way back to camp.

The empty black eyes of a porcelain mask stopped him in his tracks. All feelings of warmth and joy drained out through Beorn's feet, to be replaced with the iciness of dread. The Faceless Mother stood at a height with Beorn, her featureless white mask so close to his face that his breath fogged its polished surface. He nearly dropped the firewood in shock. How long had she been standing there? How much had she seen? All this time Beorn had been scouring the treeline for the glistening eyes of a predator watching as they slept, unaware that the watchful eyes had been so close all along.

Her obsidian robes were silent as she raised a milk-white gloved hand to her face and pressed a single finger to the lifeless lips of her mask.

"Shhh," she whispered.

# Chapter 9

Dense forest gave way to clear sky, which gave way to stone and mortar. Twenty yards from the treeline rose Gaius's Wall.

The Carthian Emperor Gaius had ordered the construction of the Wall near one thousand years prior, to mark the northern-most boundary of his empire. At the Empire's peak, the wall boasted an impenetrable curtain that cut the Far Isles in two. Near seventy miles long, ten feet wide, and fifteen feet high, the Carthians had made their Wall of solid black stone quarried by the slaves of conquered lands. A thousand years later, while still standing, the Wall had slipped into deterioration.

After the Carthian withdrawal, soldiers had left the Wall largely abandoned, and it fell into ruin. It continued to be of crucial strategic importance in the centuries to come, as the Southron kings regularly sought to expand their territory into the Northern Realms. But as time went on, and periods of peace stretched out, the wall dwindled. Some locals on either side of the divide quarried building materials from the Wall, dragging stones away to be used in castles, strongholds, and churches. The elements hammered the pillaged wall, further weakening the structure; rains washed away mortar and wind crumbled stone. But here, away from the prying fingers of greedy stonemasons, the Wall stood strong.

Shades of green moss and lichen painted a tapestry across the black stones, telling of its story through centuries. The shadows of the soldier pines danced across the battlements, so you could almost believe Carthian legionaries still manned their stations, spears in hand to fend off would-be-climbers. Beneath the face of Gaius's Wall a ditch, three meters deep and six across, ran parallel to the stone marvel. The added three meters made any attempted climb even more difficult for assailants. Now it served as a convenient path for those who wished to stroll beneath the stonework.

With a pearly grin plastered across her face, Morrigan ran her eyes over every crack and fissure.

"Why the smile?" queried Beorn.

"This wall is a great pride among my people."

"Why? 'Tis not as though they built it."

Morrigan chuckled. "Nay. But we were its cause. The Carthian Empire stretched from Old Carth, across the Continent, and ended right here. My people never yielded t' the Carthian invaders. The greatest empire the world has ever seen, and they never took us; the peak o' human civilisation brought low by an uncoordinated band o' tribes, clad in fur and tartan. This wall is their greatest failure; and our greatest pride."

"Which way?" asked Father Emanuel, walking up beside the pair.

Beorn looked left, then right. "Either will serve. Walk long enough in either direction and we ought to reach a checkpoint. I vote right." Their travels along back roads and forgotten trails had steered them left of the highroad. Finding where the highroad met the Wall would reveal a bustling checkpoint, clogged with north- and south-bound travellers; the perfect chaos for Beorn and Morrigan to slip past unnoticed. A smaller checkpoint with bored guards was more likely to result in a fuss of checking them over and wanting travel papers. Something they were in short supply of.

"Very well, Captain Lawrence," the priest said. "Lead on."

They followed the ditch beneath the south face of Gaius's Wall for half the day. Morrigan strolled beneath the masonic marvel, her outstretched hand running along the stonework, brushing creeping vines. Beorn hadn't seen her and Joanna speak since their clandestine kiss. Nor had he seen any change in behaviour by the Faceless Mother despite the sins of her acolyte. She remained a silent shadow at the back of the group, hands held in prayer, lifeless mask unreadable.

'*Shhh.*' A chill crept into Beorn's bone marrow as he recalled her whisper.

As the sun reached noon, the clamour of carts creaking, livestock protesting, and people bartering drifted along the midday breeze. A short time later, the checkpoint crested the horizon.

A small causeway crossed the southern ditch to what had once been a Carthian milecastle - a small walled courtyard, of equal height with the Wall itself, surrounding a gateway. The milecastle would once have housed a garrison of troops to man the turrets for the defence against northern barbarians. Now, king's men manned the fort, controlling and taxing the passage of people, goods, and livestock across the frontier.

Outside the courtyard, an encampment of hemp and canvas tents spotted the earth; all travellers who'd journeyed northward to ply their trade and hawk their wares now that commerce was free to flow between the Southron Kingdom and Northern Realms. Upon signing the armistice and officially ending near two decades of bloodshed, King Aethelstan had decreed any God-fearing citizen who wished to immigrate north and spread the word of the Gilded Father would receive twenty silver pieces and two acres of Crown-seized land to start a new life. The Church would preach this was all in the name of bringing heathens into the Lord's Light. Beorn suspected it had more to do with the taxes and levies the customs officers bled travellers of as they crossed the border. The King ensured those silver pieces quickly made their way back into his own pocket. Commerce lubricated the gears of statehood.

A queue had formed through the camp leading to the gates of the outer courtyard. Travellers stood irritated in line, awaiting their chance to process their papers, shuffle through the milecastle courtyard and across the border. Legs straining against the wool of his pants, Beorn climbed the embankment out of the ditch, leading Godfrey by his reins. The posse tacked onto the end of the line to await their turn.

"Beorn," Morrigan whispered. "How're we t' get through the checkpoint? We've no papers."

"We shouldn't have an issue. We've a man of the Church to vouch for us and this besides." Beorn twisted the signet ring upon his fingers, crossed keys glistening in the sun.

Shuffle, stop, wait. Shuffle, stop, wait. So it went for what seemed like the rest of the day. As they drew nearer to the gates, Father Emanuel made his way to the front of the group and began pulling leaflets stamped with holy and royal seals out of his cassock. The acolytes formed a line behind him. The Faceless Mother brought up the rear like an overbearing headmistress, surveying her students. Beorn and Morrigan sidled to Godfrey's other side, putting the draught horse between the line of holy men and women and themselves. Beorn hoped that by staying out of direct eyesight, they'd skim through without quarrel, accepted amongst the larger group.

They reached the front of the queue.

"Brother Emanuel?"

The voice held an aristocratic sharpness.

Beorn couldn't see the priest's face on the other side of Godfrey, but he could make out the hand emerging from the sleeve of his cassock. Its fingers had clenched into a tight ball and the skin was as white as sour milk.

"F-F-Father Constantine. W-w-what are you doing here?"

*Another priest? Why's the boy sound so distressed?*

"What?" sighed the voice of the unseen clergyman. "No hello? No embrace for an old *friend*?" The word sounded greasy to Beorn's ears. Something about it set his stomach roiling.

"I just... am shocked to see you so far from the King's court." A beat. "Father," the boy priest added, almost an afterthought.

The voice chuckled. "I see you haven't forgotten your manners. Tell me, Brother Emanuel, do you still sing? You truly had the single most angelic voice I've ever heard from a choir boy. So pure. So clean. Surely a reflection of your own soul, no?"

Sweat was beading the back of the boy-priest's fist. A drop fell from his knuckle.

"N-no, Father. I don't sing any longer. My clerical duties are my single focus now. And for correctness' sake, it is *Father* Emanuel now."

A high sharp bark of a laugh cut the air. It dissipated as quickly as it had erupted. "You're serious?"

"Indeed. The Church has appointed me a position among the Ministerium of Virtue and the Prevention of Vice. I am escorting these Faceless Sisters and their Mother Superior across the border to establish a convent and places of penitence for the sinners of the north. Perhaps you may be familiar with my exploits?" Pride swelled in the young man's voice. "The Madelena Laundries?"

Silence.

"Places of redemption and forgiveness for the fallen women of this land?"

"Can't say I have, Brother Emanuel. Although I've had my eyes on a slightly different crowd of women these days. And I suppose for *correctness'* sake, I should also advise you it's no longer Father Constantine. It's *Inquisitor* Constantine."

Beorn felt the earth fall out from under his feet.

*'I am the Inquisitor, Constantine Julius Herodotus.'* The words reverberated around the Brexton town square, somehow making their way to the busy milecastle on the border.

*The Inquisitor from Brexton,* Beorn thought. He looked down at Morrigan. The girl's eyes were wide as saucers. Her hands, unlike Father Emanuel's, hung limp by her side. Her arms were shaking. Tears welled in the corners of her eyes.

"Inquisitor? What business do you have at the border?"

"Well, since you ask, I am chasing a witch."

Father Emanuel chuckled. "Lose one did you?"

The earth crunched as two shining black shoes appeared closely before Emanuel's. Their toes were a hair's breadth apart. Beorn could almost feel the gaunt inquisitor's breath on his own face. "That mouth of yours always had a way of getting you into trouble." Beorn could now see the Inquisitor's arm alongside Father Emanuel's, their hands nearly touching. Where Emanuel's cassock was black in the way coal is black, Constantine's sleeve was black as sin. The Inquisitor extended a finger and traced a slow line across the young priest's knuckles. Father Emanuel did not move his hand away. "I thought we'd worked through that defiant streak. I see there is work still to do. Tell me, Brother, do you still give confession each night for your sins?"

"...Yes, Father. Each night."

"Good. Good boy." Constantine withdrew his finger. "Now, to business. It is my belief a prisoner of mine seeks to cross the border in a vain attempt to escape the King's justice. I have established thorough screenings at each crossing along Gaius's Wall."

"Ah, well, I wish you good fortune in your hunting, Inquisitor, but I'm afraid I can be of no assistance. I have here the necessary paperwork-"

"Yes, yes, I'm sure you do. Your obsessively anal nature always was my *favourite* feature of yours as a boy. However, I must be thorough; I will require the Sisters to remove their veils."

A tense silence filled the air, cut through only by the uncomfortable shuffle of the Sisters' feet.

"But… Fath-*Inquisitor* Constantine, you know as I do, it is not virtuous-"

"I care little for their virtue, Brother. Witches do not escape the Inquisitorum. Thorne, remove their veils. I need to see them."

The earth seemed to shake with each armoured footfall. The jingle of mail and clink of steel plate echoed from Godfrey's far flank. Beorn cast a tentative glance to the saddle. There, clearing the near six foot height of the Draught horse, bobbed a crown of black iron nails. The footfalls stopped at the first Sister. A short inhale was all the sound she made as the giant thorn-helmed knight pulled her scarlet veil from her brow and let it fall in the ground's dirt.

"No," called Inquisitor Constantine.

Another jangling footstep. Another red veil floated to the earth as silent as butterfly wings.

"No."

Step. Veil.

"No."

A fourth gossamer whisper fell to the ground.

"No."

Morrigan was vibrating next to Beorn. Her breaths were coming so fast and shallow, Beorn feared she would keel over and give them away. The man who hunted her, who had likely tortured her, stood mere meters away, separated by nothing more than a horse.

"And the last," Constantine ordered.

Beorn heard the girl give a gasp and a cry, and Thorne tore the veil from her head.

"Joanna," Morrigan whispered, head snapping out of her trance immediately. But she did not move. She knew to move would mean death.

"See?" snapped Father Emanuel, his sudden anger at the sacrilege done to his wards suppressing whatever fear he had of the Inquisitor. "Nothing except five terrified maids."

"And the Mother."

"You can't be serious!"

The air cracked with the sound of a palm striking face. "You will remember your *place*," Inquisitor Constantine hissed. "I care not for your position as glorified babysitter, nor for your titles, be it *Brother* or *Father*. You will always be that little choir boy, whose mouth was too big for his own good. You will recall your place in this world - *my* world - or I will *remind* you. Thorne! Remove. Her. Mask."

But the Captain of the Inquisitors' Dogs had no need. Beorn saw the glide of her black robes hemmed with gold as she strode towards the Inquisitor's shining shoes. The air was silent save for the barest whisper of the Mother speaking to the Inquisitor. Beorn remembered the darkening forest, a porcelain mask gleaming beneath a veil of black, and a whispered, '*Shh.*'

Inquisitor Constantine chuckled. "Father Emanuel, you have my apologies."

"P...pardon?"

"Perhaps you are not as useless as I first insinuated. You've brought my prize to *me*."

Crunch, crunch, crunch went the glistening shoes. A wide-brimmed black hat emerged around Godfrey's bridle. A skeletal smile grinned back at them; eyes, deep and black, as two pools of pure emptiness landed on Morrigan. "Hello there, little rabbit."

Morrigan's hand reached for her dagger before Beorn could find his axe. The silver blade darted towards the inquisitor's grim face, but before her strike could land, a giant mailed fist encircled her tiny wrist. Sir Brutus

Thorne, Captain of the Holy Order of Knights Inquisitorial, Brutus the Red, the Red Hand of God, towered over the small northern girl. A second obsidian hand reached over his shoulder, mailed fingers encircling the hilt of his massive greatsword.

Beorn lunged, catching the giant in the midriff and tackling him to the ground.

"On Godfrey!" Beorn barked. He grabbed the knight's wrists and pinned them to the ground - there was little else he could do to the heavily armoured behemoth. "Now!"

With great difficulty, Morrigan pried her eyes away from the smirking Inquisitor and leapt into Godfrey's saddle. The commotion had caused a panic among the encampment. Someone was screaming for the guards. Beorn heard the hurried shuffle of boots from within the milecastle courtyard.

Slowly, Sir Brutus pried his arms off the ground, pushing back against Beorn's own. Tendons in Beorn's neck popped as he tried desperately to keep the knight restrained, but steadily, the black-armoured man continued to break free. Beorn had the horrific realisation that he was barely struggling to do so, nor was he using his full strength. He was gauging Beorn's. With a mighty shove, Brutus pushed Beorn off him and leapt up.

"Kill the bear," Inquisitor Constantine barked. "But the girl is for the flames, and the flames alone."

"Go!" Beorn roared over his shoulder as he charged.

Brutus did not reach for his sword. Instead, as Beorn made to tackle him again - for what else could he hope to do against such an armoured opponent? - Brutus raised his fists over his head, interlocked his fingers, and brought his boulder-like strength crashing down atop Beorn's skull.

Beorn's vision dissipated. Stars skittered across his eyes. Blood welled in his mouth. Staggering, Beorn's vision returned briefly enough to see the giant fist swinging towards his head. Steel knuckles slammed into his jaw. He careened backwards, landing in the dirt.

"Thorne! The girl!"

Morrigan was in the saddle, reins in hand.

*Go*, Beorn wanted to yell, but his lips were swollen and wouldn't move. Instead, he reached out a hand to wave her away. His finger brushed leather. A stirrup. His fingers closed.

"*Hyah!*" Morrigan cried, and Godfrey took off at a gallop. Beorn dragged behind through the dirt.

"Stop them!" The Inquisitor's face was red. Guards were streaming out of the gate and running after them. Some hurled spears but with every second that passed, Godfrey's powerful legs spirited them further from harm. Captain Brutus did not run. He stood; unyielding, unending. Hunger incarnate, watching them go. He would hunt them, Beorn knew it.

Father Emanuel and the Faceless Mother watched them flee; shock plastered across the former's face, the latter's an unreadable porcelain visage. The Sisters were hurriedly scurrying to reattach their veils. One girl knelt in the dirt, her gossamer swathe limp in her fingers. Her copper coloured hair shifted delicately in the breeze. Joanna's eyes were pools of hurt, betrayal, loss, and want as she watched the back of Morrigan's head disappear into the treeline.

It took all of Beorn's strength to maintain his grip on the stirrup.

* * *

The pair rode hard to the east for as long as Godfrey could stand, stopping only once after their escape so Beorn could climb into the saddle behind Morrigan. He slumped against her, barely able to keep himself up. One of his eyes was closing over itself, his nose was a river of blood, and his lips had split like ripe tomatoes. His vision swam and his head throbbed. Godfrey could not maintain his sprint forever and eventually they all had to rest.

"How did he know?" Morrigan said, doubled over and panting from the hard ride.

Beorn had slid from the saddle and lay in the dirt where he landed. "He didn't..." he groaned. "...pure luck... figure they'll have posted men at every crossing solely to watch for us."

"But it was *him*. That bastard Constantine. He was the one who led me t' the pyre. The one who signed my death notice. The one who *tortured* me!" Morrigan was sucking down air in frantic breaths, pacing like a caged animal. Her hands were shaking. "How did he find me? He's not h-human, h-he's some m-m-monster. I winnae l-let him take me back there. I w-w-w-winnae go back… I winnae go… I winnae go… I…" She fell to her knees, struggling for air.

Beorn's wounds screamed at him as he leapt to her side. "Girl? What's the matter with you? Girl! Morrigan!"

She was panting madly, eyes glazed, her mind lost to some nightmare that she alone could see. Beorn didn't know what to do. What sort of affliction was this? He was no healer. And even if he was, the girl had taken no injuries. He thought back to his brothers-in-arms. The bloodshed of battle drove some men mad. Was this the same?

"Please, Morrigan… I don't know what to do…" So he held her. Beorn wrapped her in his arms, burying her in his tunic, her head pressed against his thunderous heart. Her hair smelt like children's sweat and pine. Small white fingers clutched fists of fabric… then slowly released. Her breathing slowed, then returned to its normal rhythm. Beorn felt her body heave with her sobs as she drenched his shirtfront in tears. Finally, she pulled away, eyes averted, shamed by her own weakness. Beorn steered her back towards his gaze with two hands gently gripping her shoulders.

"Morrigan, look at me. He will never take you again. I'll make sure of it." He nodded at the dagger sheathed on her hip. "*You'll* make sure of it."

The girl nodded, sniffing. "What now?"

She'd clued on faster than Beorn had. With the Inquisitors and their Dogs watching Gaius's Wall, there was no other way into the Northern Realms. They were trapped, hunted by the Church. It was only a matter of time before they were found. Unless…

"There's another way to cross the border."

Morrigan looked up at him, hopeful. "Really?"

"Aye. But… it's treacherous. And we need hurry." A cool wind blew through the trees, an ever-present reminder of winter's steady march toward them. Beorn turned his gaze east. The distant peaks of the Spine cut through the sky like a curtain of white and grey. His stomach roiled with unease, memories cutting like icy blades. "There is a pass through the mountains. But if the snows fall before we cross it, we'll never make it north."

Morrigan was on her feet, wiping her cheeks. "Then we best be off."

* * *

Beorn pushed Godfrey to his limit. The forest thundered with the heavy drum of the draught horse's hooves. Beorn and Morrigan rode pillion, much to Beorn's guilt.

*I'm sorry, old friend,* Beorn silently said to Godfrey's neck. *I swear I'll shower you in apples when next we have the chance.*

Each day, the mountainous wall grew closer and closer; and each day the temperature dropped lower and lower, winter nipping at their heels. Every shadow made them jump; every twig snapping in the night became a squad of Holy Guardsmen closing in around them. They stuck to thin dirt tracks and animal paths as they journeyed east. Civilisation disappeared from view until the fifth day after their escape.

"What's that?" Morrigan whispered as they rode Godfrey out of a dense crop of trees and into a grassy glade. At the centre of the clearing sat what had once been a squat little log cabin, not unlike Beorn's own. The structure appeared long abandoned. Vines blanketed the walls, the stone chimney was collapsed and smokeless, and the shutters hung limply.

"We should look inside," said Beorn.

"Why? The last thing we need is anyone seeing us."

"I doubt there's anyone around to see us." But even so, Beorn hesitated to urge Godfrey forward. The glade held a strange still air, as though preserved from a dream. An unexpected oasis, obscenely far from civilisation. Who had lived here? Why? "We'll camp here the night. It'll be good to sleep with walls around us for once."

Beorn tethered Godfrey in the remains of the barn, stripping him of his saddle and bags, before heading for the farmhouse. Beorn pushed the door open with the pommel of his axe, hinges wailing like banshees. The entryway opened onto the first and largest room. Two doors stood ajar in either far corner, leading to other smaller rooms. The air was thick with dust, cobwebs… and decay.

Morrigan gasped when she saw the first corpse. It was little more than a withered skeleton, skin clinging tightly to its frame. The remains of clothes hung in tatters, moth eaten and decomposing. What was most shocking, however, was that the corpse was pinned to the far wall by a pitchfork through its chest.

"What d'you think happened t' him?"

"Likely the same thing that happened to her."

Seated at a table in the room's corner was another corpse. Her long hair was the colour of straw. Empty sockets stared out of her skull. A rust-coloured stain spread across the floorboards beneath her.

"What's that in her hands?" Morrigan crept closer to the body. Clutched in her leathery hands was an equally leathery tome. The covers of the book were filled with uneven and rough-edged pages. Morrigan gingerly pried the book from between skeletal fingers. Pages parted in a cloud of dust, and she began to read.

*"It is the first day of summer. The days are long and hot. Eadric spends them in the woods hunting. I spend them locked in my room. My flux is three weeks late. I fear what that means. I fear to tell him. Would it change the way he treats me? Would it stay his hand, or increase the fury of his fists? Would it stop him stumbling to our bed, reeking of beer? Would I be less tempting to his ravenous desires...?*

*"It has been months since Eadric brought me here; since my father sold me to him. For that's what it was in truth - a sale, more than a match. Father parted the exchange richer one dairy cow, half a dozen hens, and a pouch full of grain. Eadric parted richer one fertile young bride. 'You should feel lucky,' Father told me before I left. 'Eadric is a rich man. King Edward has granted him a parcel of land just south of Gaius's Wall to settle. You will help him clear this land and reap its rewards. It is a better life than you could ever have hoped for with us.' But all I could think of was the widower twenty years my senior who I had never before met, who I was expected to wed, bed, and produce heirs for.*

*"We departed Lasthome to the waving hands of our neighbours... and their whispers. We had all heard them before. 'There goes another wife', 'Will this one meet the same fate?' 'Will she bear him sons or die upon his fists like the last?' Father didn't come to see us off. I wasn't his daughter anymore. I was Eadric's wife..."*

Morrigan paused, looking up from the book. "It's her journal." She flicked through the pages. "She wrote near daily."

"Likely her only escape," said Beorn, casting an eye over the skewered corpse on the wall. "I've changed my mind. I have no taste to stay here among these ghosts."

The sky cracked and split asunder. Rain hammered the ground deafeningly.

"I don't think we have much o' a choice," Morrigan observed.

* * *

The pair sat around a small fire in the centre of the room. The hearth was beyond use; the chimney crumbled. Rain had settled into a steady thumping atop the thatch. Beorn had done what he could to fix the shutters closed, but the room still suffered from a chilling draught.

Morrigan sat crossed-legged on the floorboards, the journal balanced atop her knees, thumbing through its pages, reading aloud.

*"I can no longer hide my pregnancy. My stomach has swelled too much to escape Eadric's notice. He appeared happy when I told him, though more-so for what it meant for the land than our family. 'More hands to tend the farm,' he declared. It hasn't stopped his desire, nor has it tempered his anger. He uses his fists as freely as before, though always away from my womb now.*

*"I fear what life this child will have. I fear the fate of a daughter with Eadric as her father. I fear what would become of a son, whose only role model is a drunkard and batterer. But - shamefully - I fear for myself most of all. What will become of me, now that he knows I can bear his seed? How many 'farm hands' will he force me to produce? Is this what my life is to be? A brood mare? I wanted to be a dancer..."*

Morrigan trailed off, pinching the pages between her fingers. "This ink is old. Old by the time she died. She'd been here for years. With that… man."

Eadric's corpse stared down at them from the wall.

"Why didn't she leave?" asked Beorn. "If she was so miserable, so tormented, why not flee?"

Morrigan scoffed. "To where? With what supplies?"

Beorn shrugged. "I don't know, but surely it would be better for her to take her chances than continue to endure?"

Morrigan's eyes grew hooded, descending into memories. "In our travels, my mistress and I stitched up many a wife who'd tried t' flee her husband. Each one told us they thought he would kill them. 'I'd never seen him in such a rage,' they would say."

"They feared losing their wives."

"They feared losing their *control*. Men cannae stand anything outside their control. Part o' why they fear witches so. These are women who are isolated from the world around them. Look at this farm, as far from civilisation as you can get without stepping through the veil o' death. Then there are the wee 'uns t' think of. Do these fleeing wives take their babes with them? Or leave them behind? Each choice comes with its own risks. Often the only place a mother can ensure her child's safety is by their side, despite the risk it puts her in." Morrigan returned her gaze to the journal.

"*I have given Eadric a daughter. The whole ordeal was terrifying. He would not send for a physician, and he refused to return to Lasthome so my sisters could midwife for me. He insisted on delivering the babe himself. When I questioned if he knew what he was doing, he caught me with that look he gets before he raises his fist. 'I've delivered calves before,' he informed me, as though t'were the same. I dared not argue further.*

"*The pain was unending, the feeling of my insides tearing themselves apart. I tore from front to rear, and the blood was unending. But finally Eadric drew forth our perfect baby girl and placed her in my arms. When I asked if he was pleased, he grunted; 'Two arms, two legs - all a farm hand needs.'*

"*The recovery has been the hardest. Eadric made an attempt at stitching me; somehow it felt more humiliating - him staring at my secret place so closely, candle held to light his work - than when he stumbles into bed, bearing down atop me. The stitches were not neat, and the bleeding has not ceased completely. Yet Eadric demands we continue the work. Fields need clearing if we are to plant crops before the season is out. So I must continue to labour, in the field as well as the birthing bed. The only joy to my day is our little Emma. I wear her strapped to my chest as we work, so I may sniff the crest of her head. Let it be worth it, for her..."*

Morrigan was looking around. Beorn knew what she was looking for. "Don't," he told her.

"Don't what?"

"Just don't." They sat in silence, the fire crackling between them. Beorn was holding a stick of dried beef, but could not bring himself to eat. It looked far too close to the gaunt, dried skin pulled across the corpses' frames. He threw it down in a huff. "Read on."

Morrigan flicked through the pages to the end of the journal, desperate to know how the story ended. She stopped at a page towards the end of the book. "This is the last entry. Judging from the dates, it's eight years after she birthed the girl. The ink is... red?" She brought the book to her nose and sniffed, then cast her eyes to the red-brown stain beneath the woman's feet. "It's not ink."

"In your own time."

Morrigan took a breath.

*"Eadric is dead. I killed him.*

*"I came inside from my chores and found him seated at the table. My journal was before him. I felt my whole body go cold in that moment. I don't know how he found it. I've always kept it hidden. In the barn, under the floorboards, in the rafters, always moving it so he'd never find it. But he had; and he'd read it. He didn't yell. He didn't scream. That scared me the most.*

*"He asked me why I'd written such lies. Something about having the book out in the open, my secrets laid bare... it made me brave. I told him these were no lies. These were the actions of a cowardly, small, insignificant man. Too weak, too pitiful to be anything else. These were the accounts of the hell he'd put me through. And I told him I wouldn't take it any longer. I told him I was leaving. That I was taking Emma with me. That we were fleeing to God-knows-where and he would*

*never find us again. And that the next time I saw him would be with me on the banks of the River of Penance, and he in its icy water. I told him I would wait for him to reach up a hand, begging me for help as those icy daggers cut his sallow flesh to ribbons, and I would push his head down with my boot until the bubbles stopped...*

"*I waited for him to yell. I waited for him to hit me. But he simply stood. 'You are free to leave,' he told me. 'But you will never see Emma again.' He was at her door before I realised what he'd said, locking it behind him. I heard her scream, and I pounded my fists bloody, trying to open that damned door. I ran outside and grabbed the pitchfork, thinking to leverage the door off its hinges. But when I returned, the door was open... I can't write what I saw. I can't...*

"*Eadric came up behind me, foul breath in my ear. 'Don't worry,' he said, hands on my shoulders. 'We can always make more.'*

"*I care not if I spend the rest of eternity floating down the River for what I did next. I should have done it years ago. I drove that pitchfork through his belly and skewered him to the wall. I stared into his eyes as he died and I said her name: 'For Emma.'*

"*Now I sit alone at our table. The remnants of my life around me. Everything is getting darker... the lights are going out... I have run out of ink, but I have blood aplenty. It is currently pooling beneath me, from the wounds I have cut upon mine wrists. Soon I will be with you, Emma. Soon.. mummy is coming...*"

The words died on Morrigan's lips. With tender grace, she closed the journal, fingers tracing the cracks in the leather. Beorn stood, walking to the door in the far corner of the room. It creaked open under his palm. A simple room. A wooden wardrobe in the corner, a shallow basin for washing, a lone straw mattress, and upon it...

Slowly, Beorn shut the door and returned to the fire.

"Why?" he swore through gritted teeth. "Why fathers? Why must they all be so..."

"Monstrous?" Morrigan offered. She made no attempt to ask about the room's contents.

Beorn gave a slow nod. "Do they not realise what they have to lose? How grateful they should be?"

Beorn could not take his eyes off the fire. The heat was making them water. He told himself it was the heat. Nothing else.

The shuffle of skirts signalled Morrigan's move to Beorn's side. A tender hand came to rest atop his own, curled tightly into a fist he hadn't realised he'd been making. "I know it's no consolation, Beorn. But ye daughter… she was spared the pain o' growing t' womanhood in this accursed world."

"I could have protected her." He paused. "I should have… Why is the world like this?"

"Some men wish t' see all women treated so brutishly. Whether they be kin or witch."

"I was a soldier," Beorn stammered. "I saw death. I saw violence. But that was war. This… all of this… it's just so… senseless." Was he referring to the dead family in this farmhouse? The gibbets and crucifixes along the roadside? The women executed in the town square? The corpses hanging from the message tree?

"Violence is violence," Morrigan muttered. "It never makes any sense."

They fell asleep to the thunderous pummel of rain. Beorn's sleep was as tormented as ever, phantom pains torturing his soul. Grief, regret, sorrow, shame; each taking equal turns. *Save her, Beorn.* He woke in the early hours of the morning. The rain had ebbed to a light sprinkle. Morrigan slept soundly on the other side of the cold fire. Careful to not wake her, Beorn set to work.

Morrigan awoke several hours later, sunlight dispelling the remaining storm clouds and cutting through the broken shutters. She found Beorn outside, shovelling the remaining soil on to the two graves. "You didnae need t' do that," she told him.

"No, I did." Beorn buried the blade of the shovel in the earth and turned back to the farmhouse. "Come. The day has begun, and we still have a long way to go."

Morrigan nodded. As they collected their belongings inside, Morrigan slid the leather-bound journal into her satchel.

"You're taking that?" Beorn asked.

"Aye. This is her story; she deserves t' see it endures. Perhaps I'll use the blackthorn ink I've brewed t' make some copies. People deserve to have their stories told."

They set off atop Godfrey's back, strutting past the two fresh graves for mother and daughter. They turned east and continued on their journey, leaving the farmhouse behind, Eadric's corpse still nailed to the wall.

# Chapter 10

Mountains erupted from the earth before them, harsh and unending. The peaks of the Spine's summits were frosted white with year-round snows, looming menacingly above their heads, a persistent threat of a frozen burial. Jagged cliff faces towered over them like colossal titans; brutal, merciless, unyielding-

"Beautiful," Morrigan whispered when she'd first laid eyes on the peaks.

Beorn looked again with fresh eyes. Glacial blues and luminous whites greeted the eye, whispering promises of a wonderland out of a forgotten fairy tale. Perhaps Beorn's perception was clouded with memories, long thought buried.

*A beautiful place to die, an ugly place to die; it doesn't matter, we'd be dead all the same.*

Beorn walked beside Godfrey while Morrigan rode in the saddle. As they had neared the Spine, all trails, roads and paths had converged, connecting to the Greytower Pass. That was their destination.

Gaius's Wall wasn't the only defence against northern invaders. Any army that wished to circumnavigate the once-heavily armed border would have to sneak through the mountains. The only known path through the Spine from north to south was the Greytower Pass.

"Why is it called that, anyway? The 'Greytower Pass'?"

Beorn roused himself from his brooding. As they'd neared the Pass he had slipped back into his more laconic state, withdrawing into himself until he would eventually meet Morrigan's questioning eyes and realise she'd been speaking and was awaiting a response.

"At the highest point of the Pass," Beorn replied, "sits Greytower Watch. A small fortress so named for the lone tower that stands above it. Any army that wishes to cross the Spine must be channelled through Greytower Watch, which is exactly why it exists. From the Greytower's parapets, a sentry can spot an advancing force from miles away and signal the closure of the Pass."

"Closure?"

Beorn nodded. "The Pass is rigged to collapse at the shortest of notice. Boulders rain down from the cliff sides, blocking the advance, and hopefully taking out a few of the enemy force's numbers if timed properly."

"So we must go through this Greytower Watch, then?"

"Aye." Beorn let the word hang in the air.

*A solitary stone tower rose menacingly at the centre of the card. 'There's only one tower I care about, and it has no place in my future. I will never return there.'*

"What sort of reception can we expect?"

Beorn blanched. "Excuse me?" *Reception?* Sometimes Morrigan appeared to see into his mind, an eerie sensation that made him question her reasons for being sent to the pyre that day.

"Will they be looking for us? Like on the Wall?"

"Oh. No, I don't think so. Greytower Watch is out of the way, largely forgotten about now since the northern campaigns are over. It's one kingdom now, no need to fear invaders."

As their path had converged with others near the base of Greytower Pass, they had passed other travellers headed for the Watch. The usual sort; those wishing to circumvent the rapacious taxes of the border, those wishing to avoid the litigious paperwork required to pass Gaius's Wall, or those like Beorn and Morrigan who wished to avoid scrutiny all together. All the travellers they passed told the same story; witch trials were rampant across the Southron Kingdom.

The Inquisitorum was in a fervour. The mere mention of witchcraft was enough to fan the flames of paranoia, whipping the countryside into a frenzy. Inquisitors charged with staunching the sickness seemed only to spread it. Where they went, accusations followed, like the plague behind rats. Jilted neighbours, spurned lovers, all leaping at the opportunity to accuse those who had wronged them; revenge as warm as the flames.

Omens appeared to sprout from the earth without warning. Calves born with two heads, crops that withered and died the day before harvest, babes that soured in the wombs of healthy young mothers. Across the land, folk chose not to see cows that drank downstream from dyers' mills, crops planted in weak soils, or the natural effects of an underfed mother; instead, they saw only the evils the Church told them to. The Adversary's cloven hooves scourged the land. Women ran naked under the full moon, dripping with the blood of the unborn, conducting their dark sabbaths - or so the Church claimed.

Greytower Pass was treacherous; so narrow in some places Beorn would have to pull Godfrey through the gorges while Morrigan pushed from behind, while in others they skirted along a precipice of sheer drops, the siren song of the open air tempting them to jump.

They passed a traveller journeying in the opposite direction, the width of the path requiring them to wait on the lip of a cliff side as the traveller shimmied by. Beorn bought some winter clothes from the man for himself and Morrigan. The girl insisted on keeping her Rover skirts but happily donned the warmer tunic and thick socks. By nights, they slept under whatever rocky outcropping that best blocked the howling winds. The snows had not fallen this low among the mountains yet, but the icy winds bit at their skin and carried with them stinging frozen sand.

Up and up they climbed, Beorn's trepidation growing daily. Greytower Watch sat at the highest point of the Pass. If they didn't reach it before the snows fell, they never would.

"Look!" Morrigan shouted on a cloudy morning.

Cresting the rising mountain ridges was the Greytower. Made of the same dark stones as Gaius's Wall, but bleached the colour of ash from its closeness to the sun, the Greytower stood as another ominous relic of the Carthian conquest. Angular walls erupted directly out of the rock face, nestled between the icy peaks of the Spine. The wind and sleet had worn away the crenellations, until all that remained were jagged stubs along the parapet, like the gap-toothed jawbone of a long decayed beast. Arrow slits lined the walls pointed at the northern and southern roads. As they drew nearer, Beorn spotted the jagged and perilous stairs carved into the mountainside itself leading from the Greytower's gates down to the Pass.

Nestled in the shadow of the Greytower sat the walled fortress of Greytower Watch.

Hidden from the ravages of the wind, Greytower Watch stood better preserved than the solitary watchtower from which it garnered its name. Its walls were strong, patchworks of newer mortar showing preservation and repair efforts. Behind its curtain, columns of smoke rose from multiple chimneys, and Beorn heard the bustle of men and women at work.

"Come on," muttered Beorn as he tugged Godfrey forward by the reins. "We get in, resupply, and get out. We've beaten the snows, but the trek back down will still be difficult this time of year. Autumn winds can cause rock slides and avalanches."

Morrigan sighed. "Here I was hoping for a warm bed."

They approached the gates, hoods drawn low. A single guard leaned dispassionately against the gatepost, hand hanging limply from his sword pommel. His gambeson was thick grey cloth, lined with fur trimmings for warmth. He wore a sigil of a solitary tower on his breast. "Papers?" he sighed, holding out his other hand.

Beorn dropped something golden and clinking into his palm. "Lost in the Pass."

The guard weighed the coins in his hand before nodding them through. They were hardly the first shady travellers to take the Pass to avoid customs.

Greytower Watch hadn't changed. Cobblestones carved straight from the mountainside formed the ground they walked upon. Builders constructed houses using bricks from those same quarries. The greyness created a dense maze, as though the world had been bled of its colour.

*Perhaps this is the world of greys the girl had spoken to the priest of,* Beorn considered. But Beorn knew first hand these were not the greys of ambiguity, but of cold indifference. These were the greys of turning a blind eye to the pain of a boy bleeding out in the courtyard, beaten to a pulp by the master-at-arms. These were the greys of letting the cries of a boy who'd just lost his mother fall on deaf and uncaring ears. These were the greys of disowning your son for choosing love over military servitude.

They made their way through the streets without challenge. Beorn kept his hood pulled low and his eyes on the ground, but no one paid him any heed, regardless. They stocked up on provisions for themselves and Godfrey, purchased some additional winter clothes for the coming months and were about to make for the northern slopes when Beorn heard the ringing of the crier's bell.

"Hear ye, hear ye! Good people of Greytower Watch, residents and passers-by alike; you are directed to attend the trial of Beatrice Smith for the charges of heresy, maleficium, and witchcraft."

People in the streets muttered to themselves as they shuffled after the crier, leading them through Greytower's streets like rats behind a piper. Beorn and Morrigan exchanged troubled looks as the masses swept them up.

*Will I never be rid of these infernal trials?* Beorn cursed. *Brexton, Ravensburg, now Greytower. Am I cursed to have witches herald my every step? Or is there simply no place left devoid of the Inquisitorum's paranoia?*

Greytower Watch had no town square, for it could barely be called a town. The mob had instead erected the gallows at the barbican below the Greytower itself. Behind the heavy iron gates, precarious stairs zigzagged up the mountainside to the Greytower's iron-studded doors. The tower stood silent sentry over the event unfurling beneath it; grey, impassive, indifferent.

*For the Greytower looms tall and casts a mighty shadow,* Beorn's father used to say.

As Beorn and Morrigan jostled to a stop before the platform, Beorn's mouth went dry. A knight in shining black armour sat atop the gallows platform. Beorn's dread was only slightly eased as he realised the great-helm resting beside the knight lacked a crown of thorns.

*Not the knight from the Wall.* Regardless, this wasn't good. Beorn saw Morrigan slowly raising her own hood beside him, hiding her crimson braid beneath the grey woollen cloth. As they awaited the presentation of the accused, Beorn took the measure of the Inquisitors' Dog. The knight sat with his helm on the bench beside him, revealing him to be not a monster but simply a man. Curious that he would reveal his face despite his knightly vow of modesty. Could it be the thin mountain air, or simply the leagues between him and his thorny captain?

He was meat-headed with a receding hairline, shaved close to his skull to hide the fact. His chin was non-existent and his neck was a solid slab of muscle. Beorn held no doubt the rest of him would be the same. In one hand he held a gleaming silver longsword, and in the other, a whetstone which he expertly ran down the length of the blade.

After a moment, there was a commotion at the front of the crowd and a woman was hauled onto the platform. Bruises mottled her face; several of her fingers lacked nails; someone had shorn her head. Several members of the mob immediately broke into boos and curses.

*She's as good as guilty in their eyes. The accusation alone will condemn her to the noose.*

There was no coming back from the taint of an accusation of witchcraft, innocent or not.

"Good people of Greytower Watch!" a short fellow in lawman's attire proclaimed to the crowd as he joined the witch on the gallows. "You are called forth today to see the righteous work of God take place, and see His holy justice dispensed. Beatrice Smith, thou hath used detestable arts called witchcraft and sorcery. How do you plead?"

"Innocent! I am innocent Willem and you know it to be true! End this farce!"

The lawman, Willem, gave no sign of hearing her pleas. "We have witnesses that claim thou used evil spectres and sinister visions to torment Nial Crawson - a rival smith of your husband."

"I am no more a witch than you are a wizard. And if you take my life away, God will give you blood to drink. Thick enough to choke on!"

Someone in the crowd gasped. "She tries to curse us!"

"Curses are just words, and words are but wind," Beatrice spat. "The only curses I have for you lot are to bugger yourselves for turning on me so! I am your neighbour! You know me!"

No one in the crowd came to her defence. Lawman Willem continued. "We have a witness to your crimes. Goodman Crawson step forward."

A man thick of arm and covered in wiry hair climbed the scaffold. He could be none other than the rival smith. "Aye, Beatrice Smith be a witch. I saw her spectre, clear as day, come to me in my home. She tormented me so, denying me sleep until my work in the forge grew sloppy and lax. T'was her intent! Her and her husband have always held malice and envy in their hearts for my superior talents, God knows. T'were her intent to sabotage my craft so as to drive customers to her husband."

Mutters and nods rippled through the crowd.

"Lies!" Beatrice shrieked. "Anyone who's had the misfortune of buying a sword from you knows your work is horse's shite compared to my husband's!"

"The witch is hysterical!" someone shouted. "Gag her mouth so she can't bewitch us with her mutterings-"

"I am with child!" Beatrice's plea echoed over the heads of those assembled, leaving silence in its wake. Low muttering broke the silence as the crowd contemplated what this meant.

"We can't kill a babe, unborn... can we...?"

"Surely the Church will show clemency? At least until the babe is born...?"

"But who would wet-nurse for such a creature? What if its feet are cloven, its hands clawed...?"

"Who cares, I say! We leave the hagseed to grow, we'll only be cursing our children with the same plight..."

"Enough of this." The crowd fell silent at the words from the Knight Inquisitorial. He put down his whetstone and slammed his sword into its scabbard. "I've heard all I need to hear. Witches beget witches. I will not abide you to bring more of your ilk into this world. Beatrice Smith, I find you guilty of the crime of witchcraft and order you to be hanged by the neck until dead. Pregnant or otherwise."

"No!" The cry came from the front of the crowd where a man was pushing his way through to the gallows. "You cannot, sir! The court has not granted her leave to enter a defence. This is no true trial!"

The knight stared down at the man with venomous intent. "I speak with the authority of the Church. My word is law. And I say she shall hang."

"You can't! My wife is innocent!"

"God would not let an innocent woman be led to the gallows. Her presence here proves her guilt. Would you question the will of God?"

Beorn sighed. The man was beat. He could not speak out against God's divine will without condemning himself to the noose beside his wife. But what he said next shocked everyone in the crowd.

"Then let *God* prove her innocence. I demand my wife receive a trial by combat! I will act as champion!"

The crowd gasped in unison. Trial by combat. It was unheard of for witchcraft. Trial by ordeal, yes; specifically ordeal by water and ordeal by fire. But never ordeal by combat. To be accused by the Church was to be accused by God. The purpose of a trial by combat was for God to prove the innocence or guilt of an accused by lending strength to their hand. In the eyes of the Church, God had already found her guilty - the entire scene was paradoxical. Nonetheless, the law was the law, and the court owed her the option to let God decide her fate.

The black knight knew this as well. His teeth ground together in frustration. "If you are so intent to die with your wife, then step forward, peasant, so I may cut you down. My blade is sharp and I will make it quick."

"No!" the woman screamed. "Mikkel, you cannot! Think of the children! They cannot lose us both!"

*Mikkel...* Beorn thought. *Mikkel Smith?*

Beorn shoved sideways to glimpse the man. Above them, the knight was grinning. His frustration had turned to macabre amusement.

"The challenge has been made!" he beamed. "Trial by combat, it shall be. Choose your weapon, sir."

"Mikkel, no!" Beatrice shrieked, struggling against her bonds.

Mikkel stood petrified beneath the looming knight on the scaffold above him. The enormity of what he had done was sinking in. He was about to die.

No blacksmith stood a chance of besting a Knight Inquisitorial in single combat. His wife would watch him die upon the cobbles and then follow him in death shortly thereafter.

The knight was enjoying toying with his prey. "Unless someone else would defend the witch?" he bellowed, knowing no one would take up the call.

"I will."

The crowd turned as one to stare at Beorn. It took a moment to realise the words had come from his own mouth. Morrigan was at his elbow, pulling his cloak.

"*What are ye doing?*" she hissed.

What *was* he doing? He didn't get involved. He didn't. And yet…

"I will be her champion," Beorn thundered over the heads of the gathered peasants.

The knight's eyes narrowed down at him. "And who are you to throw your life away for this witch? Some knight errant, seeking a song of his deeds?"

"No knight. I'm just a man."

"Very well. At noon you die like one."

* * *

"What the *fuck* are ye doing?" Morrigan swore.

The crowd was dispersing, likely going to fetch those who hadn't come at the crier's bell who would no doubt find a trial by combat significantly more interesting than a measly witch trial. Lawman Willem led Beatrice Smith away to await the death match that would decide her fate.

Beorn couldn't explain what had prompted his actions. Somewhere in the recesses of his mind, words bubbled forth: "*He who sees evil and does naught is just as complicit as those who stain their hands with the act. You told me that.*"

"And ye thought the best time t' trial this new moral compass was by challenging an Inquisitors' Dog to a fight t' the death? The same knight who that bastard Constantine likely stationed here t' watch for our crossing?"

"Aye."

Dumbfounded, Morrigan stood still.

"What about what ye said in Ravensburg? About what a knight in full plate can do t' an unarmoured peasant?"

"I said nothing of being unarmoured."

Mikkel Smith was making his way to them through the thinning crowd. A short man of later years, Mikkel had more hair on his arms than his head. But strong arms they were, honed from decades before the forge, hammer in hand. A coarse black beard covered the bottom half of his face, migrating down his neck to join the tuft of similar hair jutting from atop his leather work apron. Before Beorn could stop him, the smith grabbed both of his hands.

"Bless you, sir," Mikkel sobbed. "Bless you." The smith's hands squeezed Beorn's like an iron vice. "Whatever you need, you shall have. My forge is yours to plunder." Mikkel looked up at Beorn's face under his low hood, tears glistening in his eyes. The briefest shadow of recognition flickered across the smith's face before Beorn quickly pulled away.

"Take me to your forge," Beorn commanded. Mikkel was silent for a moment, but then led on.

Mikkel's smithy was built into the northern wall of Greytower Watch, made of the same basalt slabs as the Greytower. The forge sported a low ceiling, its walls covered with weapons and tools hanging from iron nails. The forge spewed sweltering heat, bringing Beorn to an immediate sweat. Despite the heat, he kept his cloak on and hood pulled low.

Mikkel was darting frantically from wall to wall, pulling down various pieces of plate armour and running to hold them against Beorn's body. This spaulder was too small, this cuirass too large. Mikkel let the pieces fall to the floor as he darted away to gather others until he had piled a full suit of mismatched armour on the worktable closest to them.

"You'll be wanting a sword," Mikkel was muttering, pulling off blades of various lengths from the wall. Each bore his maker's mark stamped upon the flat steel - the solitary tower of his liege. Two-handed longswords, hand-and-a-half bastard swords, short swords, greatswords, daggers, dirks. Blades of every size, shape, and design hung from Mikkel's walls. "Here," he said, pulling down a longsword. "This looks to be about your size. To be honest, a man as big as you could probably wield a greatsword with not much difficulty-"

"No swords."

Mikkel stared blankly at his saviour, as though for the first time considering the stranger who volunteered to defend his wife's charge of witchcraft might actually just be mad. "Um... another weapon, then. I have maces, flails, poleaxes-"

"No weapons."

Panic danced behind Mikkel's eyes. But what other choice did he have? He couldn't hope to best the Inquisitors' Dog himself. "No... weapons...?" Morrigan moved up beside him. She'd lowered her hood against the heat of the forge, sweat already beading her forehead. "Surely a man such as yourself has to care for you and your daughter on the road? You must have some way of defending yourself?"

"I have an axe."

"Oh! I can work with that. A battle-axe?"

"A felling axe."

Mikkel sank to the floor, a cloud of sawdust and metal shavings scattering in his wake. "Tell me true, sir. Is there any hope for my wife?"

"The truth? I can't promise you anything."

The smith sobbed uncontrollably. Beorn found the sight uncomfortable. Mikkel was such a robust man, built like a brick house, yet bawling on the floor of his smithy he looked like a child. As if on cue, a second child ran into the room.

"Papa?" The boy had Mikkel's looks; the same thick dark hair and dark eyes. Given time he would grow into the spitting image of his father, Beorn had no doubt.

Mikkel was madly rubbing his eyes before his son could see his father's shame. "Edmund, go back inside the house. I-I have customers."

The boy's eyes looked over Morrigan before taking in the sight of Beorn.

The boy had to crane his neck to look under Beorn's hood. After a moment's observation, he returned his innocent gaze to his father. "Where's Mama? You said you were bringing her back. We miss her." Another child, a girl, peered around the corner of a door at the back of the forge.

Mikkel looked poised to weep again. His stomach convulsed under his apron as he attempted to bite back the sobs. "She... I... I couldn't..." Mikkel didn't have the answers for his son.

Beorn slid a cold iron helm over his head, reducing the world to a thin slit of vision. "Your mother will be home tonight," Beorn promised the boy. "Mikkel, help me with this armour."

"But sir... your weapon?"

Beorn strode across the workshop, past the hanging array of weapons, to where Mikkel hung his tools. Hammers of all sizes and weights hung in their designated places. Forged not for battle, but for creation. Beorn's fingers wrapped around the handle of a medium size hammer, one side flat, the other pointed. "I'll make do."

Just before noon, the crier rang his bell and shepherded the peasantry back into the space before the barbican. Beatrice had resumed her place upon the gallows, this time with a noose wrapped tightly around her neck. The knight had donned his shining great-helm. Even without the twisted thorns that adorned his captain's, the helm was an intimidating sight. He stood with hands resting atop the pommel of his sheathed sword.

Mikkel had riveted and strapped Beorn into his motley collection of mismatched armour pieces. Some of it was fine work, with scroll inlay adorning the edges, while other was rough steel, barely hammered into shape. But all of it was Mikkel's, and all of it was solid.

"Good folk," called Willem the lawman to the crowd that had regathered to watch the trial for Beatrice's life, "we have gathered to watch the Gilded Father make his will known in the earthly trial of Beatrice Smith, who has been charged with witchery and heresy. Beatrice's own husband has invoked the right of trial by combat. A... *peculiar* choice, but nonetheless, one she is owed. Standing as champion for the Church is Sir Artorius Maximus, anointed member of the Holy Order of Knights Inquisitorial. Standing in defence of the accused is…?"

The crowd turned to Beorn. Several leaned over and shoved to get a better look at the mystery champion, but no one could see anything of worth with his helm's visor closed. "No one of any repute," Beorn called back.

Sir Artorius scoffed, the sound echoing through the grill of his great-helm. "That's not in question."

"As challenger," Willem continued, "you, sir, have the right to choose the weapons used to determine the defendant's fate. For the sake of parity, both you and Sir Artorius will use the same weapons in today's duel."

"Hammers and shields," Beorn called back.

"Fine by me," Artorius said, turning to give his longsword to a squire dressed in black with the Church's holy keys crossed upon his chest, the undersides of his hair shaved close to the skin. The boy returned a second later with the knight's shield and a long, thin war hammer. The weapon was black ebony wood, highly oiled and glistening. A silver hand balled into a fist crested its tip, grasping a long, deadly spike on one side and the flat face of the hammer on the other. His shield looked to be heavy bands of oak, fastened with iron rivets. The silver keys of his order, painted in shining silver leaf, adorned the face of the shield.

"Good men," lawman Willem continued once both men had armed themselves. "I invite you to kneel and join me in prayer before we begin." Neither of the armoured men knelt. "Very well… Gilded Father, turn your golden face towards us on this day, so we may bask in your heavenly glow. Lend strength to the hand of your champion and make your will known on these here earthly proceedings…"

Beorn let the man's words wash over him, paying no more attention to them than to the crisp breeze blowing down off the mountains. The world had narrowed through the slit in his visor, reducing his sight to what was directly before him. He had to turn his head to get a view of the crowd. Peasants mostly, come to take in the entertainment. A few Greytower men lingered here and there, a single ashen tower sewed into their surcoats and gambesons.

"… do the champions have any words they wish to say before we commence?"

Icy breath frosted through the grill of the knight's great-helm. "After I cave in your skull, I'm going to hang the witch in front of her husband, then hang the smith as well, and lastly, both of her hagseeds."

"Where is the White Bear?" Beorn called, ignoring the knight's threats. Weak men made threats. Men of conviction made promises. And kept them. "Does the castellan of Greytower not wish to oversee the justice dispensed unto his own people?"

A murmur rippled through the crowd. Where was the old man? Beorn had no wish to see him, in truth, but his absence was noted.

"The White Bear is dead." Lawman Willem's words crashed over Beorn like an icy wave.

"Dead?"

"Aye. Some months now. The White Bear died with no living issue. Therefore, the stewardship of Greytower Watch has returned to the Crown to name a new castellan. I oversee the law and order of Greytower Watch until one is named."

*Dead?* The word echoed off the walls of Beorn's skull. He was dead? He was dead. "No living issue?" Beorn stammered, voice ringing in his own helm. The world was spinning. "He… he had a son."

Willem scoffed. "Be thankful the White Bear *is* dead, sir. Everyone knows to mention his exiled son in the White Bear's hearing is to openly invoke his wroth. The White Bear's son is dead, or good as, and was never knighted besides. Only a knight may be granted stewardship of the Greytower, to defend the Pass and lead the garrison. But of what concern is this to you, stranger?"

"N-nothing," Beorn stammered. "Nothing."

"*Mmph.* Then let us prepare. Noon approaches. Take up your positions, champions."

The crowd boiled with excitement. Morrigan and Mikkel stood anxiously behind Beorn at the edge of the rabble. Beorn and Sir Artorius took up positions with the looming Greytower and the gallows to their left. It was tradition in trials by combat to begin proceedings at noon, when the sun was highest, to negate the risk of one champion benefiting from the sun's position. The Carthian hero, Adriac of the Mirrorshield, was fabled to have redirected the glare of the afternoon sun into his opponent's eyes with his gleaming bronze shield, blinding him long enough to deliver the fatal blow. The practice of 'sharing the sun' had emerged when the Church of the Gilded Father adopted trial by combat to settle troublesome cases.

*Wouldn't want the Church's trials to be seen as unfair,* Beorn mused, sourly.

The sun rose slowly into the clear and cloudless sky. Then it was gone, swallowed behind the Greytower, casting the congregation into shadow.

Artorius broke into a run. Despite his armour, despite his shield, despite his war hammer - the man moved fast. Armoured legs pumped, boots struck the ground, and the black-clad slab of muscle hurtled towards Beorn. His first strike was large and brazen; an overhead swing of his wicked war hammer aimed at the top of Beorn's helm. It was all Beorn could do to bring his shield up in time to catch the strike. The war hammer's claw punched through Beorn's oaken shield just above his arm.

*That could have been my head.*

Artorius wrenched the claw out without hesitation and began raining a hail of blows down upon Beorn's shield, not giving him a moment's reprieve for retaliation. The knight pushed Beorn back, leaving a trail of wood chips and splinters in his wake as the black knight hammered his shield. Beorn heard the scuffle of the crowd behind him move aside quickly to avoid the warring men.

*I need to get on the offensive.*

As Sir Artorius pulled his hammer back, Beorn surged forward with his shield. Artorius's hammer came down and met a much closer target than expected, bouncing off and unbalancing the knight. Beorn took a wide swing of his own, blacksmith's hammer arcing through the air to crash upon the knight's hastily raised shield. It was Beorn's turn to hammer the oaken shield with strikes of his own. The pointed end of the smithing hammer, used for riveting armour, chipped away at the painted silver keys until only bare and splintered wood remained in the centre of the heraldry.

Chance put a stone under the knight's foot and as he stepped back to brace against another of Beorn's thunderous blows, he went sprawling onto his back, shield and hammer splayed wide. Beorn raised his own hammer, aimed deftly at the black great-helm.

*The White Bear is dead.*

Suddenly Beorn wasn't a man any longer, but a boy of ten training with a wooden sword on these very cobbles. The backswing of a training sword caught him on the cheek and sent him hurtling to the ground. A tall shadow loomed over him, dark eyes staring down, dripping with disappointment.

*Pick it up.*

The shadow raised his weapon.

"Beorn, get up!" Morrigan's screams brought him back to the present. Artorius loomed above him, hammer poised to strike. Beorn had hesitated when the knight was on his back, just long enough for Artorius to crack him across the helm with a desperate blow, quickly reversing their roles.

Beorn swung his hammer at the knight's armoured ankle. A sickening crunch sounded from under plate and mail and Artorius screamed in his black great-helm. The pointed claw of Beorn's hammer hooked around the knight's ankle and Beorn gave a mighty pull, sending the knight careening onto his back.

"Beorn, get off yer arse!" Morrigan yelled.

*What a boost of confidence.* Beorn rolled away before Artorius could recover. Both armoured men slowly got to their feet. Beorn was spinning from the blow to his helm, and could feel the warm trickle of blood running from his temple. The ground rocked beneath him like the deck of a ship.

Three black knights paced towards him, all dragging their crippled ankles. The champions resumed their clash.

Injuries crippled both the fighters, but it quickly became apparent that Beorn was the worse off. Artorius's wound hobbled him, but his arms remained strong and his blows ferocious. Several times Beorn saw an opening and swung what should have been a killer blow, only for his hammer to whistle harmlessly through the air, a foot from his intended target.

*I have to end this,* Beorn thought as the knight battered his shield with blows. The time of their struggle was measured by the Greytower's shifting shadow across the ground.

*The shadow...*

"C'mon, Beorn!" Morrigan screamed, the only voice in the crowd rooting for his cause. The rest were desperate to watch the witch hang. "Put the Dog down!"

The girl's insults drew the knight's attention. The wind had blown back her hood, her thick braid billowing like a rope in the breeze. "You..." the knight panted. "You and that girl... you're the ones Constantine is after!"

Beorn seized on the knight's surprise and barrelled into him with his shield, shoving past him so Beorn stood with the Greytower at his back. As the black knight turned to face Beorn, the sun poked from behind the Greytower, blinding Artorius's narrow vision. He raised his shield to cover his eyes, but Beorn swooped in from his left and crushed his shield elbow. Bone splintered under the heavy iron hammer and the Inquisitors' Dog screamed.

*For the Greytower looms tall and casts a mighty shadow.*

Beorn threw down his splintered shield and pursued with a two handed strike to the gleaming black great-helm. Beorn cut short the scream, and the knight fell like a sack of rocks, his hammer dropping from his limp fingers. Straddling the fallen knight, Beorn brought his hammer down over and over again on the black helm. Metal caved in and red ran between the cobbles under the fallen man's head.

*He's dead,* Beorn thought as his own hammer fell from his grasp. *He's dead. The White Bear is dead.*

Beorn's head spun, and he slipped into oblivion.

* * *

Beorn woke beside the blacksmith's forge, heat bathing his face with its orange glow. Someone had wrapped a bandage around his head and staunched the bleeding. The blows he'd received had battered and bruised his shield arm, and his heartbeat pounded in his temples. But he lived.

A shadowy spectre blotted out the light of the forge.

"Morrigan?" Beorn wheezed.

"Nay," replied a voice like a wood saw, grating and raspy. Mikkel. "She's with Beatrice and the children."

"Beatrice…?"

"Aye, she's free. You saved her, Beorn. You saved my wife." The smith's voice was heavy with emotion.

*I did it*, Beorn sighed to himself. *I saved her.* Perhaps he'd finally sleep easier, knowing he'd been able to save someone, anyone. Even if not those he'd most wished he had. He doubted it.

*You saved her, Beorn.*

Beorn sat up lightning fast - too fast. His head spun, and he careened off the workbench where he'd been laying, falling with a heavy thud to the dusty smithy floor.

"Easy, boy, easy," the blacksmith cooed, lifting Beorn under the arms to lean him into an old wooden chair. "You took a nasty blow to the head. The girl said you'd best stay off your feet for some time."

"You… you know my name…" Beorn grunted. White stars exploded behind his eyelids, but when he opened them, the world would not stay still; sweeping and spinning. Mikkel's old, lined face swam into view. The man was several winters older than Beorn, but wore his years well. His face bore the creases of many a smile, and what little hair he still had was dark and thick as a mountain goat's. Beorn, in contrast, knew his face bore the weight of his travels, and his own hair and beard were waging a losing battle against time's grey advance.

"Aye, Beorn. I know who you are."

"How?" He had to leave. He needed to get Morrigan and leave as fast as they could, before word spread. He shouldn't have interfered with the trial. He shouldn't have brought the girl to Greytower. Goddammit, he shouldn't have fucking interfered in Brexton to begin with.

Mikkel chuckled. "I couldn't tell with you hooded and helmed. But after the trial was done, and we pried that helm off your head, I knew it was you at once. Aye, you're older than the boy who left here, but you have your father's features."

*So I am reminded of by every mirror I pass.*

"Plus," the smith continued, "the girl wouldn't stop hollering your name during the fight. Pretty hard to miss."

*Bloody girl.*

"And what," Beorn grunted, biting back the pain exploding in his skull, "will you do with this knowledge?"

Mikkel eyed him queerly. "What will I do? Why, whatever you'll have of me. You saved my wife's life, Beorn, and likely mine and my children's as well. But even so… you were like a brother to me. You still are. Do you think I could betray you?"

Beorn had known Mikkel since he was a boy. The 'prentice smith had taken warmly to Beorn. He had forged Beorn's first sword. And his last. Beorn had never thought he would see the man again, but now that he had, all he wished for was to be as far from Greytower Watch as his legs could carry him.

*There's nothing here for me now. The White Bear is dead.*

"I need to leave," Beorn groaned. With great effort, he rose and began pulling on his boots.

"Aye. We as well. You may have saved Beatrice from the rope, but the taint of the accusation remains. We will find no friends in Greytower so long as we remain. We make for the southern slope as soon as Beatrice and the children are ready. You are welcome to join us. You and the girl." There was a question in that last word. *Who is she? What brought you back to the Greytower? Why did the Inquisitors' Dog recognise her?*

All the more reason to leave, and fast.

"We make for the northern slope. There's nothing for us south. Ask no more questions, Mikkel," Beorn interjected as the smith opened his mouth. "It is better for you and yours if you don't know for where we head. Better still if you had never seen us."

Mikkel took in the woodcutter with deep, thoughtful eyes. "Aye. I think that is best for us all," he agreed.

When Beatrice Smith came into the room, she burst into tears at the sight of Beorn, awake and well. The woman ran to him and flung her arms around his neck, the stubble of her harshly shaved head bristling against his neck. She showered him with thanks and kisses not just on her behalf, but that of her family, and her unborn child as well. Morrigan followed her in quick succession, the relief on her face plain.

"I dressed yer wound," she told him. "A nasty knock, but yer skull seems intact. Ye'll be fine, all in all."

"Alright, alright," Mikkel conceded, ushering his younger wife and her kisses away from Beorn's awkward acceptance. "Give the man room to breathe. Are we ready, wife? Are the children prepared?"

"Well enough, husband. As well as can be."

"Good, good. See that they are dressed warmly. The days grow colder."

Beatrice left to finish their preparation, giving Beorn her thanks until she had left the room. Morrigan followed, to continue assisting. She was speaking to the woman of herbs that would ease her pregnancy, rummaging in her medicine pouch for what little she had available.

"You're a good man, Beorn," Mikkel said when the two of them were alone once more.

"Good?" The word tasted acidic on Beorn's tongue. "By what measure?"

"You *saved* my wife. An innocent woman and her unborn babe would have died if not for you."

"And how many have died because of me? How many in war, and how many after it? We burn witches because we haven't any more wars to fight. You have me and my brethren to thank for that. Maybe if we were still fighting northmen your wife would never have been on that scaffold to begin with."

"And how many northern wives might stand upon a gallows if the war was still waging?"

"You prove my point. Good men don't exist. Only those who can keep the harm they cause to a minimum."

"Why help then? Why volunteer as champion?"

"Perhaps it's my penance. To save the would-be-burnt from their pyres. To make up for the ones I couldn't." Flames danced before his eyes. Wood cracked and embers flew. Beorn's throat grew hoarse from remembered screams.

*Save her Beorn.*

Mikkel's eyebrows raised in solemn understanding. "I… I know not what sins you may have committed in the war. But people can change. We are more than our worst acts. We are… potential. And I see in that girl your potential for a brighter future."

Beorn had no answer to that, so he sat in silence.

"I was told," Mikkel continued, "that you'd met someone. Started a family. What happened?"

"They're gone." Beorn had nothing further to say about the topic.

"Then you have my deepest condolences. To have loved, and have been loved, is to have truly lived. Anything short is just existing." Mikkel eyed Beorn's haggard face; sunken eyes, the deep lines, the greying beard. The last time Mikkel had laid eyes upon him, Beorn had been a boy of twenty winters, eagerly setting off to war. The man who had returned looked defeated. "Are you living, Beorn, or just existing?"

*I died with my family years ago.*

Beorn had no desire to relive his past. It pained him enough that their journey had forced him to return to Greytower. But still… there were things he had to know.

"How did my father die?"

"He got old. He got sick. Even the strongest of us cannot fight off death forever."

"That wouldn't have stopped the White Bear from trying."

Mikkel chuckled. "You're not wrong on that count."

"Did… did he ever speak of me? Before the end?"

Mikkel looked sombre. He steepled his fingers and looked at the floor. "Only… only to curse you, I'm sorry to say."

"Don't be sorry. If you'd told me otherwise, I'd have known you for a liar. What did he say?"

"He… he called you a deserter, and no true son of his. He said you had shamed him by leaving the royal army before ever attaining your knighthood, and for leaving it all behind for some… and these are his words,

Beorn, I would not lie to you. He said you'd left your post for some whore."

"So he was a bastard 'til the end," Beorn seethed. His teeth hurt from clenching them, and his fingers curled and uncurled into fists. "He was an old sot. He never cared for me. He saw only what I could do for him, for his legacy. The future Knight of Greytower. He never…" *Loved me.* "I'm glad he's dead. I am. I hated him. And yet… why does it hurt? Why does it feel like I've… *lost* something? Something inside of me? I hated him! So why do I grieve?" Beorn would not cry, not for that man, but his voice cracked and his chest heaved.

Mikkel reached out and placed a hand on Beorn's clenched fist. Despite the calluses, it seemed to be the softest touch Beorn had ever known. "When we grieve, we mourn not only what was; but what could have been. Both are lost to us when someone dies. You did not love your father. And, perhaps it's true, he never cared for you. But in life… there was always a chance. A chance he could change. Now that he's gone… That chance is gone too."

"Then I am truly alone now. I have no family left."

"Beorn," Morrigan called from the doorway. "We should go. Once the Inquisitorum hears word that one o' their Dogs was slain, they will fall down hard upon this place. Godfrey is readied."

"I will be but a moment."

Morrigan nodded, disappearing into the doorway.

"Perhaps," Mikkel mused, "there is still hope for a family."

Beorn grunted and stood, making his way to the door. *'He's not my Da.'*

"Beorn," Mikkel called. "Before you go. I'd made a sword for you, when last we saw one another. What ever became of it? Did it serve you well?"

*I painted the Northern Realms red with that sword.*

"I have no more use for swords. I swore a vow."

*And my family died because of it.*

# III

# Monsters

*"How many more men would commit atrocities if they thought
they'd never get caught?"*
*"How many do so anyway, regardless?"*

# Chapter 11

The bright red splatter of blood was a gash upon the crisp white snow. Beorn dipped the tips of his fingers in the gore. Still warm, unfrozen; fresh. His boots crunched the fresh snowfall as he stood. The crimson trail led him down an embankment and across an icy brook.

Snowflakes clung to his shoulders like a second cloak. The snows had fallen as they made their way down the northern slope of Greytower Pass. Autumn had washed its hands of them for another year and passed the reins to its icy sister. Winter was here in all her chilling glory.

The northern slope had led them into a forest of ancient pines, wild oaks, and untamed firs. The woods looked more wild than any they'd seen south of Gaius's Wall. This was the Northern Realms. Unchanged for time immemorial. Beorn's stomach had been sinking as fast as the snowdrifts were rising. Each night was harder to light a fire than the one before. Every breath Godfrey exhaled sent plumes of steam billowing from his nostrils. But where Beorn's mood had soured, Morrigan's had flourished. That first day when the snows had fallen, the girl had stopped dead in her tracks and raised her child-like face to the sky. Snowflakes as white as her skin dissolved on her eyelids. Not opening her eyes, Morrigan reached back and untied her braid, shaking her hair free; as fiery as the snow was cold. Beorn had not seen her hair unbraided since the square in Brexton (as per his instructions). Regular meals and combing had restored some of its thickness. She looked healthy. She looked happy. She looked home.

Climbing the bank on the other side of the chirping stream, Beorn located the trail and followed on. He did not have to look far to find the source of the blood. The corpse of a deer lay limply against the gnarled roots of an oak that had been old by the time the Carthians came with their roads. The surrounding snow was stained red with its lifeblood. Something had strung the deer's entrails around it, the gaping wound showing what reward the killer beast had reaped.

Morrigan's boots crunched through the snow as she appeared from where she'd been stalking Beorn through the underbrush. "Wolves?"

Beorn nodded, kneeling to inspect the carcass. He spotted the remains of kidney, liver, and heart among the gore. "Aye. Most likely a pack. They wounded it back there and followed it 'til it could go no further. But they didn't finish the meal. Something scared them off."

"Scared them? What scares wolves?"

Beorn shrugged. "No way to tell. Snow's been falling heavy. The snowfall covered the pack's tracks and whatever spooked them." The snow was limiting his vision. A few rows of black trunks were visible, but beyond that was a white haze. "We should get back to the road, and to Godfrey."

The snow fell heavier as the day went on. Beorn had not expected it to fall so thickly so early in the season. His dread for what awaited the rest of their journey only grew. Until this point, Beorn's only goal had been to get them across the border. Mostly due to the fact he hadn't truly believed they'd make it any further. But now that they had passed that hurdle, he would need to extract the specifics of their destination from the girl. But the priority for the moment was warmth.

They found a shallow cave to huddle in as the night fell. It was little more than an overhang in truth, but deep enough to shield them from the biting wind and keep the fire from sputtering out. They hadn't seen the sun itself for several days, and the only signifier between night and day was the changing shades of the opaque sky. The day's trek through the snow had tired them all, and Morrigan slipped into an untroubled sleep as soon as she curled up beside him. Beorn fended off sleep a while longer by staring out into the void beyond their firelight.

Shadows danced across the black tree bark. Shades from the fire or… something else? Something skulking in the dark? Something that hunted its prey until it fell exhausted and could run no more. Godfrey gave a distressed snort and tugged against his reins. Somewhere far off, a long howl pierced the silence. Beorn's fingers wrapped around the icy haft of his axe.

The snow fell lighter the next day, something to be grateful for. Beorn broached the subject of their destination. "How far to your village?"

"Not much farther in truth," the girl replied.

"And how far is 'not much farther'?" Morrigan worried at a strand of hair, avoiding his eyes. She'd let her hair fall free since they'd descended the Pass, signalling her freedom to the world. Beorn stopped and grabbed her lightly by the elbow to signal her to do the same. "Look at me, girl. I care not how much further the destination is. I need only know where to point us." She looked up at him. "I'm in this 'til the end."

Her lips turned upwards. "I'm sorry. It's just… I didnae expect us t' make it this far, in truth."

"You and me both."

"The Horns."

Beorn blanched. "Pardon?"

"Well… just shy o' the Horns in truth. My village lies at the lip o' the Frostline."

Beorn stared blankly at her. *The Frostline? We've still half the Isle to go.* The Horns were the north-most tips of the Far Isles. Clad in snow year round, they were some of the harshest environments any explorer had laid eyes upon. In the dead of winter it was said even the sea froze over, and across the ice-bridges came monsters from the Bitter North. Sea beasts with tusks that could skewer a man, direwolves the size of oxen, bull moose with antlers wider than Beorn was tall, and ice bears that could swallow a man's head in their jaws.

"Beorn?" she asked tentatively. Beorn realised he'd not responded.

"Oh. Well… guess we'd better keep moving." And together they continued to stride north through the snow.

That night the howl was closer, and Beorn was sure the shadows flitting through the trees were more than just the light of the dying fire. When Morrigan awoke in the morn, Beorn sat awake beside her, axe resting across his knees.

"Beorn? Did ye not sleep?"

"I slept enough," he lied. "We're being hunted."

Panic flickered behind her grey eyes. "The Inquisitor?"

"Nay. Wolves, I think."

"Oh," she sighed, the panic dying behind her eyes.

*How interesting*, Beorn thought. *Alone in the woods with wolves on our trail is cause for relief, yet the thought of that black-robed man...*

"Are ye sure it's wolves?"

Beorn nodded. "Aye. I heard them howling last night. They're scouting us. Gauging our strength against the pack's."

"Then best we'd get a move on," she said, standing, adjusting the dagger on her hip for a quicker draw.

It was just after noon that they came across the second carcass. The scene was similar to the last; red on white. But in place of a deer lay a great brown bear, dead black eyes staring unblinking into the sky. It was the largest animal Beorn had ever seen. Blood matted its thick fur. Something had ripped deep claw marks through its hide, tearing fat, muscle, and bone. Like the deer it had been gutted, the contents of its insides lay steaming in the snow before them. It had died with a snarl on its snout, lips peeled back to reveal long yellow fangs, each the size of Beorn's fingers.

"No wolf did that," Morrigan said.

"Aye," Beorn agreed. But if not wolves, then what? What had killed the bear? And what was hunting them...

But later that night, Beorn heard the howls again. More of them this time, and closer than before. Shadows danced just outside of his view and every so often, a pair of golden orbs would reflect the light of their fire. Over the crackle of kindling, he could hear many paws lightly crunching through the snow. Beorn touched Morrigan lightly on the shoulder, rousing her from a shallow sleep.

"We're being watched," he whispered. Morrigan took his meaning, and making no sudden moves, placed her hand on the hilt of her dagger.

Godfrey was panting nervously, whinnying every so often, desperate to flee. His reins tethered to a nearby tree were the only things keeping him from doing so. *Easy old friend,* Beorn thought calmingly, but made no move to vocalise the reassurance. He dared not break the silence. A light snowfall began near midnight. The fire began to choke and sputter, the ring of light creeping smaller and smaller, retreating from the treeline to be replaced with shadowy veils. Past Godfrey, tied to his tree, the light receded, past Beorn's boots, Morrigan's skirts, and finally died with a pitiful hiss smothered by a layer of wet snow.

A dark, lithe shadow darted forward in bounds. Beorn moved as quickly as he could, but the snow had chilled his joints, and his axe only barely came between the wolf's jaws and his throat. White canines clamped down over the hardwood haft, a pair of golden eyes locking with his own. Beorn intentionally let the weight of the beast carry him onto his back and used the momentum to fling the creature over his head. The wolf released its bite on the axe as it flew through the air and crashed into a tree trunk with a whimper.

"To Godfrey!" Beorn shouted and Morrigan was running by his side through the snow. Morrigan wasted no time untying his reins, instead cutting through the leather straps with her dagger before leaping into the saddle. Beorn was about to leap to join her when red hot pain lanced his ankle and he fell crashing into the snow. Slipping, he saw the curled lips of a wolf around his ankle, fangs biting through leather and wool. The beast shook its head frenziedly. Drops of scarlet flung like spittle from its mouth and Beorn roared in pain.

"Beorn!" Morrigan screamed. Silver cut the air as Beorn brought his axe down in an arc and split the mongrel's skull, killing it instantly.

"Go!" he roared as he lumbered onto the saddle with his wounded leg.

"*Hyah!*" Morrigan screamed, as if Godfrey required the motivation. The giant horse flew through the woods, black earth and white snow erupting from where his hooves gouged the forest floor. Pine needles and oak branches whipped at their faces as they darted through the hazardous brush, leaping over snaking roots that threatened to bring them down in an avalanche of horseflesh. All around them, black shapes darted and snarled.

Godfrey hurtled through a gully, steep earthen walls looming above them. From the tip of an overhang lunged a black-furred wolf, slaver spraying from its drawn-back lips, fangs angled for Morrigan's throat. Beorn's hand moved of its own volition, axe head cleaving the wolf's skull in two while mid-air. The limp mass of its corpse slammed into Godfrey's flank, sending the horse into a frenzy.

Beorn tried to rein the horse in, but it was no use. Godfrey was bolting anywhere he thought would take him away from the predators, but they were everywhere. Up and up a hill he bolted, Morrigan and Beorn desperately holding onto the reins. They crested the rise, clearing the trees into what looked to be the remains of an ancient ringfort. The fort's circular shape was still discernible, marked by a raised earthen bank. Where walls had once defended the hill, they now gave way to thickets of thorny bushes, brambles, and spiny gorse. The remains of the circular walls were now nothing more than knee-high crumbled rings. Godfrey vaulted the uneven crumbling stone and earthwork defences and made to continue through the ruin and down the other side of the hill. But the wolves had other plans.

As Godfrey neared the other side of the ringfort, a great grey beast leaped atop the tumbled stone wall and snapped at the draught horse's neck. Godfrey reared, hoof catching the wolf in the face and crushing his skull, but sending Morrigan and Beorn stumbling to the ground. Beorn wrapped a meaty arm around the girl before they struck the earth, cushioning the fall with his body. Godfrey's eyes were wide and white, and he paid no heed to his sudden lack of passengers. The horse disappeared over the wall in a flurry of hooves and mane.

A howl came from deep in the forest.

"Get behind me," Beorn barked and Morrigan sidled in behind him. But where was front and where was behind when surrounded in the circular centre of the fort? Nature had reclaimed much of the ruin, grasses and weeds sprouting from the relatively flat area beneath their feet. Beorn turned in a low circle, axe in hand. "Put your back against mine!" He ordered, and Morrigan obeyed. He heard the telltale sound of her dagger hissing as

Morrigan unsheathed it. They would die here, in the ruins and snow. But they would die with blades in their hands.

Despite the centuries since the ringfort's construction, the ruins still exuded an air of silent strength. This was a good place to die.

"There," whispered Morrigan. The first wolf slunk atop the low, crumbling wall. He was black and brindle, eyes of gold catching the moonlight and reflecting it back. Beorn's knuckles tightened on his axe. Another soon appeared atop a different section of the decrepit ring wall. Dark grey, with icy eyes. Another, on their other side; black as sin. Another and another appeared until they completely encircled them, the strength of the wall resurrected from dead stone to living flesh. Flesh with fangs that would tear and claws that would rend. "They're waiting for something," Morrigan observed. They quickly saw what.

Dead ahead of Beorn appeared the largest wolf he'd ever seen. Its fur was deep red, near black in the moonlight, but glistening as though slick with blood. Fangs the length of Beorn's fingers hung from his mouth, eager to tear out his throat. Pointed ears angled towards them, snout creased in a savage snarl. This beast would be his end.

The red giant gave a bark, and the pack moved in. Beorn tried to shield Morrigan with his body, but the beasts were all around them. They would kill her easily.

*No, no, no,* his mind frantically spat out. *Not again, not again, not again. I can't save her, I can't save her, I can't save her...*

The great red raised his head, staring off into the distance, ears pointed as though listening. His nostrils flared, taking in the scent on the wind. A wolf to Beorn's left whimpered. Another joined the chorus to his right. The beasts' heads were low now, ears pressed flat against their skulls. The great red barked a command, and they were off, leaping over the ringfort walls and disappearing down the hill.

"What the fuck?" Beorn swore in astonishment.

Something snapped deep in the forest's gloom. Heavy, thumping footfalls echoed through the trees. A deep, guttural roar echoed off the snow.

A hulking mass emerged from the swirling frost like a malevolent spectre.

Its ivory coat glistening with snow as though the hill itself had come alive. The air hung heavy with the noxious stench of death and decay, clinging to the beast like a shroud. Long, black dagger-like claws splayed across the snow with each lumbering step, leaving deep bloodied impressions as it moved with an unholy gait.

A pair of blood-red eyes stared out of the giant skull, burning with unnatural hunger, craving the warm, pulsing flesh of its prey. It couldn't be; not here, not this far south, not when the snows had only just fallen. Yet there it was: a colossal ice bear.

As the ice bear closed in, its hot, rank breath hit them like a wall. This was what had spooked the wolves from their prey. This was what had killed the brown bear.

The axe fell limply from Beorn's fingers.

The monster advanced at a leisurely pace, freezing them with its blood-red stare. The ice bear reared up on its hind legs, towering over them; eight feet of death and terror. Its black muzzle pulled back to show long yellow teeth.

Before Beorn could stop her, Morrigan had pushed herself between him and the bear. "Roooooooooooooaaaaaaaaarrrrrrrr!" Her bellow frosted the air before her face, echoing through the night. The girl who stood frozen in fear at the gates of Gaius's Wall when faced with the skeletal Inquisitor stood defiant against the ice bear. "Rooooooooooooooooaaaaaaaaaaarrrrrrrrrr!!!" she bellowed again. Her courage was infectious.

Beorn sucked in an icy breath and bellowed: "ROOOOOOOOOOOOOOO AAAAAAAAAARRRRRRRR!!!"

They screamed until their throats were hoarse and then screamed some more. They stood in the centre of the ringfort panting, snow piling up around them. The beast from the frozen ends of the world stared down at them, unblinking. No emotion swam behind those dead red eyes. No rage, no anger - only hunger. Its lips were stained red with its last kill. It took a step forward with a heavy limb, then another… then shuffled past them, over the ring wall and off into the night.

The night was silent. The snow fell.

"We need to get out of this fucking forest," Beorn said, before collapsing in a heap, the blood from his shredded ankle staining the snow red.

* * *

Beorn awoke propped against the crumbling wall of the ringfort, his ankle wrapped tightly in cloth bandages. Morrigan had staunched the bleeding and dressed the wound. The bandages smelled strongly of herbs.

"A poultice," Morrigan said when Beorn had asked. "I used some of the comfrey I picked back with the Rovers for the pain, and yarrow to slow the bleeding."

"Yarrow?"

"I used t' always keep some in my herb pouch when I travelled with my mistress. We'd use it in tisanes for heavy menstrual bleeding. Applied directly t' a wound, it will slow the bleed."

Godfrey had come cantering back after the ice bear had lumbered off. *Fat lot of help you were*, Beorn had grumbled as the horse nuzzled into his chest, but in truth, he was nothing but glad to see his friend unharmed. They mounted up as the sun cut through the snow clouds and went in search of warmth and safety.

Morrigan took the reins; partly as she'd said she knew of a small village close by where they could find an inn, but also due to Beorn barely having the strength to keep himself in the saddle, let alone steer the draught horse. They rode for most of the day, at times through light snows and at others through freezing winds, but never once did they hear the howling of wolves or the crunch of an ice bear's paws upon the snow. As they crested a white rise, a golden sword of sunlight cut through the grey clouds and struck the bell tower of a church. Beorn had to blink to clear the snow from his eyes. Was it the blood loss? No, on the other side of the rise, down a small hill stood a bell tower glistening in God's glory. The church struck out over the roofs of the surrounding town - smaller than Brexton, but larger by far than any settlement they'd encountered south of Gaius's Wall. No guards challenged them as they entered the town, but Beorn noted the wary eyes the townsfolk cast their way. They were entering from the south, of course.

While technically north of the border, the town bore all the hallmarks of a southern settlement. The freshly thatched roofs, the still mostly white plaster walls, and of course the newly erected stone chapel. The town had likely stood for generations, but the southern settlers, granted land nearby, had added the enhancements. Beorn doubted the locals would have sung the southern migrants' praises for them, though. Is that why they glared at the horsed duo so venomously? Did they see more settlers come to make off with their land?

*Better they see settlers than two fugitives of the Inquisitorum*, Beorn thought. The one benefit of the snows was that no one would look twice at the pair of hooded figures. Anyone wanting to preserve their ears would have their hoods drawn. Unfortunately, this was where their luck ended.

"A room?" the inkeep of the first tavern they'd tried had spat incredulously.

"Well, we're nae here for yer shining wit, are we?" Morrigan had barked back at him. While both northerners, Morrigan's accent was degrees courser than the inkeep's. Beorn figured the drawl got thicker the further north they were bred. And seeing as they were headed for the Horns, Beorn doubted they'd find thicker than hers.

"Can't say I can help yous there," the inkeep continued. "Better fuck off and look somewhere else."

A few locals at the bar chuckled as Beorn held the door open for Morrigan. Their second stop fared no better. "Can't spare the space I'm 'fraid," the fat bartender had proclaimed, not raising his gaze from the counter he was shining. "Might be ye's could try Devon's down the road." Devon's had turned out to be a pigsty. When they'd asked the farmer (Devon, Beorn figured) about board he'd laughed and told them to get fucked.

The third inn proved equally fruitless, though the proprietor was marginally more forthcoming with his reasons for refusing them. "Listen here, ye foreigners. I could be swimming in empty rooms with debtors at my threshold and I *still* wouldn't give you two a room under my roof. Bugger off, the pair of ye." It was then he'd smiled. "But if ye really that desperate for a bed, ye could always head on down to *Rosie's*."

Beorn fixed him with a chilly stare. "If I find out you're sending us to a pigpen, I will come back here, and you won't appreciate what I do next."

They were winding their way through the darkening alleys, looking for *Rosie's*, when Morrigan asked Beorn what was on his mind. "I can understand why they're kicking me out. But you? I thought these were your people?"

The girl threw her head back and laughed. "HA! *My* people? We're still leagues away from *my* people. These southern whelps are closer t' *yer* people than mine. That's the thing about you southerners - ye always saw us as a single kingdom, but never stopped to ask why we didnae have a king. There's a reason it's called the Northern *Realms*. The lands north o' Gaius's Wall are - *were* - ruled by half a dozen thanes before yer southern conquest. My people were the last t' bend the knee. This lot basically rolled over the second yer soldiers crossed the border."

Disdain laced her voice. Her derision for her southern neighbours almost neared that for Beorn and his ilk. As they rounded a corner, Beorn discovered that *Rosie's* was indeed not a pigpen, and certainly did contain beds.

"It's a whorehouse," Beorn said, eyeing the single red lantern swinging over the door. Candles were busy being lit inside the establishment, casting the street in a sensuous red glow as the light filtered through window panes made of the same crimson glass. A similarly deep red splashed the eaves and door, as if the building were a painted lady for sale. "Well, I made a promise. Time to go kill an innkeeper."

"So melodramatic," Morrigan sighed, already striding towards the establishment.

The snows had turned the streets to slurry, and Godfrey's hooves squelched through the mud as Beorn led him to the hitching post. Morrigan was already crossing the threshold while Beorn was tying off the reins. *Hard-headed witch*, Beorn cursed as he ran after the girl.

The inside of the brothel was warm and inviting. Maroon wallpaper stretched from floor to roof, detailed with the silhouettes of naked women. Somewhere in a dark corner, atop a small raised stage, some minstrels were fingering a harp and blowing a windpipe, while a bard sung a bawdy tune.

Red cushions covered every surface of the common area. Atop the cushions lounged women of every shade and shape entertaining their male patrons; stroking their arms, batting eyelids, laughing too loud at jokes that weren't funny. The men themselves were a motley bunch. Some looked like locals, spending their hard earned coin on a warm bed and warmer company. But the majority looked like roadmen, scars aplenty across sun-baked leathery skin. Daggers, short swords, and hand axes hung from hips while the hands that would wield them were busy grasping tankards and waists.

Beorn found Morrigan at the bar, trying to hail the barmaid. She was too busy darting between patrons, pouring their drinks and drinking their compliments to notice the small redheaded girl waving her down. Beorn reached into his purse and drew out one of the few remaining gold coins from Brexton. As it clinked against the wooden bar-top, the buxom serving maid appeared before them. Hooded eyes stared up at Beorn's.

"What can I get you, handsome?" she purred. When Beorn looked down, his coin had vanished.

"A room," Beorn said.

The tips of her fingers reached across the bar and brushed the backs of his knuckles. "And someone to warm it for you?" Her voice was thick and husky, smooth as honey and inviting as a blazing fire.

Beorn drew his hand back and hid it under the counter. "Just the room will do."

The sparkle disappeared from her eyes. "Look pal," she snapped, the magic faded from her voice, "this isn't an inn. You want a bed, you rent a girl."

"None o' the inns will have us," Morrigan chimed in. "They sent us to ye."

"Via a pigpen," Beorn grumbled.

The serving maid rolled her eyes and called over her shoulder: "Rosie! Clyde's sent us another pair of outsiders!"

A second woman appeared behind the bar. Where every other woman in the brothel was barely out of girlhood, she was a woman grown and wore her years well. A tight corset cinched her waist and pushed her bust high under her chin. She had hiked her skirts to her waistband, scandalously displaying her stocking-clad legs. Her mop of rich auburn hair, streaked with silver, was tied high upon her head, and she ringed her eyes with smokey black khol. She touched the barmaid on the shoulder, relieving her of the troublesome newcomers so she could go back to applying her trade.

"Greetings, handsome," Rosie said, sex dripping from her voice. The way she gazed up at Beorn made him uncomfortable - in truth, it made him *very comfortable,* but that was the problem. No one had stirred him so in a long, long time. "How can I help?"

"We need a room," Beorn repeated, hoping for better results.

"We have rooms to spare, and girls aplenty to keep you company." Her eyes flitted over Morrigan appraisingly. "Although I'm afraid we don't cater to the likes of your friend. Children, I mean. Women are, of course, also accommodated within *Rosie's* walls." Beorn noticed a blush creeping up Morrigan's neck.

"We don't need girls," Beorn re-explained, "we just need beds. None of the inns will take us."

Rosie nodded, an auburn curl falling across her face. With the tender care of a well-practiced performer, she tucked it behind an ear. "I can believe it. The people of our quaint little town are not especially accommodating to foreigners - from the north or the south. But alas, those aren't the services we provide."

Beorn gritted his teeth in irritation. "How so? You rent rooms - by the night, hour, or I imagine by minute when needed. How is this different? Just because we don't need anyone to join us?"

"You don't rent the room, you rent the girl, and she takes your coin. In turn, for providing her a safe locale, she provides the house a cut of her earnings. So if you want a room, you'll need a girl - and for an entire night she'll put you out of pocket mighty more than any inn."

"I have the coin," Beorn admitted hesitantly, wary of wandering ears. Truth be told, the Holy Guardsman's purse was growing light. "But I'll not be buying one of your girls."

"And why ever not, brown-eyes?" She battered him with her long lashes.

"Are my wares not to your taste?"

"Your 'wares' are to my *distaste*. Call it a moral aversion."

Rosie rolled her eyes. "A Pious Pete. Fine, you don't have to fuck her, but if you want a room, you pay a girl."

"I won't partake in your flesh-trade."

During the exchange, Morrigan had been leaning against the bar, casting the occasional glance at the passing ladies. While Beorn debated the ethics of prostitution, one of the weapon-clad patrons came sauntering up beside her, pressing uncomfortably close to her body as he signalled the barmaid for another tankard. While he waited for his drink, he took the time to take in a tall drink of Morrigan. He undressed her with a look, raping her with his eyes.

"Well, well. Looky, what we got here? Do the girls in here get younger as I get older? Haha! Not that I'm complaining." He ran a calloused hand of short fingers down Morrigan's back. "How much to take you upstairs for a tumble, sweetheart-?"

As his hand brushed over Morrigan's buttocks, her own hand swatted it away and lanced at his face. A deafening crack filled the room. Conversations died, music stopped, and eyes turned towards the bar. Anger swelled in the man faster than the hand print appearing on his cheek.

"You little slut!" he roared, hand whistling as it raced to return the strike. A second crack of skin on skin filled the room. The short-fingered man's hand hovered centimetres from Morrigan's cheek, Beorn's iron grip wrapped around his wrist. They stood there a moment, silently looking at each other, then Beorn gave a shove and the man stumbled clumsily backwards, knocking over a bar stool. Several locals snickered, but the other armed men were on their feet, glaring at Beorn. Women across the room sat anxiously, awaiting the fallout.

"Raise that hand again, and I'll take it from you," Beorn stated. It offered no chance of debate; it was a fact.

"The little whore struck me," the man spat. His face was twisted and rat-like. Beady black eyes, a fraction too close together, stared hatefully at them both.

"Call her that again and I'll take your tongue, too." Another fact. Another promise.

The tension in the room grew, time wading slowly through the smoke and hate filling the brothel.

"Boys, boys!" said Rosie, batting her eyelids at them both, leaning over the bar to give them a generous view of her God-given assets. "What a pair of big burly men you both are. Now, now, there's plenty of Rosie's girls to go around, no need to fight! Chastity, can you take dear Renulf here, up to his usual room? And grab Guinevere while you go - my treat for you, Renulf, for any inconveniences you might have received."

Rosie bit her finger salaciously as Chastity led Renulf away, but the whole time, the rat-faced man never once took his eyes off Beorn until he disappeared up the stairs.

"Back to merriment, all! The next round of drinks is on me!" That seemed to cut through some of the tension in the room and slowly, music and conversation returned. Though more than a few of the hard-looking men in the room continued to stare at Beorn.

Rosie fixed him with her cool gaze; flirtation and whimsy vanished. "Helga, our friend here, would like a room. Take him to mine. Find the girl suitable accommodation in the ladies' lodgings. Don't kick up such a fuss," she interjected, as Beorn made to voice his aversion. "I'm not going to sell her while you're not watching. But you and I need to have a talk." And with that, she vanished into the shadows and smoke of the room.

"This way, sir," a warm voice urged from Beorn's shoulder. Helga was a tall, mousy-haired girl with deep doe-brown eyes. Beorn could only hold her gaze for a moment before his eyes dropped lower. A smile played across her pink lips. "Do you see something you like...?" While they most definitely were impressive, it was the bulging stomach below that had caught his gaze. "Or have you just never seen a pregnant whore before?"

"Honestly? No."

"Well, food still costs coin, so the work goes on. To tell it true I mostly just wait the tables now and help behind the bar. Few men ask for me in my current state, which is more the shame as I've never been more rowdy in my life. Honestly, I'd prefer to earn my keep on my back rather than on my feet; my ankles are swollen something awful."

Helga waddled off with Beorn and Morrigan in tow, the trio disappearing into a door behind the bar. The hall beyond was bright where the common room they'd left was dark and smoky. Lush carpets overlapped down the hallway. The wood-panelled walls were broken up by doorways leading to various back rooms. Many of the doors were closed, and of those that stood open, many were in the dark. While passing one ajar door, Beorn glimpsed a slender brunette woman in a state of undress. Her unlaced shift dropped to the floor, revealing skin as smooth and flawless as porcelain. She leaned forward, rolling down her hose to display a pair of long slender legs…

Beorn hurried past the voyeuristic display, neck blazing and eyes forward. As Helga reached the end of the hall, she opened a door on the right and ushered Beorn inside. "The Madam will see you shortly. Make yourself comfortable. You come with me little miss, we can wait in my room while yer Da and Rosie talk." And then they were gone, leaving Beorn alone in the opulent room.

Lacquered hardwood panelled the walls, lit generously by multiple sconces. Ornate golden frames opened portals to a range of fantastical scenes, picturesque scenery, and a myriad of graphic sexual escapades of Carthian design. A fire was burning in the fireplace, a series of books lining the mantle, each title more explicit than the last. Rich, lush carpets from the Continent covered the floors. In the room's corner, a large round copper tub sat filled with lukewarm water, rose petals of every shade dancing across the surface. Beorn was staring at the massive four-poster bed when the door behind him clicked open and closed.

"Wondering whether the feather bed is as comfortable as it looks? I'd be happy to show you if you'd like?"

Beorn turned to look at the Madam. "Is that the only reason you wanted me alone?"

"Not the only reason. I believe we can help each other."

"How do you figure that?"

Rosie moved away from the door frame and over to a paper-screen room divider. "Don't mind if I get into something more comfortable, do you?" Without waiting for an answer, Rosie slipped behind and undressed. A candle cast her shadow across the screen, displaying her every movement. "That gregarious gentleman you managed to insult was Renulf, colloquially called Renulf the Bloody to those with the misfortune of knowing him well."

The black corset Rosie had been wearing appeared over the top of the divider, the shadows of her hands going to work at unlacing her dress-front.

"He and his band of brigands have made a habit of frequenting my establishment. I take no issue with parting them from their pillaged coins, but unfortunately they have been... *unkind* to some of my girls. Renulf especially."

"He hurts them?" Beorn asked.

"Yes... Oftentimes my girls leave his rooms with dark bruises 'round their necks, and need to ice betwixt their legs for a whole day before they are ready to work again."

Beorn felt uncomfortable with the topic. "Why not go to the reeve or sheriff? Surely they could spare a watchman or two to set the brigands straight?"

Rosie gave a warm chuckle. Beorn enjoyed the sound of it. "You and I have obviously walked vastly different paths in life. You, likely down a path where evil-doers and ne'er-do-wells are metered out justice? Me, well, I've walked a path where whores tend to their own affairs. We don't benefit from the protection of local lawmen in this establishment."

"You have my sympathies," Beorn said, eyes watching the shadow of Rosie's dress fall soundlessly to the floor. Candlelight illuminated a figure defined by supple curves. "But what interest is this to me?"

"You want a room, yes? Fine; you can have a room, along with food and shelter till this snowstorm passes. All you have to do is handle Renulf and his thugs."

"No," Beorn said immediately. Shadow-hands pulled on a thin-looking shift, smoothing the fabric flat against her body. Rosie rounded the partition. She had shed her Madam facade of busty dresses and tight corsets for a loose fitting gossamer shift and velvet robe. Her breasts, no longer pressed together and held aloft by the corsets, now hung naturally lower, outlined clearly through the thin material. They were as though made of uncooked dough - soft, warm, and nourishing. Dough to be kneaded and needed.

She had scrubbed her face free of cosmetics, showing her true age; thin lines carved from years of smiles adorned her eyes. Her auburn mop hung loosely over her shoulders, showing even more silver than Beorn had first noticed, glistening in the candlelight. Without the corsets, her waist was wider, her shift clinging to a small pouch of stomach fat. She was even more beautiful than Beorn had first thought.

Rosie sat in a high-backed ornate armchair and gestured for Beorn to take the matching one. After a moment, Beorn obliged. The Madam poured them both a glass of dark velvety wine from a decanter on the table between them.

"The way I see it," Rosie continued after a sip, the wine staining her lips, "is you now benefit from Renulf's demise as much as me and my girls."

"How so?"

"You don't know the man. He's a monster. A butcher. He kills and maims without hesitation. Yes, he pays for the company of my girls, but no amount of coin could be enough for the state he leaves some of them in. He's a beast. He needs to be put down."

"How is that my concern?"

"You made him look a fool in front of his men. In his eyes, the only course of action is for you to die."

"All the more reason to reject your offer and leave tonight, while your girls are *entertaining* him." Beorn couldn't keep the derision from his voice.

"You would die in the cold. If you somehow survived, Renulf and his band would hunt you down. The last man who crossed him was Arthur, my stable boy."

"I saw no stable boy outside."

"Nor would you. Renulf killed him." Hatred flared behind her eyes. "Arthur walked in on Renulf and one of my girls. A simple mistake. Arthur's true misstep was repeating some... unflattering remarks about Renulf's *person* to some other patrons. Specifically, its size. Word got back to Renulf."

Rosie paused, her eyes cast down. Amber light flickered off the tears welling in her eyes. "I found Arthur crucified to the brothel's door. Renulf had flayed the skin from his body. The only way I recognised him was his eyes, devoid of eyelids. He'd always had such beautiful eyes…" Rosie's gaze found Beorn's. Sadness turned to hatred. "Renulf needs to die; the sooner the better. Tonight, preferably. And if you don't do it, you can expect the same outcome for that redheaded lass who struck him. He's not a man to let a woman spurn him. He'll hunt her to the ends of the earth to hurt her in return, and when he catches her, you can be sure he'll deliver it tenfold."

Beorn's hand tightened around the glass in his hand. "I won't let that happen."

"So you'll kill him?" Hope layered her husky voice.

"If he tries to hurt me or mine, he won't survive the encounter. But I'm not a murderer." Beorn envisioned the notches on the haft of his axe. *People can change. We are more than our worst acts…* "Thank you for the drink. But I want no part in your quarrel."

Beorn stood to leave, walking towards the door.

"Wait," Rosie called, reluctantly. "You can stay the night. That girl will die out in the cold. Stay. I'll give the girl a room. You can join her if you wish." Her eyes darted towards the four-poster bed. "Or I can answer your unasked questions about my mattress."

Beorn scoffed. "You have no shame. I won't trade my morality for your body."

Rosie rolled her eyes. "You stubborn headed *man*. It is possible for me to want something from you *and* to want you. And I wasn't offering my body as a trade; I have desires of my own, you know." Her eyes wandered up and down Beorn's frame. "The room is yours, regardless. Hide away until Renulf and his men are gone. I'll have one of the girls feed and water your horse." And with that, Rosie turned away, done with Beorn.

As he opened the door to find Morrigan, he couldn't help voicing his mind. "If you really cared about the safety of these girls, you'd let them leave to find other work. Work that doesn't bring them into contact with such beastly men."

Rosie stared calmly back at him. *"Let* them leave? You think I in any way force my girls to work for me? I provide them with a roof and safety. If not working here, they'd be plying their trade on the streets, sleeping in gutters and freezing in the snow. I force nothing upon them they wouldn't be doing, regardless. Every one of them is here by choice."

"Is it really a choice when poverty and death are the alternative?"

Rosie's calm stare turned hot. Her chest heaved under her shift and Beorn shamefully was powerless from casting a furtive glance at her breasts.

"You think you're a smart man? A morally superior man because you've never sold your body for coin? Answer me this; if not whoring beneath my roof or in the streets, what trade would my girls pursue? Smithing? Tanning? Hunting? What trade do you know that permits girls to 'prentice freely? And which of these trades would supposedly keep them free from *beastly men?"* When Beorn didn't respond, she continued. "There is nowhere in this world for girls to hide from men like that. They will always find us out, hunting us like dogs through the snow to take what they want. You ask, is it really a choice when poverty and death are the alternative? No - it's survival. It's fine for you to preach that we shouldn't have to sell our bodies to survive - but that's not the world we live in. And I'd rather my girls be alive and safe under my roof, doing what they need to survive, than dead for your moral paradise.

"Now fuck off."

# Chapter 12

Beorn found Morrigan in a room down the hall. As he shouldered open the door, he was met with the sight of Helga's massive stomach bared to the wind, skirts hoisted under her breasts. A dark brown line stretched from naval to groin. Red streaks clawed her stomach's sides, indented where her skin had stretched from carrying the babe.

*God, does no one wear clothes in this place?* A somewhat stupid question to ask in a whorehouse, Beorn quickly realised.

"Apologies," Beorn stammered, looking anywhere around the room but at the pregnant woman's stomach. "I'll wait outside…"

Helga waved him off. "Don't worry, handsome, I'm not shy." She flattered him with a wink. Beorn's neck grew hot again. He found himself a seat on a stool in the corner, Helga's stomach obscured by Morrigan's body as she worried away at the whore's swollen belly.

"Yer time is very close," Morrigan mused, slender hands gliding over Helga's pregnancy. "The babe's definitely dropped. Feel here-" Morrigan said, fingers pinching the fatty mound above her groin, "-the babe's head is in position for birthing. Have ye had a show yet?"

"A what?"

"A thick discharge o' blood and mucus from yer vagina?"

"Oh. Um, I don't think so? To be fair, I've been running like a tap these past weeks…"

*God. Put me back on the battlefield.*

"Contractions?"

"A few, but never frequent enough to be genuine. Just phantom pains, I think."

"Hmm. Have ye soap 'n water? I want t' do an internal examination."

Beorn's eyes found a knot in the wall's wooden panelling that suddenly occupied his attention.

"Wouldn't be so sure 'bout those 'phantom pains.' Yer dilated."

Helga's face froze between shock and excitement. "I… I am? The babe's coming?"

"Soon," Morrigan assured. "Could still be days, could be weeks. But yer time is here." Morrigan moved away to scrub her hands in a bowl on a wooden chest of drawers. Helga cradled her stomach in both hands, fingers trailing over the taut skin. Her face was aglow with emotion. Her eyes shone silver with tears, lips tweaked in the faintest of smiles. Beorn knew what she was feeling. Joy, fear, excitement, worry; all rolled together in a churning sea of expectation.

"Boy or girl?" Beorn asked. "For which do you hope?"

Helga smiled at him as she lowered her dress. "I know you're meant to say it doesn't matter. Long as they're born happy and healthy. But in truth, I'm hoping for a little girl - a daughter."

Beorn smiled sentimentally. "Daughters are a blessing."

A phantom scream behind a closed wooden door. A wail. An older woman in a blood-stained apron. *'It's a girl.'*

Beorn's smile dropped and his brow furrowed. "Aren't… aren't you worried about what your child will think? Of your… profession?" *Or what others will think of them? The child of a whore?*

Helga's eyes were kind and patient, as though talking to a child who knew not what they said. "My child will know only the world it's born in to. I can't change that. But I can make sure they know what it means to treat others with kindness and compassion. If it's a boy, I'll raise him to be a lad who treats women with respect. Who takes care of them, is kind, asks before he takes. And if it's a girl, I'll raise her to know her worth. Know it in a way only a mother who's had her own worth measured in coppers and pennies can know. I'll teach her to be strong, resilient. And I'll teach her how t' say no. Something I wish I'd known myself."

As Helga lamented the babe to come, hands cradling her belly, Beorn looked at her properly for the first time. Swollen breasts and bulging stomach had added the appearance of maturity to her slender frame, but in truth, she was barely more than a girl. Eighteen years? Nineteen? How long had she whored under Rosie's roof? How much longer had she done so on the streets before? At what age had she realised a starving girl couldn't eat modesty; but that there would always be men willing to pay to eat a starving girl?

"Helga... are you happy? Here at *Rosie's*? Doing... what it is you do?"

"Whoring?" She said the word plainly, as if it were no different a profession to a baker or wainwright. She took a minute to consider Beorn's question. "Well enough, I think. The money I make is mine to spend on what I wish, and with no husband to take it from me. That's more freedom than many women know."

"But don't you ever feel... used?"

Helga shrugged. "To be a woman is to perform. Whether I was a whore or a wife, I'd be used for something."

Helga lowered her skirts over her bump, stood, and thanked Morrigan for her time. On her way out the door, she cast Beorn one final bawdy wink.

When Helga was gone, Beorn turned to Morrigan. "What do you make of all this? This 'profession'?"

"In truth- I dinnae have an opinion."

"That's a first."

"Why should I? Who am I t' judge the choices other women have made?"

"You don't think the practice tempts men to violence? Brings out their basest instincts?"

*I saw no rape*, he'd told the girl when recounting his years as a soldier. That had been the truth. Though, how much of that was because of his choices to skirt the tents of certain known bastards? And in the instances the girls were paid? How did that factor in?

Morrigan considered. "You give a man power over you once, he'll think he's owed it. He'll keep coming back; again and again, until there's nothing left t' take. But then again, how many men need to be tempted t' violence?"

"So, as a woman yourself, you think it's better to serve and survive, rather than fight the natural order of the world and die?"

That was Rosie's argument. *'I'd rather my girls be alive and safe under my roof, doing what they need to survive than dead for your moral paradise.'*

"In truth, I think most women give nary a thought t' the power dynamics they are born into. It is an agony t' be fully conscious o' the chains we wear; so much easier t' bear them in ignorance. I cannae begrudge them their survival. But nor can I abide a chain."

*'The easiest prisoner to keep is the one who can't see his own chains.'*

Morrigan sat busying her hands, arranging her medicine pouch. Beorn saw she'd given Helga some herbs, just as she'd done for Beatrice Smith before they left Greytower Watch. Whenever the girl spoke of babes and birthing she seemed at ease, as though performing her God-given purpose. But Beorn could not help but remember their first meeting in the Brexton town square. *'Her greatest sin... the murder of the innocent; of the unborn!'*

"Morrigan?"

"Mm?" She didn't raise her eyes from organising her pouch.

"Why… why were you on trial in Brexton?"

She looked up at him at that. "You know why. I was a cunning woman's 'prentice. We travelled around, selling cures and remedies, birthing babes. We were taken in a hamlet close to Brexton."

"Yes, but… why?" Morrigan stared back at him with her stone grey eyes. "What did you do?"

"Ye want to know about the babe I *killed*?" she asked solemnly.

"If… if you would tell me."

Morrigan sighed and took a breath, deep through the nose, as though steeling herself for the story to come. Beorn sat patiently, waiting, ready to listen.

"When… when my mistress and I first rolled into that hamlet, we saw much and more o' the same as we did everywhere else we roved. Boils needing lancing, rashes needing easing, fevers needing quelling. As was our practice, we set up just on the outskirts and let folk come t' us with their ailments.

"One afternoon, while my mistress was gathering water from a nearby creek, a young girl came slinking into our camp. She was a wee thing, maybe younger than I. She told me she was the stonemason's daughter. I asked her what she needed of me, expecting maybe she'd gotten her first period and needed something t' ease the discomfort. Instead, she told me she had a babe in her belly; and it was her father who'd put it there."

Beorn's stomach roiled. He felt ill. Morrigan went on.

"I knew, o' course, what it was she had sought us out for. I'd done it for other women before… though never one so young as her, and never… Well; I brewed her a tisane with the usual aborticides - tansy, rue, pennyroyal, mugwort. I warned her it winnae be pleasant. There'd be spasms and bleeding and pain. But she insisted, and drank. She left our camp, and I thought that was the end o' it. Another girl helped. But it weren't.

"The settlers came for us a week later while we slept. They came with torches, and farm tools, and rope. The bleeding was especially bad for the girl. Her mother found her in her bed, skirts soiled with blood, tears running down her cheeks. The girl had told her Ma what she'd done… what her father had done t' her. She would nae believe the girl. She cursed her, threatened t' hand her over to the Inquisitorum for incest and then for killing the babe. She said they'd burn her; her own daughter. The girl panicked.

"She told her Ma it was us. That we'd somehow bewitched her into seducing her own father. And that when she'd gotten with child, we had murdered the babe, as a sacrificed to yer Church's Adversary."

"She sold you out?" Beorn was shocked.

"Aye."

"You must hate her."

Morrigan fixed him with her storm cloud stare. "Why? For saving herself?"

"But she sold you to the Church, knowing you would die. She condemned you to death."

"The Church condemned me for their own hypocrisy. You saw how quickly the Inquisitors' Dog sent the blacksmith's wife t' the gallows, despite the child in her belly. They care not for the life of the unborn babe, only for the control it grants them over the mothers. And best believe if alter boys could get pregnant, the Church would have a mighty different outlook. After all, it's not sacrilegious when the Church does it. Divine obedience is only for the sheep; not the shepherds.

"Nay, I cannae hate the poor girl. I hate her father, who defiled her. I hate her mother, who chose to protect him over believing her own daughter. I hate that bastard Constantine and his mongrel knights. I hate the whole stinking Inquisitorum. I hate the Church. I hate yer whole *fucking* kingdom. I *HATE* your soldiers who sacked my home and its people and brought your hate-filled religion into my lands… but I cannae hate that girl."

Beorn didn't know what to think. Morrigan had just been trying to help. And that bastard of a father… Beorn's mind couldn't cope with the image. How could anyone do that to their own daughter? And yet… Morrigan had killed a babe. "You… you feel no… guilt? For killing the child? Not that I could comprehend… the choice… I just… a babe…" Beorn's mind was a tumult of thoughts and values that had been ingrained in him since he was a child.

"I refuse to feel guilt for what I did. Men do worse every day and still believe themselves virtuous. I saved her from the stake for her 'adultery and seduction.' Or I saved her from a dive, belly first down the stairs, pushed by her father to hide his sin. He'd have done it too; they always do. There's nae justice for men like that."

Justice was a fallacy, a beautiful lie they told themselves to sleep easier at night. That wicked men were punished for their actions, and the innocent were protected. How wrong they all were.

"How many more men would commit atrocities if they thought they'd never get caught?" Beorn lamented.

"How many do so anyway, regardless?"

Beorn felt sick. He wished he'd never asked. But there was at least some small part of him that was relieved to know the truth. That Morrigan wasn't some bloodthirsty woods-witch who murdered an unborn babe in cold blood. "I suppose… given the circumstances, no one can fault you for your actions. The babe beget of such an act should never have been born."

Morrigan gave him a slow shake of her head, crimson curls swaying side to side. "Oh, Beorn. I'd have given that wee girl the tisane, even if it hadn't been her father's get. I'd have given it t' her if she were a woman grown and madly in love with her husband. The same as I've given more times than I can count t' women above and below Gaius's Wall. I did it because she asked. Because it was her choice to make."

They spoke no more on the topic.

*   *   *

As Beorn settled in to fall asleep, a soft knock rapped on the door. Cracking the door, Rosie's warm smile and kind eyes greeted Beorn. Morrigan was already asleep, and not wishing to wake her, Beorn slipped into the hallway to see what the Madam wanted. Beorn had somewhat of an idea.

"How are you finding the room?" Rosie purred.

"Comfortable enough." Beorn had no wish to be obtuse, but he feared the message he might send if he were overly kindly. The truth was, he could only tell her no up to a point.

"I came… to apologise," Rosie said. "It was unkind of me to put you in such a position. You know me not, nor I you. What I asked was… well, it was not a simple request. And I am sorry for dismissing you so coldly. You struck a nerve, but a host should not speak so to their guests."

Rosie had left her robe behind and stood in naught but her gossamer shift. In the light cast by the hallway's candles, it was nearly transparent. Beorn struggled to keep his eyes level with hers.

"It is I who should apologise. I had no right to critique your trade. You said I thought myself morally superior because I'd never sold my body for coin. But that isn't true. I was a soldier. I sold my body, my soul, to King and country for a purse of coin. I killed for that coin. If you ask me, it's you who has the moral high-ground here."

Rosie gave him a smile. Her lips looked so soft. "How about we keep our apologies and try to start over?"

"Sounds good to me." Beorn's heart fluttered quietly in his chest. Was the hallway warmer than their room?

"I have to ask… just once more. There is truly nothing you can do for me about my… problem?" Rosie was a strong woman, Beorn could tell by the way she commanded a room. It hurt him to see such vulnerability in her eyes. To be reduced to relying on another, on a man, to solve her problems. But Beorn could no more help her with her problems than she with his.

"I'm sorry, Rosie. My priority is the girl. I cannot risk what a fight with this Renulf and his men might mean for her, should I fall."

It hurt him even more to see the flicker of disappointment and failure in her eyes. Almost enough to make him march upstairs and throw Renulf out, bare-arsed, into the snow.

"I understand. But I owed it to my girls to ask once more." She turned to leave, her shift sliding down her shoulder, leaving it bare in the candlelight. "And what of my… *other* offer? It still stands, you know."

She blinked a slow blink. Images of the four-poster feather bed danced before Beorn's eyes. Images of pillows, Rosie's pillows… *Soft*, he thought. *They look soft.* "My answer… remains," he said, albeit with more difficulty than last time.

"I understand," Rosie said, and walked away; the sway of her hips a silent seduction. Beorn waited until she disappeared behind her door before re-entering their room. Morrigan was awake and sitting upright on her bed.

"What was that about?"

Beorn rubbed his hand through his beard, hoping to hide the flush in his cheeks. "The Madam wants me to help her with a difficult client. He's causing trouble with her girls. I refused her."

"Why?"

"I don't get involved, remember?"

Morrigan stared at him with her cunning, grey eyes. "I dinnae think that's true. Least, not anymore. Ye saved the blacksmith's wife. Ye saved that woman outside o' Ravensburg. Ye saved *me*. I think for all ye talk o' not getting involved, there's a part o' you that wants to help people."

"Not a part large enough to risk dying for them."

Somewhere above them came the slow steady rhythm of a headboard banging against a wall. Beorn sighed. "I shouldn't have brought you here."

Morrigan chuckled. "I'm a midwife, remember? I've delivered plenty o' babes; I know well enough whence they come from." She pulled the covers back on and lay down to sleep.

Beorn did the same. The rhythmic banging persisted. It made Beorn think of Rosie and her four-poster bed. Perhaps he'd dream of her… Alas, that was not the case.

A woman's scream penetrated Beorn's dreams. Not in itself an unusual occurrence, but this scream sounded as though it had come from *outside* his head. Beorn was awake and upright in a flash. Morrigan had heard it too, her hand resting on the dagger she'd hidden under her pillow. It had come from upstairs.

The last of Renulf's men were shuffling out the door as Beorn raced past the common room and up the stairs, chuckling amiably to themselves. Dawn had come and the pink rays of the rising sun filtered through the brothel windows.

Beorn found Rosie slumped to the floor in one of the upstairs rooms. Strewn across the bed was the naked, lifeless body of Chastity, the girl Rosie had directed to entertain Renulf the night before. Her eyes stared lifelessly at the roof, her lips parted ever so slightly, and her golden hair splayed around her head like a gilded halo.

Encircling her throat was a line of dark mottled bruises, in the unmistakable shape of a man's hands. Placed in the middle of the dead woman's chest was a single silver coin, resting directly over her heart.

Rosie's tear-filled eyes stared hatefully up at Beorn.

*'You could have stopped this,'* they screamed.

*'I don't get involved,'* he might have refuted, but even he knew now that was a lie he could no longer hide behind. Here lay the cost of his inaction. His feet were moving of their own volition, taking him down the stairs, through the common room, and out into the yard. Renulf and his men

were meandering across the snow-covered courtyard, some still lacing their breeches and tying up boots.

"*RENULF!*"

The rat-faced man was chuckling with a companion. He rolled his eyes as he turned back to the door of the brothel. "I paid the whore for damages done. A whole silver piece. More than what she was worth, if I'm being honest." His goons laughed. He looked at Beorn blankly, all memories of him from the night before lost. Until his eyes drifted to Beorn's elbow and the redheaded northgirl standing there. "*You,*" he said through curled lips. Two long knives appeared in his hands, the kind a butcher might use to carve up a pig. "You're the little whore who struck me last night."

The band of brigands were cluing on that there was violence on the morning breeze. Hands were creeping to weapon hilts.

"I told you what would happen if you called her that again," Beorn seethed. "But for what you did to that girl inside…"

Renulf laughed. "What do you plan to do? Drag me before the constable? Turn around. Pretty sure I saw him back upstairs."

"No," Beorn said. "No constable. No lawmen. Sometimes the only true justice comes at the edge of a blade."

"What d'you think you're gonna do?"

*What I should have done last night when Rosie asked me.*

Renulf nodded to one of his men, who was leaning against a pitchfork by the stables. Beorn could see Godfrey over the man's shoulder, as well as his axe hanging from the saddle.

*Shit.*

The man took up the pitchfork and swaggered towards Beorn. The men he passed slapped his shoulder and egged him on.

"*Stick him!*"

"*Put him on his arse!*"

The brigand was twenty years younger than Beorn, leaner and fast, and he knew it. The man gave a lazy right feint with the three-pronged pitchfork before lunging forward to bury it in Beorn's chest. The wooden haft vibrated with the impact.

Beorn's fingers had caught it just below the rusted iron head, red prongs inches from his shirtfront. The group was silent. Beorn swiftly pulled the weapon from the cocky youth's grip, only to return it when he broke the lad's nose with the haft's wood.

Everything happened in an instant after that.

Renulf's men closed in, weapons singing through the air. Beorn danced away, pitchfork darting back and forth like a spear. The pitchfork had the advantage of reach, rusted prongs cutting through the brigands before their short swords and axe blades could get close to Beorn. They fought crudely but savagely, relying on their numbers to overwhelm their prey. Beorn held his own, slaying the bastards left and right, but they just kept coming. Beorn caught a swing from a short sword in the pitchfork's prongs, but as he did, another assailant darted under his arms with a dagger pointed to his stomach.

*Shit, I was too slow...*

The wicked point sliced through the air, but before it could bury itself in Beorn's flesh, a small red blur barrelled into the brigand, opening his throat. Morrigan held Brown Tom's dagger the way he had taught her, its blade now slick with the dying man's blood. The fight was over near as quickly as it started. Against scared women and unarmed whores, the brigands may have been fearsome, but against Beorn and Morrigan, they fell like autumn leaves.

Only Renulf remained.

"He's mine," Beorn told Morrigan, stepping forward with pitchfork raised.

The rat-faced man slunk forward, his carving knives dancing in his hands. His lips were curled in a sneer. "I'm gonna bleed you," he spat. "You and the *girl.*"

"Girl?" Morrigan called from behind Beorn. "Is that meant as an insult? I'd call ye *boy,* but from what I hear, ye fall short by even those standards."

Renulf bared his teeth like a feral dog and lunged.

Beorn thrust the pitchfork forward, but Renulf darted away, twin blades feinting left and right. Beorn had the better reach, but Renulf was the faster man. Half Beorn's size, he was twice as fast, dancing away from Beorn's thrusts and sweeps to dart in like a wasp, stingers at the ready. Beorn had to close the gap, and do so soon. His lungs were screaming as they drew breath, his arms afire with the effort of swinging the pitchfork. Twenty years before, Beorn had fought from dawn till dusk, swinging his sword until his arms were leaden, only to rise the next morn and do it all again. But Beorn was an old man now, and whatever fight he had was only available in short bursts. He had to end this.

After a feint to the left, Beorn barrelled forward within arm's length of Renulf. Beorn expected the rat-faced man to careen backwards, thrown off balance by the hulking mass bearing down on him. This would give Beorn the opening he needed, and he'd open the man from neck to groin. But Renulf did not blanch. Instead, he planted his feet, dodged the pitchfork's prongs and struck like a viper with his two silver fangs. Beorn caught one with the pitchfork's haft but the other bit into his upper thigh, cutting through muscle.

*Fuck.*

*'You've only got a foot of steel in your hand, which means in order to use it, you'll need to get close. The easiest way to do that is to let* them *get close to* you.' He had told Morrigan as much when they first started training. *Can't even listen to my own fucking advice.*

Beorn's thigh was growing wet and warm with his blood. Each beat of his heart sent another torrent of scarlet running down his leg.

"I was a butcher's boy once," Renulf gloated, waving his knives about like a deranged magician. "First thing I learnt was how to bleed a pig."

Beorn made to lunge, but his bleeding leg buckled under him, and he fell to his knee.

"Bleed, piggy, bleed," Renulf chuckled.

Beorn knelt, his blood mingling with the snow on the ground. The pitchfork fell from his fingers, his strength fading fast. The world was growing blurry.

Renulf stepped in close, lifting Beorn's chin with the tip of his knife. "After I carve you up, I'm going to do the same to your little whore. But not 'til after I've had my fun." Renulf leaned in close, his rancid breath hot on

Beorn's face. "You should say goodbye," he whispered.

"Goodbye." Beorn's hand was viper-fast. He wrapped his iron grip around Renulf's hand and made him disembowel himself with his own knife. The brigand staggered back, knives falling from his hands as he struggled to grab at the guts spilling from his belly. Renulf fell. Beorn stood.

*Let* them *get close to* you.

Renulf dragged himself bloody through the snow, a deep red streak smeared behind him. "Please…" he begged. "Lord… God save me…"

A spasm of bloody coughs cut his pleading short.

"Save your prayers," Beorn growled, limping up behind him. "The sky is deaf. If you want to pray, pray to me."

"Mercy!" Renulf pleaded, but Beorn had no mercy to give.

Renulf died on his belly, the pitchfork skewering him to the ground.

Beorn swayed on his feet, blood pumping down his leg. *One, two, three, four…* Beorn counted the dead to tally on his axe.

*Death follows me wherever I go…*

Morrigan was cleaning her blade on the tunic of a corpse, a red wound weeping from its side. "Kidney," Beorn observed. "A good strike."

A small smile graced her face.

A scream erupted from the brothel behind them. Beorn broke into a run, his thigh pulsing with pain. Morrigan was faster and was through the door and up the stairs while Beorn trailed behind. He followed the cry across the landing to a doorway at the end of the hall. They found Helga doubled over, hands clutching her stomach.

"What is it?" Beorn demanded, eyes scanning the room for threats. Had he missed one of the brigands? Had they directed their anger towards the whores?

"It's the babe," Morrigan said, scrubbing her hands with soap from a nearby basin.

"The… should we… call for a surgeon?"

Morrigan threw her head back and laughed. "Why? Do ye want a haircut?"

*She's going to deliver the babe,* Beorn realised. "What do you need?"

A soft hand pressed against his chest. "You've done enough," Rosie whispered.

"I want to help." The memory of a scream behind a wooden door. A newborn's wail. The door opened. *'It's a girl.'*

"I know. And there are spaces where your help is welcome. But not in this. This is women's business. We'll take it from here." A gentle push and the door closed in his face.

*I was on this side of the door once before,* Beorn thought.

The world was spinning. Darkness was creeping into the corners of his vision with every beat of his heart. A pool of blood was steadily growing at his feet, the wound in his thigh afire.

The last thing he thought as the floor swam up to greet him was, *Why am I always fucking fainting?*

* * *

A woman was screaming. Inside or out of Beorn's dream, he couldn't tell.

*Save her Beorn!*

Fire turned the night red. As red as her hair. How he wished to run his fingers through that hair one last time.

Beorn awoke in the same room he'd spent the previous night in. The bed was soft under his back and for a moment he lay there enjoying the peace, the quiet, and the softness he'd found himself in. The dull ache in his thigh slowly brought him back to the here and now. He tried to rise, but a tender hand on his chest kept him at bay.

"Easy now," Rosie cooed. "You lost a lot of blood."

Beorn's bare leg was jutting from beneath the thin sheet atop of him. Someone had expertly sewn the wicked gash that Renulf's dagger had opened high on his thigh with a series of neat stitches.

"Morrigan...?"

"Me," Rosie answered. She placed her hand on his thigh, tracing the scar with her finger. "Your girl was somewhat preoccupied with Helga. Plus, given the location of the wound, I thought you'd prefer someone with a bit more... *experience*, to tend to it."

Realisation dawned that under the sheet Beorn was naked. Rosie's hand rested high upon his thigh.

"One of my girls is sewing up your breeches," the Madam continued.

"You have my thanks," Beorn stammered.

"And you have mine. You and Morrigan both. You've done my girls a great kindness. Both for Renulf and for Helga."

"I should have done something when you asked. My inaction…"

Rosie looked sadly away. "The fault lies with Renulf. And you served him the justice he deserved. For that, I thank you. I owe you an apology also. Last night, when I came to your room and… *propositioned* you, I was not being completely truthful." She smiled coyly. "Not that I'd be *dis*interested in your sharing my bed, but… I thought I might have convinced you to help us. I should not have misled you so."

"We use the tools that are afforded to us." Rosie's hand was remarkably close to Beorn's own tools.

She was leaning forward, face close to his own. "The offer stands," she whispered. "Stay with us. We could use a man of your talents close at hand. I could find work for the girl. Work you deem appropriate, of course. You have my gratitude, Beorn. You need only reach out and take it."

Something was throbbing under the sheet. *The wound*, Beorn lied to himself.

"I can't… I have to get the girl to her home."

Rosie nodded sadly. "The girl told me what you did for her. Don't worry, your secrets are safe with me. I would never hand a girl over to those monsters in cassocks. You know… the Frostline isn't so far. You could… come back?"

He felt the weight of her hand where it remained high on his leg. He felt the longing, the desire. The Church would name it temptation. He looked at her lips. But all he saw was another's.

"I can't…" he said, turning his gaze away, painfully.

"I understand," Rosie said, and Beorn knew she did. "Will you tell me about her?"

"…Who?"

"This woman who lays claim to your heart. A woman divine enough to make a man hold to his vows even in the den of a whorehouse. Dare I even say, one who's…*memory*, drives a man to escort a young girl across the country, hounded by the Inquisitorum?"

Beorn closed his eyes. Images swam up…

The vibrant vermilion of her hair: a glimpse of eyes the colour of storm clouds brewing over a raging sea; the pale porcelain skin of her hands. Yet her face…

"She was… how can I even describe her? She was my world. I would have known her across aeons; the ravages of time could not change her such, that my eyes would not recognise the shape of her soul. Even in total darkness, my fingers would know her form by touch alone. I would know her by the sound of her footfalls, and the trill of her laugh. Had God struck me deaf, I would know her by her scent… by her taste…

"But for the life of me, no matter how hard I try, I cannot recall her face." Tears welled in Beorn's eyes. He had not spoken of her since… since the fire… But once started, the words poured out of him.

"I remember the way she lit up a room, the way she would sing to the birds. I can recall the sound of her cries as she brought our daughter into the world, and the taste of our mingled tears as we held our babe and kissed for the first time as parents.

"She comes to me in my dreams, tormenting me with her absence. I see her standing in a forest glade, her hair the colour of falling autumn leaves. The wind whips it around her shoulders, obscuring her face. I try to walk around her, to glimpse her, but no matter how fast I walk, the wind shifts and changes, constantly obstructing her from my sight. In other dreams, I stand above her. She holds our daughter, dead in her arms, her hair falling like a veil. When she looks up at me, all I am met with is a countenance devoid of any features. No mouth, no nose, no eyes; yet even without, tears of blood streak her cheeks with grief.

"Time has taken her from me. That is the worst of it. I lost her once in life, and now the years have slowly stripped her from me, even in death. I fear that eventually I will recall her as nothing more than a shade. At which time, I pray to finally have the strength to fall on my axe. For what other purpose will I have to go on?"

Without meaning to, an image of Morrigan flashed behind his eyelids for barely a second.

Rosie stared back at him with dewy eyes. "Well then, I can hardly take offence at your rejection. How could I ever live up to such a woman? Even the shadow of one." She leaned forward and laid a gentle kiss upon his cheek, hand still resting near his wounded thigh. The softness of her lips was at stark odds with the coarseness of his face. The blankets near her hand stirred slightly. "Even so, we will never forget what you have done for us. There will always be a place for you here."

A fire burned inside him. He was too stunned to speak, until finally: "…Perhaps one day, I will take up that offer."

That brought a smile to Rosie's lips. He enjoyed making her smile.

They found Morrigan in the birthing room. Beorn had to lean on Rosie to limp up the stairs. Helga lay abed, a swaddled mass pressed against her breast. Morrigan sat up at the sight of Beorn, relief upon her face.

"Yer awake," she sighed.

"That sounds almost like concern," he teased. She did not deny it. "How went the birth?"

"As well as could be hoped for. Helga was amazing."

The blonde-haired girl smiled bashfully. "I did nothing special, really. In truth, I felt like I was just along for the ride, my body acting on its own."

"The memories o' yer foremothers live within ye. Be proud o' what ye did today."

"And the babe?" Beorn asked.

In response, Helga held out the small swaddled mass. Beorn limped closer, just to look, but when he did, Helga pressed the bundle into his arms. A small pink face looked up at him through slitted eyes. Five small digits were grasping at the air until they found Beorn's fingers. With remarkable strength, the babe brought Beorn's finger to its mouth.

"There's a man who's held a babe before," Rosie mused.

Beorn had not realised, but he was rocking slowly from side to side, a slight bounce and dip with each swing. It had been years, but some things never left you.

"I was thinking," Helga ventured, "if it were born a boy, I'd name the babe after you. But Beorn doesn't quite suit a girl. So instead, would you like to pick the name? Maybe someone who meant something to you: mother, sister...?"

"Daughter?" Morrigan offered.

Beorn had not taken his eyes off the small pink bundle. The babe had closed her eyes, fallen asleep sucking his finger. So innocent, so peaceful, so full of potential. A creature devoid of any ill-will or evil deeds. A soul untainted by the world and free of sin. He remembered another swaddled babe years ago, filled with the same potential.

"Althea," Beorn whispered. The babe opened her eyes and stared at him, responding to the name he had not said in years.

"A beautiful name," Rosie agreed.

Beorn handed the babe back to her mother. "Althea," Helga cooed. "What a beautiful name. I will make sure she always knows whence it came. Thank you, Beorn."

"No, thank you."

"What for?"

*For giving Althea a second chance at life.*

# Chapter 13

Rosie sent them on their way, well provisioned and well fed. The snows had kept them for another four days. At first Beorn had argued they must be away immediately before the corpses in the courtyard drew attention, but Rosie claimed to know somebody who knew somebody, and at noon a cart came and went, laden with the corpses of Renulf and his brigands.

It was nice to fall asleep each night with a fire and a full stomach. They each got the chance to bathe in hot steaming baths of fragrant lavender water. Rosie had kindly offered to accompany Beorn to 'help scrub the hard-to-reach bits', but Beorn had politely declined. Morrigan kept close to Helga's side, making sure her milk came in smoothly and that any physical trauma from the birth was healing well. The other whores had swarmed the babe as soon as Helga was stout enough to leave the birthing bed. Little Althea may not have had a father, but she had a dozen aunts who would drag themselves over broken glass for the babe. When Helga was well enough to bathe, Brida jumped at the opportunity to hold the child. When Helga needed to sleep after the ordeals of the birth, Ethel held the babe all night, swaying in her arms as she strolled around the back hallways of the brothel. At one point, a patron had complained of the babe's wailing, disturbing his experience. The young woman servicing him politely informed him that if he had an issue with the establishment, he was welcome to head home and suck himself off. The man stayed and kept any further complaints to himself.

The morning Beorn and Morrigan had left the brothel, a line of girls lined up to embrace Morrigan and kiss Beorn on the cheek. The latter stoically endured the procession until Rosie stood before him.

"Remember my offer," she whispered and planted the lightest of kisses in the corner of his lips.

The skies were clear of cloud or snow as they made their way further north, but the temperature had dropped dramatically. Winter was well and truly here.

They wrapped themselves in their warmest garb, woollen travelling cloaks wound tightly around them. Thick woollen scarves covered their mouths and noses, staving off the frostbite, their breaths coming in thick white clouds through the fabric. Now they were north of Gaius's Wall, Beorn felt more comfortable travelling along main roads. Having never been conquered by Carth, the Northern Realms lacked their roadways. Instead, even their grandest roads were dirt and gravel - albeit wider and better maintained than the winding goat paths and game trails they had grown used to.

They passed travellers migrating from town to town, selling their wares, buying up others, and moving on to sell those. Farmers moved in circles around the shires, distributing the wares they'd toiled in the fields to produce before the snows had set in. Children made snowknights and snowmaids in the fields they passed. Rowdy boys played warriors with wooden staves, gallantly defending their sisters and cousins, while the latter rolled their eyes as they went about making winter-daisy crowns.

The temperature may have dropped, but Beorn had never seen Morrigan warmer than when she was looking at those children at play. Travelling along the highroads offered greater opportunities to shelter in barns and inns where they were available and the elements demanded. When they lacked for shelter, they would make camp in natural gullies, rocky outcrops, and under thick oaks to stave off the worst of the biting wind. A large enough fire and their tightly wrapped cloaks would fend off the worst of the chill, but Beorn regularly woke with Morrigan pressed close against his back. One night, as he lay struggling to sleep, he felt her nuzzle into his side. He didn't know why he did, but Beorn gently slipped an arm behind the girl's head and pulled her close, wrapping his own cloak over her shivering frame. The girl settled into the crook of his arm and slept soundly through the night. It wasn't until the following day, riding pillion atop Godfrey over snowy hills and under low-hanging branches, that Beorn realised he had not awoken in a cold sweat. He had no recollection of tormented dreams or phantoms of his past. He let Morrigan sleep with her head upon his chest from that night on.

Days turned into a week, and a week turned into two before they trotted into the abandoned village. It had once been a quaint little settlement. Beorn could hear the echoes of a smith's hammer striking an anvil as they rode past the empty smithy. Beorn could hear phantom peddlers hawking their wares as they rode through the forsaken market street. Everywhere he looked, nature had reclaimed the long-vacant buildings; vines crept up walls, weeds grew through cracks in the pavers, and a family of deer scattered as they turned the corner into the village centre.

"What happened here?" Beorn pondered.

"They all left after the occupation," Morrigan answered. "There's nae Church, which means ye southerners never settled here. Money follows the Church. Without the revenue with trade t' the south, small villages like these died. Assimilate or perish."

Beorn was looking at the water fountain in the centre of the square. The water had long since dried up, but the fountain itself was still a remarkable piece of stonework. The basin was wide and deep, and at its centre a woman stood holding a gourd. Beorn knew that when the water was running, a continuous stream would have flowed from the gourd into the pool around her feet.

"I… I danced here," Beorn said.

"When?" Morrigan asked, taken aback.

"A lifetime ago." Beorn was certain of it now. Here was where the vendor had sold his salted nuts, rich and warm. There was where the wine-seller had set up his stall, fencing mulled wines rich with cinnamon and nutmeg. During harvest festivals, everyone from the entire valley would converge on this little square and dance and sing and make merry. This was where he'd met her. This is where his life had changed.

Without another word, Beorn was reining Godfrey to the left, heading out of the village to the west. Morrigan did not ask questions, and for that, Beorn was thankful. Perhaps she saw in the set of his mouth or the tension in his shoulders that this was not the time. He rode them down a dirt track for the better part of an hour before he saw what he was looking for. A familiar knot in an old oak. Looking carefully, Beorn could still see where the dirt track branched off into a smaller path, unused for many a year now. He spurred Godfrey on through the thick grass. They dipped down a small gully, then up a steep rise and, out of nowhere, it was upon them.

The collapsed ruins of a burnt down shack sat solitary upon the hill's crest. Charred beams poked through heavy underbrush like the ribs of a long dead animal. Beorn slid from Godfrey's saddle and paced towards the ruins. He walked down what had once been a cobblestone path before the forest floor had reclaimed it. He followed it past the beams and rubble to a tall apple-blossom tree. Pink remnants of its autumn petals littered the ground beneath the tree. At its base stood a small cairn of piled stones.

Beorn had never intended to return here. He had piled these stones in a lifetime past, and walked away into obscurity, alone.

"I'm sorry, Dorthea," Beorn whispered. "I didn't bring any flowers. I'm sorry…" Beorn hadn't felt himself kneel until the snow had soaked through his breeches. He scooped up a handful of fallen petals and placed them atop the cairn. It was still standing after all these years. That gave him solace, that at least no one had disturbed this place since he left.

"Beorn?" Morrigan said from behind him. "Who's grave is that?"

"My… my wife's." His voice caught in his throat. "This was our home. Many, many years ago."

"Yer wife?" Morrigan took in the sight of the decimated hovel. "There's only one cairn. What of…?"

*My daughter?* "There wasn't anything left to bury." Beorn couldn't bring himself to say anything more. He didn't think he could survive it.

Snow crunched as Morrigan knelt beside him, moisture seeping into her Rover skirts. He didn't want to answer any more of her questions. He didn't want to say what happened here, all those years ago. Thankfully, Morrigan didn't ask. Instead, she sang. The song was not in a tongue Beorn knew. It was low and guttural, untamed and wild. It was full of sorrow and longing and grief. Tears Beorn hadn't realised he'd been crying fell from his cheeks onto the snowfall. Morrigan finished her lament, and the pair sat together in silence, alone but for Godfrey and the wind. They knelt there for hours, but Morrigan never asked to leave. When Beorn gave a final sniff and stood, Morrigan stood with him, and they left that place together.

* * *

A thousand discarded swords littered the field before them.

*The Final Field.*

A decade prior, the last great battle between the Northern Realms and the Southron Kingdom had taken place here. Thousands of men from both nations had perished. The boots and hooves of the two great armies had churned the earth into roiling mud, watered with the blood of fathers, brothers, and sons.

What had once been rolling moors had degraded over the years into leagues of treacherous bogs and deadly mires. The toll had been beyond anything the Far Isles had ever seen. Too massive was the list of dead, that their bodies could not be recovered for burial; not without risking the lives of further men to the sinking bogs of earth and blood. Instead, each man's sword was pierced in the earth above him as a makeshift headstone. Carrion crows had made away with the earthly remains of southerners and northmen alike, their armour sinking beneath the mud until only a field of rusted swords remained to remind the world of what had occurred here.

Godfrey's hooves echoed across the Final Field as they made their way across the stone causeway. The Field itself was still too treacherous to cross ahorse, even all these years later. Sinking mud would swallow man and horse whole in seconds, dragging them to a muddy death with no chance of escape. Then there were the ghosts.

"How much further?" Beorn asked. A thick fog hung above the ground, making it impossible to see more than several yards on either side. The causeway stretched out in front and behind them into the white abyss, with no hint of how much further it extended.

"*Shhhh*," Morrigan hissed. The northgirl was superstitious. Legend said the spectres of those who had fallen here still walked the Field, and would take up their rusted arms against any who desecrated their resting place.

"To think, such a smart girl as you believes in ghost stories."

"I believe in respect for the dead. My countrymen died by the thousands upon this field. They deserve our respect."

"On that, we agree. You forget, my brothers died here too."

"I didnae forget. But it is hard t' muster sympathy for the men who ravaged my homeland." The girl took a breath, quenching her fury. "Did ye fight in this battle?"

"No. I'd met my wife before my brothers ever reached this far north. We met in the village back yore. There ended my career as a soldier."

All around them, swords red with rust, erupted from the red clay earth before disappearing in the fog behind them. Some had helms rested atop their pommels. Southron longswords and northern claymores stood side by side where their wielders had slain each other.

"So much death," Morrigan lamented. "So much pain…"

"That's war."

"It's selfishness," she snapped. "War is just mass violence orchestrated by those who seek power and buy it at the cost o' others' lives."

"What else are two enemies expected to do?"

"*What* enemies? I have nae enemies in the Southron Kingdom. So why do southerners hate me and my people? Why did they march north and spill our blood? The north and south have nae quarrel. 'Tis our *rulers* who insist we do.

"The northern people's greatest enemy is nae the Southron Kingdom - it is their king. The Southron Kingdom's greatest enemy is nae the Northern people - it is the *Southron King*. The deaths o' yer brothers and fathers who marched off t' war shan't be laid at our feet - that sin falls upon yer king's shoulders."

"Surely there must be some purpose to war? Some rationale? Otherwise, why have we been doing it since the world was young?"

"Men of the weaker land are put to the sword. Their women raped then put to the sword. Their children enslaved, or if too weak to work, put to the sword. It's a cycle that started with Old Carth and persists t' this day. A cycle o' gluttony and savagery. War is indiscriminate. It cares not for innocence or guilt. Tell me, have ye ever seen a child's skull?"

"Yes." Burnt and blackened in the charred shell of the home they had just left behind.

"Then ye tell me: *is* there any valid reason for war?"

"No."

Then what was it all for? The death, the blood? The pain? For what purpose had he stained his soul with the blood of countless northern soldiers? Morrigan noted Beorn's sullen silence after a time.

"I'm sorry," she sighed. "I dinnae mean t' lay the sins o' yer king at ye feet. Ye were a soldier. Ye followed orders." Did that absolve him of the blood on his hands? "In truth, the war ended long before my birth. All I know o' it is from these relics, and the state it left my homeland in. Was it... was it terrifying?"

"War isn't terrifying. Fatherhood... fatherhood is terrifying."

"Would ye... tell me 'bout her?"

What was there to tell? A girl of ten, with hair the colour of autumn leaves, the same as her mother's, taken too soon by a world that cared not for cosmic injustice. "No," Beorn said at last. "I'm sorry, but no."

"I understand. What o' the war? Will ye tell me o' that?"

"If I must choose one or the other, I suppose I'd rather speak to that." Beorn pondered for a moment, wondering how best to describe the experience. "My father... he made me join the army during the northern campaigns. He wished for me to receive my spurs during the invasion. He had trained me, since I was a lad, with sword and spear and shield. I squired for one of my father's sworn swords during a campaign on the continent. But my father saw in the northern campaigns an opportunity to prove myself and gain my knighthood."

"He was a knight himself?"

*The White Bear.* "Aye, a landed knight with castle and peasantry. Knight-hoods are not like lordships, though - they aren't hereditary. My father always planned for me to take on his duties after he'd died, but without a knighthood I could never have hoped to hold the honour. Therefore, I must need prove myself in battle, through some great deed, and earn my knighthood from the King.

"I must have been twenty winters when we marched north? In the beginning, it was exhilarating. The energy, the camaraderie. We marched to the beat of war drums and trumpets. When we passed through towns and hamlets, the people ran out of their hovels to line the road for us. Young boys brought out sticks and played at sword fighting, pretending to be heroes of old. The girls threw flowers at us, the more daring even stealing a kiss from a passing soldier. These were people with nothing, but they gave us whatever they had; shelter at night, food from their tables, the warmth of their fires. We were living legends to them, shielding the kingdom from far-off heathens who would steal their women and cook their children.

"We marched day-in, day-out without complaint, singing our marching songs. At night, my brothers and I would dice, and drink, and talk of the glory to come. I made friends, close friends. We were closer than blood, our rank and station before we were soldiers meant nothing. I was a knight's son, Gregor was the get of a tanner, Pip's parents were farmers, and Clyde was a street orphan. We'd all walked a different path in life, but they all converged to bring us together. My brothers. The only other high-born amongst us was Richter… but he was another story.

"Our sergeant marched us north, all the way to Gaius's Wall. He was a stern man, but fair. He never marched us harder than he had to, and let us talk and sing as we pleased. Our provisions were ample, and we slept with full stomachs every night. For a boy like Clyde, it was the best he'd ever eaten. Our uniforms were new and clean - Pip had never owned anything that didn't have half a dozen holes in it and patches on the elbows. We were happy. That changed once we reached the wall.

"Our sergeant handed us over to a lieutenant with the Northern Brigade.

He was a harder man than our sergeant-at-arms had been. He marched us longer and further than we had before the Wall. We'd replenished provisions before crossing the border, but what we got was worlds different from what we'd left camp with. Hardtack, stale breads, and mouldy oats. Gregor knew dried meat, and seemed to think the hardtack was horse. Clyde didn't complain - he'd eaten worse on the streets. We marched and slept, marched and slept. The nights grew colder the further north we went. Our brand new uniforms couldn't keep the cold out. The ground grew hard, and there were no longer any parades of flowers and kisses and warm hearths. Even so, we were content. We were going to be heroes.

"The fighting started in the shadow of the Spine. There was no field, no agreed upon time and place. There was us and a dark wood, and demons in the mists. Northmen descended on us in the gloom, cutting through boys who'd never killed a pig, let alone a man. Giant claymores and slender dirks cut my brothers to ribbons. As soon as we'd form up a defensive perimeter, the northmen would vanish back into the trees. We begged leave to bury our dead. Our lieutenant denied.

"We marched. On and on, we marched. Our uniforms grew ragged, our boots fell apart in the mud, our stomachs grew hungry. Again and again the northmen descended on us, killing us in scores. Pip took a flail to the skull, dead before he hit the ground. A northman's claymore took the top of Clyde's skull off. I found Gregor dead beneath a tree after one skirmish, his entrails ripped from his belly. I tried to close his eyes, but they just kept opening...

"I gave as good as we got. Out of the peasants and farmhands who filled our ranks, I was the most skilled. My sword was castle-forged and well-honed. I carved through the northern guerillas like a butcher. I grew wild without my brothers beside me. I grew hateful. I killed and killed, painting the forest floors red. March, kill, march, kill. We didn't sing as we marched anymore. We didn't dice and game of a night. We took what little sleep we could, afraid some northman was going to gut us if we closed our eyes. I oft heard boys weeping of a night, calling out for their mothers. Some prayed; though they never got an answer..."

Morrigan was watching him intently. Beorn feared to look her in her eyes, feared what he would see there. Anger, disgust, revulsion? But when he met her gaze, all he saw was pity.

"I'm sorry, you know," Beorn said. "For what we did to your people. We were told we were fighting for peace… but that's hypocritical; you can't *fight* for peace. We were fed a lie, one of glory and fame. But all we received was martyrdom."

"Martyrdom," Morrigan said, mulling the word over in her mouth. "The true martyrs are the women forced t' lie beneath their husbands, stinking o' barley beer, tasting o' sweat. Forcing their bellies t' swell and bear them sons who will grow t' find their own wives t' make martyrs of. Ye were just babes, keen t' make yer fathers proud. But in the end, aren't we all?"

"I made my father anything *but* proud. By the time my company reached the abandoned village behind us, the experience had jaded and bloodied me. It, by contrast, was bustling and full of life then. It was there I met my wife, Dorthea. She was Southron-born but had come north to settle the new frontier. I won't bore you with our courtship, but needless to say, I fell for her, hard. I asked for her hand. The only problem was, she refused to marry a killer. She said she'd not start a family with a violent man."

"What did ye do?"

"I gave it all up. My career as a soldier, my inheritance as a knight's son, and most importantly, my sword. I swore I'd never again raise a weapon, as long as I lived."

"That's why ye didn't take up that sword in Brexton…"

Beorn nodded.

"We had a child together; a daughter. I left my life of soldiering behind, and we spent ten beautiful years together. But… some things can't be put behind you. You reap the violence you sow in this world." Beorn would say no more.

As they neared the end of the causeway, a rotten acidic smell permeated the air.

"What is that?" Beorn asked.

"Mire gas," Morrigan answered. "Careful breathing it in. It's known t' cause visions."

"What about you?"

Morrigan smiled. "We northerners have higher tolerances. But a southerner like ye with yer weaker constitution will take one strong whiff and be off chasing wisps across the moors."

Eventually, the causeway's end came into sight and they were once again enveloped in the dark embrace of tall pines, firs, and oaks. The fog had kept the sun's rays hidden, so the shift from day to night was only marked by a drop in temperature and the emergence of the nightlife's cacophony of chirps, croaks, and growls. They made camp amongst the gnarled roots of an ancient oak; the canopy had kept the worst of the snowfall off the forest floor, the ground beneath them softened by a bed of fallen leaves. The day's journey had been long, and neither Beorn nor Morrigan had the energy to build a fire. Beorn was asleep moments after laying down, the acidic smells of the mires drifting into his nose.

*Save her Beorn!*

Beorn sat up with a start, heart hammering against his ribs. His hand shot out beside him, searching for the bundle of warmth he had grown so used to feeling at his side of a night. His hand found only empty air.

"Morrigan?"

The girl was gone.

Beorn took his axe in hand and sprinted into the forest. The fog was heavy, a thick white blanket that hung between the dark trees.

"Morrigan!"

She couldn't have gone far. She'd be fighting every step of the way. But who was it that had taken her? The Inquisitors? But how had they found them? The Northern Realms were massive, a labyrinthine expanse of forests, moors, mires and mountains. Bandits? Had some of Renulf's men fled during the fight and followed them away from Rosie's village, waiting for the chance to take their revenge? It didn't matter, Beorn had to find her. He had to.

*"MORRIGAN!"*

His voice echoed off the trees, disappearing into the misty void. A shadow darted through the whiteness to his left.

"Who's out there?"

The clink of armour jingled on his right.

"Hand over the girl, or I swear by whatever infernal gods you worship, I will cut you into pieces your own mothers won't recognise."

No one answered his threats, but the darting shadows continued, always in the corners of his vision. A metallic clang resonated through the forest. Then another, and another. The sounds of swords striking shields echoed all around. A battle, and close by, just over that rise from the sound of it. Beorn ran at the nearest slope, stepping deftly over loose stones and clawing roots that threatened to break an ankle. His legs burned as he ran up the slope through the fog, the sound of clashing growing louder. He crested the hill, axe at the ready, eyes scanning the scene, searching for the vibrant red of Morrigan's hair-

But there was nothing.

No battle, no swords, no shields, no Morrigan. Far off to his left, the sounds started again. Beorn had no time to consider what was happening. With each wasted second, Morrigan potentially moved farther away. He would not lose her. He would not lose anyone, ever again. The cacophony of battle, of dying men and wounded horses seemed to be all around him, as though the Final Field were once again alive with the murderous clash of two colossal armies fighting for freedom, for conquest, for *blood*. Branches clawed at his face as he ran, raking scratches down his cheeks, twigs tangling in his hair and beard. He couldn't slow, he couldn't, not for a second.

A rock under his boot turned unexpectedly, sending Beorn careening down the slope he had been sprinting over. His face ploughed into the snow and mud, the axe sliding out of his hand. He spat out a mouthful of autumn-red leaves, reached for his axe's haft… but a boot pressing on his wrist stopped him. The cold tip of steel bit into the nape of his neck.

"Well, well, well," mused his captor. "What have we here? Running back to your guerilla companions? You can't have expected to evade us forever."

Beorn had no clue who was talking or what they were talking about, and nor did he care. "Where's the girl?" he demanded.

Something shifted in his assailant's posture. "You're Southron-born?" he asked, doubt creeping into his voice.

That inkling of trepidation was all Beorn needed. Spinning as fast as his old bones would allow, Beorn swatted the sword blade away with his free arm, lunged from under the off-balance ambusher and dived for his axe, rolling into a coiled squat. The flash of silver cutting through the foggy night nearly caught Beorn off-guard, but his body's long-dormant reflexes saved him, the axe rising just in time to intercept the sword swing. They stood, weapons locked, glaring at each other in the dark.

A pair of dark eyes stared back at Beorn. His own eyes, twenty years younger.

The ghost of Beorn's younger self wore his dark hair short, and his face cleanly shaved. A man fully grown, his younger self was of a height with Beorn but was leaner, more lithe, hardened by the long days of marching and soldiering. But the resemblance was unmistakable, like looking through a mirror in time.

"This can't be..." Beorn stammered. "You're..."

His younger self lowered his sword. "You *are* Southron," he muttered. *Southron?* Could the boy not see with his own eyes their resemblance? But then again, the years had been cruel to Beorn. Would he have recognised himself in his younger self's place? And what was an old man in the forest to a young soldier in his prime, but a passing thought? The young never thought of the old. To do so was to acknowledge one's own frailty, the borrowed time we all have on this plane.

Somewhere behind Beorn, the sounds of fighting resumed. Beorn could hear the war cries of the northern guerillas, that terrifying wail that had kept him and his brothers so afraid of sleep on the long march northward.

The shadow of his younger self tightened his grip on his sword. "I don't know what you're doing here, old man, but you need to leave. It isn't safe. Those northern savages are out for blood. I have to go help my brothers."

Beorn couldn't help but note the apprehension on his younger's face. Is that really how he'd looked all those years ago, striding into battle? A scared little boy? Beorn came to a realisation as that boy made to shove him aside and rejoin the battle.

"You haven't killed yet."

The boy snarled at what he perceived as an insult. "Oh, and you're some great killer, are you?"

"Unfortunately… yes." Beorn bent and retrieved his axe, thumb brushing the notches on the haft.

The boy noticed the marks and seemed to put two and two together. "Any advice?"

"Don't," he answered immediately. Could anything he said here change this boy's future? Change his own past? "Just don't do it. Put down your sword before you ever bloody it. Be something - *anything* - else. Become a farmer, a baker, a blacksmith… a woodcutter."

"*Pfft*," the boy scoffed. "Where's the glory in that?"

Beorn looked at his own face, unlined by the years of pain and tormented sleep. What did this face need to hear?

"This won't make him love you. You'll kill a hundred men and he'll still never say the words."

Suddenly, he was no longer a man of near fifty winters, talking to a boy of only twenty; but also himself a boy of twenty, looking up at a face so similar to his own and also remarkably similar to their father's.

"You are a good son," the older face said to the younger. "You did everything that was asked of you and more. It isn't your fault that it'll never be enough. Stop trying to prove yourself to him - find your own happiness. Find peace. Before this path that you walk takes the option from you forever. Find family; one who will love you for who you are, not what he wants you to be."

Beorn the Younger stared back at Beorn the Elder, dark eyes peering into dark eyes. It was the younger man who looked away first.

"You know I can't."

"I do. And I'm sorry for everything that you've been through. And everything yet to come."

The two men who were one gave each other a final longing look, and the boy turned and charged into the fog. The sounds of war faded until Beorn was alone with his silence. Snowflakes fell from the heavens, landing lightly atop Beorn's shoulders, but when he made to dust them away, his hands came back ashen.

*Ash. It's not snow, it's ash.*

The white fog lingering between the trees took on a hellish glow. Hues of red and black bathed the forest. Snow had turned to ash, fog had turned to smoke.

*"Save her Beorn!"*

Dorthea's cry made his ears bleed. He knew it wasn't real, but he couldn't ignore it, not if there was even the slightest chance he could change things. Beorn burst through the underbrush onto the scene that haunted his nightmares.

Their home stood before him in flames, red tongues lapping at the night, casting demonic shadows across the woods. Dorthea lay where she always did, flat on her stomach and faceless, a Southron soldier's knee in her back. Tonight she wore a Faceless Mother's porcelain mask, featureless and devoid of emotion, but for the crimson tears that bled from the eyeholes.

Soldiers loitered around the glade, flinging their burning torches onto the pyre that had been his home, cinders sparking as beams cracked and collapsed into the inferno. At their head, Richter stood in his resplendent raiment, black and silver. He had risen high in the decade since the war had ended, all the way to the Inquisitorum. But time and promotion had not been enough to make him forget the brother-in-arms who had abandoned him for some common woman.

This was hell. Hell was not some freezing river of daggers and pain. Hell was fire, and memories, and guilt.

"There he is!" Richter called, catching sight of Beorn. "The deserter!"

Beorn ran straight towards the inferno, hoping, praying, that this time, *this* time, he wouldn't be too late. Holy Guards converged on all sides. He swung his axe, and it passed through them like smoke and shadows, but when their hands grasped hold of him, their grips were iron.

"No!" he roared. "No! Get your hands off me! Althea! I'm coming! I'm coming, baby! *ALTHEA!*" But as in life, the crackle of flames drowned

Beorn's cries. He tried to console himself, tried to lie, and make himself believe that the smoke had gotten to her first, that she had fallen peacefully to sleep before the flames ever kissed her delicate skin. But that was all it was - a lie. A way of coping, of surviving every day that came after this horrific night. He could not know for sure, for only bones, dust, and memories would remain of his sweet Althea.

When Beorn had screamed himself hoarse, Richter knelt before him, his blue eyes as piercing as they always were. Part of Beorn wondered, as he did every night, if it was Beorn's desertion that had inflamed Richter so - or was it that Dorthea had chosen Beorn over his handsome brother? How much bloodshed boiled down to the bruised egos of little men?

"You've grown soft, Beorn," Richter spat. The red light from the burning home danced playfully across his dark oiled locks. "There was once a time where no one could stand against you. But your desertion has made you weak. No wonder your daughter fled into the house; a coward, just like her father, without the spine to stand and fight."

"I fought plenty for one lifetime," Beorn seethed. Spittle and tears clung to his face. "I laid my sword down."

"And here I am to offer you a chance at redemption. There is no putting your sword down for a true soldier. You die with it in your hand, as God intended." Richter drew his steel and threw it at Beorn's feet. "Die like a soldier, Beorn. Pick it up."

He stared down at his own reflection in the sword's blade. The eyes of his younger self stared back at him in anguish. *How could you let this happen?* they asked. "I... can't. I won't. I swore... I swore a vow. That's not who I am anymore."

Beorn dared to look over at Dorthea and, for once, was thankful that he could not see the look upon her face. He could not bear to see her hurt, her shame, as she looked at the husband who could not save her daughter. *I'm not that man anymore.*

Richter picked up his discarded sword and paced to where Dorthea lay. "A man who cannot even protect his family is no real man." And he thrust his sword through Dorthea's back.

*"NO!"*

But there was nothing Beorn could do to change the events of the past. Fate went ever as it must. After the shades of his past had dissipated into the night, Beorn lay among the ash and dirt, Dorthea's lifeless body held tightly in his arms. His chest heaved with sobs, the kind that men pushed down their entire lives through heartbreak, and anguish, and grief. The sobs no man would ever let another man see. The sobs of a truly broken man.

Beorn raised his hand to his wife's face, fingers sliding beneath the edge of her Faceless Mother's mask. *Please, just let me look upon her face one more time, even this cold, lifeless version of it.* But when he pulled away the porcelain mask, Dorthea disappeared into smoke.

"Such a disappointment."

The voice was unvarnished, full of wood grain and splinters. A voice that could command armies and scold sons. If the spectre in the forest had been Beorn's past self, then this was surely his future. That was what he wanted to believe. But alas, the river of time was cruel, and where it had eroded the features of Dorthea's face entirely, it had preserved his father's pristinely in its icy waters.

"I thought I trained you better than this," the White Bear spat derisively.

His father was as tall as Beorn and just as robust, despite his advanced age. His hair and beard had gone to white when Beorn was still a boy, earning him his famous moniker. He wore both closely cropped, ever the soldier. His surcoat was slate grey with the emblem of the Greytower stitched into the chest. Two longswords hung from his hip, a hand resting atop one's pommel. Eyes filled with cold indifference bore into Beorn's soul.

"What happened to the soldier I raised?"

"He died, marching north."

"Oh, how I wish that were true. Instead, you had to shame me by deserting for some *woman.*"

"That woman was my *wife!*"

"I hope she was worth your honour."

"She gave me things you never could."

His father snorted. "Aye, her cunt."

"*Love!* She gave me a family. She gave me a daughter."

"I don't even recognise you. Who are you under those masks? Son, soldier, husband, father, widower, woodcutter… witch-lover?"

"You don't recognise me because I stopped being the weapon you forged me into."

"*Hmph.* More's the pity. You were always a better soldier than you were a son."

"On that, we can agree."

The White Bear's sword whistled as he drew it. "Do you still remember how to use one of these?" He threw the naked steel at Beorn's feet.

"I took a vow."

The White Bear unsheathed his own blade. "To a dead whore."

Decades of swordcraft came rushing back.  From northern guerilla fighters, to squiring on the Continent, to the courtyard of the Greytower, broken and bruised, his father telling him to pick up his wooden training sword.

*Pick it up.*

Fingers wrapped around wood and leather.  It had been near on two decades since Beorn had felt the balanced weight of a longsword in his hand. It felt good - it felt *powerful.*

Beorn sprang. Steel sang and steel clashed, ringing out through the silent night. Again and again Beorn and his father's swords met, darting this way, dashing that way. Beorn instantly knew he was outmatched. He had never been a match for his father in life, and it appeared he would fare no better in death. The White Bear was ferocious. His strikes swung, intending to cut through Beorn's own sword and into the meat behind. Into his own son.

Beorn made a desperate lunge under his father's swing to drive his own sword-point through the chinks of the White Bear's mail.  Alas, Beorn's father saw through his attack and, with a twist and a flick, disarmed his son's sword, sending it flying away into the red fog that still enveloped them.

"Sloppy!" the Bear yelled, catching Beorn's face with a savage backhand. His armoured gauntlet sent Beorn reeling, falling down the forest slopes until his back crashed against hard, flat ground. The acidic stench of mire gas flooded his nostrils. All around him, the red iron of discarded swords stood like silent observers. Beorn took the hilt of a two-handed claymore into his grasp just as his father lunged from the fog with an overhead slash. Beorn parried once, twice, but the third time their swords clashed, the rusted claymore shattered under the weight of the Bear's castle-forged steel.

"A man is only as good as his weapon," the White Bear barked. "And it appears your weapons show this plain."

Beorn wasted no time in taking up another sword, this one a chipped Southron longsword, whose tip had long ago snapped off against some northman's ribs. On and on the fight between father and son raged, Beorn's breaths coming in ragged gasps while the White Bear remained poised, stoic, unyielding. Sword after sword shattered in Beorn's grip. He wondered if each one he pulled from the earth released the ghost of its fallen owner. Would they haunt him till the end of his days? He would know soon enough, as he too made his last stand upon this field of red bogs and fallen warriors.

The White Bear's steel sheared through the seventh rusted relic Beorn had pulled from the earth, sending his son sprawling to the ground. Beorn's father levelled the tip of his blade at his son's throat.

"I thought I'd trained you better. Your defeat is as much my failure as yours. The law is the law, and the sentence for desertion is death."

Beorn never could beat his father with a sword. The White Bear was a knight, the castellan of Greytower, defender of the Pass. He'd been slaying northmen before Beorn was born. Beorn was just a soldier. Just a man.

But a much younger man.

As the White Bear raised his sword over his head for a final devastating strike, Beorn launched himself at the knight, bearing all his weight down upon him. Beorn's fists became hammers, crashing into the old man's face, snapping his head back and forth with the force of their blows.

All throughout, the White Bear laughed.

"Shut up!" Beorn bellowed, but his father just continued to cackle, laughing at the cosmic joke he considered his son to be. "Shut! Up! *SHUT! UP!*"

Beorn took his father's skull in an iron grip and pressed his thumbs through the bastard's eyes. But instead of blood, thick red clay seeped out around Beorn's fingers. His father laughed through broken teeth.

"Beorn!" his father cried, but Beorn just squeezed, his father's head malforming into a red mass.

"Beorn!"

He wouldn't stop, he *couldn't*. He couldn't keep letting this man laugh at him. Berate him. Beat him down. He couldn't keep living in the White Bear's shadow. Why wasn't he good enough for his father? Why was he not *enough*? *Father, why wasn't I ENOUGH?*

"Beorn!" Morrigan's hand slapped him across the face. The world spun, and the northgirl's visage slowly swam into focus standing over him. Beorn looked down at himself. Mud and snow soiled his clothes. Seven swords lay flung about him, but each of their blades remained intact - rusted, warped, notched, but intact. Beorn raised his hands; thick blood-red clay clung to his fingers.

"It… it wasn't real? None of it?"

Morrigan stared at him with concern. "Ye breathed in the gas ye great dolt. I awoke t' find ye sprinting out the camp like a bat out o' hell."

Beorn's lungs ached. His feet ached. His hands *ached*. His cheeks, he realised, were wet with tears.

"What did ye see?" she asked.

"Everything." And Beorn broke down, sobs racking his frame. Morrigan's arms enveloped him, barely able to reach around his shoulders. The girl held him as he cried. She offered no warm words of sympathy. She did not tell him it was just a vision. She knew better than most how deep the scars of the past could cut.

When his sobs had stopped, Morrigan drew him up and took him by the hand. As she led him back towards the treeline, Beorn cast one last look over his shoulder at the Final Field. The White Bear stood beside Beorn the Younger, who stood beside a white-masked Dorthea. In front of them all stood a girl of ten, vibrant crimson hair falling over her shoulders. Althea's emerald green eyes watched him go. In front of him, Morrigan's own locks of resplendent red trickled down her back, eyes of grey set steadfastly ahead.

*'You are at a crossroads Beorn,'* Sibella had foretold, *'staring ever back at the road you have travelled without taking the time to glance at the path ahead... and who is at your side as you travel it.'*

# Chapter 14

They put the Final Field behind and let the northern woods enfold them in its leafy embrace. The verdant greens and rich browns had slowly disappeared the further north they ventured. The trees they passed beneath now were as white as the snows they trudged through, sapped of colour by the edge of the world. What few leaves remained on their branches were vibrant reds or violets.

When Morrigan had seen the first white trunk amidst the dark forest firs, she had dismounted Godfrey and gone to rest her forehead against its bark.

"What, uh, are you doing?" Beorn had asked.

"We have nae *'one true God'*, like yer Church preaches," Morrigan replied. "Our druids tell us a god exists in each o' our trees. These White-Barks are sacred to us here in the True North. I am beseeching the trees t' guide us safely home." As she left the tree, she rapped her knuckles twice upon the wood. "T' ward off foul spirits," she explained.

They saw no more game; the snows having either driven them south or into hibernation, and made do eating what meagre provisions remained to them. When they made camp, Godfrey would drag his muzzle through the snow like a pig hunting truffles, but what little grass remained beneath the snowfall was brown, dead, and spindly. Their oats were running low and Beorn had to pull the feedbag away from Godfrey's ravenous lips to prevent him from emptying it. Each time he did so, the giant bay horse would look pleadingly at him with those massive brown eyes.

*I'm sorry, old friend. Not much further now.*

Morrigan was growing more restless with each passing day. She sat high in the saddle, as though expecting her home to appear before them after each hill they crested. After fording a shivering stream, Beorn noted a change in the trees they passed beneath. Though they were bare, the shape was unmistakable.

"These are apple trees," he told Morrigan.

Her eyes were afire with excitement. "We're close. These are the orchards of Applethorpe. They produce the sweetest, juiciest green apples ye'll ever taste. Folk travel from across the north on market days to taste the products o' these orchards. Apple wines and apple ciders. Apple pies, tarts, cakes, cobblers, and crumbles. Appulmoy and apple sauce. Children go apple bobbing and eat caramel-glazed apples on sticks. I've heard it said on some farms, he who has the good fortune t' find the first fallen apple of the season might present it t' their beloved as a way o' engagement."

*I used a ring*, Beorn mused, *but an apple seems nice as well.*

Godfrey gave a frustrated snort, plumes of hot steam bellowing from his nostrils. *Sorry buddy, we picked the wrong time of year.*

The barren orchards stretched on for leagues in all directions, divided by narrow dirt paths that marked the boundaries of one farm to another. They passed several farmhouses that looked quiet and dark, with snow covering the thatch roofs. Beorn wanted to seek shelter in a barn if they could find a farmer who'd allow them, but Morrigan would not have it. She said they were too close.

"My village is small and nameless, but Applethorpe is the largest settlement in the region. All the local villages and hamlets go t' Applethorpe for their needs, us included. Once we reach the settlement, it'll be a short day's ride t' my home. To my family." Morrigan was smiling like Beorn had never seen her smile before. "Ma will likely be making broth t' heat the bellies o' my sisters. Millicent will be knitting by the hearth, Melina and Mathilde maybe playing dice. I imagine Marigold will be throwing a fit in this weather. She prefers the warmer seasons - lets her show off a little more skin, haha! Once they know I'm back, they'll send word t' Margery. She'll come running through the snows barefoot if she has to, t' get a look at her wee sister returned. I wonder if that archer's put a baby in Marian's belly yet?" Lost in her daydream, Morrigan wore a smile.

"What of your parents?"

"Ma will probably cry herself hoarse. She never wanted me t' go in the first place."

"And your father?"

*Pa wanted sons... Millicent said it was after the fifth he started to beat Ma.*

"Compared t' the monsters we've met on the road, even Pa will be a welcome sight."

*And after you're home... what becomes of me?* Across all the leagues they'd journeyed, Beorn hadn't once thought about what would happen once they reached Morrigan's home. Could he really hand the girl over and then be on his way, as if they hadn't fought their way through Holy Guardsmen, brigands, bandits, Inquisitors' Dogs, and even an ice bear together? Where would he go? Maybe, if he was lucky, Morrigan's village would be in need of a woodcutter.

Applethorpe appeared like an oasis in a desert of white snowdrifts and naked apple orchards. It was not the largest of towns, but more civilised than they had grown accustomed to on their journey. The northern houses and cottages were distinct from their Southron counterparts; where the latter favoured exposed timber frames with wattle and daub walls, the northerners built their homes with stones mined in the Highlands. The singularly unfitting piece of architecture was the church bell tower that peeked over the slate cottage roofs, evidence of the Gilded Father's presence even here at the end of the world.

Candles flickered behind closed windows. Those that were opened were hastily shuttered as Godfrey trotted past.

*To keep out the cold?* Beorn pondered. *Or the two unknown travellers rolling into town?*

Morrigan did not notice. Her eyes drank in the first true sight of her people since she had set out with the travelling woods-witch long ago. Beorn, on the other hand, could not help but notice the distinctive *lack* of people about to greet them. The sun was making its slow descent to kiss the horizon, but there was still light aplenty for hard-working folk with chores to finish. But Beorn saw no milkmaids milking, no swineherds herding, no shepherds coaxing bleating lambs. Daylight remained, yet the forges had fallen silent, the bakeries had grown cold, and the vendors had ceased to hawk their wares despite the two potential customers.

"Morrigan," Beorn spoke from where he walked beside Godfrey's bit. "Something is about. Where are the townsfolk?"

"Hiding from the cold?"

"This town sits on the cusp of the Frostline. The town is cold most of the year. No, there is something else."

Their answer came in the form of a black-plated knight emerging from the fog like a wraith, a red hand aglow upon his chest.

"Thorne," Beorn swore.

"Beorn!" Morrigan's cry drew his attention to the other shades emerging from the fog. From every alley, every wynd came soldiers in grey mail, silver keys crossed upon their surcoats. They came armed with swords and spears and shields. Beorn made to wheel Godfrey around, but Holy Guardsmen appeared like rats out of the darkening streets, closing off any avenue of escape.

"Beorn?" Morrigan's unasked question hung ominously in the air. She could see it, too. There was no way out. There were too many to fight.

*No. Not now. Not this close. Not after all we've been through.*

The black knight lumbered forth, an avalanche on two legs.

"Tell the girl to get off the horse," he thundered.

Godfrey was whinnying and stomping his hooves upon the cobbles, the scent of danger filling his nostrils.

"Beorn? What are we gonnae do?"

There were too many. Beorn was skilled, of that there was no doubt. The tallies on his axe spoke to that fact. But this was an unwinnable fight. Standing their ground or throwing down their weapons would lead to the same destination. Knowing what he did of the Inquisitorum, Beorn suspected it would be a kinder and swifter end to die fighting here in the street, rather than in an Inquisitor's cold dungeon, whipped and racked and cut. Beorn saw no escape but death. At least for him.

Morrigan was shaking as he pressed Godfrey's reins into her hands. Was she recalling her own time spent in such a dungeon? Looking at her now, Beorn could hardly recall the frail and broken creature who he'd first seen atop that scaffold in Brexton, porcelain skin glistening in the rain. No, not porcelain. Porcelain was brittle, quick to break. She was wood of the White-Bark trees that housed her gods. She was steel. She would understand. She would survive. That was all that mattered.

"Morrigan, you have to go. You know these lands better than they do. You can disappear. Godfrey is faster than any nag they've dragged this far."

"What are ye saying?" She slowly registered the reins he'd pressed into her hands as Beorn unslung his axe from the saddle. The first wave of Holy Guardsmen were closing in, hands gripping their still-sheathed swords. *Idiots.*

"Fly, Morrigan. Fly. And tell your father what a lucky man he is."

Beorn's large, flat palm cracked Godfrey across the flank. The draught horse reared, hooves punching the air, and set off at a gallop at the nearest alleyway.

"*BEORN!*" Morrigan cried as two guards jumped aside of the tonne of horsemeat descending on them. He held her betrayed grey gaze until she disappeared around the bend.

"After her!" Brutus commanded, but Beorn's axe stopped the responding officers, cleaving their faces in two. The remaining soldiers turned on him, steel bared. He could not stop them all. He knew this. But they must face him, lest he cut them down from behind as they ran after the girl.

Captain Brutus fixed him with a baleful stare from beneath his thorned great-helm. "Put down the axe."

"Come and take it from me."

Come, they did. In ones and twos they crashed upon him like waves upon a cliff side, and in ones and twos Beorn cut them down like the dogs they were. The Guardsman's steaming viscera painted the white stones red, heavy steel axe head splitting mail and shattering bones. Beorn slew the men who would do Morrigan harm without contrition, his grin half exertion, half malicious ecstasy. Beorn's hot breath frosted before his face, melting the hoarfrost in his beard.

The fervid tumult of steel echoed through the empty streets with nary a witness but the rising moon.

*Keep her safe,* Beorn prayed to the White-Bark gods of Morrigan's druids. *I could not save Althea. Let me please save this one.*

"C'mon you dogs!" Beorn thundered, axe cleaving limbs and rending flesh. "Die you bastards!"

Beorn swung his axe, silver blade singing through the air. A mailed black fist caught the haft mid-air, wrenching it from his grip. The shock elicited the tiniest of gasps before the back of the axe head cracked Beorn across the face, rendering him insensate. His last sight was of a glowing red hand, before the blackness swallowed that too.

*Please, you fucking trees. Let me have given her enough time.*

* * *

The world was black.

Beorn awoke in a black cell with black walls. He could see nothing, hear nothing. His body felt numb but for the splitting pain across his face, dealt by the backhanded blow of his axe. With no light and no mirror, he could not imagine what his face looked like. Despite the pain it caused, he couldn't help but laugh.

He had always hated his own reflection. Hated how similar his face was to his father's. Perhaps now he would be able to stand the face that gazed back at him from the looking glass.

Beorn had tried to stand after his strength had returned in some measure, only to find someone had shackled his hands and feet together. He meandered through the darkness with small half-steps until his outstretched fingers found the smooth bricks of a wall. With one hand on the wall, he shuffled along until he reached a corner. He limped the length of this one as well until he found another corner, repeating the process until he'd found all four corners of the cramped little room. At one point, his fingers had slipped from rough brick to smooth polished wood, back to brick. A door.

He'd groped through the darkness to find a handle without success.

*A small dark room, a door that opens only from the outside - I'm in a cell.*

Somewhere in the cell, a continuous drip leaked from the roof into a shallow puddle. *Drip, drip, drip.* Devoid of all his other senses, the sound was maddening. What Beorn assumed was hours passed in total blackness with nothing but the *drips* to signify the passage of time. After an age, Beorn's bladder was bursting. On his hands and knees, he searched the dark cell for a chamber pot or bucket, but to no avail. Once significantly desperate, Beorn decided on a designated corner and relieved himself against the wall.

Hours stretched into what could easily have been days, but Beorn had no means of telling but for the ache in his stomach and the thirst burning in his throat. Shuffling around the cell with his face turned skyward, Beorn could finally locate the dripping and stood for an age as the continuous drops filled his mouth for a single unsatisfying swallow.

After so long in the darkness, a sudden appearance of light blinded him. He squinted through raised fingers as the cell door groaned open on rusted hinges and a hulking black shape bent under the lintel and placed a burning torch in an iron sconce fastened to the wall. The iron thorns atop his helm made him look like a horned devil come to torment Beorn for his past sins.

Beorn sprinted toward the Inquisitorial Captain, but he tripped over his ankle fetters before he could take three paces. A mailed fist to his nose sent him sprawling.

"You would be wise to remain seated in the Inquisitor's presence," Captain Brutus spoke.

From the shadowy hallway outside the lone door slid the skeletal shape of Inquisitor Constantine. He placed a simple wooden chair atop the cell's stone floor and perched himself upon it like a vulture staring down at his next meal, waiting for it to die.

"You," Beorn cursed.

"Me," the Inquisitor smiled.

The torch sent shadows flickering beneath his comically large hat, pooling in the gaunt recesses of his eye sockets. A grinning skull stared down at Beorn.

"Where is the girl?" There was no malice in his voice. The Inquisitor asked the question as a guest may ask his host where they kept the salt.

Beorn spat blood at the Inquisitor's slim pointed shoes by way of reply. Brutus had broken his nose, and the bottom half of his face was red.

Inquisitor Constantine sighed, pulling a black square kerchief from a hidden pocket of his cassock to wipe the blood from his shiny pointed shoe. When he was done, he cast the cloth into a dark corner of the cell. He fixed Beorn with his beetle-black eyes.

"You thought you could get away? No one escapes the Inquisitorum. Not once our Dogs have the scent. You didn't make it easy, I'll grant you. After you fled Brexton, I thought that was it. We'd never see you or the little witch again. But then, as luck would have it, Captain Brutus was fortunate enough to be held up by a witch trial in Ravensburg. While he was there, a haggard band of Rovers came limping into town, bloody and beaten. Apparently, they'd run afoul of a small settlement on their way through. Something about trying to steal a cart from the local wainwright? It makes no matter - what interested us, were the pleading questions of a young Rover girl, desperately wanting to know if her redheaded friend had passed through the town. A redheaded girl accompanied by her broody guardian, a man of *large stature*."

*Esmerelda.* Beorn silently cursed.

"Yes," Constantine continued. "I can tell by the look on your face you knew her. Hearing you were so close, Sir Brutus sent out his scouts to find you; but ultimately we knew where you would be headed, so we planned to intercept you at Gaius's Wall. We both know how that turned out. Given the young witch's tenacity, I knew she'd not let you abandon your headstrong quest, and like you I was aware the only other option before you if you were hell-bent on making it into the Northern Realms was to pass through Greytower Watch. I was right, of course, and had already dispatched Sir Artorius to secure the crossing. Unfortunately for him, he underestimated your devotion to protecting *witches*. The fool should have never humoured the blacksmith's whore with a trial by combat. There was, of course, one benefit of that complete fiasco. When we caught your little blacksmith friend on the road, he had the most interesting story to sing about you... *Beorn.*

*Mikkel!*

"I swear, if you hurt them-"

"Oh, hurt them I did. They're all quite dead. The smith, his witch, and their little hagseeds, as well. I find the flames so purifying, don't you, Captain?"

Sir Brutus silently nodded his approval.

Beorn struggled to rise, spittle flying from his bared teeth, but the black knight pressed him back down with an armoured boot. "You bastard! You *MONSTER!* She was with child!"

"And the world will thank me for sparing it from such a monstrosity. But let us speak more of you. I was quite interested in the song the blacksmith sang as we were burning his children. Wayward son of the famous White Bear, castellan of the Greytower. What a disappointment you must have been to your father. You might have one day been the sword that guarded the Southron Kingdom; but you threw it all away. And for what? A *woman?* *Tut tut tut.*

"But back to my conundrum of how to find you. The Northern Realms are a vast territory, and largely untamed. It was as my men were scouring the villages closest to the Northern Pass that we caught your scent. You left quite the mess in that madam's courtyard."

*No, not Rosie.* Beorn's face must have shown his shock, for the Inquisitor laughed venomously at him.

"Oh, you poor simple man. Smitten with a whore? No wonder you abandoned your post as soon as a woman flashed her lashes at you. You're an imbecile if you thought that whore wanted anything more from you than your wanton propensity for violence. The north is vast, but the Frostline narrows that down quite a bit. All we need do was ride ahead and station hosts in every major settlement along the snows and wait. Eventually, you would bring the little witch to us. And so you did.

"Your walking right into the settlement where Thorne and I had stationed ourselves was... fortuitous. Call it providence. Now I may deliver the justice you so heinously robbed me of in Brexton."

"You're a monster."

"I do only what my God commands."

"If your God commands you to burn women and girls alive, then your God is evil!"

"Evil is a matter of perspective. Where I stand, it is you who is evil; aiding and abetting a witch, a murderer of the unborn."

"*You* are the only murderer here." He'd killed Mikkel, the smith's wife, and their children. What had happened to the others he'd questioned? To Esmerelda and the other Rovers? To Rosie and her girls?

The Inquisitor smiled. "It isn't murder if sanctioned by Church and State. And besides... the *only* murderer?" He eyed Beorn knowingly. Could he weigh the guilt of Beorn's soul?

"That was war."

"So is this. But where you killed for the land rights of some spoilt kingling, I kill to preserve the morality of this kingdom and its people. That is the Church's holy mission; its righteous responsibility. We cannot expect humanity to steer itself alone. Humanity is tired - so let the Church take the reins." The Inquisitor leaned closer, the torchlight making sunken black holes of his eye sockets again. "And if humanity will not conform by choice, I will fill the River of Penance with every witch and witch-lover on these wretched isles if that is what it takes to bring the Lord's peace."

Beorn thought of Danior and his philosophising. '*Witch hunting at its core is an instrument of Church-ordered control.*' "You'll never get that peace. There'll always be someone for you to vilify. Without fear, your God loses his control."

The Inquisitor winked. "Perhaps you're not as thick as I originally thought. Here's the thing, Beorn - I *can* call you Beorn? The Church is morality. The Church is order. The Church *is* control.

"You were told the Carthian Empire fell, but that is merely a half truth. Carth conquered half the known world, but cannibalised itself trying to hold it. It would never last, but we couldn't simply relinquish control of such a large portion of the world for them to return to a hundred quarrelling kingdoms. Mankind needed to remain united. So the Empire 'evolved.' The Church of the Gilded Father sprouted from the ashes of the pantheon of old gods to usher mankind towards an age of prosperity and unity. A seamless continuity of power. Yes, borders were redrawn. The illusion of power returned to a multitude of puppet kings, but *we* remained. The infrastructure was there; Carth's roads, its walls..."

"Its crosses," spat Beorn, staring daggers at Captain Brutus.

The Inquisitor chuckled. "Well, yes, we still needed to make examples now and again. But no longer was the Empire controlled with force through legionaries and centurions, but through *faith*. Faith in something greater than us. Something that watched over us, protected us, and above all *judged* us.

"Generals became priests, senators became advisers to kings, and the Emperor, well, he became High Pontiff. The Church was designed to be a continuation of Carthian imperial authority. The state religion of an authoritarian regime - we just traded the swords for cassocks." Constantine laughed. "Of course, once, now and then, swords would still be necessary. But that's where you come in. These northern savages wouldn't welcome the Lord willingly, so we brought Him in by force."

"Sounds more like fear than faith to my ears."

The Inquisitor mulled this over. "Perhaps that observation is half right. Fear is a powerful motivator. Hence, the need for the Inquisitorum."

"To round up 'witches' as your scapegoats. To keep the populace afraid."

"The Lord is the light that ushers his flock through the darkness of this world. We of the Inquisitorum merely display this darkness to the masses." His voice held a mocking tone, as though reciting a long rehearsed speech. Realisation dawned for Beorn, down there in the dark.

"You don't believe in any of it, do you?" Beorn thought back to the knight on the mountain, the helm so flippantly resting at his side, steel bared to the world. These men had no genuine regard for the Church's decrees; they just wanted the freedom to inflict violence in the Church's name.

The Inquisitor gave him a chilling grin. "Captain Brutus, leave us." The Dog obeyed with characteristic servitude. When he was gone, Constantine continued. "Do I believe in an Omnipotent Father who guides our actions?" He shrugged. "I believe in power. The Church *is* power. And I am the

Church. I will let nothing strip me of that power - so tell me: where is the girl?"

"That's what this is about? Why you've hunted us all this way?" Beorn let out a rattled laugh.

Constantine pierced him with those black beetle eyes. "The Church is the earthly manifestation of God; and the peasantry believe God cannot err. You and that heathen showed weakness in the Church. You showed we can be defied - that *I* can be defied. I will demonstrate this as false, to the largest crowd we can find with a pyre that reaches the heavens. Our laws are made of iron, cast from God's will. Suffer one criminal, one *witch*, and ten more follow suit."

"The laws of today are the shame of tomorrow. Laws change. Right and wrong do not."

Constantine's scorn was palpable. The Inquisitor sighed irritably. "I see this conversation will get us nowhere." Constantine stood and banged a fist on the small cell's heavy door. Rusted hinges screamed as Captain Brutus returned. "Captain, I leave the extraction of information in your capable hands. Do not disappoint."

"Yes, Inquisitor."

* * *

They started first with whippings. Brutus shackled Beorn's hands to an iron ring in the ceiling and stripped him naked. *To search for the mark of the witch*, they'd told him. To humiliate him, more like.

Beorn had known pain in all its different forms. The cutting bite of blades, the blunt crush of cudgels and maces, the vision-splintering blows of fists. But nothing could have ever prepared him for the sting of the whip.

He stood naked as his name-day, awaiting the whistle of leather through the air. His body tensed as he waited. The first lash seemed to come and go without his notice. The second came in quick succession, lacerating his shoulders. It was as the third strike came that the pain from the first made itself known. The sheer sting of the initial lash seemed to shock his body into numbness. Only as the pain seeped in and the wound peeled open, like the skin of an over-ripe fruit, did the hot-white pain erupt behind Beorn's eyes. The breath was driven out of him and his knees buckled beneath him. He bit back a scream and planted his feet, only for the pain from the next lash to come stinging into existence. All the while, Brutus was lining his shoulders, back, and buttocks with fresh wounds.

Somewhere near fifty, Beorn's feet gave out from under him. He wanted so badly to fall to the hard floor and quench the fire upon his back with the icy feel of the stones. But alas, he could not. The ring atop his head groaned as it took the weight of his slack, the shackles around his wrists biting deep into his flesh. The pain in his shoulders made him desperately try to stand, but he lacked the strength. At some point, the ordeal ended, and they unchained him from the roof to the sweet relief of crashing to the floor. Beorn lacked the strength to drag himself to his corner. He pissed where he lay, a puddle spreading beneath him.

At the end of each day (or what Beorn assumed was each day - he had no way of knowing if it was day or night), Constantine would return, perched atop his chair. The effect was obvious; Brutus asked no questions as he tortured him, and Beorn suspected even if he offered to speak, the knight would not grant him respite until the Inquisitor returned for his nightly confessional. *Speak now or suffer another day of torment*, the act suggested. But speak, Beorn would not.

"Where is the witch? Confess."

Beorn held his tongue.

"Your silence, while commendable, is futile. I have men scouring the countryside looking for her. She will be found. What happens to her afterwards is dependent on the time and energy expended in her apprehension. Assist us in her recapture, and I will be inclined toward... leniency."

He gave the Inquisitor only silence.

Constantine sighed and held out a glass. A dark-haired serving girl scurried forward from behind the Inquisitor to pour thick red wine from a pitcher. Her hair hung loose around her face like blinkers shielding her from the scene. She kept her eyes cast on the stone floor, as invisible as possible.

"I hope you don't mind me taking refreshment," Constantine said after the girl had melted back into the shadows. He raised the glass and took a long swig. The wine was thick as Morrigan's blackthorn ink and stained his lips red like some demonic vampire from the stories Rovers brought from the Continent. "I have quite a fondness for the grape, one of my many vices. But the Lord forgiveth."

*And what of your other vices?* Beorn thought.

*'That mouth of yours always did have a way of getting you into trouble,'* Constantine had told Father Emannuel. *'You will always be that little choir boy, whose mouth was too big for his own good.'*

Morrigan may have believed the world was made of shades of grey, but some of those greys were darker than others.

The following day, Brutus used hot irons.

Beorn resumed his tether to the roof, watching the iron rods glow among the coals of the blazing brazier. Captain Brutus stood on the other side of the fire, red enamelled hand print glowing with the heat of the coals. Beorn stood silently watching the knight, trying to prepare himself for the pain. The whipping had stolen the breath from his lungs with every lash. The irons made him scream. The small room stank with the rancid smell of burning flesh. Tears streaked his cheeks.

*Is this how it felt, Althea? When they burned you alive?*

That night when Constantine came, Beorn looked like an exotic cat, blistered and oozing stripes lining his ribs. Brutus was an expert in his craft - he did not heat the iron rods to an extent that the skin would slough off the body, but just enough to sear and burn without the threat of death.

"Where is the witch?" the Inquisitor demanded. He paid more attention to the wine in his glass than he did to his prisoner.

"Go fuck yourself," Beorn seethed.

"*Tsk tsk tsk.* I must admit, it is saddening to see such a proud beast brought so low." Constantine smiled his skeletal smile and downed the rest of his wine. "Until the morrow then."

The next day, Beorn had his wrists shackled to a low wooden table. Brutus Thorne sat across from him, a hammer in one hand, an iron nail in the other. He was rolling the thick carpenters' nail back and forth between his fingers, deep in thought, when finally he spoke.

"Do you know how I earned this crown?"

Identical black nails, twisted and melted together, formed the ring of thorns. Beorn remained silent, but Brutus continued regardless.

"After earning my spurs and being appointed to the Knights Inquisitorial, I served in the capitol… in the Leyanite Quarter." Beorn had heard tales of Cronwic's Leyanite Quarter, one of the last Leyanite ghettos tolerated in the Southron Kingdom. Most others had been sacked, torched, and their residents run out or crucified. Many considered Cronwic's Leyanite Quarter to be the most dangerous place in the Southron Kingdom, riddled with crime and poverty. Residents were required by law to wear evidence of their race, under pain of death. Beorn recalled the Leyanites they'd seen crucified on their journey to Gaius's Wall; they looked so similar to Far Islers, you'd never be able to tell if one slipped through the checkpoints…

*If Morrigan were here, she'd berate me for my ignorance. They're just people,* she'd probably say. Another scapegoat for the Church to vilify in their quest for domination of the populace. Another unseen enemy to stoke paranoia, another monster that lurks in the dark. And why? Because it's impossible to truly police an entire kingdom - unless they themselves are policing their own neighbours.

How could Beorn ever have been gullible enough to fall for any of it? Leyanites, the northmen, witches?

*Because everyone else believed it*, Morrigan would have said.

"One day on my rounds," the knight continued, nail rolling between thumb and finger, "a young woman approached me. Torn and tattered clothes covered her, and bruises mottled her face. An honest Far Isle woman who worked in a bakery. Every day she brought the stale loaves from the day before into the Leyanite Quarter and sold them for pennies on the groat. She was an honest, God-fearing woman, and do you know what she got for her charity? Some Leyanite scum raped her bloody."

Nothing in Beorn could excuse such an act, but there was a part of him that understood. Some affluent Southron woman traipsing through the cordons of the Quarter at will while the Leyanites were crammed within like penned animals, covered in their own filth, so she could bask in her righteous charity as she sold them stale bread.

*Every single revolution in human history has been about one thing: food. Those who lack for it, those who are abundant in it, and the divide between.*

Back and forth, back and forth, the iron nail rolled between Brutus's fingers.

"My Captain at the time wanted me to round up every Leyanite male who matched her description and present them to the poor woman, so we could execute the offender. I didn't think that sent enough of a message. I crucified them all, any male who matched the description. They were Leyanites after all. They'd all be guilty of something.

"After their bodies had rotted off the crosses, I went back and retrieved every single nail, and had them fashioned into this crown upon my helm. The blood of all those kills still stains the iron. I wear it to remember that day, to remember that bloodied, ragged woman sobbing in my arms. To remember what I am capable of, and for whom I meter out such harsh justice."

But Beorn had his doubts; was it for justice that Brutus had crucified those men, or for the simple act of violence? Beorn recalled the limp and lifeless bodies crucified aside the road to Gaius's Wall.

With a swift swing, Captain Brutus brought the hammer down atop the nail's head, driving it through Beorn's palm and into the wood of the table beneath. Beorn's screams echoed through the tiny cell.

"*Agh! Fuck you!* And your fucking Church! Fuck you all to fucking hell!" Blood was pooling beneath Beorn's pinned hand, running along the grain of the wooden tabletop. The nail had unlocked some strongbox of emotion inside of him, upending it through his mouth. "What sort of God burns women and girls alive? What sort of God allows war, and rape, and murder? What sort of God would steal a wife and daughter from a husband and father? What sort of God would make a bastard like *you*?"

"A just God. He took your family from you for your sins, your desertion. And he made me to meter out justice to the wicked."

"You're a monster."

"The crow calls the raven black."

"That's not who I am anymore," he panted, but even as he spoke, images of dead northmen dragged themselves from the mires of his memory. "I … I've changed."

"Why? Because you feel ashamed? Shame doesn't unburn villages, unkill northmen, unwidow their wives, or unorphan their children. Your guilt doesn't absolve you. It's valiant what you've tried to do, I admit; starting afresh. First with your family, again with the girl. But you can't. You cannot change. You're as much of a monster as I, and you always will be."

Constantine looked sallow when he attended the shivering cell that evening, skin pale and eyes sunken more than usual. He looked as though he wanted for sleep. He took his wine as usual, the serving girl hiding in his shadows.

"Your silence is growing irksome. Tell us where the girl is now and Sir Brutus will kill you quickly. Defy me further and it will take an eternity. You will beg for death's release."

"Go. Fuck. Yourself." Each word was an agony, his body screaming for release. Brutus had left him shackled to the table, nail driven through his left hand. He was saving his right for the next day, but it appeared the Inquisitor lacked for patience.

Brutus took a knee beside Inquisitor Constantine. "What will it be, Inquisitor? Thumb screws? Flaying? Trepenation?"

Constantine swirled his wine as he contemplated Beorn's fate. "Pressing." He gave no further explanation as he stood and exited the cell.

Death by pressing was a remnant of Carthian occupation; a remnant the Church had seized with malicious zeal. Under King Aethelstan and his father, King Edward's law, a man who refused to admit his guilt could not be tried. The lawmen found a few rounds of torture usually loosened the tongues of difficult felons, but for those who stubbornly continued to proclaim their innocence, a more robust method was required.

After the Inquisitor left, Brutus unshackled Beorn and pulled the nail from his hand. A fresh gout of clotted black blood pumped from the wound and new cries escaped Beorn's throat. The small amount of joy of the cold iron leaving his skin was short-lived.

Brutus kicked Beorn onto his back, wounds from the whip burning as they pressed against the filthy stone floor. Brutus found fresh shackles to tether Beorn's arms and legs asunder, crucified on his back. Beorn's torturer laid planks of splintered timber fastened with cold iron nails across Beorn's chest and stomach.

Last came the stones.

Brutus lumbered into the cell with a heavy basalt boulder fastened with an iron ring in each hand. The knight wasted no energy lowering the stones delicately, but threw them both onto the boards with the ease a father might playfully throw his son onto a hay bale. The air was driven from Beorn's lungs like a bellows. It took a constant tension of his stomach muscles to stop the boulders from crushing his rib cage. Each breath was a labour.

Brutus's black armoured legs appeared in the periphery of Beorn's vision. He could not turn his head, the tendons in his neck taut with the effort of keeping the board from flattening him.

"Every day you do not tell us what we require, another stone will be added. This will continue until you perish. Tell us the witch's whereabouts and I will end this with one deft swing of my sword. It will be mercy."

Beorn gritted his teeth and did what he'd always done best; disappoint.

That night Constantine's dark haired serving girl stole into the cell with a bowl of watery broth. Beorn could not raise his head, so the girl dripped small spoonfuls into his mouth. The Inquisitor did not intend for Beorn to perish from hunger. Constantine would allow nothing to occur other than what he had ordained.

"Hold in there," the girl urged before slipping from the room.

When Constantine next visited the cell, Beorn's face was purple from exertion, the capillaries in his eyes bloody and shot. Constantine looked no more hale than his captive, but the sight of Beorn's discomfort appeared to bring him some measure of satisfaction.

"Have you anything to confess?" the Inquisitor asked.

Beorn opened his mouth and let out a stifled croak. Constantine nodded to Captain Brutus, who removed the stones to allow Beorn the air to speak. A fit of coughs instantly racked Beorn's lungs, red spittle flying past his teeth.

When the coughing stopped, Beorn made another attempt at answering.

"Pardon?" the Inquisitor asked. "You'll have to speak up."

"I…said…" Beorn wheezed. "More. Fucking. Weight."

The Inquisitor's teeth grated together in unbridled detestation. "Thorne. Give the prisoner what he wants."

Captain Brutus complied. The first stone pressed the breath from his lungs, the second pushed his blood into his eyes and the third drove his tongue from his mouth. Beorn was once again encoffined, a living corpse interned in his stone tomb.

Instead of leaving, Brutus pulled the Inquisitor's chair beside Beorn's purple face. The knight held Beorn's axe in his mailed fingers, tracing the notches engraved down the haft.

"A soldier without a sword. What a paradox," the knight mused. "For the longest while, I couldn't understand it. You've killed aplenty along your journey, but never once with a sword from what I could gather. You even took the time to pilfer a troop of slaughtered Guardsmen south of Lasthome, taking the Captain's signet to impersonate him. But you didn't touch their weapons. Slowly, I realised. You think you're above them. Weapons, I mean. That's how you justify your killing.

"I laughed at first - what sort of distorted version of morality must you live by to convince yourself this absolves you of your violence? But then, I realised - we're not so different."

The hulking black knight reached behind his head and pulled forth a greatsword, five feet long. No man of normal stature could hope to swing such a blade, but Captain Brutus was no normal man. He raised the sword over Beorn's face so he could see the blade hovering above his neck like a guillotine. Like a promise of sweet release.

"Do you know what this is?"

Beorn studied the blade through bloodshot eyes. Ebony wood formed the handle, wrapped in boiled black leather; the circular pommel bore the stamped crossed keys of the Holy Seal, and a pair of straight quillons separated the steel from the hilt. The blade itself was a hand's width across, but unlike a regular sword, it did not taper at its end. Instead, the blade was entirely rectangular, the end bereft of a point.

"An… executioner's… sword," Beorn struggled.

"Correct." Forged for the sole purpose of parting criminals from their heads, an executioner's sword was longer, wider and flatter than any other conventional blade. And as its sole purpose was beheading, it lacked any need for a point. "You see? We are alike, you and I. I do not wield a longsword or spear like some common soldier, whose sole purpose is pillage and murder. This is no mere weapon. It is a symbol of my judicial power, bestowed upon me by God. It is a *tool*."

*'My axe isn't a weapon,'* he'd told Morrigan what seemed like a lifetime ago. *'It's a tool with a specific purpose.'*

What a hypocrite he was. What did it matter the manner of tool he used? The outcome was still the same. Valiant or violent, he was still a murderer. A single tear trickled from his bloodshot eye.

That night, as the serving girl was spooning watery gruel into his mouth, Constantine burst into the cell, Brutus Thorne close in tow.

"Thorne, remove those stones for the nonce. I have something our guest will be most eager to see."

The girl shrunk into the corner, eyes on the ground as Brutus took to his task with religious zeal. The knight uncuffed Beorn's hands and feet, only to re-shackle him to the iron ring in the ceiling.

"Good. Now retrieve the girl."

*The girl?*

Beorn's heart turned to stone the second Brutus brought her in. Her dishevelled hair was paler than Beorn remembered, bleached a beaten copper by the sun, not her usual scarlet. Someone had bruised and battered her face, bound her hands behind her back, and gagged her mouth.

*Morrigan!*

Brutus dumped her gracelessly on the stones before him. Beorn lunged at the knight but jerked to a stop by the chains at his wrists. How had they found her? Why was she here?

"Quite loyal for a witch. We caught her skulking around the Church. It appears she's returned to liberate you." The Inquisitor held a wicked grin across his face.

*No Morrigan, why?* Why had she come back? Everything Beorn had endured, all of it in vain, just for the girl to walk right into the Inquisitor's hands.

"What... what will you do to her?"

"That," Constantine grinned, "depends on you." He appeared to be relishing every second of Beorn's discomfort. "The witch has not deigned to inform us where she fled. I would be remiss in my duties as Inquisitor if I allowed her coven to go... *unmolested.*"

*Her family. He wants her family.*

Millicent, Marigold, Melina, Margery, Marian, Mathilde. What would happen to her sisters if Beorn gave them up? After all, the sister of a witch was a witch.

"As Inquisitor, it is my duty to rid these Isles of heretics and heathens. Sometimes, I must need choose between the fate of a few and the fate of the many. It is for this purpose I offer you an accord, a final chance of rectitude." Captain Brutus reached over his shoulder and drew forth his headsman's sword. The flames of the torch danced along the length of the naked steel. Fear blazoned behind Morrigan's eyes as she saw the sword. She began shaking her head frantically, a silent plea. "Tell us for where you and the witch were heading, and I shall spare her life. You and she may depart our company so you may continue this father-daughter fallacy you have convinced yourself of. Deny me what I want, and Captain Brutus will part her head from her neck."

A muffled scream escaped from behind the gag. Brutus raised his sword, its edge desperate for blood. Could Beorn really trade the lives of seven girls for one? In a heartbeat.

"Wait!"

Constantine smiled. "There is a village to the east, two to the west, and another to the north. To which were you headed?"

Morrigan and Beorn locked eyes. She was desperately shaking her head, pleading.

Shame bloomed in Beorn's chest. "The north."

Morrigan stared back at him with those huge green eyes.

*Green. Not grey.* Morrigan's eyes were grey. Something was wrong.

Constantine chuckled, running a finger along the girl's cheek, catching the gag and pulling it down. Disbelief flooded Beorn as he took in the sight of the Faceless Sister, Joanna, sprawled across the floor before him. The flickering light of the lone torch and the days of sleep deprivation had obscured the truth that sat before him. The girl's orange hair was lighter than Morrigan's, her arms - devoid of Morrigan's rigorous training - lacked the northgirl's musculature, and her eyes, her *eyes*, they were the wrong colour. Beorn was a fool, and he'd played directly into Constantine's ruse.

"Thorne," the Inquisitor commanded, "send forth a contingency of men. They will find the witch in the village to the north."

Beorn had failed her.

"What of the Faceless Sister, Inquisitor?"

"She is of no further use to us."

The headsman's sword whistled through the air, parting hair, flesh, and bone. The serving girl screamed into her hands, trying desperately to muffle the sound. Beorn could hear her choking back sobs from the dark recesses of the cell.

Constantine and Brutus paid the girl no mind. "Such a shame. Her Faceless Mother bequeathed her to our purposes after our altercation at Gaius's Wall. She informed us of the girl's...*transgressions*. Such a shame. Such a pretty young thing. Those supple young lips, wasted on another girl."

Beorn had not the energy to respond. The pool of red spread across the stone floor. Joanna's decapitated head stared vacantly up at him from the floor, green eyes bereft of light. How long until Morrigan met the same fate? He had damned her. He had failed.

# Chapter 15

"Beorn," the darkness whispered.

His ghosts visited him of a night, speaking to him from the shadows.

*Pick it up.*

*Save her Beorn!*

But his past failures didn't matter any longer, compared to his failure of Morrigan. The girl would burn, and it was all his fault.

"*Beorn,*" the darkness continued to hiss.

His eyes were too weary to open, and he had no desire to see whatever torment his mind had conjured up for him. Would it be Dorthea, faceless and begging him to save their daughter? Althea, screaming from within their burning home? His father, come to express his utter disappointment in the man his son had become?

"*BEORN,*" the darkness urged. Sheepishly, he opened his eyes. The dark-haired serving girl was squatting before him, staring back with her grey eyes.

*Grey eyes.*

"Morrigan?"

She had dyed her hair and wore it out around her face like a veil, rendering her practically invisible. She'd been here the entire time, standing in the same cell as Beorn, and he'd not even noticed. But then again, neither had his captors. After all, what business would an Inquisitor have to inspect the face of a lowly serving girl? More intent on inspecting the wine than who had poured it. To men like Constantine, girls such as Morrigan's alter ego were beneath their attention - they were maids to clean, cooks to prepare their meals, laundresses to clean their robes, nurses to tend their wounds, whores when they needed a fuck, mothers when they wanted a son. But they weren't people. They weren't worthy of their notice, let alone scrutiny.

Morrigan set to work removing Beorn's fetters. The heavy iron key turned in the lock, releasing the shackles with a loud *click*.

"The guards...?"

"Won't be waking. How do ye think I got the key?" She wore her dagger at her hip.

The chains fell heavily to the stone floor. Beorn's wrists were bloody where they had chafed his skin raw. Morrigan slid her body under his, hoisting him onto his feet. Beorn's back burned where his wounds reopened as he moved, clinging to the filthy linen shift they'd dressed him in. He hissed a curse and his legs buckled under the pain.

"I need ye to help me," Morrigan groaned, as his weight bore her down. "I cannae move ye on my own. Please, Beorn. We have t' move."

Summoning the deepest reserves of his strength, Beorn stood, Morrigan under his right arm like a crutch. They shuffled across the cell, Beorn's bare feet dragging over the stone. A large brown stain remained where Brutus had taken Joanna's head.

*She was here*, Beorn realised in horror. *Morrigan saw.*

"Morrigan... I'm so sorry... Joanna..."

"I know," the girl whispered, her voice layered with pain and grief. "I know."

The guards outside his cell sat in pools of their own blood, throats opened like gaping tongueless mouths.

"I'm tired," Beorn groaned. "I'm so... so tired." The weight of the years was crushing down upon him. His external injuries were only half the issue. Decades of wounds to his soul were bleeding out inside him.

"Just a wee farther," Morrigan pleaded. "Godfrey's outside. We just need t' get out o' the Church. Just a wee farther, Beorn."

*Father.* The word echoed around Beorn's skull. *I'm nobody's father. I couldn't save Althea. I couldn't save Joanna. I can't save you, Morrigan.*

"…father… just a little farther…"

*Father.*

The hallway outside Beorn's cell led to a set of ascending stone steps, which led to the sanctuary of a church. They'd had him in the dungeon of the Applethorpe church the entire time. But why would a church require cells and a dungeon? For heretics and blasphemers, obviously. The Lord offered forgiveness, but only through penance.

Hundreds of candles sat flickering beneath the altar of the Gilded Father. His likeness stood stoically above them, cast in gold. His lined, paternal face gazed down at them benevolently, a billowy beard flowing down his chest. Beorn could not help but notice the similarities to the stone guardian they had seen holding aloft the remains of the Carthian aqueduct. Constantine's words rung out in the silent halls of the church: *'You were told the Carthian Empire fell, but that is merely a half truth. The Church of the Gilded Father sprouted from the ashes of the pantheon of old gods to usher mankind towards an age of prosperity and unity. A seamless continuity of power.'*

How much of the Church was simply the recycled remnants of Old Carth?

The pair stopped under the altar, Morrigan returning the Father's loving gaze with one dripping with derision.

"Ye have nae place here," she said, and spat up in the face of God. Spittle dripped from his gilded nose. The girl reached out and swept a dozen candles aside. The rich linen cloth that lined the altar erupted in flames, warming their backs as they shuffled down the nave towards the Church's heavy oaken doors. Smoke rose to pool in the high steepled roof. Orange flames spread from the altar over lavish carpets and up hanging tapestries. The pews closest to the blaze began to smoulder and smoke. Black streaks lined the walls where the fiery tongues lapped at the red bricks.

The square outside the church was aglow as they shouldered open the heavy doors, flames lapping at the colourful stained glass windows. Saints and apostles stared down from the glass panes in judgement. The sight of the flames caused Godfrey to rear and whinny, his eyes rolling in terror as he remained tethered to a post not five yards away.

"We're almost there, Beorn. They've sent the Guardsmen away."

*To your village*, Beorn lamented. *Because of me.*

"Almost there, almost there… once we're on Godfrey, we're free. We'll disappear into the woods until they give up the chase, then find our way back to my family. Then we'll-"

Morrigan was cut off with a cry as someone dragged her out from under Beorn's arm, sending him careening into the snow.

Morrigan was screaming.

Captain Brutus towered over Beorn, the Church aflame behind him. Light from the inferno danced across his obsidian enamelled plate, his thorned crown backlit like a demon's horns. Morrigan's feet kicked at the air frantically as he held her aloft by her hair. She clawed desperately at his wrist to stop his mailed fingers tearing loose her dyed locks.

"Look who's come scampering out of her warren," Brutus chuckled. "The Inquisitor will be pleased to see you, little rabbit."

"Put… her down!" Beorn groaned. Speaking was pain, his ribs bruised and tender from the pressing. Ash and snow were falling in equal parts from the sky now, the church's red bricks aglow with the heat from within.

Brutus unslung something from his back and threw it at Beorn's feet. His axe skidded to a stop in the grey snow. "I'll make you a deal, woodcutter. I'll put her down; if you pick it up."

Brutus twisted his fist, causing Morrigan to scream anew.

Beorn's fingers wrapped around the axe. "Fine," he groaned, staggering to his feet. "Let's see who's the bigger monster."

The captain threw Morrigan aside like a sack of flour. She hit the snow with a thud. Brutus unsheathed his mountainous sword, steel whispering against the leather.

The two men rushed at each other, weapons swinging.

Beorn's wounds were forgotten, the icy breath of the wind was forgotten, the blinding heat of the inflamed church was forgotten. All that remained was the fight.

Brutus was an unstoppable force, two hundred pounds of religious zeal bearing down upon Beorn. The executioner's sword cut through the air, rapaciously attacking. Beorn parried the thrusts and swings, batting them away with the heavy head of his axe.

"Blasphemous heretic!" Brutus roared, irate and venomous. Despite his mass and the size of his sword, Brutus moved with agile speed, righteous fury made flesh. Beorn ducked under a horizontal swing, darting forward to strike, but Brutus was faster, reversing his blow and slamming the sword's pommel into the woodcutter's face.

The sword rose, the sword fell, with Beorn just barely rolling aside and limping out of arm's reach.

"You stand against a knight of the Inquisitorum," Brutus said, resting his blade upon an armoured shoulder. "I earned my spurs on the Final Field. My hand ran red with the blood of heathens and northern savages, and I put them down in the name of God."

"A knight? Knights protect. Knights defend. Knights meter out *JUSTICE!*" Joanna's head rolled across the icy floor. "You are no knight. You're just a Dog."

"And you are nothing more than an old man."

Beorn gripped his axe with white knuckles. "No. I am no man. I'm a monster, remember?"

The snow fell and steel sang.

The reach of Brutus's sword gave him the advantage. Try as he might, Beorn couldn't close the gap and get close enough to land a blow. The knight's strength was unparalleled, and Beorn had no hope of overpowering him, even without the injuries he nursed.

Again and again, their steel clashed, sending sparks flying into the night. Beorn dared not look around for Morrigan, lest Brutus's colossal blade shear his head in two, but he was desperate to know she was okay. How his father would have laughed at him. Brutus was the son the White Bear had prayed for. Brutus was the son the White Bear had deserved; every bit the monster he was. And how Beorn's father would have relished the fact. This man would never have forsaken his duty for love. This man would have been worthy of the seat at Greytower. This man would not have begged his father's mercy for a wounded deer in the snow.

The edge of Brutus's blade slid past Beorn's defences, slashing him above his left eye. A gush of crimson blood cascaded down Beorn's face. He ducked under Brutus's next swing and danced away to give himself a second's respite.

Beorn's heart was thumping in his ears. He couldn't do it. He couldn't beat Brutus. The knight was too fast, too strong, too determined. A dog with the scent of blood on his nose.

Was this what it had all come down to? All those years of training beneath the Greytower? All those lessons learnt at the dull edge of a training sword?

*'Pick it up!'* his father had yelled as Beorn's blade rattled against the cobbles. *'Again! Again, until you land a strike.'*

*'How?'* Beorn had roared back, a boy no older than ten. *'You're too fast, too strong. I'll never match your reach!'*

*'There will always be an enemy faster or stronger than you. The more you dance away from their attacks, the more power you give them. You'll need to get close. The easiest way to do that is to let* them *get close to* you.*'*

The opportunity came without warning. Brutus swung his sword back, preparing for a strike. Beorn darted forward. Brutus swung, but too late, Beorn was inside his circle. The blade battered off the haft of Beorn's axe, allowing him the time to bring the axe head arcing down upon his great-helm.

Steel grated against steel, and blood splattered across the snow.

Then Brutus stepped forward.

Steaming blood dripped from his armoured hand, mailed fingers wrapped around the axe head, caught in his grip. Beorn tried to wrench his axe free, but the knight's grip was iron.

"You lose, woodcutter." Hot breath frosted through the holes of Brutus's great-helm. Moonlight glinted off the blade in his right hand. "You should have stayed in your cabin."

*No,* Beorn thought, staring at his death. *I hid there long enough. I should have stepped out of the shadows long ago.*

Brutus raised his sword.

*"Ahhhg!"*

The knight dropped his sword, hand darting to his side. Morrigan's dagger had slipped through the chinks in his armour, parting leather and flesh and sinking up to the hilt.

*Kidney,* Beorn thought. *A good strike.*

The northgirl twisted the blade and snapped it off at the hilt.

*"YOU LITTLE WHORE! I'LL KILL YOU FOR THAT! I'LL KILL Y-!"*

Beorn snatched up the executioner's sword, spun in a full circle, and took Brutus's head.

His decapitated corpse dropped to its knees, then collapsed in an awkward heap beside his thorned helm. The world was silent but for the crackle of flames at their backs.

Unoiled hinges cut through the silence like a scream.

"Thorne! Thorne, where are you?" Constantine coughed as he limped down the church's steps. The fire had singed and smouldered his cassock. He was limping down the stairs, holding his gut. When he reached the bottom, he collapsed into the snow. It was then he seemed to notice the scene before him; Thorne's headless corpse an island in a red sea of his own blood. Constantine glared at Beorn with cold black eyes and started to curse, but a coughing fit stopped him. Red spittle flew from his thin lips, smearing the white snow in front of him.

When he lifted his head, Morrigan was crouching before him. For a long moment, all he saw was her disguise, an invisible serving girl with unkempt dark hair. Realisation dawned slowly, like the sun cresting the horizon.

*"You?"*

"Me."

Constantine reached out with clawed fingers as if to throttle the northern witch who had given him so much grief, but another fit of coughs wracked his body. His black wide-brimmed cloth hat fell from his head, revealing a pate of slick silver hair. The blood staining his lips now was a dark, clotted red, almost black. This wasn't just the effects of the smoke, Beorn could tell.

"What's wrong, Inquisitor?" Morrigan asked, sarcasm dripping from her voice like venom. "Perhaps ye'd like some wine t' clear ye throat?"

Constantine's skeletal hand clutched at his neck like some drowning beast. "What... what have you done to me?" With every word, more and more blood fell from his red maw.

"Ye appear t' be in need of a healer," Morrigan said, ignoring the man's accusations. "Let me see what I have in my pouch."

Morrigan unlaced the red pouch from her hip and pulled forth an umbrella of small white flowers. Beorn had seen those flowers once before, on the road north with the Rovers.

"What… is… that…?" wheezed the Inquisitor.

"Hemlock."

"You… witch… you… poisoned… m-"

Another painful fit of coughs cut the Inquisitor's accusation off.

*'The ability to heal and the ability to harm are so intimately linked,'* Danior had mused. *'It's no wonder so many cunning folk are strung up or burnt these days.'*

The irony of the Inquisitor hell-bent on the girl's death being brought low by the very skill-set that had seen her marked for the pyre.

Morrigan reached out and picked up Constantine's fallen hat, placing it reverently atop her head.

"That's… not… yours…"

"And who is going t' stop me, Inquisitor? Yer Dog is dead. Yer Holy Guards dispatched at yer own orders. What sort o' threat are ye without yer lackeys? Ye had no *real* power, did ye? It were the mob that handed me t' ye. It was yer Dogs that tortured me in the Brexton cells. All ye've ever been is a sadistic old man; a voyeur o' pain."

Morrigan's taunts looked to re-energise the Inquisitor; at least enough to speak. "Look… at you. Some wild… beast, who doesn't know her… betters. You need to be broken in; *domesticated*."

"Yer kind have been trying t' beat us into submission since Carth was young. And yet every woman ever born is still born wild; untamed. Yer kind have t' beat us, bend us, and break us into subservience. Yet under the surface, every one o' us are still just feral creatures waiting for our chance t' bite the hand that strikes us. Ye're a failure, Inquisitor."

"It's *you* who's the failure! A failed product of… societal conditioning. A horse who can't be broken must be put down!" The effort sent Constantine into a fit of laborious coughs, retching up tar-like blood, staining his chin red.

"I am nae failure," Morrigan replied coolly. "I am the product o' generations o' women who drowned on their own blood from biting their tongues. I am the product of their sacrifices. I am their rage incarnate. I am their vengeance."

By now, Inquisitor Constantine's breaths were coming in ragged and raspy. Sweat beaded his forehead, pooling beneath his sunken eyes to run rivulets down his face like streaming tears. Morrigan stood and turned to leave.

"Wait... please... kill me..."

Morrigan stared down at the pitiful man who had once held so much power over her, who had caused such fear in her heart, who had tormented her waking and sleeping mind. Constantine's body was convulsing. A steaming pool was melting the snow beneath his waist as he lost control of his bladder. The man was pathetic; a wretch. Beorn did not know how long the effects of the hemlock would take to kill the man. Death would be a mercy.

Atop the church's smoking bell tower, a hungry, fat crow *cawed* loudly. The sound echoed through the silence of the night. Black wings flapped as more of the carrion birds appeared on adjacent roofs, dozens of beady black eyes staring down at the corpse that hadn't realised it was dead. For Constantine was a dead man, whether he knew it or not.

*An unkindness of ravens; a murder of crows. What had the black feathered birds done to warrant such unfortunate plurals?* Beorn had the distinct feeling that if they stayed much longer, he would receive an answer. Carrion birds did not observe a mourning period.

"Goodbye, little rabbit," said the northgirl, and left the monster to die in the snow.

Beorn, with much help from Morrigan, climbed onto Godfrey's back. Together they rode off into the cold northern night, the flames of the church warming their backs as they left.

* * *

The night sky was a black blanket above their heads, the moon a perfectly circular hole of light in the fabric. It hung like a giant eye in the sky, the only witness to their shadow-clad escape. Godfrey's hooves sent up plumes of snow as he raced through the freezing night, clouds misting before his billowing nostrils. It took all of what little strength remained to Beorn just to stay upright in the saddle. Morrigan rode pillion in front of him, reins in hand. She rode Godfrey through thick undergrowth, around the gnarled remains of fallen White-Barks, soaring over frozen streams and brooks, and down winding game trails.

Beorn was sure he lost consciousness more than once, his shirt-back rubbing his lashings raw, the hole in his hand throbbing with every hoof fall. But he held on. He held on to Morrigan.

"I know these paths better than those Southrons," she was saying, through the haze of Beorn's mind. "We'll reach my village 'fore they do. We'll warn my family. We'll flee."

How similar optimism and denial could sound. But Beorn could make no answer. Life was a dream.

*Your family. Your sisters. I told the Inquisitor where they were... I thought I was saving you. I'm sorry.*

Godfrey's neck was lathered, his mouth frothing, but Morrigan did not relent. A day's ride north of Applethorpe, the girl had said her village lay. They made it there by sunrise.

But sunrise was still too late.

Morrigan's village was a quaint little place. Or it had been once.

*...it'll take days for him to die,* Beorn had said when first he'd started her training. *He can hurt you in that time. Better to end it quick.* Morrigan had waited too long, slowly poisoning the Inquisitor over the days that Beorn had been tortured. She should have slit his throat from the shadows. She'd given him time to hurt her.

Brutus's detachment of Holy Guards had been and gone. Stone and timber houses had lined a single avenue winding around and overshadowed by the hill of a barrow. The ancient burial mound had probably been old when Carth was young. Generations of Morrigan's people lay beneath its soil, and atop the hill's crest stood a solitary White-Bark, its branches bare but for a single red leaf, waving in the breeze.

The houses now lay smouldering; piles of rubble and ash. Bodies lay strewn across thresholds and half out of windows. The hooves of holy destriers had churned the earthen path into slurry.

Morrigan wouldn't let herself cry despite the carnage, despite what every logical part of her mind must have been telling her. She reined Godfrey around the broken corpses of her neighbours and down the avenue, to the last squat little hut at the very back of the barrow hill.

They had crucified Morrigan's parents to the lintels above their windows. Their corpses hung limp from the nails through their outstretched hands. A dog had taken to chewing at her father's toes, but scampered away as Godfrey trotted near. The scene was reminiscent of stories Beorn might have been told as a boy about northerners and their brutal pagan ways. But this carnage was signed by Southron hands.

A pile of ash lay in a heap at the threshold. Cinders flew from the pile, carried by the breeze.

*One... two... three... four... five... six. Six skulls.*

Morrigan slid from the saddle and collapsed before the ashes that had once been her sisters. Millicent, Marigold, Melina, Margery, Marian and Mathilde stared out of the remains of their pyres with vacant, bottomless eyes. Morrigan's mouth dropped open in a silent scream. Tears streaked lines through her ash-covered face, her hand beating an erratic rhythm against her chest, but no sound could escape her throat.

*'The Tower... Danger. Crisis. Destruction.'* Sibella had tried to warn him, but he was too blinded by his past to heed her words.

Morrigan's fingers found their way to her face and began raking red lines across her eyes. When her fingers brushed against her dyed hair, they balled into fists and began tearing at the roots, all the while her mouth hung open in a soundless cry. Beorn's arms were barely strong enough to pry her fingers out of her hair and keep her nails from clawing her eyes out. When she squirmed out of his grasp, he expected her to return to her self-mutilation, but instead she spun, hand striking his face like a viper. The blow sent him reeling, stumbling into the mud.

*"This is yer fault!"*

The look in Morrigan's eyes froze Beorn. A look he had previously seen reserved for the Inquisitors and their Dogs. For Southrons.

*"Ye told them! Ye told them where my family was!"* Beorn had never heard Morrigan's voice so high, so shrill, so unrestrained by the iron facade she kept up so that no man would ever see her so vulnerable, so emotional, so *female.* There was a time, not too long ago, that Morrigan would have been right, and Beorn would have interpreted her emotion as weakness. His ghosts visited him every night, but he did not cry. He sequestered himself away from the world, shuttered in his lonely hut with naught but an old draught horse for company. Until the Final Field. Until Morrigan.

But it was not only sorrow that laced her tears; it was *hate.* Pure, unbridled hate, all directed at Beorn.

"I thought... I thought they were going to kill you..."

*"Then ye should have let me die! Ye saved one girl at the cost o' my entire people!"* She dropped to her knees, sobbing, this time as loud as a birthing sow.

Beorn reached out his one good hand to try and embrace her, but she flailed her arms, shrieking at him. "Don't TOUCH ME! Yer no different t' THEM! Ye're all MONSTERS!"

Her words stung worse than any slap. Brutus's words hung over Beorn's head like a spectre. *'You cannot change. You're as much of a monster as I, and you always will be.'*

"Morrigan... I'm not like them."

"Of course ye are! Ye only act when there's the promise of violence! Ye dinnae want t' help people, help *women,* ye just want to fight! Ye saved me in Brexton, aye, and Beatrice at the Greytower. But what o' Esme, what o' Joanna and her Sisters?"

"That's not true. I acted because it was the right thing to do. Perhaps once, I may not have. It's true. But you opened my eyes-"

*"Why did ye need me to?"* she screamed.

Images flashed behind Beorn's eyes. Corpses hanging from the message tree, a baker's wife tumbling into the dirt, an old woman's kindling stolen. What did he do? Nothing. But he'd saved Morrigan... why? Because she looked like his dead daughter? Or because of the promise of a fight? The clash of steel? The chance of redemption... or an honourable death.

"It's performance!" she continued to roar. "It's theatre." Beorn had thought the same of her execution. Perhaps any act done in front of others was performative. Did that make it any less right? How much did their intentions matter when compared to their actions?

*Save her Beorn.*

"Everything I did, I did in the memory of Dorthea and Althea. I did it to make them proud. I did what I couldn't do for them in life."

*"And why did ye need t' wait? Why could ye not have been a man t' make them proud while they were still alive? Yer no different from the men who shunned Lucetta of Carth, driving her t' open her own wrists! Why does it take our DEATHS t' spurn men t' action?"*

"I'm not like them. I'm... I'm not a violent man." But even as he said the words, he knew them to be false. The notches on his axe told the truth. Did he really believe just because he didn't use a sword that he was better than all those other monsters? That he was better than he himself had been?

*'Your guilt doesn't absolve you.'*

"Nay," Morrigan spat back at him, "not a violent man. Just an indifferent one. *'I don't get involved.'* That's what ye say, isn't it? And what is the cost o' yer inaction? That family in Ravensburg - *dead!* A generation o' women gone! That poor girl in *Rosie's* - *dead!* Before she'd even had a proper chance at life."

"We are more than our worst acts. We are potential." He said Mikkel's words like a prayer, begging them to be true.

"The only potential ye have is for pain, like all men. Leave me be. I must bury my dead."

"Morrigan, we can't stay. Once the Holy Guard find out what happened in Applethorpe-"

"*LEAVE ME BE!* For the sake o' the gods, listen t' me for once! Get *AWAY!*

I winnae go *anywhere* with ye!"

Beorn watched silently as she stumbled towards her parents, stopping to rest her forehead against her father's chest, sobbing into his bloodied tunic.

"Da... Daddy..."

*I'm not her Da,* Beorn thought morosely. *I never was. I never will be.*

* * *

Beorn found Morrigan atop her people's funeral barrow, beneath the shade of the lone White-Bark.  Beorn's footfalls crunched through the freshly fallen snow as he came up behind her.

Morrigan didn't turn. Who else would it be? Everyone else in the village was dead.

"Have ye ever sat down and considered, *really* considered, that all the dust in this world was once other things?" she mused. The snowfall had buried her skirt, her dyed hair covered with an icy white veil. Ashes that had once been her sisters covered her hands. "The walls o' ancient cities, monuments t' kings whose kingdoms nae longer exist, books o' poetry written by long-dead lovers. Their creators probably thought they would be eternal, standing in testament t' their genius until the last star in the sky died. But dust is always the ultimate destination. And now my family, who had once been flesh and blood, warmth and love - are dust." She curled her ashen fingers closed.

Beorn knew the pain of watching your legacy crumble into ash. There had been nothing left of Althea to bury when the fires of his home burned out. Morrigan had taken her mother and father down and interned them in the tomb beneath the barrow. Her sisters she had collected in a hessian sack and taken to the top of the hill. Handful by handful, she let the wind snatch up her sisters six, and carry their souls to the horizon. What bones remained she had laid to rest bedside their parents. With the heavy stone door closed upon the tomb, she was now truly alone in this world; a solitary red leaf clinging desperately to its branch.

Beorn stepped closer to Morrigan's side. He had thought long and hard about what he might say, but he knew better than anyone that words would never be enough. Instead, his feet had taken him to Godfrey, his hands rummaging under his saddlebags for a cloth-wrapped parcel he had hidden there, even from his own mind.

Kneeling in front of Morrigan, he placed the parcel between them. The heraldry was old and tattered, but in the right light you could still make out the slate-coloured sigil of the Greytower.

"I won't ask your forgiveness," Beorn began. "I know I will not find it. But nor will I apologise for what I did, for I did it for you."

The hatred had subsided in her eyes, but malice still lingered. She listened intently to what he had to say.

"When you asked me to train you to fight, I told you… I told you I had no desire to make you into a monster. That I wouldn't do what my father did. That I wouldn't turn you into… me." Beorn shook his head. "For all the good that did you. Well, perhaps this world needs a few more monsters; monsters to make even the Inquisitorum scared."

Beorn unwrapped the cloth. Hidden inside was a sword. It was simple in design, a regular hand-and-a-half sword; blade, crossguard, hilt, pommel. Stamped upon the flat of the blade just above the hilt was Mikkel's maker's mark. He had made this sword for Beorn years ago, before he left to fight in the north. It was the only piece of Greytower that remained to him. Despite his vow, he had never given it up.

"I made a vow that I would never again raise this blade. I held true to that promise all these years. Even after they came for my wife… my daughter…

"I swore it to Dorthea. I will never again raise this sword. I cannot unmake that promise, any more than I can bring your family back to you. But I can make a new vow; to help you take your vengeance. I cannot raise this sword against your foes. But I can teach you to wield it yourself."

Morrigan's grey eyes stared back at her from the blade. Her sisters' eyes, her mother's eyes.

*But not Althea's eyes.*

"What are you waiting for?" Beorn asked, flinching from the pain as he stood. Beorn could not tell if this was the right thing to do. But Beorn had never been very good at doing the right thing.

"Pick it up."

# Afterword

Hello again dear reader,

Hopefully if I've done my job right, you'll be feeling some sort of way about what you've just read - the purpose of storytelling is, after all, to illicit thoughts, emotions, *some* response. You may even be thinking what a horrible imagination I have, to write all these terrible things that befall the women in my story. It may then be pertinent to pick up where our last conversation ended; me telling you *I didn't make them up.* But this is fantasy; surely I've done some embellishing to better get my point across? Let's zoom in on just one chapter, and have a look at the facts.

In Chapter 7 we are introduced to Father Emanuel, as he sketches the busty statue of Lucetta of Carth. Lucetta's story is a direct plagiarism of the *Rape of Lucretia* and the subsequent revolution her suicide inspired that resulted in Rome's transition from kingdom to republic. Do a quick image search for artwork inspired by Lucretia's suicide - spot what they all have in common.

What about Father Emanuel's ingenious solution to the scores of 'fallen women' plaguing the kingdom, his Madelena Laundries? Again, these are directly inspired by the real life *Magdalene Laundries:* institutions run by the Catholic Church, in which thousands of women died while forcibly confined, and the last of which wasn't closed until 1996. Symbols of religious and colonial control, that spread across the globe, even to my home of Australia.

What of the good priest's appointment to the Ministerium of Virtue and Prevention of Vice? Surely here we've reached the level of absurdity that demonstrates the shift into fiction? Alas, no. In August 2024, while already writing the early chapters of this book, the Taliban's Ministry for the Propagation of Virtue and Prevention of Vice banned the women of Afghanistan from showing their faces or speaking in public. The Ministry mandated that women were to veil their body at all times in public and that a face covering was essential to avoid the "temptation of men into vice". A woman's voice was deemed to be a potential instrument of temptation, and so should not be heard singing, reciting poetry or reading aloud - even within the confines of their homes. All these examples are from but one chapter of this book.

What of the other atrocities? The truth is, there is nothing done to women in this book that I have not personally seen with my own eyes in my professional career.

So why did I write this book? I wrote this book for one simple reason: I am fucking angry. I am angry that I have to go to work every day and read about the women who are stabbed, beaten, strangled, and burned to death by their partners. I am angry that to speak out about this topic is to be viewed as some radical feminist or misandrist, and that I should "really consider men's mental health in all of this". I'm angry at the cyclical nature of the news, which comes out of the woodwork once a year to report the tragic slaying of a young woman by a man of "great potential", ignoring the women who aren't white, middle-class and conventionally attractive who die daily at the hands of men. I'm angry that instead of making progress, we seem to be going backwards, with a rise of conservatism and harmful patriarchal rhetoric amongst the young men of today, fuelled by the toxic ramblings of every *manosphere* alpha male with a podcast and an opinion.

We look back on the witch trials of the middle-ages and recognise the awful phenomenon it was. At the peak of the European witch trials, one to two women were executed daily. Today, at least two women are killed per day in the European Union by a family member or intimate partner. We used to think these women were witches, devil-brides, evil incarnate. What are we thinking now, for femicide statistics to remain so high?

The truth is we never burned witches. We burned women. And we still do.

# About the Author

L.S. Walker holds academic degrees and a decade's worth of professional experience in gender-based violence and the broader criminal justice system. His work in death investigations, including intimate-partner homicides, has provided him with firsthand experience of how destructive patriarchal ideology can be. This professional experience served as the inspiration for his debut novel, *The Witch and the Woodcutter*.

L.S. Walker lives in Australia with his family.